OPERATION ANNIHILATION

James K. Burk
writing as
Rob Jackson

WolfSinger Publications ~ Security Colorado

Published by WolfSinger Publications

ISBN 978-1-942450-77-1

Printed and bound in the United States of America

Dedication

This book is for Rob Fertner, Bill duPlessis, and John Dixon, who were there in the beginning.

Chapter 1

A man who'd just stepped out the door of a bar shouted, "Holy shit! Would you look at what just got off the boat."

Reynaud studied the man a moment. The Texan, a lean man with a hard, weathered face wore, like most of the men they'd seen, jeans, cowboy boots and hat, and a jeans jacket over a nondescript shirt. Most importantly, he also wore a large, silvery revolver in an open holster.

"I told you we should have brought all the artillery instead of stashing the long arms outside town," Logan muttered.

Steve grinned. "Logan, I think he's picking on you because of that Hawaiian-print shirt you're wearing."

"What's the matter with Hawaiian shirts?" Logan demanded.

The stranger had apparently heard the question. "Not a single damn thing, if you're going to a pimp's funeral, but we don't have much use for them around here. They scare the stock and keep honest folk awake at night."

Logan's grin seemed frozen on his face but all traces of humor had deserted his eyes. "What're you worried about then, asshole? You won't lose a minute's sleep over it."

The group spread out with Logan, who'd been standing nearest the bar, stepping forward, turning as he moved, so he directly faced the Texan. Steve had moved from Logan's left by three paces, and the Deacon had backed up two paces, also facing the man. Reynaud had continued another half dozen paces then he, too, turned to face the gunman.

"Hey, furriner," the Texan drawled. "We don't much like damnyankees and we really don't like 'em when they got a big mouth on 'em." The man stepped out to the edge of the sidewalk facing Logan, his hand hovering over the butt of his revolver.

Logan had just swung his coat open and held it out of the way with his left hand, reaching across his lower back. The movement displayed a military-styled holster and, suspended by a sling, an Ingram MAC-10. "If you reach for that hog-leg on your hip," Logan said, "I'm going to shoot enough holes in you my friends will be able the draw the Last Supper on you just by connecting the dots."

Suddenly they heard another voice, behind Logan and to his right. "Hey, bushwhackers, if you don't like getting shot at, you're in the wrong line of work."

Reynaud spun. Two men with rifles or shotguns had moved into position behind them and no more than twenty yards away, almost invisible in an alley. The ambushers also pivoted to face the source of the voice then, at what sounded like two shots only a split-second apart, they tumbled and were flung to the street. Reynaud looked at where the shots had come and a man stepped into the street, reloading a revolver. He stood six feet tall in Navajo moccasins, with broad, strong features, deeply tanned skin, black hair hanging past his shoulders. He wore a flat-brimmed, flat-crowned black cowboy hat with a beaded hatband, dressed in black and orange and wearing enough silver and turquoise to open a trading post. The pistol he twirled back into its holster was one of a pair of ivory-gripped single-action revolvers and the holsters were a crossbelt rig. Apparently, the stranger was there to cover their backs.

Reynaud turned to face the man who'd started the argument. "You didn't say this was an open party," Reynaud said, as he loosened the flap of his military holster.

The man had, like Logan, reached across his back with his left hand although he wore no coat but a short jeans jacket. "Maybe we'll all just call it a day," the Texan said. "I'll stand for the dri—" Suddenly, his left hand swept out, clutching a small revolver.

Reynaud had just begun to reach for his .45 automatic when the MAC roared and spat flames. The man spun and jerked spasmodically, flapping his arms as though he was trying to fly. The pistol in his left hand spun into the air and flecks of blood were spattered across the whitewashed front of the bar. With a final twitch, the corpse fell, a heap of bleeding meat.

Logan pulled the empty magazine out of the Ingram, shoved a fresh one in, and hauled back the bolt.

Seeing Logan was more than ready to deal with anything in front of them, Reynaud turned and walked back to where the stranger was bending over the bodies. "What're you doing there?"

"Putting a shell in each of their mouths," the stranger replied. "It's sort of a calling card. Less messy than taking ears or fingers." He looked up at Reynaud. "Slattery figured you might run into some trouble and he sent me to keep an eye on you. My name is Hasteen O'Ryan."

Hasteen nodded at the bodies. "If any of their stuff appeals to you, take it. Spoils of war." He dug wallets out of hip pockets, glanced into them, put them in his belt, and stood waiting.

One of the would-be ambushers had carried a strange bullpup weapon and a glance at the bore was enough to let Reynaud know it was twelve-gauge or larger. It had two pistol grips, the one behind the trigger equipped with a grip safety and the other on the forearm and had a perforated jacket around part of the barrel. A carrying handle doubled as the sights. He picked up the shotgun and pulled the bandolier of shells from the body. As he removed the bandolier, he found the two bullet holes in the man's chest, near enough together they could be covered with an old silver dollar.

The dead man also wore a pistol, a double-action revolver in what looked like a police holster. Reynaud had to fumble with the belt before he finally figured out how to operate the dummy buckle and tug the belt loose. Taking off his own military pistol belt with its .45 automatic, he slung it over his left shoulder and strapped the dead man's belt around his hips. Pulling the corpse's pockets inside out, he found nothing until he felt something solid in the watch pocket. Digging the objects out, he discovered one was a large silver coin and a smaller gold one, about the size of a quarter.

"You can stand drinks," Steve said. He'd just strapped on the other body's high-ride fast-draw rig with a single-action revolver. Bending down, he slipped the Beretta M-9 he carried out of its military holster and shoved it into his waistband, pocketing the extra magazines. He groped through the body's pockets and flashed another gold coin. "I guess we can both stand drinks for the crowd."

"Christmas came early this year," Logan announced. He was grinning broadly and tossed and caught something that flashed with a yellow light, and Reynaud noticed he had two more pistols thrust into his belt.

"Hey," Logan said, apparently noticing Hasteen for the first time, "it's a faithful Indian companion."

Hasteen stared coldly at him. "I'm not in the market for a Caucasian sidekick but you can submit an application if you think you can handle the comedy relief." He glanced at the others. "If you're ready, I'll take you to see Slattery."

"What about the bodies?" Steve asked.

"Leave 'em. You aren't cannibals, are you? We've got no use for them and, sooner or later, somebody will get tired of walking around them and dump them outside of town."

Reynaud, examining and experimenting with the bull-pup, had figured out it was a pump-action shotgun. "It's just that this is a little less formal than we're used to. Since we got out of a Russian prison camp we've spent most of our time in Polish cities or in a sub."

Hasteen led them on a zig-zag route until he shoved open the door of a garage, where several pickups, their hoods agape, stood in ranks, being ministered to by four men in greasy coveralls. "Slattery has a decent business, converting pickups to run on alcohol and replacing electronic ignition systems when they burn out."

Logan shook his head sadly. "Seems like a helluva waste of good booze."

"Well, they're trying to get the oil patch producing again but it's hard to find enough people to help rebuild the oil-cracking plants, and distribution is going to be shot for a long time." Hasteen strode to the office door, pulled it open, and waved them inside.

The man sitting behind the desk looked as if the chair in which he sat had been built around him. Sitting in a chair in front of the desk, a Mexican with hard eyes stared at them.

The man behind the desk stood and thrust out a massive hand. "I'm Buttercup, better known as Jim Slattery." He reminded Reynaud of a fifty-gallon drum with knees and topped with a head that had grown through most of its hair.

Each member of the group shook the hand and introduced themselves. After they'd finished, Slattery nodded to their "guardian angel" and the Mexican. "You've already met Hasteen, and this is Paco Morales." The Mexican nodded and seemed to be studying them.

Hasteen shoved his hat back and let it hang by its latigo,

mounted a chair backward, and sat with his arms crossed on the back of the chair. "You were right, Slattery. They managed to get themselves into a dust-up."

Slattery sank back into his chair, which protested with a creak. "I thought I heard gunfire. What happened?"

"They got paid for." Hasteen dug the wallets out of his belt and tossed them onto the desk. "It was a set-up, an ambush. All three of the ambushers had gold. Someone wanted them dead badly enough to pay top dollar."

"I was afraid that might happen," Slattery said.

"What do you mean?" Reynaud demanded.

"I mean we don't have a secure radio here, so if the Russian you're chasing—Chernikov is his name, right? If he or some of his contacts had been listening to the right band, they'd have known you were going to hit town." He turned to Hasteen. "Did you recognize any of them?"

"One of them was Toby Wells." Hasteen glanced at Logan. "That was the one you killed. Wells got himself fired from Gorman's a few days ago—at least, that's what I've heard."

"Think you could find out who did the hiring for the jobs?" Slattery asked.

"Maybe." Hasteen stood. "Paco, why don't you come with me? We'll make the rounds of the bars and see what we come up with."

The Mexican stood and picked up the straw hat on the desk, patted it into place, then drew his .45 Colt automatic and checked the chamber. "I could stand a drink."

As soon as the two men left the office, Slattery pulled a fifth of Bourbon out of a drawer of his desk. "Sorry, boys, but I don't have glasses. We'll just have to pass the jug around." He took a drink, held out the bottle to the Deacon, who scowled and shook his head, then to Logan, who accepted it and took a long pull on the whiskey. "I know you boys are just brimming with questions, so ask away."

Steve had just accepted the bottle from Logan and took a short drink then handed the bottle to Reynaud. He pointed at the door the two men had just done through. "Who are those guys?"

Slattery's predatory grin was broad enough it looked like a gash in his reddish beard. "Just two of the best gunnies you boys are liable to run into for a long ways around. Hasteen's from Arizona. He's half-Irish, half-Dineh—what us whites call Navajo—and all hell-on-wheels. Paco, he was originally from San Antone. He was visiting family down in Mexico when the Russians popped the nuke over near Lackland. Neither of those boys are real friendly or talkative, but they'll both do to ride the river with. I hear you guys had sort of an interesting time of it, too."

Reynaud had sniffed at the bottle. It smelled like very good Bourbon. Tipping it back, he took a swallow, feeling the welcome burn in his throat and belly.

Logan wiped his mouth with the back of his hand. "Interesting if you consider riding back from Europe in a leaky bucket that couldn't dive more than sixty feet interesting. And we got to worry about whether we'd have kids or, if we do, whether they'd have all the standard equipment and nothing optional—say, a spare head or tentacles instead of fingers, yeah, it was pretty interesting."

"What was the trouble with the boat?" Slattery asked.

Reynaud watched the progress of the bottle around the circle. "It got hit by an air-launched torpedo during the war and the crew only had time for makeshift repairs, so they had a dive limit. They told us the reactor hadn't been damaged but it's a little unsettling to have an officer run a Geiger counter two or three times a day through the area where you sleep."

~ * ~

Slattery passed the bottle on to Logan again, studying the men around his office. He was the head of the Reconstructionists in Texas for several reasons, but the most important of those: he was an excellent judge of men.

Billy Joe McCluskey, the teetotaler, looked to be the most military of them. He was clean-shaven and wore the navy dungarees like a uniform. He was a good six feet tall and he was lean and hard. He had the piercing eyes of a hawk, even a hooked nose that suggested the beak of a bird of prey, and a thin-lipped mouth set in a disapproving line above a lantern jaw. He looked twice as tough as a tree stump and gave the impression of having less mercy than one. He reminded

Slattery of a Japanese lantern, lit from within by a flame. He was a thoroughly dangerous man, a sputtering fuse, but with too closed a mind to be a leader.

Steve Villareal was, like McCluskey, thin, but whipcord lean and flexible, less angular and craggy, and shorter, no more than five-eight. He wore a fine moustache and had the air of a well-bred man who'd become used to slumming. He moved with feline grace and the manner of a decisive man.

The Cajun, Dechaine, was about five-ten with a medium build, maybe a hundred seventy-five pounds, with a lush moustache and tightly-curled hair that suggested, along with a very light chocolate complexion, that some of his forebears were African. He had a watchful, calculating look about him.

Logan Reid was the shortest, no more than five-seven, and the heaviest, at near a hundred eighty-five pounds, all of it rock-solid. He wore a short beard, a sort of ginger color a couple of shades lighter than his hair. He seemed to like to grin and laugh but Slattery suspected he wanted to be far away when Logan stopped laughing. He was the only one wearing anything other than the navy denims and plain black boots.

Slattery had been given some information about these men, and he'd dug up a little more. They'd all been fighter jocks except McCluskey, who'd flown a bomber, and they were just about the last survivors of a Russian POW camp that had once held over two hundred men. They'd escaped, along with three or four others, and made their way to Krakow where they'd learned the camp commandant and his lieutenant had also gotten out. The lieutenant had remained in Krakow to assume command of the local FSB—the new name for the KGB—apparatus, but the commandant had gone to Texas.

When the escaped prisoners had learned what had happened, there'd been hell to pay, and those boys had done a thorough job of collecting the bill. With some Reconstructionists in Krakow they'd crippled, if not killed, the FSB in Krakow. Now they were in Texas to track down Chernikov, the commandant. It was a business trip as well as for pleasure. He'd heard rumblings of an FSB plan, something called Operation A or Operation Alpha. It seemed to be time to take the bull by the tail and face the situation.

"What's this Operation A I've heard about?"

The Cajun looked at the bottle before lowering the level a

good half-inch. "Damned if I know. I wish I did. About the only things I can tell you about it for sure is that it's what Chernikov came to Texas to work on, and if he's a party to anything it's got to be dirty and dangerous." He handed the bottle to Slattery.

Slattery took another good pull and held up the bottle. When all the men shook their heads he screwed the cap back on and replaced the bottle in the desk drawer. "That doesn't narrow it down much. That sorta describes a lot of Texas. I guess the first thing we gotta do is get some clothes for you boys so you don't look so much like pilgrims. The Wellington boots will pass, I guess, but you're gonna hafta chuck the navy cast-offs. And, Logan, I'd advise you to lose that shirt unless you like to fight."

The one named Steve laughed. "Hell, Logan would go three rounds with the devil with a stick, and he'd give Old Scratch the stick. What we'd really like, though, is some decent food. Since we broke out of the p-camp we've only had half a dozen meals that weren't military rations. You ever eat freeze-dried peaches? And they were a delicacy. The worst rations beat the hell out of the slop the Russians gave us in that camp."

"Let's get the clothes first, and I'll take you to a café. I'd also better bring you up to date on the doin's here in Texas."

~ * ~

To Reynaud, Slattery seemed to rise from the chair like a titan rising from the earth. As the man rounded the desk Reynaud saw, for the first time, the long-barreled single-action Colt he carried in a crossdraw rig. "How come so many of you Texans pack those rattling antiques?"

"Better not let Hasteen catch you talking like that," Slattery said. "Some of it's tradition, some of it's comfort, and then there's the gunslinger who can make one of these things really sing an aria."

Slattery led them down two blocks of buildings which were mostly abandoned shells or burned-out hulks, although they passed two bars, a café, and a saddlery. Slattery opened the door of a clothing store and gestured the others past him.

A tall, thin man with a white moustache and dressed like a drugstore cowboy who sold used cars advanced toward them, rubbing his hands together. "Help you, gentlemen?"

Slattery stepped forward. "Wes, these boys are friends of mine. They just got their discharges and I think they've forgotten how to dress like civilians. Would you see they get what they need?" He sat in a chair in the boot department. "You boys be sure to get slickers and cold-weather gear while you're at it. It's pretty wet around here and if you start headin' for west Texas this time of year, you'd better pack a spare pair of mukluks."

Reynaud chose a couple pairs of jeans, socks, shorts, two nondescript shirts, a jeans jacket, a bandanna and a spare, a slicker, and a gray cowboy hat. Remembering Slattery's advice, he added a sheepskin-lined leather jacket. After looking over the boots he decided on a pair of cowboy boots with riding toes and heels and, after taking off the Russian army boots, flung them at a trashcan. "Burn those damned things."

Steve had selected a similar outfit but chose a cream-colored cowboy hat. McCluskey had kept the Russian army boots and picked up two pairs of black pants and two plain black shirts, along with accessories, topping it off with a high-crowned, flat-brimmed black hat.

Slattery grinned. "You look like you're dressing for a funeral or to preach a sermon."

"You got it in the wrong order," Logan said. "First, the Deacon reads to them from the book, then he buries them." He held up a pair of brush-finished jeans. "You got these in burgundy?"

Wes stared at Slattery. "Is he shittin' me?"

Slattery rolled his eyes upward, perhaps praying for patience. "Would you just pick some clothes out? Preferably something less 'scintillating' than that shirt you're wearing."

"I'll bet you live on a second floor just so you can piss on parades," Logan grumbled. He finally chose a paisley shirt, two pairs of jeans, and a charcoal-colored cowboy hat. He also selected underwear and almost a dozen pairs of socks. "God bless America," he said, "the country that has socks. You know what the Russkys do? They wear diapers on their feet." He strolled along the racks and finally pulled out a heavy jacket and an unbleached linen duster, a long, loose coat that reached below his knees.

He disappeared into a dressing room and emerged wearing the hat, jeans, and the duster over his Hawaiian-print shirt. "Okay, let's go get some grub."

"What do I owe you, Wes?" Slattery shoved himself out of the chair.

Wes jerked his thumb in Logan's direction. "The comedy show almost paid the bill." He scratched some figures on a sheet of paper and did a quick bit of addition. "Looks like it's gonna come to about three bits. Your marker's good."

Slattery signed the bill then led the way to the café they'd passed and the party took a table in a corner. They all ordered the special, a huge steak with mashed potatoes, gravy, and corn, and they had the waiter leave the pot of what passed for coffee at the table.

As they waited for the food, Slattery leaned forward, bracing his powerful forearms on the table. "I guess you fellas have a pretty good idea what happened to the country, what with the war and the plague." He ignored the nods from Steve and Reynaud. "Most of the cities went to hell in a handbasket and a bed sheet. You dump a plague in a place where you got thousands of people living' cheek by jowl and you get a real disaster. If you get lucky and nobody drops a bomb on you, you still got about half the people dying of the plague, a lot of the survivors crazier than Panama hats, and you get looting, riots, fires, and all the rest.

"Water and sewage go down their own tubes so you get secondary plagues—typhus, cholera, whatnot." He took a sip at a glass of water and frowned at it. "I think they finally caught Charlie the tuna.

"When everything went to shit, the country broke up like a taco shell. It was everybody for themselves, each little community for itself. Forget politics. There were enough people sore about the mess that any politicians were likely to be shot—if they were lucky. I know of a senator got skinned alive. 'Course, Texas has always been sort of a special case anyway.

"When push came to shove, we had to go it alone. A lot of Mexicans saw gringos keeling over, and even after the plague there was a lot more Mexicans than the land there could support, so some of them headed north. Even had a few Mexican army units jump north. One headed this way but what was left of the National Guard and a few troops from here and there, along with locals—Chicanos and Yanquis—busted them up at Corpus. I hear there's still about a company loose in west Texas, though.

"Colonel Whiteacre, of the Guard, thought he had the best claim to run the place so he sorta nominated and elected himself president of the New Republic of Texas. He's gotten away with it because he knows his shit. He's even got coinage being minted and he's doing a pretty good job. There's some grumbling about having a 'military dictator,' but the fact is he's helping hold the eastern and northern parts of the state together. I hear he's been doin' some hagglin', with the Mexicans in the south and a lot of them in the west are willin' to talk—the government in Mexico City ain't in such great shape, either."

The waiter brought them their meals. Logan looked up at him and said, "Start another one of these for me." He cut off a piece of steak, forked it into his mouth, and chewed, an expression of beatific rapture spreading across his face.

"Hey, go easy," Slattery said. "I ain't got all that much ready capital."

"Sounds like Texas weathered the storm pretty well," Reynaud observed.

"Better'n a lotta places, I guess, although some parts are pretty nasty," Slattery replied. "And you'll notice everybody is packing iron. It ain't just ballast to keep 'em from sailin' off like tumbleweeds. You'll also notice people don't pay too much attention to gunplay, beyond gettin' behind good cover. This coastal area is pretty well settled down, but further west you'll find bandit gangs—Mexicans, rednecks, and even mixed, not to mention the crazies."

Logan had finished his first plate of food. "Slattery, you don't know how good that tasted." As the waiter brought him his second plate, he held up the coffee pot. "We need a reload on this, too,"

"So, what's the program?" Reynaud asked.

"That's kinda my question for you." Slattery finished his potatoes and gravy and wiped his mouth with his napkin. "I guess the boys in the network found out something that told 'em Chernikov was headed this way. My guess is, he's the one who put out the contract on you boys, which is why I sent Hasteen and Paco out to try to dig up something. We're supposed to get some other help, too, a former Texas Ranger. Fella by the name of Wade Patterson. He's a good man of the old breed. You know—one riot, one Ranger."

"Maybe we ought to be out seeing the sights," Logan said, already halfway through his second meal. "And the sight I most want to see is a Russky dressed like a cowboy."

"If the guy you're after is around, he's probably crawled into a hole and pulled it in after him. Just meeting him by chance is awful unlikely, and he might spot you first. If that happens, the best you can hope for is to only have blown the element of surprise."

"What are the local customs?" Reynaud asked. "I don't want to spend all my time playing gunslinger."

"Usually you'll know when trouble's brewin'," Slattery said and finished his coffee. "Just don't go around with a chip on your shoulder, and it's a good idea to steer clear of bars and cantinas. That's where most of the action happens. A couple of boys get tanked up, and a fight starts. Most times, it's just knuckle-dustin', but now and then somebody pulls a knife or a gun. Oh, and watch out for dogs. A lot of 'em have gone feral, and they're a lot smarter and more dangerous than mutts born in the wild."

The waiter began to clear the plates from the table. "You want anything else?"

"Nah." Slattery dug out a small leather pouch. "What's it come to, Ernie?"

"Five ROT dollars will cover it."

Slattery fished out five of the silver coins about the size of the old silver dollar and laid them on the table.

"I'd like to get some leather for my new guns," Logan said.

Slattery looked into his poke. "The well's fixin' to run dry, boys."

"Don't worry about it," Logan said. "We picked up a little change along the way. All we need to know is how much the coins are worth."

"Well, the ROT dollars I paid the bill with have half an

ounce of silver in them, and they're worth about three dollars old money. "There's a gold coin about the size of the old quarter that's worth about what you could buy in the old days for a hundred and fifty dollars, and there's another gold coin about the size of the old half dollar that's worth three hundred. Cartridges are used for change a lot, along with almost any kind of barter.

"Some places still use the old currency and change but only for local trade. Any old silver change is still good, at about twice the face value." Slattery stood. "Alright, let's go to the saddlery. That's where you'll find almost anything leather."

The saddlery was two doors down and, as they walked through the door, Reynaud breathed in deeply, inhaling the aroma of worked leather. Half a dozen saddles mounted on sawhorses stood along the wall to the left and eight or ten pairs of chaps, both batwing and shotgun styles, hung from the rafters. Belts and holsters hung on racks.

A thin young man with a dense moustache and wire-rimmed glasses hustled out of the back, wiping dye-stained fingers on a suede apron. "Howdy, Slattery. What can I do for you and your friends?"

Logan opened his duster and laid the large, silvery pistol on the counter, and a smaller, blued revolver beside it. "I need leather for these."

The young man picked up the larger weapon. "Ruger Super Redhawk, .44 mag. Going Cadillac-hunting?"

Logan shook his head. "Just picked it up. I thought it looked pretty. You got a shoulder holster for it?"

The leather worker bent his head and peered at Logan over the frames of his glasses. "Shoulder holster? That's a slow draw. I hope you never need to reach it in a hurry." He carried the pistol to one of the racks, this one holding a number of shoulder holsters and tried the weapon in three holsters before he found one with what he considered an acceptable fit. He brought the holster back and tossed it on the counter, set down the Ruger, and picked up the smaller revolver. "What do you want for this one?"

"I'd like an inside-the-belt holster that clips on. Better make it a right-hand draw so I can reach across with my left hand."

"My name is Ron," the young man said. "This piece is a Charter Arms Bulldog, .44 Special. An adequate little hideout gun." Ron checked the fit of several plain holsters with metal clips before he finally placed one beside the shoulder holster. "Anything else?"

"Yeah," Steve said, "I'd like a shoulder holster for this." He drew the Beretta M-9 out of his waistband.

Ron barely glanced at the weapon. "Good gun. You want it for the right hand or left?"

"Right hand, just in case I need more than six shots." He patted the holster he'd taken from the corpse.

Ron pulled another shoulder holster from the rack and showed Steve how the pistol was drawn from the back of the holster and helped him fit the rig so it rode comfortably and held the pistol securely. "Okay, how are you going to pay for these goodies?"

Logan drew the Russian Makarov out of its military holster and laid it on the counter. "How much is this worth to you?"

"Souvenir?" Ron asked. He picked the weapon up and looked it over. "I'm afraid it's worth more to you than to me. It's a glorified pocket pistol and the ammo for it has never caught on here. It'd make an impressive paperweight but I couldn't give you enough for it to cover more than a billfold."

Reynaud unslung the web pistol belt and laid it on the counter. "How about this? It's a .45."

Ron drew the pistol, dropped the magazine, drew back the slide, ejecting the cartridge in the chamber, then held the pistol to his ear and shook it, grimaced, then, with the tip of his little finger in the chamber, squinted down the barrel. "It's pretty shot-out. Got any extra magazines?"

"Two."

"I can swap you one of the shoulder holsters for the gun and the magazines."

"Okay," Logan said. Fishing in his watch pocket he dug out the gold coin he'd taken from the body of the man he'd killed. "What can we get for this?"

"Besides what you've already picked out, I've got three steel magazines for the MAC you're packing, and I can let you have a hundred fifty rounds of pistol ammo or seventy rifle cartridges. And you can get three pistols cleaned and tuned."

"How long will you need the pieces, and can we get

loaners?" Logan asked.

"Yeah, leave your pieces tonight and pick them up tomorrow afternoon. They should be ready by three. What're you leaving here?"

Logan handed over the Ruger and the hideout gun. "Rennie, why don't you let' im work on that Smith you picked up?"

Reynaud took the revolver out of its holster and laid it beside Logan's guns. Ron picked it up and swung the cylinder out. ".45 Long Colt. You got yourself a good piece here." He handed Reynaud a well-worn revolver. "This 'm is kinda like my girlfriend, not flashy but tight. This is a .357 mag. I'll let you have six rounds and you can get more from your buddy, there, with the single-action." He pointed at the cartridges in the loops of the gun belt Steve wore. Bending, he brought up another old revolver and placed it in front of Logan. "The best I can do for you is this old Colt New Service. It's loaded, and I can loan you a couple extra half-moon clips. It takes the same .45 ACP round as the MAC. For a hideout gun, I've got a Chief's Special." He handed over a much smaller revolver in a hideout holster.

As the group left the shop, Slattery swung his head in the direction of Ron. "Ronnie's a good man, and his brother is probably the best pistol smith in Texas."

"Yeah?" Logan asked. "Where was he?"

"Probably in the back room. He don't come out much since he lost his legs. He's one of the vets of the battle of Corpus Christi."

Hasteen and Paco sat waiting for them when they got back to Slattery's office. "What have you got for me, boys?" Slattery asked.

Hasteen, who'd seemed to be dozing, stretched and said, "It was Toby Wells all right. He and Red Britten had been canned from the Gorman farm a couple of days back. Charlie Silvers was another of the gunnies. He must've gotten tired of doing odd jobs around town. The three of them had been hanging around with a drifter called Stan Klein. Klein and Silvers were the two I shot. They'd been hanging out in a warehouse west of town, the old Capital Plastics place. We thought we'd check with you before we went out to have a little chat with them."

"I appreciate the consideration, boys." Slattery said. "All we want is the name of the man who hired them. The disposition of the body is up to you."

"We'd like to go along," Reynaud said. "We're the ones they tried to kill."

Hasteen glanced at Paco then nodded. "We don't want to look like a war party, though. Two of you come with me, the other two go with Paco. We'll come in from two sides, and you take orders from Paco or me. Clear?"

They all nodded.

"All you boys are getting a little hot," Slattery said. "After you got what you need, get out of town. I'll meet you this evening at the old Hermann farm."

"You two," Hasteen pointed at Reynaud and Logan. He stood and strode out of the office. Reynaud got a good look at the town of Freeport as they walked along asphalt or gravel streets or cut across lawns that had reverted to weeds. Hasteen said nothing but his eyes seemed to be constantly moving, taking in a hundred small details. Abruptly he stopped and turned to face the men with him. "As soon as we round this corner, we'll be looking at the warehouse. You can stay here or you can follow me but, if you go, I want you well spread out. Britten's probably a rotten shot but that's no excuse for clumping together and making it easy for him to get lucky."

"I'll go along," Logan said. He checked the bolt and magazine of his Ingram.

"All right," Hasteen said, "but no shooting unless I call for it, and keep your hands away from your guns unless I give the word. Got that?"

Logan nodded, trying to hide his disappointment.

Reynaud's mouth felt dry and tasted metallic, and he wasn't sure he could trust his voice. He was intensely aware a man with a gun, possibly several guns, was hiding in the building around the corner but he couldn't let his friends take all the risks. "I'll walk with you," he managed to say, knowing his voice was pitched slightly higher than usual because of the anxiety pinching his throat.

"Paco and your friends are going to be coming toward that building from our right, so don't get antsy." Hasteen settled his hat firmly, slightly tilted forward to keep his eyes in the shade, then stepped out from the building sheltering them.

As Reynaud followed Logan, all his senses seemed preternaturally sharp. He could hear the whisper of Hasteen's moccasins as they churned the sand of the driveway. Paco, Steve, and the Deacon appeared around the corner of another building to the right and their weapons were also holstered. His attention shifted back to the warehouse toward which they strode. The sun stood low behind the structure so the building was darker against the glare than it would be after sunset but he seemed to clearly see each rusted nail head, each spiderweb-cracked window then he noticed the rifle barrel thrust through a broken pane of glass. "Gun barrel," he said softly, "second window left of the garage door."

"I see it," Hasteen replied. "Just stay steady." He raised his voice to call out to the building. "Give it up, Red. I'm O'Ryan. Even if you pull that trigger first, you're only about twenty yards off. I think I can get a shot or two off at you, and Paco, over there, will be sure to get you."

"Stay where you are," came a shaky voice from the building.

Hasteen halted and said, "We just need a few words with you, Red. We can make it as easy or as tough as you want it." He began to move slowly ahead again. "You'd better raise that gun barrel. You know a chest shot won't keep me from killing you. Of course, a head shot is an awful tricky shot. And you'll only get one chance. If you miss me by a hair, you're dead, and even if you make the money shot, Paco will get you or one of these other fellas will get a notch."

Reynaud had already decided Hasteen was crazy or suicidal, which came to the same thing. He wanted to rub his moist palms on his shirt but was afraid of making any move that might start the shooting.

"You know the only way you're going to walk out of here is to put that rifle up and talk to us." Hasteen was now less than twenty feet from the window.

The rifle wavered then was pulled inside.

Hasteen continued his unhurried advance and stepped to the open door to be met by the man inside. "Toby and the others took on more hay than they could fork. They won't be coming back."

"That's what I hear." Red was obviously making an effort to keep his voice steady. He was a little shorter than Steve, about Logan's height, and built wiry, with bowed legs, a square face, and a shock of red hair that gave him his nickname.

Paco stepped up beside Red. "Aren't you going to be polite

and invite us in?"

Red's face worked as though he were trying to raise some moisture in a very dry mouth. "Why don't you boys come in an' set a spell?"

"Right nice of you, Red," Hasteen said, and gestured for Red to walk ahead of him, following him to a break room in the back of the building. The large windows, some of them still unbroken, admitted enough light to see four long, plastic-topped tables, a number of chairs scattered around the room, and a vending machine that had once held colas. The machine was dark but they could see it was empty.

"Have a seat, Red," Hasteen said, and turned the back of a chair toward the seat Red had chosen, swung a leg over his own chair, and sat, facing Red. "All I need to know from you is who gave the contract to Toby."

"What makes you think I know?"

"C'mon, Red." Hasteen stared at the man from just under the brim of his hat. "You and Toby have been hanging around together since before the plague. You worked for Gorman together, and you got fired together. Toby got hungry for some money and he thought he'd found an easy way to make it. He'd have tried to get you in on the deal, but you had better judgement than that. Use your good judgement again and tell us who paid for the job."

"If I had good judgement, I wouldn't say nothin'," Red mumbled. "He'd have me killed. He could probably get that job done for pocket change." He looked at Reynaud and the rest of the group. "Somebody figgered you boys were awful tough or awful important to drop that kinda money to be rid of you."

"We're flattered," Logan said, "but we'd kinda like to thank him personally, or maybe return the compliment."

"You give us the name," Hasteen said, "and you got a ticket out of town, and by this time tomorrow you won't have to worry about the subcontractor."

"Sounds real nice but, somehow, I don't think you boys know what you're talking about."

"This is getting us nowhere," Paco snapped. He grabbed Red by the hair and dragged him to the wall, fifteen feet from where Hasteen sat. "Here." He handed Red an old half dollar then grinned at Hasteen. "I don' think you can make the shot and two ROT dollars says you can't do it."

"You're on." Hasteen stood. "Red, hold that between your thumb and first finger." He loosened his right-hand Colt in its holster. "If you make me miss because you wobbled, I'm going to be real upset."

With a hand that trembled slightly, Red held the coin as far away from himself as he could reach.

The Colt appeared in Hasteen's hand. It roared and spat flame, and the coin flashed in the dim light as it spun away and fell, ringing, to the floor. Hasteen twirled the gun back into its holster.

"Aw, shit," Logan said, "that was too easy." Standing beside the vending machine, he swung up the MAC and fired a short burst into the machine's lock, pulled open the door, and hauled out the coin box. After rummaging in the box for a moment, he tossed Red a quarter. "This ought to make it more of a challenge. Double or nothing?"

Hasteen stared at Red. "How about it? Has your memory gotten any better?"

Red stared back then slowly held up the quarter.

Again Hasteen's pistol appeared in his hand as if by magic, and again it roared. The quarter hit the floor and rolled under one of the tables. "That was a little trickier," Hasteen admitted. "I wasn't real sure I could make that shot, myself."

"Aw, hell," Logan said, "let's go for the whole wad." He dug through the change box again, tossed a dime to Red.

"Now that's going to be a real trick," Hasteen said. "That thing isn't much bigger than a .45 slug. I'm liable to take a little skin off this time. Of course, the odds get steeper that I'm going to make some little mistake and Red, there, is going to have trouble either pointing out the sights or doing much of anything that requires a thumb. How about it, Red? Memory jogged yet, or do you need another loud noise to help it along?"

"Okay." Red dropped into a chair. "The one you're after is Mike Donovan."

"Where do we find him?" Hasteen demanded.

"He keeps a back room at the Lucky Slug. I hear he owns the place, that Gerstner is just a cover. Before you get too excited, I oughta warn you he keeps enough gunnies in the place to start an army."

"Why din't he just have his pistoleros do the job instead of farming the work out?" Paco asked.

"He's real slick, that one is," Red answered. "You won't find anything in or around him that'll tie him to anything."

"All right, *vacquero,* we've kept you here long enough." Paco said. "You've got a horse out back getting fat eating the grass here. You need to give him some exercise. Clute, Jones Center, and Oyster Creek are all about five miles away. If you ride hard, you should be able to reach any of them by dark."

"Hell, I'm not likely to stop this side of Houston." Red began to gather up his few belongings and stuff them into saddle bags.

"Paco, Logan, you can pay up now," Hasteen said softly. "Pay Red. I couldn't have done it if he hadn't held 'em steady."

Paco hesitated a moment then dug two ROT dollars out and handed them to Red. Reynaud took out the ROT dollar he'd found on one of the corpses and gave it to Logan. "You're still light," he said. "Next time you'd better check your poke before you raise the bet."

"Hey," Logan said, "Hasteen never shot the dime away."

"You're right," Hasteen replied, "but since Red's done his part, you hold the dime."

Logan only paused for a deep breath. "You know, a fella has to have confidence in his friends. I'm sure you could've done it, no sweat. Any way you can take it out in trade?"

"I'll cover it," Hasteen said, and tossed another coin to Red.

Paco had slung Red's saddle over his shoulder and caught up the saddle blanket. "I'll help you with this." He strode out the back door.

Reynaud was surprised how quickly they had Red ready for the road. "You take care of yourself, Red," Hasteen said. "Pick your friends real careful. You're too good a man to get killed for some damned fool."

Red touched a forefinger to the brim of his hat in a sort

of salute then shot the spurs to his gray mare, which reached a gallop in three strides.

As horse and rider sped away, Logan turned to Hasteen. "I like your style. You're the kinda guy the Lone Ranger would've liked."

~ * ~

Hasteen stared at Logan, not sure whether the blocky little man was making fun of him but Logan's broad, bearded face seemed open and genuinely friendly. He nodded at the compliment then glanced at the others. "I suggest we ought to have a few words with Slattery before we go talk to Donovan."

Chapter 2

Colonel Alexei Fydorovich Chernikov stared out the window. He raised the glass of vodka and sipped, without pleasure. It was too warm, it lacked the purity of good vodka, and it lacked the taste of the flavored varieties. He'd once tried squeezing the juice of a pepper into American vodka but the result was even more unpleasant than the plain vodka. His finger flicked at a piece of lint on his carefully creased trousers and he found himself growing increasingly angry at the delay.

He'd activated four sleeper agents and he considered the term most appropriate—these people dozed and slumbered, lacking purpose. Operation A was the last, deadly stroke of the war, the blow that could destroy what remained of the United States, could finish the collapse of the country and set back efforts to rebuild for more than a generation.

These fools wanted to know how it could help Russia, missing the point entirely. His own nation was in no better condition than the United States but the resilience of the Russians would see them rise again in power, and this was a chance to neutralize their greatest rival and danger, now that most of China was radioactive ash or scoured by plague. These fools didn't understand the power of hatred, like a shining, naked blade that could cut away all the flab and soft muscles down to the clean bone.

The sleeper agents were too soft to understand, or perhaps they'd become soft from having lived too-comfortable lives for too long. The power of hatred was best demonstrated in killing a wounded enemy, making sure it couldn't rise again. That was his purpose in being here, on taking over Operation A.

He began to sort through the intercepted messages and frowned at the sheet on top. Recon 9. The team that had been sent to find him. One of the questions that message raised had probably already been answered. Benton had been certain the man he'd visited could dispose of this Recon 9, whatever it was. But other nagging questions remained. Who were the people who made up Recon 9? He was sure the CIA were at least as disorganized as the FSB, and as discredited. But, if not the CIA, who? Who was the local contact? He only had a code name; Buttercup.

Recon 9 could've come from anywhere but Europe was most likely, and they'd known his name and that of Operation A, although they didn't seem to know what constituted Operation A. But how could they even know of the mission? His briefing on the project with Colonel-General Damieten, had been face-to-face in the colonel-general's office, and the message to activate the project had been sent on a scrambled line. Also, he hadn't used his name since the identity farm prison camp at Zheltyye Vody.

He scowled at a memory. Eight prisoners had escaped on the day Operation Passport had been terminated, using a prison riot as a diversion. That riot had killed most of the guards as well as all the prisoners. He'd directed the hunt for the escapees himself, and they'd found one body, a German named Schiller, then he'd turned the matter over to the MVD and he and Lieutenant Oshevsky had left for Krakow, the first step in both their operations.

Oshevsky, at least, had appreciated the power of hatred. Now he was busy turning the remains of Poland into a client state under the control of the FSB or, at worst, a wounded creature biting at its own vitals with the church and government and army all at each other's throats. If ever Oshevsky was discovered, Chernikov was certain he'd more than decimate his attackers, dying on his feet with a gun blazing in his hand.

That was the way for a man to die; fighting, asking no mercy and giving none.

He saw Benton approach the house, heard the rattle of the lock, and then the man was inside. From the way he held his head and from the expression on his face, the news was bad. Chernikov drew his suppressed Makarov from its shoulder holster and placed it on the table before him. "What's the problem?" he asked.

Benton eyed the pistol and cleared his throat, a fine sheen of sweat appearing across the bridge of his nose and just above his upper lip. "The men Donovan hired are dead. I told him I did not pay for failure and he would have to finish the job at his own expense."

"Does this Donovan know who you are?' Chernikov asked.

"Yes, but he understands discretion. It is essential to his business. We might hope the people you want dead find a trail back to Donovan. That would be the best way to be sure they all die."

Chernikov shrugged and stood, leaving the pistol on the table. "That seems direct enough. Just the same, you have a pistol, haven't you?"

Benton patted his shirt.

"Very good. Keep it to hand, just in case." He moved away from the table. "Have you learned about Doctor Schmidt?"

"He must have died of plague; his brother has not heard from him since the outbreak."

"That's too bad." Chernikov began to pace. "What about Professor Baker?"

Benton relaxed a bit. "He runs a veterinary clinic near Victoria. I have two of Barnes' men to escort you to Victoria and help you find him. There was to be a third man but he went with the men Donovan hired and he was killed. The other two will meet you in Clute. There's a bar there called the Yellow Rose. Tell the bartender you're looking for a man named Randy."

"Very good. You won't mind my taking your automobile." It wasn't a request.

"No," Benton seemed eager to please. "Here are the keys." He reached into his pocket and held out the keys to his car.

"When can I leave for this town—Clute?"

Benton had poured himself a glass of the vodka and took a deep drink "You may leave at any time. Barnes' men should be there by now."

"Excellent." Chernikov took a step toward Benton, holding out his hand for the keys, then drove the edge of his hand into the man's throat. He felt the cartilage collapse then he slammed the heel of his palm into the bottom of Benton's nose, driving the septum up into the brain. The man dropped like a bag of rocks without making a sound.

Chernikov sneered down at the corpse. Benton was probably as unreliable as he was stupid. To assume he was safe because Chernikov had moved away from his pistol was no less stupid than dealing with a man who could identify him. Now, at least, his silence could be relied upon. Chernikov had broken enough men himself to know that no one was immune to pain or the threat of pain.

He gathered the papers and tossed them into the fireplace, lit them, and watched to be sure only ashes remained. He'd already cleaned the place of any clues, even wiping off the few fingerprints he might've left. Taking out his handkerchief, he carefully wiped off the bottle then wrapped Benton's dead fingers around it, since the total absence of prints was almost as much a clue as leaving his own. He carefully cleaned the glass he'd used, wiping away all traces.

He glanced outside. The darkness was deepening enough for him to leave without anyone being able to tell he wasn't Benton. He picked up the Makarov and slipped it back into its shoulder holster then, using the handkerchief to avoid leaving prints, he opened the door and left.

~ * ~

Slattery listened intently to Hasteen's terse report then leaned forward. "There's something I ought to tell you boys about Donovan. He's got an insurance policy. To get into his office, you gotta go through his bar, where he keeps a bigger rogues gallery than you could find on a post office wall. And his office has its own little surprises. I talked to a fella who did some work for him. His desk is one huge claymore mine."

"How's that?" Hasteen asked.

"It's a steel desk, with heavy steel plates welded on. He's covered that with a coating of explosives and a layer of shrapnel over that, the whole thing covered with a veneer shell. Knowing what I do about him—he's a sure-thing shooter—I'd guess his desk has a deadman's switch."

"I've got one of those, too," Hasteen said, and reached behind his back to draw a much-modified single-action revolver. The barrel had been cut off at three inches, the ejector rod and tube had been removed, along with the trigger, the grip had been re-shaped to form a bird's-head grip, and the hammer spur had been cut off and replaced with a tiny spike spur mounted lower. Reynaud could see that if the pistol were cocked, the slightest slip would release the hammer.

"I don't like it," Slattery said. "If he's jumpy enough to touch off his desk we might wind up burying the both of you, along with any information Donovan might have."

"Is there a back door to the place?" Reynaud asked.

"Yeah, but it'll be sure to be booby-trapped too." Slattery frowned. "He ain't what you'd call real accessible."

"No problem," Reynaud said. "We go in the front door with Paco. I'd guess if we make our presence known with a little gunfire, this Donovan might scurry out the back. He might have a bodyguard or two, so maybe someone should stay with Hasteen, but the two of them ought to be able to nab the guy."

Slattery frowned again. "It's iffy, but it's probably the best shot we've got. All you fellas think you can handle this?

"I still think I can handle my part alone," Hasteen said.

"I think he can, too," said a voice from the shadows cast by the wall of the farmhouse. A tall, thin man stepped into the dim light. He wore a white cowboy hat, what looked like a tan military-styled uniform, and a pistol belt with a pair of .45 Colt automatics. The man approached the group. "Howdy, Slattery," then, to Hasteen, "You must be O'Ryan. I've heard of you." The stranger glanced around the group until he saw Paco and a grin slowly spread across his face. "Paco Morales, nice to see you again, and I'm glad to be on the same side with you this time." He shook Paco's hand, which Paco had extended after a slight hesitation.

"This is Wade Patterson," Slattery said, "former Texas Ranger." He introduced the rest of Recon 9 and Patterson shook hands with each of them, studying each man closely.

"Looks like you've got yourself a real good group here, Slattery. Whose scalp are we hunting?"

"Ever hear of Mike Donovan?"

"Yeah, he's no amateur," Patterson replied. "He's usually got a pack of gunnies hanging around him. What's he into this time?"

"Contracts," Slattery said. "He paid top dollar to have these boys bumped off."

"Sounds like the Mike Donovan I know. Well, let's go

talk a little business with him."

"Hold on," Reynaud said. "What do we do once we get the information? You want to meet us in town right after the interview?"

"Use your judgement on that," Slattery replied. "I'm going to spend the night out here. If the information is hot, follow it up right away then get back to me here. Or just meet me here as soon as you finish chattin'."

~ * ~

Reynaud was third in the line, after Paco and Logan, to step through the doors of the bar, and he wiped his hands on his jeans jacket and almost reached down to be sure the thumb-break snap on his holster had been released but decided to keep his hands away from his weapon unless he needed it. The Deacon strode right behind him, his .45 automatic out of its military hip holster and thrust into his pistol belt. Steve came next, with Patterson at the rear of the line.

Paco strode to the bar and, without waiting for the bartender, said, "Tequila. Give me that bottle." He pointed to a bottle on a wall rack, "And a glass. I'll pour it myself."

The bartender stared at Paco for a long moment and looked as though he might refuse then he turned and reached for the bottle. When the bottle and a glass stood on the bar before him, Paco reached for a saltshaker. "And I want a lime."

A second bartender backed away from the group, keeping both hands in clear view. Reynaud looked around the room and saw several men edging for the door. Three men sitting at a table had thrown down their cards and began to stand. Two other men, who'd been leaning on the far end of the bar, straightened and let their hands drift toward their gun belts. Four other men at another table had stopped playing cards and their hands slowly crept toward the edges of the table.

Logan had also noticed it. He faced the table and swung his duster open. "Naughty, naughty. We wouldn't want anybody to think you boys were playing with yourselves. Time for a hand check."

The bartender's voice was very quiet. "That'll be ten ROT dollars for the bottle and the lime."

"Get your boss out here. Tell him we intend to pay the bills in lead." Logan kept his eyes on the men at the table, who had all placed their hands flat on the wood.

"I'm the manager here," said one of the men at the other end of the bar. "Get out of here and leave the bottle."

The crackling sound of the bottle's seal being broken was loud in the room. Paco used his left hand to pour himself a glass of tequila then, with the salt and the lime, took a drink.

"I've heard of you, I think," the manager said. "Paco Morales, isn't it? You're supposed to be a real badass peppergut. I don't think you're that damned bad."

Paco stared at the man and smiled, showing a flash of white teeth under his heavy moustache.

"Bill," the manager said to the other man at the bar, "you stay where you are." He began to slowly sidestep to his left until he stood halfway between the bar and the table Logan faced.

Suddenly the nearer bartender reached under the bar. Paco's automatic was instantly in his hand, blazing and roaring, and the bartender spun and fell with the racket of breaking glass.

Reynaud snatched at his own weapon then saw the manager, who'd started to draw, stagger backward, his pistol dropping from limp fingers. Almost at the same time, the man at the end of the bar doubled over and dropped, falling to his knees and the top of his head then rolled away from the bar.

Logan's MAC made a loud, ripping noise and all four of the men at the table were flung away, tumbling across the floor. One of them lunged for the automatic he'd dropped.

Reynaud pointed his revolver at the figure and jerked the trigger three times. One bullet hit the floor, sending up a spray of splinters, while the others smashed the man's right arm and tore into the side of his neck. Reynaud wasn't even aware of his weapon's recoil. He'd only dimly heard the viciously sharp report of the .357 magnum and scarcely heard the other shots fired.

He heard another single shot and wheeled to face the bar but Paco had already shot the second bartender.

"Get down!" Paco shouted, and ducked below the level of the bar.

Reynaud threw himself to the floor then caught at the

Deacon's leg, pulling him down, too. He waited for whatever danger Paco had warned them about. He'd just decided the battle was over and started to his feet when an explosion behind the bar hammered at his ears and sent chunks of wood whistling past him.

Paco slowly stood. "He'd pulled the pin of a grenade but I shot him before he could toss it out here."

Everyone spun as a .45 roared and the manager, who'd reached his gun and raised himself up on one arm, rolled onto his back. The Deacon slid his automatic back into its holster. "'Those who live by the sword will die by the sword.'"

Paco gazed sadly at the broken bottle of tequila then finished the drink in the glass beside it. "Maybe Hasteen's right. Maybe I should start double-tapping them." He nodded to Patterson who, with Steve, had killed the three men at the other table.

Patterson was already pulling gun belts off the bodies. "Let's make a quick grab and get out of here. I don't want to have to explain this to the local sheriff."

~ * ~

Hasteen stayed in the shadows at the back of the building. He knew when the rest of the group entered the bar because the babble of conversations suddenly stopped. He could barely hear voices then the gunfire began, with sounds like two or three submachine guns firing short bursts with a few ragged pistol shots as counterpoint. He heard Paco's voice, shouting, then an explosion shook the building. After a moment, he heard a single pistol shot.

Before the sound of the shot had died away, something rattled at the door inset in the back of the building and the barrels of a sawed-off shotgun were thrust through the opening.

A man crept into the alley, swinging the shotgun's muzzles through an arc that covered the entire back wall of the building. A second man appeared in the doorway and stepped into the alley. He waited for the first man to take the lead, staying motionless while the bodyguard started for the shadows where Hasteen waited.

Hasteen stepped into the dim light cast by a window. Both men saw him and the man with the shotgun swept the weapon around but Hasteen drew and fired before the guard could bring his shotgun to bear. The shotgun bellowed and the muzzle flash was followed by roiling dust as the loads went into the alley.

"Don't try it, Donovan," Hasteen said. "You'd never live long enough to put your hand on it."

Donovan slowly raised his hands.

Hasteen spun his Colt into its holster. "You don't want to leave yet, Donovan. The party hasn't really started." He stepped up beside Donovan and whipped out the slip gun and pressed it against Donovan's side. "This is a slip gun so, if you have any ideas about setting off any booby traps, you'd better plan on a double funeral."

Donovan led the way back into his office, where Hasteen had a chance to study the man. He wasn't the weasel Hasteen had expected. He stood nearly six feet tall and broad-shouldered and he wore an expensive, well-fitted suit. His features were sharp and regular but with thin, cruel lips and a coldness in the eyes. Hasteen waved him to a position in front of the desk then sat in Donovan's chair. "Just a couple of little questions. Who paid you to rub out some people just off a boat?"

Donovan crossed his arms. "Surely you don't expect me to betray my business ethics."

Hasteen snorted. "If you've got ethics they probably belong to someone else and if you have morals, they've probably got the serial numbers filed off." He slid down in the chair to be able to examine the desk while still watching Donovan. "There's a switch down here, and a button. Now, what would happen if I were to flip this switch?"

"Don't do it!" Donovan shouted. "That's a deadman's switch. There'll be an explosion that'll take out the building if you turn on the switch without pressing down the button first and keeping it down."

"Interesting." Hasteen carefully lowered the hammer and set the pistol on the desk then pressed the button with his right hand and flipped the switch with his left. "Now, who did you say hired you?"

"If you let go of the button, we both go up."

"Nice bluff," Hasteen said. "You're called."

"No!" Donovan raised his hands to placate. "We can make some kind of deal. You know I can't let it get around I talked about a client, right? Now, you got to keep it quiet where you heard this, understand?"

"Quiet as the tomb."

Donovan swallowed. "All right. The guy you're looking for is named Benton. Carl Benton. He used to manage the plastics plant."

"You wouldn't lie to me, would you?" Hasteen demanded.

"No, no." Donovan spread his fingers nervously. His courage, which had begun eroding, was in a state of collapse.

"I'm glad to hear that," Hasteen said. He started to stand. "Well, so long."

"Wait! You've got to throw the switch!"

"Oh, that's right," Hasteen said, and removed his finger from the button. The roar of the explosion was like a huge club, hammering his ears and the concussion hurled him back into the chair. For a moment he was too stunned to think then he lurched to his feet. Something tickled his upper lip and he wiped away the line of blood that ran from his left nostril. He reached out and flipped the switch off. "Sorry about that," he said to the mess on the floor that hardly looked as though it had ever been human. "I could never get the knack of all these high-tech gadgets."

The building seemed to wobble as he walked back the way he'd come, slipping out into the alley. The flash of the explosion had left an afterimage that barely let him see the shadows, much less anything hidden in them. His coordination returned before his night vision and he slowly made his way out of town and to the farm.

By the time he reached the house he was finally able to see clearly in the moonlight and starlight, and the glow in the window was a sign the others had returned. Alone, Slattery was too cheap to waste kerosene, or even a candle,

He shoved open the door and, without a word, walked to the table where Slattery had a bottle. He poured himself a drink, swallowed it, felt the alcohol burn away the dust and shock in his throat. "Carl Benton is our man."

"We heard the blast," Paco said. "I don' suppose we need to worry about this Donovan deciding to not leave his work unfinished."

"He looked pretty unfinished, himself, when I left," Hasteen said. "Are you ready to go find your man?"

Slattery pursed his lips. "All this action in one night is liable to leave you boys in worse shape than something that's been rode hard and put away wet but it's probably best to move fast. I'm afraid brother Donovan's demise was sort of noisy, not the sorta thing you can keep quiet, so the longer we take to get Benton, the more likely he is to vacate the country."

Hasteen ejected the two spent cases and reloaded. "I'm afraid I didn't have time to leave my calling-card on the bodyguard." As though he'd forgotten he had to reload, Steve drew his own revolver, opened the loading gate, and pushed back on the ejector rod.

"What the hell is this?" Steve asked, as a small tube of paper was pushed out the back of the chamber.

"Probably hungry money," Wade replied. "Back in the old days, cowboys used to leave an empty chamber under the hammer, in case anything bumped the hammer. With the Rugers you don't need to leave need to leave an empty chamber but old habits hang on. A lot of them would use the dead chamber as a sort of safe-deposit box—keep a ten or twenty-dollar bill rolled up in the chamber."

Steve shrugged and inserted a cartridge, rotated the cylinder to the next chamber, punched out a dead case, loaded a fresh round, and repeated the operation until the weapon was loaded. Without thinking, he slipped the paper into the watch pocket of his jeans.

"You know who this Benton is, and where he lives?" Hasteen asked Slattery.

"Yeah, he took over a house right at the northern edge of town. It's almost due north of the saddlery. The place is made to look like a cross between a log cabin and a high-dollar hunting lodge. One thing I can tell you for sure; he had a gray over blue '18 Camaro. He's had it in the shop."

The group filed out of the farmhouse, Paco in the lead. He took them around the town, staying among trees and brush as much as possible and, after nearly an hour, he pointed at a house. "That's the place, but I don' see the car."

"Maybe he's already skipped," Steve said. "I guess the only way we're going to find out is to go look."

"I'll take point," Wade said. He crept out of the brush and strode straight toward the dark house. When he reached the metal-framed screen door he paused a moment then pulled it open. He twisted the doorknob then glanced back at

Steve, who stood at his elbow. "Not locked. Not a good sign. You stay here while I go in and check the place out." He shoved open the door and slipped inside. After a few minutes he returned to the door. "Y'all can come in but don't leave any prints or tracks."

"Is he gone?" Steve asked.

"In a manner of speaking." Wade replied, with a grim smile.

As soon as everyone was inside, Wade lit a lamp and they could all clearly see the body on the floor. "Looks like he's been here a while, probably since around sundown."

"Chernikov was here," Reynaud announced. "Look how neat the place is. It obviously wasn't a robbery." He glanced down at the corpse. "And this is his style. He likes to kill with his hands."

"Looks like the end of the line," Wade said. "The best we can do is try to cut a circle. There's three towns pretty close around here. We know the car we're looking for, and somebody must've seen it."

"Now you know what we're up against," Logan said. "This guy gets a hard-on from killing, and he likes to do it with his hands, like he could feel the life slipping out of his victim."

"No percentage in wasting our grief on this one," Paco replied. "He was a player and someone raised the ante."

Logan nodded. "You're right about that. But Chernikov doesn't care who he kills, so be warned."

"Let's get out of here," Wade said. "Slattery can decide what he wants to do about this—whether he wants the local law to get on it right away or let it lie."

They returned to the farmhouse and reported the killing to Slattery who slammed the table with a fist like a ham. "Damn! This Chernikov sounds like someone I really don't want to let get out of sight. You boys bed down here. I'll get one of the boys from the shop to check around in the morning."

They found enough blankets for everyone and, after several coin tosses, Reynaud, Paco, Hasteen, and the Deacon occupied the beds while Logan tried to sleep on a couch that had almost collapsed. The others slept on the floor.

Reynaud got little rest. He dreamed he was turning over bodies whose faces were covered by masks that looked like Chernikov's face. When he peeled away the masks he found the features of men Chernikov had killed in the prison camp or those of his friends and allies. He kept hearing Chernikov's voice, sometimes speaking

Russian, sometimes speaking English, and often laughing. The last mask he peeled off had covered his own face.

He woke, sweating, his pulse racing. After a while he fell back into a fitful slumber, only to dream again and wake again.

Finally he woke to a room growing lighter. After rolling out of bed he pulled on his boots and buckled on his pistol belt then walked outside, where he found Hasteen making what smelled vaguely like coffee. He hunkered down next to the gunfighter, sniffing the aroma from the pot and warmed his hands from the chill of the brisk morning. After a companionable silence Reynaud pointed to the revolvers on Hasteen's hips. "I've been meaning to ask you—I only heard two shots when you killed those two guys who were trying to ambush us, but I saw two bullet holes in one of them."

"There should've been two in the other body, too," Hasteen replied. "I always try to double-tap my kills. It's just a little insurance. As for your having heard only two shots—well, let me show you." He stood, drew his right-hand weapon, and emptied it, replacing the live rounds with what looked like blanks. "These are snap-caps, to keep the firing pin from being damaged by dry-firing."

Hasteen twirled the Colt back into its holster. "The single-action revolver is actually the fastest gun to get into action. A lot of people, when they draw, thumb-bust the gun like this." He slowly drew the pistol and thumbed the hammer back then pulled the trigger as the pistol came level. "Hammer-slapping is faster." He replaced the gun then drew slowly again. This time he dragged his thumb along the front of the holster until it reached the hammer, which it drew back while the revolver was still holstered. His lower fingers curled around the butt and drew the gun while the trigger finger was held straight and stiff along the side of the trigger guard until the gun was out and level, then the trigger finger snapped back and tripped the trigger.

"Now, when you want to fire several shots rapidly, you can fan it." Hasteen chopped at the hammer with the edge of his left hand while his right index finger held the trigger down. "If you really want to speed it up, you 'roll' the hammer." Still holding the trigger down, he held his cupped hand over the hammer and rotated his wrist so he tripped the hammer with the base of his thumb and the edge of his palm. "There was a fellow—he might still be alive, although I haven't heard anything about him since years before the plague. He could draw a single-action and fire five shots in a little over half a second. I'm not sure I'm that good, but I get by."

Reynaud whistled. "Now that's impressive. I've noticed Paco's awfully fast, and Wade seems pretty good, too. Which of you do you think is the best?"

Hasteen unloaded the snap-caps and replaced them with live ammunition. "You couldn't live on the difference."

Logan stepped out onto the porch of the farmhouse and rubbed the sleep from his eyes. "The rest of the gang are still trying to get their asses in gear."

Hasteen pulled up a sack and began to fry bacon and eggs. "There's only three plates and three forks in the house, so we'll have to take turns eating."

One by one, the rest of the group joined them. Each of them, in turn, downing the eggs, bacon, and fry bread and washing it down with the chickory with its trace of coffee. Steve was the last to eat. As he finished, he leaned back with a sigh. "My compliments to the chef. Here; here's your tip." He dug into his watch pocket and felt the piece of paper he'd found in his revolver. He drew out the paper, unrolled it, glanced at it, and handed it to Hasteen. "Here you go, a fifty-dollar bill. If you don't mind the glasses and fangs the guy drew on General Grant, you got some real money there."

Hasteen glanced at the "artwork" then studied the bill more closely. "It looks like the man who had this was using it as a scratch sheet. Do the names Robert Schmidt or Paul Baker mean anything to any of you?"

Wade considered the question for a moment then said, "Schmidt rings a bell with me. Seems to me he was at one of the universities doing research."

"Which university?" Steve asked. "And what was he researching?"

"Damned if I can remember. Maybe Slattery knows or can find out."

Hasteen turned the bill over. "Do any of you know of something called The Yellow Rose? Looks like it might be in Clute."

Paco stood. "Is a bar in Clute. Rough place. I don' think I'd be welcome there again. I had to kill a couple of gringos there."

Hasteen rose to his feet. "Paco, you stay here. Give this bill to Slattery and tell him where I went. I'll be back as soon as I've got something."

"Hold on," Wade said. "I'm going along. There's just the outside chance you'll need some help."

"We'll all go," Logan added. "We've got to be back here by two in the afternoon but our morning's free."

"You going to walk?" Hasteen inquired. "We've only got three horses here."

"I can ride a horse," Steve said, "and I think you'll need someone along who knows what Chernikov looks like."

Hasteen paused only long enough to look at Paco, who nodded, then Hasteen gestured from Steve to the corral. "All right. Let's go."

It took them only a few minutes to prepare Hasteen's lean black horse, Wade's large gray, and the wiry sorrel Paco had ridden into town. Hasteen changed out of the rust-colored silk shirt, black headband and pants, and charro-style jacket into jeans, jean jacket, gray shirt, and a gray cloth around his head, under the hat, but he still wore the silver and the turquoise.

The three who were leaving for Clute mounted and shot spurs to their horses and, within minutes, had disappeared from sight.

Paco turned to the others. "You stay out of sight while I go get Slattery."

"While you're gone," Reynaud said, "I thought the Deacon and I might go pick up the guns we stashed yesterday. It's only a mile or so away. We should be back by the time you get back from town with Slattery."

"All right, but be careful." Paco tossed Logan a .30-30 lever-action rifle and pointed to a low ridge behind the house. "Get up there and find yourself a good place on that ridge where you can see all around. And don' skyline yourself."

Logan moved the lever enough to check the chamber then lowered the hammer to the safety-cock notch. "If anybody gets too close, you want me to pop 'em?"

Paco shook his head. "Not unless you know a *brujo* who can speak with the dead." He turned on his heel and strode away.

Reynaud and the Deacon set out for the highway sign they'd used as a marker. After almost losing their boots in the marshy ground of the fields, they stayed to the road. The day was clear and bright and Reynaud managed to walk some of the kinks out of his back and memories, as the dreams receded, banished by the day.

Reynaud was familiar with coastal Texas, having grown up in Port Arthur, and the familiarity of the country caused a bout of homesickness but a sense of renewed youth.

They found the highway sign, bullet-pocked and rust-freckled, and from there they could see the hedge trees in which they'd stored their long arms. Reynaud climbed the tree and lowered the piece of camouflaged tarpaulin in which they'd wrapped the guns.

By the time the Cajun had climbed back down, the Deacon had pulled on the pouches of magazines for his AK-74 and the bandolier of grenades for the BG-15 launcher mounted under the rifle's barrel and had slung the weapon over his shoulder. Reynaud picked up the rifle he'd brought back, an ancient Russian army Winchester 1895 with a fore end like a musket.

The Deacon picked up Steve's AK-74 so Reynaud slung Logan's stubby AKR across his chest in the style he'd learned from the Frenchman in Krakow then both he and Billy Joe loaded themselves with web gear holding extra magazines and ammunition.

They were gone less than an hour and, as they returned to the safe house, Reynaud waved toward the ridge, wanting Logan to know who was walking in. They'd just finished cleaning and oiling the weapons when a maroon van pulled into the farmhouse's driveway.

Reynaud and the Deacon took cover but the van stopped in front of the house and Slattery hauled himself out of the driver's seat while Paco exited the passenger's side. Walking around to the right side of the van, Slattery opened the sliding door and, after rummaging around inside, emerged with an armful of books.

"When Paco told me what you boys had found, I decided to visit the library. They've got a couple of pre-war *Who's Who*s, including an academic listing. Let's see if we can find the names in here."

He laid the books on the porch and opened the top volume

then consulted the fifty-dollar bill. "Let's see, …Schmidt…Schmidt…" He flipped through the pages. "Here it is; Robert Schmidt." He read the section and frowned. "He was working on recombinant DNA. Says here, he patented a virus that only attacks certain kinds of plastics."

"That doesn't make a hell of a lot of sense," Reynaud said. "Chernikov isn't going to hurt anybody much that way. As I understand it, nothing is being made of plastics anymore; it takes too much manpower, machinery, and petroleum."

Slattery shot him a grim look. "I don't think this Chernikov is interested in that particular aspect of his work. Schmidt was an expert in recombinant DNA and that has biological warfare applications. Let me check the other name." He glanced back at the bill and thumbed through the pages. "Paul Baker isn't here. Let me check another book."

While Slattery dug through the books, Reynaud stared at the Deacon. "I don't like the sound of this. Chernikov seems to want to start another plague."

"To loose again the horsemen of the apocalypse," the Deacon said.

"Here it is," Slattery announced. "I thought he might be listed in the medical guide but his field is veterinary medicine. His forte is—or was—diseases affecting grazing herd animals—cattle, sheep, goats." His frown deepened then he snapped his fingers. "I think I've got the answer, or I'm afraid I've got it. I'm willing to bet everybody's left nut that "Operation A" is "Operation Anthrax.""

Paco spat. "The son of a bitch. We have to stop him, soon."

"I vaguely remember anthrax from old westerns," Reynaud said, "where they had to shoot all the cattle. I gather it was pretty bad. Just how bad is it?"

Slattery maneuvered himself around on the porch. "The basic disease is bad enough. It's spread by spores—it can even be dust-borne—and it has several forms. The most common is cutaneous anthrax, or skin anthrax. The death rate from untreated skin anthrax is from five to twenty percent, but with some dickering around with the bacillus, I'll bet it can be boosted to near ninety percent, and be made antibiotic-resistant to boot.

"A second form is inhalation anthrax. At the beginning, it hits like a cold or flu, but kills in three to five days. Intestinal anthrax is pretty rare but happens in explosive outbreaks. The first sign is a bellyache, then fever and septicemia. It kills pretty quickly, too."

"What would it take to get a project like that off the ground?" Reynaud asked. "And what would it take to spread it?"

Slattery stood and began to pace. "It'd take some kinda research facility to crank it up. Not likely to be a university lab. More likely, it's some sort of stock station on one of the bigger ranches in west Texas. At a guess, most of the facility is already set up and Chernikov is going to activate it. As for how he's going to spread the disease, I'd guess he's gonna need a lot of men who can drive cattle. The easiest way is just to have an affected herd driven north, cutting some into local herds and picking up local stock to replace them. I'm not sure how the drovers are supposed to survive and, somehow, I don't think Chernikov stays awake nights worrying about it."

Reynaud grinned. "I've noticed you seem to slip in and out of the 'good ole boy redneck' jargon pretty easily."

"No big trick. Around here, anybody too well-educated is suspect, and I grew up on a farm and later a farming town. Don't get to thinking anyone who calls suspenders 'galluses' or who turns 'shit' into a two-syllable word is necessarily dumb."

Reynaud smiled. "Your point is taken. So, what do we do now?"

"Not much we can do except wait. Hasteen and the others should be back before two. If they aren't, you and Logan go pick up your artillery. Better get lots of ammo, too. Like I said, Chernikov is liable to have a lot of men around him, and all armed to the eyeballs."

"How about transport?" Reynaud asked. "We're going to need a way to get to west Texas."

"How well do you ride a horse?" Slattery asked.

"Not real well. Most of them I rode, you dropped a quarter into it and rocked for about two minutes."

"You'll learn on the trail. Where you're going, horses are the common means of getting around. Trucks and jeeps and such take gas. You can come up with diesel fuel pretty easily, just by letting crude oil set awhile, but most new machines are so damned complicated that if anything goes wrong with them it takes a PhD to find the problem and fix it."

Suddenly Logan shouted, "Better take cover. Three riders coming in."

Chapter 3

Steve had forgotten how long it'd been since he'd ridden a horse and how many muscles were used for nothing else. He realized he was going to be in for a bout of saddle-sores. The other two set a good pace, a mile-eating trot, staying to the shoulder of the old four-lane highway.

Passing fields of sugar cane and paddies of rice, Steve reflected again that eastern Texas was an almost tropical place. The land in this area was mostly flat, the greatest rises and depths being mere gentle undulations.

They passed a few houses then the houses became more numerous and closer together. When they rode by the shell of a convenience store he guessed they were on the outskirts of Clute. The highway became a four-lane street. A rider approached them and Hasteen hailed him, talked to him a moment, and waited for the other two, who'd dropped twenty yards or so behind him, to catch up. The rider continued on his way past Wade and Steve.

"He said the place is four blocks ahead and a block and a half east," Hasteen informed them. He stretched his legs, standing in the stirrups, then relaxed. "Do you want to do the talking, Steve, since you know the man we're after?"

"Happy to." Steve took the lead, slowing to a walk to spare the horses. As he rode he counted off the next four blocks, turned right, and had covered the next block before he saw the place. Aside from the garish yellow rose painted on the window the place looked as though it'd once been an upscale pool hall. Steve drew rein in front of the building, noticing the door stood open except for a screen door and two horses stood tied to a pipe welded between two broken parking meters, and a blue and gray late-model Camaro was parked across the street.

Steve dismounted and whipped his horse's reins around the pipe then carefully removed from the hammer of his revolver the thong that secured the Ruger in its holster. Glancing back, he saw Hasteen and Wade were right behind him and similarly primed.

Steve drew open the screen door and stepped inside. The right half of the room was taken up with pool tables, with card tables on the left. A twenty-foot bar, lined with stools, faced the door. A man in the back was shooting pool while another leaned against the bar, talking to the bartender.

Steve walked to the bar, observing the other customer had started the day's drinking early. A sign above the bar listed prices and a pot of coffee sat steaming on a small expedition stove.

"What do you want?" The bartender wiped at the bar with a dirty towel, smearing some of the stains on the wood.

Steve put three cartridges on the bar. I'll have a cup of coffee. How are the cackleberries?"

"All right for being out of a box." The bartender held up a box of dehydrated eggs and Steve shook his head. The bartender poured a cup of coffee and set it in front of Steve. "Same thing for your fellows?" he asked Hasteen and Wade, who nodded and placed old dimes on the bar.

The man with the drink sidled toward them, leaning on the bar for navigation, staring at Hasteen. "You an injun? We don't see many injuns around here."

Hasteen ignored the comment until he'd taken a sip of what passed for coffee. He made a face and put the cup down on the bar. "I'm not surprised, considering the lousy coffee and the worse company."

"Hey, was that supposed to be a slam?" the drunk demanded.

"We're looking for someone," Steve said to the bartender. "Big man, wears his hair cut short, and he's a real snappy dresser. If he wore jeans they'd have a crease."

"Who the hell do you think we are," the drunk asked., "the fuckin' triple-A tourist service?"

"I think you're an obnoxious drunk," Hasteen replied. "Unless you have something worthwhile to add to the conversation, keep your mouth shut."

"Hey, you can't talk to me like that. I know some really bad people, important ones."

Suddenly Hasteen's revolver was in his hand and he'd used the barrel to chop down on the glass in the man's hand, smashing it. The drunk jumped back with a squeal, shaking his hand and spraying bloodspots over the bar.

"Dammit," the drunk screamed. "You're dead—"

"You could've fooled me," Hasteen snapped. "Now, you want to start telling me something worth my time, or do you want me to see how many slugs I can put through your belt buckle?"

The bartender leaned to his right and Steve whipped out the gun on his hip. "I hope you were reaching for a box of bandages for your friend there. Put your elbows on the bar."

The man playing pool stopped his practice and stood staring at them. Wade strolled to where the man clutched his cue stick and set a coin on the edge of the table. "How about a game of eight-ball for a ROT dollar?"

As soon as he saw Wade had distracted the other man, Steve turned back to the bartender. "This guy I'm looking for probably came in last night. He drove into town in the car parked across the street. The bastard is a Russian agent, and I want some straight answers in a big hurry."

The bartender slowly raised his hands. "Look, mister, I'd help you if I could but I didn't work last night. I can give you the night bartender's home address."

"Would this sot know?" Steve asked, pointing a thumb at the man who'd finally fumbled the kerchief from around his neck and wrapped it around his cut hand.

"He might." The bartender swallowed. "Dale's a regular. He was probably here last night."

Hasteen gave the drunk what could only be called a smile because it showed his teeth. "Convince me you're important. Tell me what you saw."

The drunk had finally focused on the muzzle of Hasteen's Colt. His eyes grew wider as he realized he was staring down the bore of a loaded weapon and Hasteen's hand was rock-steady. "Okay, yeah, the big guy came in last night and asked Sweeney to see Randy. Randy wasn't here but Clell was, and the two of them left together."

"Who're these characters, Randy and Clell?" Steve asked.

"Randy Simmons and Clell Vickers. They both ride with Phil Barnes."

"This is a little far east for Barnes, isn't it?" Hasteen spun his Colt back into its holster.

"Barnes goes where he wants to go, and wherever the money

is." The drunk tried to thrust out his chest.

"And where is that right now?"

"Somewhere west of here. I don't know where Randy and Clell went, but they're probably gone already."

They turned to see Wade walking away from the pool table while the hustler pocketed the ROT dollar. "You know what they say," the former Ranger commented, "a good pool player is the sign of a misspent youth."

"I wasn't jerking you around about the big guy being a Russian agent." Steve told the bartender. "If you see him again, it's open season and you can even keep the pelt." He turned and strode from the bar. The other two followed and together they untethered their horses, mounted, and slowly rode out of town.

As soon as they were clear of town, Hasteen drifted ahead again and Steve found himself riding knee-to-knee with Wade. "Who's this Phil Barnes they were talking about?"

"He runs a gang of bandits. Mostly, they stay in west Texas. Whiteacre's put a price of a thousand ROT dollars on his head. He's a piece of work. He and his goons will hit a little town, take what they want, and, if it amuses them, leave most of the town still standing. I figure they've wiped out about six or eight little villages and burned what was left on their way out."

"How many men's he got?"

"About forty cavalry under a guy named Gregorio Sanchez, who must've majored in rape and murder. Then Barnes has about three hundred men, most of them in trucks, plus a following in some of the other towns. I hear he's even got one of those little French scout cars the Mexican army bought back in the eighties."

They rode another mile or so in silence then Steve said, "You said something last night that puzzled me. You sounded like you knew Paco from before, and he'd been on the other side. What did you mean?"

"Nothing much. He used to be a smuggler." Wade drew out a cake of chewing tobacco and bit off the end.

"You mean he was a *coyote*?"

"Don't you think that for even a minute. Far as I know,

Paco didn't make dime one on his operations. He was running Latin Americans; Nicaraguans, Panamanians, Hondurans, people who were desperate to get out of their own countries with their families and their lives. Paco'd pick 'em up somewhere in southern Mexico and run 'em across to where one of the church groups would get 'em on the new underground railroad. The Border Patrol knew about him but they were never able to catch him. No, he was no *coyote*. I've heard he had run-ins with a *coyote* or two and left 'em toes-up."

"If you had so much respect for him, why were you on opposite sides?"

"Nothing personal. He had his job and I had mine."

Steve spent the rest of the ride back to Freeport in reflection. He'd always felt apart, a Hispanic from an old and well-to-do family who wasn't quite Anglo, nor truly Hispanic. He could feel compassion for those who had to scramble merely to survive, but they were like people from a completely different world. He wasn't sure he liked Paco, who seemed as dangerous as a coiled rattlesnake, but he decided he respected him.

He'd also found much to respect in the others. Wade was solid and level. He'd enforced the law, but fairly, and he also knew and understood the limits of the law. Hasteen might only be a *pistolero*, but he was a *pistolero* with a code, not a bully who was fast with a gun.

After half an hour or so the ridge ahead looked familiar and he realized they'd arrived back at the farmhouse outside Freeport. When they neared the building he noticed a van in the driveway, then Reynaud and the Deacon stepped out of cover. "It's our boys," the Cajun shouted.

Hasteen rode his horse to the corral, dismounted, stripped the gear off the animal, then began to rub him down with an old towel. Steve copied the gunfighter's actions, wanting to return Paco's horse in the same condition he'd borrowed it.

"Well, boys," Slattery asked, "what's the word?"

"Gone," Hasteen replied. "The Russian linked up with some of Barnes' men. I'd guess some money's already changed hands, and it's a pretty safe bet they have at least forty men to jump when he says, 'frog.'"

Slattery brought the three up to date on the guesses they'd made about Operation A then, "Any idea where they're headed?"

Hasteen shook his head. "Eventually, probably west."

"They're not likely to try to hit what's left of the King Ranch," Wade said. "It's south of Corpus and pretty well-defended. The people there'd shoot Barnes' crowd into hamburger."

Slattery tossed the books into the back of the van and shut the side door. "They must be either picking up stock as they go, or they've already got the herd together."

"Maybe they haven't got their operation running yet," Reynaud suggested.

"It never pays to be an optimist," Slattery replied. He dug into a pocket and dragged out a small leather pouch. "You're gonna need four more saddle horses and a couple of pack animals. Hasteen, you're pretty good at shopping for horseflesh. Why don't you go with 'em and make sure they get what they need. You can get the tack at the saddlery. And make sure you get enough ammo."

"When do we see you again?" Logan asked.

"You probably won't. You boys are getting right warm, and it's probably best for my cover not to be seen with you. If you find you need something or you've got something to report, have Hasteen or Paco come see me."

Slattery started to walk, around to the driver's side of the van then turned to face them. "One more thing; I want you boys to pick out a leader. You're going after a bunch of murderous rabble who'll have you outnumbered, so it'd help if you're organized."

"Who do you recommend?" Wade asked.

"That's up to you boys—I don't have to live with your choice but you gotta live or die with him. As far as recommendations go, for what it's worth, I'd suggest either Rennie or Steve. Most of you are loners, while they tend to think like members of a group." He strolled around the van, climbed inside, and drove away.

"Congratulations, Rennie, it looks like you're stuck with it," Steve said.

"Now hold on." Reynaud looked from one face to the other. "You three Texans, or Texicans, or whatever you call yourselves, you know the area, you know the people—"

"Don't worry, hoss," Wade said with a grin, "we'll tell

you when you're eatin' with the wrong fork. Slattery's recommendation is good enough for me."

Logan had descended the ridge earlier and now he faced the group. "Let's not get too excited. I'd be a damned good leader, and I'm a better hand with a gun than Rennie is."

Paco tipped his hat forward. "If all it took was being good with a gun, you would be fourth in line, or maybe lower. I will go with what Slattery said, and if Steve don' want it, my vote goes to Reynaud."

Steve stood with his hands on his hips. "Logan, you're a good man, but your biggest strength is also your biggest liability. You have no imagination. You can't imagine yourself being killed or wounded, so you're ready to charge hell with a bucket of jet fuel. Well, I'm not ready to charge hell. I'm not the kind of guy they made movies about starring clowns who looked like they popped steroids down like candy. I can imagine being shot, and I'm not eager to find out if I guessed right about how much it hurts.

"Besides," Steve added, "you really don't want to nursemaid us, do you? You're a lot more useful to us on point or covering a flank. You'd have to give that up. Being the leader doesn't mean leading the charge, it means directing the action, which means you have to stay out of most of the action yourself."

Logan stared at the ground for a couple of minutes then looked up and grinned at the rest of them. "Okay, you've convinced me. Congrats, Rennie, better you than me."

Reynaud frowned. "I hope you know what you're doing. And I'm going to need the help of all of you. Right now, I guess we'd better go get some legs. Paco, would you and Wade mind staying here and keeping an eye on the place? Do you need any ammunition?"

Paco had taken his rifle back from Logan. "I would like another forty rounds of thirty-thirty. Wade?"

"I don't need anything, and I'll be happy to keep the home fires burning."

"Great. Hasteen, I'm going to need your judgement. About all I know about horses is that they have four legs, and when you're buying one you're supposed to look in his mouth. What for, I don't know. Hell, I'd probably buy the damned thing if I looked down his mouth and couldn't see out his asshole."

Hasteen actually smiled. "Be glad to help."

Hasteen led them to a corral at the western edge of town and they peered through the poles of the fence at a number of horses milling around. One by one, Hasteen studied the animals, checking teeth, hooves, legs, and temperament. Two of them were rejected when they spooked at a shot fired in the air. He narrowed the selection to eight, which were led to a smaller corral then he gestured at them. "Take your picks. They'll all do."

Steve chose a rangy buckskin, the Deacon picked a chestnut, and Reynaud decided on a half-Morgan mouse-colored mare that Hasteen called a blue roan. Logan studied the remaining animals through narrowed eyes. "I'd really like to have a white horse."

"I thought you'd rather have a horse with their own teeth," Hasteen said quietly. "The only white horse in the other bunch has three hooves in a glue factory and the fourth on a banana peel."

"Well, okay," Logan grumbled. "I'll take the dappled gray, but I'm not gonna call him 'Tarnished Silver.'"

"How about 'Lead?'" the Deacon inquired.

"Or 'Zinc?'" Steve asked.

"'Aluminum' has a nice ring to it," Reynaud suggested.

"Gimme a break," Logan snapped. "I think I'll call him 'Kato.'"

"Strange name," Hasteen commented. "What's it mean?"

"Never mind," Reynaud said, "it's a long story. I'll tell you later. Just pick the pack horses and we'll pay for them and get the hell out of here. You know where we can get a bite to eat? We've got some time to kill before we pick up our guns, and I'm famished."

"Maybe later," Hasteen replied. "First, we need to pick up the saddles and other gear at the saddlery."

At the saddlery, Hasteen chose the gear for them then, carrying the loose gear while the others hauled the saddles and bridles, and led them back to the corral. They fitted out the horses and still had some time before their guns were ready so they found a house, the lower part of which had been converted to a restaurant where they were served a gumbo.

Reynaud sampled a bite then stuffed himself with Cajun food. "I haven't had food this good since the cooking of my mama." He used the Cajun pronunciation of the word.

Logan ate more slowly and drank often. "Damn fine, but they oughta keep an extinguisher handy, and it's not the house I'm worried about."

As they ate, Steve gave them a more complete report of what had happened in Clute, with some embellishment of Hasteen's smashing of the glass in the drunk's hand.

As they stood to leave, Reynaud nudged Hasteen. "We'll probably need supplies anyway, so how about we get a few bottles of their hot sauce? With enough of that stuff, even I can cook."

"Just be damned careful with the stuff," Logan said. "If it ever eats its way out of the jar, or something shakes the pack, we're gonna be out a pack horse."

When they returned to the saddlery Ron laid their revolvers on the counter and took back the loaner guns. "How about ammo?" Ron asked Logan. "If you use that MAC much—" he pointed to the bulge under Logan's arm, "you'd better get at least three hundred rounds of forty-five ACP. That thing goes through caps in a hurry."

"I'm convinced," Logan said, "and I'd like some pills for the other stuff as well." He picked up the Ruger, checked the cylinder, closed it again, then worked the action. "Nice job on the pistol. What've you got to stoke it with?"

"We've got a box of fifty rounds of .44 Special for the belly-gun and a hundred rounds of like-factory for the .44 Mag." Ron set the boxes on the counter.

"Have you got any real hot loads for the Mag?"

"You're not liable to run into elephant or Cape Buffalo between here and, say, San Antone," Ron shot back. "What the hell are you hunting, anyway?"

"Trouble," Logan replied, "and I hear it sometimes comes armor-plated."

Ron disappeared into the back room and returned with another box of cartridges. "We've got these." He pointed at Logan's Super Redhawk. "That's a stout piece you've got there, but I don't think I'd feed even that one a steady diet of these. These are hot-loads and the bullets are full-metal jacketed. They're for silhouette shooting. You need something with a little extra oomph to nudge over a quarter-inch steel plate at a hundred yards." He looked over the metal rims of his glasses. "Still, I'm not sure this is such a great idea. I'd feel awful responsible."

"Can the crap," Logan snapped. "I'll take 'em." He opened the box, loaded six of the hot-loads into the Ruger, and shoved it into its holster.

"What else?" Ron looked at the rest of them. "Or were you just thinking of finding a shady spot and calling in the artillery, there?" He pointed a thumb at Logan.

Hasteen, who'd been leaning on the counter, looked up. "We'll need forty rounds of thirty- thirty, and I'd like another two hundred rounds of forty-five long Colt." He glanced at the revolver Reynaud was putting away. "Make it two hundred and fifty."

"Black powder or smokeless for the forty-five?" Ron inquired. "That's one of the nice things about that caliber; you get the option. It's liable to be the wave of the future, as they say."

"Make it smokeless," Hasteen said. "Most times I don't care but there are rare cases when I'd rather not be sending smoke signals. And I might have trouble cleaning it sometimes."

They also bought two hundred rounds of nine-millimeter parabellum. "Better use that wisely, boys," Ron advised. "When the loaded ammo and smokeless powder for reloading is all used up, that cartridge is going to get real scarce."

Hasteen paid for the ammunition, partly with four pistols from his saddle bags and with one of the small gold coins.

"One last stop before we head out," Hasteen said, and led them to a former convenience store where they bought beans, rice, a couple of slabs of bacon, flour, and coffee. "The stuff is at least half chicory," Hasteen admitted. "Real coffee is getting pretty scarce, but it's black and it wakes you up screaming."

"After we get the other fellows, what then?" asked Reynaud.

"Well," Hasteen said, "the trail, cold as it is, begins in a bar in Clute."

~ * ~

Chernikov had learned to ride a horse long enough ago he'd almost forgotten again and, after over half a day in the saddle, had remembered why he wanted to forget. The two cutthroats ahead of him seemed to know where they were going and, indeed, within the next few minutes, followed an overgrown driveway to an abandoned house hidden in a grove of trees.

They drew rein while still sheltered by the trees, drew carbines from their saddle scabbards, and approached the house warily. One of them, standing beside the door, twisted the knob and swung the door open. The other man, Clell, slipped inside against the wall. Within a minute, he returned to the door and waved.

Simmons, a short, ugly man with a long seam of scar snaking down his left cheek until it was lost in his beard, returned and took the reins of Chernikov's horse. Chernikov dismounted and Simmons led all three animals to a patch of grass, where he picketed them.

Chernikov looked at where the sun still stood above the horizon. "We've still got at least an hour of daylight."

"We've made good time today, starting at dawn. There's no place ahead for the next dozen miles as secure as this." Simmons took the saddles and saddle blankets off the horses and began to rub them down with a handful of grass. "And the horses have about had it for the day. You push too hard, and you'll kill 'em. That'll slow you down a damn sight more, unless you can walk faster than you can ride." He drew a bucket of water from the hand pump and let each of the horses have a single, deep drink.

Chernikov met the bandits well before the trip to Victoria and was angry with them and himself that he didn't just leave them to make their own way to Victoria while he rode there in a car. He could have waited for them in comfort. It was an unusual weakness and he was annoyed with himself for allowing himself to be persuaded, and with the two bandits for arguing with him.

By the time he'd entered the house, Clell, a tall, angular man with straw-like hair, had two kerosene lamps shedding their glow over dust-covered furniture. Immediately, Clell began to break up a collapsed chair and tossed the pieces into the fireplace then strolled outside to return with an armful of wood, which he added to the pieces of the chair.

Chernikov found a chair that still appeared solid and a rag with which to wipe it clean. After he'd made sure the dust had been wiped away, he sat.

Randy Simmons strode through the door, saddle bags slung over his shoulder. He set them near the fire, opened one of the pouches, and began to make coffee. "What do we need to go to Victoria for?"

"I need to meet a man." Chernikov stared coldly at the ugly, scarred little bandit. "You have no need to know even that much. You need only do what I tell you."

Simmons carved off a piece of bread and began gnawing at a strip of jerky. "You're the boss," he mumbled around the mouthful.

"That is correct," Chernikov said, slipped a knife out of an ankle sheath, and whittled at the bread. The meal was a quiet one. After he'd wiped his fingers on his handkerchief, Chernikov stood. "I will take the bedroom opposite the living room. Whatever sleeping arrangements you make will be your decisions."

He heard Simmons mutter something as he left the room but ignored it. Carrying one of the lamps, he strode to the bedroom, carefully gathered the upper sheet and quilt from the bed, carried it outside, shook it out, then, after he'd returned, closed the door and blew out the lamp.

Using the pillows and the quilt, he sculpted something resembling a sleeping form on the bed then took the upper sheet and curled up in the corner of the room by the closet, his pistol and knife by his hand. He trusted neither of the bandits, especially Simmons. Clell looked like the sort of man who always followed the line of least resistance. Such a man was not to be trusted, but could be useful.

Simmons was another matter entirely. He was a brutal man, with a twisted sense of pride and a strong sense of his own power. It hadn't escaped Chernikov that if these two men killed him before he'd met Barnes, they could offer some excuse and probably wouldn't even be disciplined. The promise of wealth was an inducement to a man like Barnes but it was only a promise, given to men who'd probably left a trail of broken words as well as burnt-out villages in their wake. Perhaps he should've brought more than a few gold coins with him but he was certain that would've only sped the confrontation.

Memories came back to him as he lay on the floor, fond memories of the large, squarish building on Dzerzhinsky Square the headquarters of the *Komitet gosudarstvennoy bezopasnosti*. He'd risen quickly in the KGB, later the FSB, and had gained the reputation, very early, as an interrogator who could make a kiosk confess to treason.

He also remembered his first failure; Afghanistan. Most of the interrogation was done by the GRU, the army intelligence unit, but he'd volunteered. He still remembered the first Afghan rebel he'd questioned. The man would not talk. He would scream, but he would not talk. After almost forty-eight hours the Afghan died without ever having broken.

His second case had been easier; a Soviet soldier from one of the Muslim republics who'd deserted and gone over to the rebels. He'd been captured by a Spetznaz team. It'd only taken Chernikov half an hour to drag out of him everything he knew, but it'd taken the deserter three more days to die. Neither Chernikov nor the GRU major had been in a hurry, and the body had served as an excellent example to other soldiers who might've considered deserting.

Another warm memory; he'd gone as an operative with a Spetznaz team in a raid on a rebel camp. It'd been the first time Chernikov had seen combat, the first time he'd killed a man who was also trying to kill him, and he'd found it a heady experience. They'd left the enemy bodies where they'd fallen, but booby-trapped.

His combat tour in the Second Great Patriotic War, after the plague, had been brief. He'd been the political officer of one of the reserve tank armies that had reached the front. After executing the General for defeatism, Chernikov had taken command and led the men against German and American units. The tank army had taken hideous losses but had seized its objective.

It was then he was recalled to take command of Operation Passport, the prison camp for downed NATO flyers serving as an identity farm for the FSB. Chernikov had found it frustrating to simply pass on the identification and information to the high command, not even knowing if the material was being used.

Operation A was far more satisfying. In English, it was Operation Anthrax but since Chernikov spoke the language fluently, it amused him to think of it as Operation Annihilation. He'd be responsible for more American deaths than any general in the army, and the deaths he'd cause would be much more damaging than merely killing soldiers. He'd kill not only men but the women who might bear the next generation of enemies, even the few children who might be part of the next generation.

Suddenly he was totally alert. He didn't know how long he'd been lost in reverie, or even if he'd dozed off, but now each sense was straining to give him perceptions and information. His hand closed on the grip of his knife and his muscles bunched for sudden action.

The bedroom door slowly swung open enough to admit a body. Even in the darkness of the room, Chernikov could make out a shape slipping through the door and, as the form passed in front of the window, pale with moonlight. He could see it was Simmons.

The stocky man had a large knife in his hand. He crept beside the bed and reached down, probing the decoy, then recoiled from it as he realized he'd been fooled.

"Fool!" Chernikov hissed. He raised his knife, pointed it at the shape, and pressed the release. Simmons grunted as the blade of the ballistic knife caught him in the chest then, with a gagging sound, staggered toward where Chernikov lay. Simmons' knife clattered on the floor after it slipped from his hand and the Texan fumbled for his pistol.

Chernikov sprang to his feet and chuckled. "So, little man," he said softly, "you came to kill me. How does it feel to know you are dead, even as you stand there and ache to take me with you?" He stepped forward and drove his foot into the side of the man's knee. He heard and felt the joint give way, and Simmons fell heavily.

A sleepy voice in the next room made a noise that ended on a higher note, evidently a question. Chernikov squatted and found the knife Simmons had dropped. Gripping it tightly, he crept into the living room, where Clell lay on a couch. Chernikov reached the resting figure in three strides.

He slapped Clell across the face with the back of his hand and, as the Texan started up, jabbed him in the groin with the point of the knife. "I will assume you were really asleep. Now, get up; there is work for you. You have to bury Simmons."

"What—what are you talking about?"

"Simmons thought to kill me and take what little gold I carry. He is dead and I want him buried. Find a shovel and bury him under the floor."

"Now?"

"Immediately. We will want to leave at dawn and I want the body and his saddle buried before we leave. His horse and the rest of his equipment we will take." Chernikov gave Clell an icy smile. "And if you are entertaining the idea of killing me or running away, let me tell you that Simmons disappointed me. He died in a few minutes. Do we understand each other? Good. Now, find a shovel and bury the garbage."

Chapter 4

Steve noticed that as they entered the Yellow Rose a tide of silence seemed to have followed them in and now it flooded the room around them as the laughter and babble of voices died out. The place was crowded tonight, with perhaps thirty-five men and women standing at the bar or sitting at the tables. Most of the women in the place looked rather the worse for wear, just as most of the men showed the marks of rough weather.

Two men stood behind the bar, neither of them the morning bartender. The drunk they'd gotten the information from earlier had just stopped talking to another man as he saw the group stride into the bar. He stared at them a moment then Steve clearly heard him moan, "Oh shit." The drunk snatched up his glass with his good hand, bolted down the liquor, then ricocheted through the maze of tables to the back door.

As Steve continued to look around the room he recognized the pool shark at the back of the room, playing pool with two other men, walking around the table and twirling his stick.

Reynaud had taken the lead and had reached the bar, Hasteen to his right, Paco on his left. The rest of the group had fanned out in a rough semicircle.

"What'll you have?" the bald man with the tattooed arms asked. He tried to hide his nervousness but a tic made his left eyelid flutter.

"We're looking for a couple-three men. One of them is a big guy. Always dresses neatly. The other two are Randy Simmons and Clell Vickers."

"They ain't here."

"We've already noticed that," Reynaud said. "We want to know where they went."

"What's it to you?" They turned to face the man who'd interrupted, a large blond. He held a drink in his right hand.

Logan tapped Hasteen on the shoulder. "It's my turn.

Let me show you how to do it right." He took two steps toward the man then his left hand shot out and grabbed the man's right hand, which was wrapped around a tall, thin glass of white mule. Logan jerked the man's hand upward, flinging most of the drink into the man's face then his knuckles whitened as he tightened his grip.

Suddenly the glass shattered in the man's hand, and the blond screamed "Shee-yee-yit!"

"He must be a real Texan," Reynaud observed pleasantly to the bartender. "He managed to draw that out to three full syllables."

"See," Logan explained to Hasteen, "if you do it that way, more glass stays in." He released the big man's hand, which bled freely.

Reynaud raised his voice. "Look, boys and girls, we really aren't looking for any trouble, but we need to find these guys yesterday. Now, who wants to tell us where they went?"

Steve noticed the men playing pool with the hustler had slipped the hold-down thongs off the hammers of their pistols and were turning to face the group. Suddenly, the hustler swept up a ball and beaned one of the players then swung his stick at the other man's forearm. The lead-weighted handle smashed into the player's arm and Steve heard the bone crack.

"What the fuck—?" the man screamed hoarsely.

"I've seen those boys draw," the pool shark said, "and you haven't paid for the game yet."

A pistol roared from under one of the tables and instantly Hasteen, Paco, and Wade were all firing. The body was hurled backward, taking the chair with it then fell clear and lay face-down in the middle of a widening puddle of blood.

"See what I mean?" the hustler asked. "You'd a had about as much chance as a celluloid snowball in hell."

"Anybody hit?" Reynaud asked.

Steve stared down at the hat he held in his left hand. It was now marked with a bullet hole through the crown. "No, but I'm glad I wasn't wearing it when it got holed."

"It'll make a hell of a good campfire lie," Hasteen said. He twirled his Colt back into the holster. "Now, just so's we don't have to feel all uncomfortable, why doesn't everybody just put their hands on the table in front of them?"

As hands were laid flat on tabletops. Reynaud walked slowly

around the end of the bar. As the bartender backed away from him the Cajun pulled a sawed-off double-barreled shotgun from under the bar, broke it open, pulled the shells out and tossed them into a spittoon then laid the open shotgun on the bar. "Let's try to avoid temptation. My friends and I don't want to have to leave a lot of leaky bodies behind us. Just tell us where the men we were asking about have gone and we'll be out of here."

"Mister, I really don't know," the bartender said. "If I knew, I'd tell you." He looked around the room. "If any of you know, just tell these guys."

The silence seemed to drag out for hours, although it could only have been seconds, then Reynaud said, "Well, how about where I can find a man named Paul Baker?"

One of the men at the nearest table worked himself slowly to his feet and let his hand swing down just below his gun butt. "I don't give two hoots in hell about a couple-three two-bit gunnies, but Paul Baker is the best vet around, and a damned good man. If you want him, you're gonna hafta go through me."

"I don't want to hurt you or Paul Baker," Reynaud said. "The one you should be worried about is the big guy with the creased pants. He's Russian—used to run a prison camp. My friends and I knew him then, and that's why we're worried about Paul Baker. One of the big guy's men had a list with Baker's name right at the top."

The man only stared at Reynaud then the Deacon spoke slowly. "As God is the witness and judge of us all, my friend is telling the truth. Your friend is in danger, but not from us."

The Texan stared at him a long moment then let his hand drop loosely, well below the butt of his weapon. "Why the hell didn't you say so in the first place?" He didn't wait for an answer. "We better be on the road to Victoria at first light."

"Why not right now?" Reynaud demanded.

"The roads around here ain't for travelin' on after dark. Besides, Simmons and Vickers go everywhere by horse, while I got an alcoholic pickup out back. We ought to be able to reach Victoria in four, four and a half hours. Can I buy you boys a drink?"

Reynaud grinned. "All of us but the Deacon. He'll probably take milk if you've got any, and water if that's the best he can do." He stepped to the bar, nodded to the bartender. "I'll take a beer." As he drank he turned to the Texan. "Do we have to worry about the local law showing up to find what the shots were about?"

"Nah. If you'd done it in the respectable side of town, he'd come lookin', but nobody gets too concerned about what goes on in bars."

"Any idea where we might spend the night?"

"Down to the corner," the Texan indicated north, "and four blocks west is what's left of a HoJo's. It'll cost a couple ROT dollars but they change the sheets at least once a week."

~ * ~

Reynaud and the group returned to the Yellow Rose as dawn was trying to burn its way through the overcast. Steve pointed out the car Chernikov had driven into Clute was gone. As they walked into the bar, Reynaud caught a flash of movement as someone at the side of the bar ducked below the level of the counter. The Texan they'd met the night before sat waiting for them, a stained mug of something hot and black before him.

"Howdy, boys," the Texan drawled, "I'm Slim. Slim Watkins. You better tank up on hot coffee before we go out there. It's fixin' to come down like a cow pissin' on a flat rock."

The morning bartender poured what they called coffee into mugs for all of them. Reynaud sniffed the steam rising from his cup and decided the stuff might help and probably wouldn't do any permanent damage. He sipped then nodded to the Texan. "I was hoping there'd be more wheels available. The car across the street is gone today."

"Yeah, I got a couple tires, myself. Nothin' much goes to waste around here. I can haul up to five of you to Victoria."

"Aren't there any other trucks available?" Reynaud asked.

"'Fraid not. After a while, all the parts get cannibalized."

Reynaud looked from face to face. "I'm going. Logan, I'll want you along, since you also know Chernikov, and we might need the firepower. Hasteen, you and Paco come along, too. That ought to be enough of us—"

"We earnestly hope." Slim added, almost piously.

Reynaud turned to face him. "What does that mean?"

"We'll be goin' through 'Injun country.'" Slim settled the brim of his hat lower over his eyes. "Bandits and crazies could be thick as buzzards on a carcass along the road."

"Great," Reynaud snapped. "All we need are some asshats wasting our time. Okay, the rest of you bring the horses. Try to stay within sight of the highway, in case we have trouble."

"We'll have to stay on the highway," Wade said, "unless our horses have webbed feet."

"I'm going with you," the Deacon said suddenly. "God made three mistakes—flies, mosquitos, and horses, which are dumber than the insects."

Reynaud stared at Billy Joe, trying to detect even a hint of a smile then shrugged. "All right with me, if it's okay with Steve and Wade. They'll have to bring the horses."

The Ranger touched the brim of his hat. "We'll meet you in Victoria."

~ * ~

Logan had cut a king and was riding in the cab with the driver while the others crouched under hats and ponchos in the bed of the pickup. They were headed into the wind and the rain pummeled them.

"What did the driver mean—about crazies?" Reynaud asked Hasteen. He had to shout to be heard above the wind, the downpour, and the wheels churning the wet asphalt.

"They came with the plague. Some of them might have some brain damage from the sickness. Some of them were probably crazy before, and the plague riots gave them a chance to become really dangerous. Others were changed by having to watch their families dying around them."

Reynaud noticed the storm had slackened a bit. "What kind of crazy are they?"

"What kind do you want?" Hasteen asked. "Aren't we all different from what we were before? Some of the ones we call crazies are harmless, or only territorial. Others are loners—cannibals have few friends, even among fellow flesh-eaters. Some of the others have become something like new barbarians; they raid and kill as much for pleasure as for what they can take."

"Sounds like it's hard to tell them from any other kinds of bandits."

"True. Then there's the Damnation Army. They believe the war and the plague were sent by God to cleanse the earth. For them, it's a sacrilege to have survived, and they justify their own survival by claiming they do God's work, killing everyone else. They may be the most dangerous because they place no more value on their own lives than the lives of others."

Reynaud glanced at the Deacon, who noticed it. "'Beware false prophets'" Billy Joe said, "'for they shall come in the last days and preach a false gospel.' Now is the time for repentance and the firm resolve to do better. If the Lord of Hosts had wanted to end the world, He would have done it. The only mistakes he made were flies, mosquitos, and horses."

Paco pointed at the cab with his thumb. "You forgot Hawaiian shirts."

"Blame not the Almighty for the madness of men," the Deacon intoned.

Reynaud was trying to decide whether it was safe to laugh when the truck suddenly lurched then he heard the sound of a gunshot. The truck skidded as the tires failed to grab the rain-slick pavement, and bullets and shot punched into the truck and cab. Reynaud heard the heavy pounding as other slugs slammed into the motor and the gunfire was heavy enough to sound like a battle.

The truck began to slow then one of the tires blew up. The pickup bounded then went into a screaming skid, the rear wheel grinding the blacktop. After what seemed hours the truck squalled to a stop, slanted across the highway.

Reynaud scrambled out of the bed as more bullets buzzed around him or smacked through the sheet metal. As he bailed out, Reynaud saw someone had strewn the highway with nails. He crouched, ready to spring for the ditch then froze as he noticed the running water in the ditch was swirling around something submerged. He caught Paco, who'd already started for the ditch, After a glance at the water, Paco roared a curse then fired three fast shots at the log, fifty yards away, lying across the road.

Hasteen was laying down rapid fire at the log with a lever-action carbine and the Deacon was stuffing a Russian grenade into the launcher mounted under the barrel of the AK-74 he carried. Reynaud darted past them and ripped open the door of the cab. Logan was slumped forward in the seat, his face covered with blood, and more blood smeared the shattered windshield.

Reynaud grabbed Logan's duster and dragged him out of the cab and onto the asphalt then dived back in to get the driver out but the driver was buckled into his seatbelt. Cursing in Cajun French, Reynaud found the buckle and released it.

He heard the dull report of a grenade launcher and pulled the driver down just as the grenade exploded halfway between the truck and the log. The gunfire from the ambush stopped long enough to get the driver out. Slim had a few shallow cuts on his forehead and face and his left sleeve was drenched with blood. Reynaud found an ugly bullet hole that looked as though it'd chopped through part of the shoulder muscle. The man was stunned but his breathing was deep and steady.

Billy Joe launched another grenade, this one falling long, and the firing from behind the log began again, although it was more scattered and less accurate. Reynaud heard only a couple of rounds hit the fender near him.

Logan had come around and was sitting on the highway, his back against the pickup's rear wheel. He wiped his face and swore and Reynaud saw he had a gash above his right eye and a lump on his forehead. He looked around, as if wondering how he'd gotten there then fumbled out his MAC-10.

"Give us some cover," Hasteen whispered then hurled himself at the side of the road, flinging himself across the ditch and almost burying himself in the mud of the field, a revolver in either hand.

Reynaud suddenly realized he'd forgotten his long arms in the back of the pickup. He sprang up, the revolver in his hand, and blazed away at the barricade while groping in the pickup's bed for his shotgun. His fingers closed on the Mossberg as the hammer of his pistol clicked on an empty chamber. Shoving the Smith back into his holster, he pumped a round into the shotgun and fired all five rounds as fast as he could pump the action.

As he ducked back behind the pickup, the Deacon touched off another grenade, this one exploding just behind the log. Screams could be heard, even above the blast. One corpse was thrown forward to lie draped over the log, and an arm sailed up and away in a lazy arc.

A man behind the log leaped to his feet, clutching his left arm and screaming. Hasteen's Colts roared and the man jerked back down, the back of his head blown away.

"You done with that?" Logan demanded, as Reynaud hurriedly stuffed more shells into the shotgun.

"Just about." Reynaud shoved the last round into the underside of the gun and pumped the action. "Now, I'm ready."

"Then cover me," Logan shouted and sprinted toward the log.

Reynaud saw a head begin to appear over the log and squeezed off a shot and the Deacon fired a burst with his AK. The head disappeared behind the log again and Reynaud wondered if one of them had hit the bandit.

Logan, who'd made his dash crouched as low as possible, threw himself forward, over the log then ducked out of sight.

~ * ~

Logan cleared the log just as a one-armed man snatched at a shotgun. Logan threw himself down as he pulled the Ingram's trigger. The weapon stuttered for only a split second then the plastic magazine split, spilling cartridges onto the highway.

The man with the shotgun slumped and the gun went off with a bellow, tearing a gouge in the asphalt.

Logan tried to pull the magazine out of the weapon but it was stuck in the magazine well in the grip. A man lying at the edge of the road raised his head and grinned at Logan with a rictus full of malice. "You're going to fry, you bastard." He drew himself into a half-kneeling position, staying below the level of the log, and reached back, adjusting the handles of the tanks on his back. Flicking a cigarette lighter, he made fire shoot out the nozzle of the wand he held. "What'll it be, asshole?" the man asked. "Regular or extra crispy?"

Logan dropped the MAC and whipped out the Ruger Redhawk from his shoulder holster. "Smoke 'em if you got 'em," he shouted, pointed the pistol at the man's chest, and snapped off a shot. The weapon boomed and recoil whipped the barrel up.

The full-jacketed bullet tore through the bandit's chest, smashing ribs and making shrapnel of the bone chips, blew the heart apart, then crashed into the tank on the man's back. The bandit didn't even have time to scream before the tanks exploded in a fireball that swirled around the body then blossomed upward. Logan buried his face in the crook of his arm and waited until the heat became bearable.

When Logan finally looked up, what was left of the body lay charred and still burning in a circle of flickering, crackling flames. "Pity," Logan said to the corpse, "you had some of the snappiest repartee I've heard in a while. It's almost a shame that being an asshole can be terminal."

The rest of the group moved forward, Paco and Hasteen crawling like water lizards until they could finally gain the side of the road.

"Looks like they're all done," Logan said, as he rifled the bodies for money or ammunition.

Reynaud motioned for Logan to follow him back to the pickup. "We'd better see how the driver is," the Cajun said. "What happened to you guys?"

"Damned if I really know." Logan squatted beside Reynaud, who was tearing the driver's shirt open. "All of a sudden we were getting shot at then we saw the log. Slim yelled something then the truck began to skid. I remember seeing my little Russian chopper slide off onto the floor, then the brakes must've caught because the next thing I know, I was trying to put my face through the windshield."

Reynaud studied the wound in the driver's shoulder, an ugly, ragged hole. "It looks like the slug that hit him had already bounced off something else." He gestured toward the pickup. "Look inside and see if he's got a first-aid kit or something."

Logan popped open the glove compartment and noticed a ragged hole in the back of it. He pulled out a bottle of whiskey and a small plastic case then saw a deformed bullet laying in the bottom of the compartment. "Jeez," he exclaimed, "if that round had had just had a little more zip, I'd be talking to you out of my belly-button." He set the bottle down and opened the case, which contained dressings, pads, several tubes of ointment, and a bottle of aspirin.

Reynaud poured some of the whiskey on a pad and cleaned the wound as best he could, then bound it. The cuts on Slim's face were superficial, although one had just missed his right eye. After cleaning up Slim's face he covered the Texan with a blanket from the back of the pickup.

The Cajun had just finished dressing the gash over Logan's eye when the rest of the group returned. "We only kep' two rifles and three pistols," Paco said. "The rest was junk." He handed Reynaud one of the rifles, an odd-looking piece with a perforated jacket around the rear of the barrel that looked like it was part of the receiver, a bulging rotary magazine that gave the weapon a pregnant appearance, and a stock that showed some resemblance to a baseball bat. Paco showed him how to load it through a spring trap on the side of the action and how to operate the bolt. "It's a thirty-aught six. I thought you might like something a little newer than your Russian antique."

"Thanks," Reynaud said. "To what do I owe the favor?"

"Saving my ass." Paco pointed to the ditch "These *hijos des putas* had put stakes in the water in the ditches. If I had fallen on them—"

"Jeez," Logan interrupted, "you'd a' been a spick on the stick; nailed like a corn dog."

Paco turned to stare coldly at Logan. "I am a man, and I will be treated like a man, with the respect due a man. Or would you rather shoot with me?"

"No," Logan said, "not unless we're on the same side. I didn't mean any offence, or to piss you off."

"Relax, Paco," Reynaud said. "Logan's just envious because his own ethnic background is so bland." He looked around at the ambush site. "It looks like the clowns who ambushed us knew what they were doing."

"Very true," Paco said. "They had a barricade to stop anything on wheels. If we'd been on horseback, they'd have shot us to pieces. They spread nails on the highway to spike tires, or perhaps men who fell from horses, and stakes in the ditch to deal with whoever lived to take cover. Yes, these bandits planned very well."

"What do we do now?" Logan asked. "In case you haven't

noticed, the clouds have been getting darker again. Looks like it's ready to storm on us some more."

"We're about twenty miles out of Clute," Slim said, his voice still weak. "They's a place about five miles ahead, a village called Old Ocean. They's still about two hundred people livin' there."

The metal shrieked and groaned as Paco raised the hood then he slammed it shut again. "This won' be taking us anywhere. About the only thing salvageable is the battery. There might be a hose or a belt left, if you look long enough."

Hasteen had used some water from the ditch to rinse away most of the mud from his face and clothes. "You stay here. Those bandits must've had some way to haul off loot, and there's a hedge less than half a mile from here." He dug his carbine and his poncho out of the bed of the pickup, shouldered the gun, and set off down the road to the trees.

Reynaud slipped another blanket under Slim's head and tried to make his as comfortable as possible. "What happened?"

Slim swallowed and Reynaud gave him a drink of water from one of the canteens. "I was pumpin' the brakes and they finally grabbed. We'd just gotten stopped when somethin' exploded next to my head. I think it was the rear-view mirror. Anyhow, somethin' smacked me upside of the head and the lights went out." He stirred under the blanket then winced. "How bad's the shoulder?"

"I can't tell," Reynaud admitted. "It looks like it's just the muscle and I don't know how badly the muscle is screwed up, but it might've clipped the collarbone. I think I got the bleeding stopped."

"Hey, Slim," Logan announced, "the bandits around here are armed to the teeth. Hell, the last guy I wasted had a flame-thrower. Any of these clowns pack pocket nukes?"

"It's probably not a military flame-thrower. They use burners out west to burn the needles off cactus so the cattle can eat it."

"Sorry about the truck, Slim," Reynaud said. "We got some stuff off the bodies to help pay for it, some guns and ammo—"

"—And about a hundred ROT dollars worth in gold and silver," Logan interjected.

"Thanks, boys," Slim said. "Right now, I just hope we can get back on the road before the rains start again."

Reynaud managed, using a strip torn from the blanket, to rig a makeshift sling for Slim. By the time he'd finished adjusting it to fit properly he heard the slow clatter of horses walking on pavement and Hasteen, riding a piebald horse and leading four more horses, approached.

"They're mostly crowbait," Hasteen said, handing reins to the others, "but they'll get us where we're going." He shifted to sit behind the saddle. "Haul Slim up and I'll ride double with him so's I can hold him in the saddle."

After they got Slim astride Hasteen's horse, Reynaud found one of the nags had a saddle scabbard that looked as though it was built for his new rifle. In a few minutes they were riding down the highway and hoping the lightning they could see in the distance would keep its distance.

~ * ~

They were all soaked to the skin and shivering when they finally reached Old Ocean, a village small enough to keep sentries watching the highway. Slim knew one of the men on guard duty and was able to get them into the hamlet and directions to the home of a former army medic, the nearest thing Old Ocean had to a doctor.

While the medic, a thin man with prematurely gray hair, checked and replaced Slim's dressing the rest of the men crowded around the stove, drying out and warming themselves. When they felt nearly human again Reynaud sent Hasteen to join the highway guard to watch for their friends, and Paco and Logan to the town's only bar to find out how long ago Chernikov had gone through the place.

The medic looked up at Reynaud. "Not a bad job."

"We'll leave the horses here for Slim. Does anybody around here have wheels for hire?"

"Orrie made a run to Bay City this morning. He should be getting back any time."

"Anybody else?" Reynaud asked. "We're really in a hurry to get to Victoria."

The medic shook his head. "The nearest place you might find another truck is Van Vleck. There's still about four hundred people living there. It's about ten miles down the road. Sugar Valley's closer, about five miles, but it's been abandoned since the plague. From what I hear, the place's been stripped." He closed the drapes of the window and motioned Reynaud out the door ahead of him. As he closed the door behind him, he nodded toward the bed. "I'll let him rest a day or so then get him to the doctor in Bay City."

"What's the bill?"

The medic led the way to the kitchen. "Call it ten ROT dollars, but, hell, Slim can pay me later."

"We'll take care of it." Reynaud dug some silver out. "Any idea what's on the road ahead of us?"

"No way of telling." The medic poured Reynaud, the Deacon, and himself cups of passable coffee. They'd just finished when Paco knocked at the back door then slipped inside, Logan behind him.

"They were through here yesterday morning," Paco said. "They probably made it to somewhere around Bay City last night."

Reynaud turned again to the medic. "How about horses? Does anybody here have horses for sale?"

"You might check at Neal Bryant's. He runs a livery stable and takes care of sales for locals."

"Never mind." Logan shouted from the front room. "Steve and Wade just rode in with our horses."

"Thanks again, Doc. Sell the horses and saddles we rode in on and get the money to Slim, if you would." Reynaud caught up his gear and dashed outside.

The riders drew rein as Reynaud darted into the street. Wade let his horse walk to the Cajun and stared down at him. "We saw the mess you boys left, about five miles back. That was damned near felony litterin'. Took us twenty minutes and almost all the horses to get that log off the road. Looks like your ride was more interestin' than ours. Have you found out anything more about the men we're following?"

"Paco says he thinks they made it to around Bay City yesterday. Can we get at least that far today?"

"We might, but we'll have to work the horses pretty hard," Wade replied.

Reynaud stowed his gear, including his new rifle and its scabbard, then swung into the saddle. "Let's do the best we can. Maybe we can get the use of another truck somewhere."

"We should be able to make better time this afternoon," Wade said, staring up at the clearing sky. "This morning was too chilly and the highway was too slick. It would'a been easy to lose a horse or two. If the rest of the afternoon stays clear, we oughta be able to make another ten miles or so."

~ * ~

Van Vleck had been preserved—or perhaps rebuilt—in clusters. Reynaud found a livery stable where a man with a wild blond beard was pounding a horseshoe into shape. He dismounted and limped to where the man leaned on the anvil. "We're in a hurry to get to Victoria. Does anybody around here have a truck they'd rent out?"

The blacksmith shook his head. "I don't think there's a truck in town up to the trip but there's a freighter in Bay City, a fella by the name of Robichaux."

"Can we at least water our horses—give them a swallow or two?"

"Sure. It'll cost you a ROT dollar or ten rounds of ammo."

They let the horses have just enough water to replace what they'd sweated out and rode through the town. Some sections had been abandoned and stripped for salvage and the land used for gardening.

"What do you think, Wade?" Reynaud asked. "Do you think we can get another five miles out of the horses today?"

"Maybe," Wade replied, "but it's gonna be near dark by the time we get to Bay City. It'll help if we can swap horses for tomorrow's ride."

"Wish I could swap asses for it," Reynaud grumbled.

At the edge of town, Logan suddenly held up a hand to signal a halt, pointed to an armadillo slowly crossing the highway, then pulled out his Ruger. He sighted for a split-second and the pistol roared. The bullet whined as it caromed off the pavement about a foot away from the armadillo, which scuttled into a bush at the side of the road. Logan spent the next few minutes bringing his horse, which had shied at the concussion, back under control.

"What was that all about?" Hasteen demanded. "That armadillo wasn't bothering us."

"Not enough traffic out here anymore," Logan griped. "It doesn't look like a real highway without roadkill. Besides, I thought maybe Rennie'd want to eat it." He grinned at Reynaud. "Somebody told me God made armadillos so Cajuns could eat possum on the half-shell."

"Logan," Reynaud said, "you keep pushing it, and the next firefight, when you ask for cover, somebody's liable to toss you a blanket."

Logan swung out the cylinder, dug out the empty case, and loaded a fresh round in. "You guys are all getting testy. You gotta loosen up a little."

Hasteen and Paco moved forward to take the lead, taking opposite sides of the highway, the rest of the group strung out behind them. Perhaps two miles out of Van Vleck, Hasteen suddenly whipped his carbine out of its scabbard and slipped out of the saddle.

Paco, across the road, instantly copied Hasteen's actions and knelt beside his horse, his rifle pointed in the direction Hasteen was staring.

"What's the matter," Reynaud asked, as he slid out of his own saddle. Hasteen didn't answer except to slip like a ghost behind a clump of brush then cautiously advance on some forms in the shadow of a young oak. While he was still eight to ten feet from the shadow he stood and waved for the others to join him. "It looks like your Russian has been here."

As Reynaud drew nearer he saw the body of a short, sandy-haired man and the carcasses of three horses. He approached and saw the horses had all been shot through the head, while the dead man had been shot twice in the chest and finished off with a bullet through the right eye. Flies buzzed around the bodies and the group's horses rolled their eyes and shied.

"They've been here since early morning," Hasteen said. He moved away from the bodies. "We may as well get to Bay City, although Chernikov's regained a lead. If he isn't already in Victoria, he's close."

"We can't leave the body here," Reynaud said. "Wade, you and Paco move the gear to one of the pack horses. Steve, you keep the horses steady. Hasteen, give me a hand with the body."

Hasteen continued to walk away. "No."

The Deacon dismounted. "I'll help you." While Paco and Wade transferred the supplies, Billy Joe recited the twenty-third Psalm over the body then helped Reynaud wrestle the stiff form onto the horse's back, a task made more difficult by the apparent terror of the animal. Finally, Wade helped tie the corpse firmly on to keep it from being tossed off by the nervous horse.

Hasteen led by a hundred yards along the road when the group started again on the way to Bay City. The party strung out again and Reynaud drew beside Wade.

"What the hell got into Hasteen?" Reynaud asked.

"He's Navajo," Wade said, as though that explained everything.

"Only partly," Reynaud corrected. "Besides, what does that have to do with anything?"

Wade kept his voice low so Reynaud had to strain to hear him. "Navajos don't have burial ceremonies; they don't even like to touch the dead. They take their dead out someplace and leave them, then leave the body by a roundabout path so the spirit can't follow them back,"

"But Hasteen doesn't believe that." Reynaud wasn't sure whether he was trying to convince Wade or himself—or maybe even Hasteen.

"Y'ever watch a high school basketball game?" Wade inquired, in his soft drawl.

"What the hell brought that up?"

"Catholic kids almost always cross themselves and bounce the ball a couple-three times before they shoot a free-throw. Hell, I've seen kids I knew were Protestants doing the same thing. Tell me what they believe or don't believe. It's like their muscles and bones have learned it, even if their brains tell them God doesn't really care whether or not they make the free-throw. That's how Hasteen is. Maybe he doesn't believe in the old way with his brain, but the rest of him still has the old sweats around the dead."

They rode in silence for a few minutes before Wade spoke

again. "Maybe that's why he puts shell cases in the mouths of the men he kills. Maybe it's his way of trapping a spirit. I hear Apaches are scared to death of hanging 'cause they think if a man's hanged, his spirit can't escape out his mouth. I don't know if they figure the spirit dies too, or what, but it's supposed to be some heavy magic." The ex-Ranger lapsed into silence until they reached Bay City.

After leaving the body at the sheriff's office, which seemed to have been abandoned, they found a cantina where they could buy some indifferent Mexican food and inferior homebrew beer. The middle-aged woman who brought them the food and beer also told them where they could find Charles Robichaux.

Robichaux, who answered their knock at his door with a pistol in his hand, was a short man who wore his dark hair with long sideburns and spoke with a faint accent.

Reynaud stepped into the dim arc of light cast by a kerosene lamp. "We need to get to Victoria, preferably with our horses, and we need to get there as soon as possible. Could you take us there tonight?"

Robichaux lowered the pistol. "I can take you to Victoria, and your horses, too, but it will cost you two hundred ROT dollars, and nobody drives these highways at night."

Reynaud turned to Hasteen and Paco who each showed one of the small gold coins. "Would you drive after dark for four hundred ROTdollars?"

Robichaux smiled. "Four hundred would buy a real nice funeral, but I'm not in that market and don' wanna be. You can leave your horses in the corral out back and you can sleep in the house to the right. I use it for the occasional two-legged passengers. It isn't much but it'll keep you out of the weather."

~ * ~

Chernikov, his face set, as if in concrete, could almost feel the furtive glances Vickers sometimes shot at him. The truck had broken down twice, as the badly converted motor choked on the alcohol fuel. Chernikov had only limited knowledge of converted engines and Vickers had the contempt of a horse-riding nomad for anything more complicated than a weapon.

Darkness had already fallen and was deepening as they drove through Victoria. For the last two or three miles they'd been passing cars shoved off the shoulders of the road, some of them still occupied by skeletal corpses, and the town itself seemed almost what Americans called a "ghost town." Several streets of houses near the edge of town had been burned and many other buildings were mere shells, stripped of everything that could be used. Chernikov guessed this town, which had once held over seventy thousand people, was now probably inhabited by three or four thousand.

"Where does Baker live?" Chernikov demanded.

"It's an estate southwest of town."

"Find a place to stop for the night."

Vickers rubbed a calloused hand over his lower face, the stubble making an audible rasp. "I thought you was in a hurry to get this done."

"I want it done quickly. That does not mean it should be done in a hurry. We can't leave before dawn tomorrow, and I would prefer to protect our trail." He drew out a small pouch. "After we've selected a place for tonight, I want you to go hire some men." He handed the bandit five small gold coins and six of the larger silver ones. "Spend these well. Get me men you think can be trusted to earn the money. Tell them to let no one through from the northeast for two days."

"Do you think anybody is following us?"

"Probably not, but I'd rather not leave the matter to chance. Just use the money well."

"You mean you're gonna trust me with that money?"

"Of course." Chernikov smirked. "You will want our trail guarded because if we are captured, you will be hanged, and if you try to run away with the money I will have you tracked down and killed—slowly—if it costs me five times that."

Vickers swallowed, and took the money. Two blocks further down the street he pointed out a house. "I guess that's as good a place as any."

Almost everything in the house that could be carried away had already been stolen, so little cleaning needed be done before the bedrolls had been laid out and both men left; Vickers for a bar,

Chernikov to find a restaurant.

Chernikov had discovered he enjoyed spicy Cajun food. He found, within four blocks, a place that catered to the local Cajuns, and he ate slowly, savoring his meal. He used the opportunity to watch and listen but learned nothing of interest he hadn't already known. He noticed another diner staring at him as he sipped his coffee, and he realized he must be squinting. He'd rid himself of his old Russian habit of leaving the spoon in the cup while drinking, but the habit of closing his right eye to avoid being poked by the spoon handle was an unconscious reflex. The American might've stared at him for some other reason but, as he'd told Vickers, some matters were too important to be left to chance.

He paid the check and left the bar and had walked no more than fifty yards when he heard the building's door open and close again. To his right lay an alley only a few yards deep that led to a parking lot. He turned abruptly and strode down the alley, drawing the silenced Makarov from his shoulder holster. Where the alley widened he turned and waited.

The footsteps slowed as they approached the alley then moved down the narrow passage.

Chernikov waited then spun around the corner, exposing himself as little as possible, and pointed his pistol at the figure. He snapped three shots into the form and watched it spin halfway around then drop, a pistol falling from its hand to clatter on the concrete.

Chernikov darted forward and hauled the body around the corner and against the wall he'd used for cover, leaving it where it'd be unlikely to be found before sunup, then he followed the cross-alley to the next street, which led to the house he'd chosen.

Once in the security of the house, he reloaded the Makarov and lay down on his blanket to wait for Vickers. Perhaps an hour and a half later he heard unsteady steps approaching the door and fumbling at the doorknob then Vickers staggered in.

"You found some men?" Chernikov asked.

"Got twelve of 'em," Vickers said as he lurched to his bedroll and sat down heavily. He cackled. "I guess you could say I bought us a jury."

"Good. Now go to sleep." Chernikov tried to ignore the odor of bad whiskey and drunksweat, and closed his eyes.

~ * ~

Leaving Vickers waiting at the driveway, Chernikov walked up the steps of the wide veranda and rapped sharply at the door. After waiting a few seconds, he knocked again, louder. A boy with tousled hair answered the door and Chernikov almost grinned. This was almost too easy. The boy looked as though he were about nine years old. "Is your father home?" he asked.

The boy gestured, indicating the stable behind the house. "He's out back, tending Charley Lester's bay mare."

The boy's eyes widened as Chernikov whipped out his pistol. "Who else is here?"

"No—nobody."

"We will go see your father. You lead. If you make a sound, I will kill you, then your father. Lead." Chernikov followed the boy through the house and out the back door, staying close enough the boy couldn't try to snatch a weapon or get away. These people had lived a soft life. Baker's profession, because it was essential, had protected them from the worst of the barbarism and left them complacent and unprepared for danger.

He and the boy went out the back door of the house and across the open space to the stable where a thin man with wire-rimmed spectacles was tying a fresh bandage around a horse's right foreleg. The animal was held up in a body sling.

Chernikov gestured with his pistol. "Baker, step back and put your hands on your head."

Baker's head snapped up and the horse flinched, too ill to shy at the sudden movement. The veterinarian's eyes finally focused on the pistol and he slowly raised his hands. Putting his hands, fingers laced together, on the crown of the straw hat he wore, he slowly moved away from the animal. He glared at Chernikov. "You're a real hero, aren't you, waving a pistol at a boy and an unarmed man?"

"I'm not interested in heroism," Chernikov's voice grated. "I have work for you to do, and you can't do it if you're dead. This was simply the best way to get you to cooperate."

"At least let me give the mare some antibiotics. She's got an infected cut."

"I can take care of that," Chernikov snapped and whipped the pistol around, firing at point-blank range.

The mare screamed and thrashed in the sling. She shook her head, flecking blood over the man and the boy, then slumped, breathing raggedly.

"At least finish her off," Baker raged. "There's no excuse for letting the animal suffer."

"There's no sense in wasting a bullet," Chernikov replied. "She'll die in her own time. Now, unless you want your son to die in my own time, you'd better pick horses—", he motioned at the corral beside the stable "—and get them ready for traveling." He waved at Vickers to bring the saddles from the back of the truck.

Chapter 5

Robichaux had been trying to sing an old blues song for what seemed the last hundred miles, and Reynaud had tried to sleep through it. He'd given up trying to sleep but continued to lean back, his hat tipped over his eyes. Logan, beside him, was humming along with the blues sufficiently off-key for the sounds he made to be described as noise.

"Hand me that canteen," Robichaux said to Logan.

As Logan handed over the canteen, he asked, "How much further to Victoria?"

"We're almost there. Notice all the dead cars?" He drank then gave the canteen back to Logan. "Have a drink. It's water with a touch of lemon. Cuts a thirst better than anything—get down!"

Reynaud shot upright and shoved his hat back. A couple of dead cars had been shoved nose-to-nose, and he saw a man behind them. Fire of a muzzle flash flickered then the windshield seemed to explode, showering the three men with bits of glass.

Reynaud crossed his arms in front of his face and tried to get lower in the seat as more bullets thumped into the body of the truck. The truck was jolted as it slammed into the cars and Reynaud was tossed around the cab. Something hit his shoulder with bruising force and he slammed his elbow against the dashboard. Metal shrieked and grated, and the motor died.

"Find something to hold onto!" Robichaux shouted. He fought the steering wheel and cautiously pumped the brake. "This oughta be a first. I ain't never seen a really bad accident before."

The cab lurched again as the right front tire was shot out and the semi slowed to a stop. Reynaud tried the door but it was stuck. Twisting the handle down, he turned in the seat and kicked at the door, which finally flew open, glass shattering as his kick dislodged the window, which had already been cobwebbed by a bullet. He tumbled out and down, his new rifle in his hands. The door that had been added to the front of the trailer was already open and Wade had dropped prone, firing short bursts from his M-14 under the body of the trailer.

The nose of the truck cab lay almost in the median strip and was turned at a slight angle to the trailer. The lines of cars along both sides of the highway were gapped and all the fire seemed to come from the cars on the left shoulder. The rest of the team had bailed out of the truck by then and Robichaux was screaming curses as he fired through the gap between the cab and the trailer. He emptied the sawed-off autoloading shotgun from the rack in the cab and started stuffing more shells into the action.

The nearest car was within twenty-five yards. A figure popped up on the other side of the car and a pistol, perhaps two, roared, flinging the body back. Wade, shoving a fresh magazine into his rifle, shouted, "They're trying to close up on us!"

Hasteen, staying low, dashed for the near car, flinching at the sound of a shotgun blast from down the highway then hurled himself forward to roll over the hood to the other side of the car.

The Deacon had taken up a position at the back of the trailer and launched a grenade into the mass of sheet metal along the highway. "Only four of these left," he shouted, as he dug out another grenade.

Paco, at the rear of the trailer, fired twice then looked back at Reynaud. "Some of them are trying to cross the road. We have to stop that or we're going to take fire from both sides." He ducked back after a quick look and a couple of near misses. "There's a wrecked car on this side of the road, maybe forty yards away. I'm going to try to get to it."

Reynaud joined Paco at the back end of the trailer. "Let me cover you. Deacon! Wade! Try to keep the rest of them on their side of the road—" He was interrupted by Hasteen firing at a figure that spun and fell. Steve dashed to the car sheltering Hasteen, firing as he ran.

"They'll work their way up the line of cars," Paco said. "You ready to give me that cover?"

Reynaud considered using the tire for cover but if it was hit, it was likely to be messy. Instead, he copied Wade, going prone and firing down the line of cars to discourage anyone from looking for targets. Staying low, Paco dashed for the car forty yards away.

Finding his rifle empty, Reynaud frantically dug out cartridges and shoved them into the loading gate until the rifle would take no more then looked up at the sound of a blast. Paco had almost reached the wreck but was caught by the edge of the blast, leaving a puff of smoke and a cloud of dirt thrown up. "Logan!" Reynaud shouted.

"Right here," Logan replied, from only a couple of feet behind him.

"Cover me," Reynaud snapped and started to get his feet under him.

"Bullshit!" Logan roared. "You can't run worth a damn. You cover me. I'll take care of anything on this side of the road, you just keep the clowns on the other side too busy duckin' to screw with me." Without waiting for an answer, he shouldered his way past the Cajun and flung himself forward.

~ * ~

Still a dozen feet away from where Paco lay a bullet whined past Logan's ear, and he sprayed a burst from his AKR and almost tripped. He threw himself into the roll, dropping the submachine gun. From the other end of the car he could hear someone wailing. He caught Paco around the chest, dragged him to the questionable cover of the front of the car. "You okay?"

"I'll do." Paco seemed dazed, with blood running down his face from a cut along one eyebrow. He wiped some of the blood away from his eyes. "Homemade grenade. It didn' do much damage but the asshole behind the car almos' put it in my hip pocket. I'll be all right."

The wail at the opposite end of the car had faded to moans and whines. Logan drew the silenced Makarov from its holster. "I'm going to get us a little peace and quiet," he whispered to Paco and crept along the side of the wreck and peered around the end of the car. The bandit had his hand cupped over his left eye, and blood ran in streams between his fingers.

Logan paused. The man was no longer attacking, was no longer really an enemy: he was wounded, perhaps fatally, and wasn't even able to save his own life. He was almost certainly dead if he didn't get to a doctor soon, but if he did survive, he was more likely than not to ambush again. Logan raised the silenced pistol until the sights were centered at the back of the man's ear and squeezed the trigger. The bandit's head snapped toward the shot and the suddenly silent corpse toppled, his hands falling away from his face, revealing a bloody cavity where his right eye had been and a ragged hole in his right temple. Logan's shot had cut a nick out of the man's right ear and torn into his head. The body, after a final twitch, lay still.

Paco had followed Logan around the wreck and the two of them, using the machine as cover, looked across the highway. From their vantage, they could see the fire from the line of vehicles was slackening. Logan looked back to see the rifles they'd both dropped, heard another dull explosion from across the road, then ducked as a bullet plowed a furrow in the car's trunk.

Logan ducked behind the car. "Paco, are you feeling up to watching them trying to cross the road or creeping up on us?"

Paco nodded, his automatic in his hand.

"I'm going to try to find our rifles. Be back in a few."

As Logan crawled to the front of the car he noticed Reynaud, Wade, and the Deacon keeping up covering fire at the machines on the other side of the medial strip. Staying low, Logan followed the drag marks back to where he'd found Paco. The Mexican's Winchester lay, its lever down, resting on a clump of weeds. Finding his AKR took a moment longer, as it was obscured by other weeds. He crawled toward them and returned to the front end of the car where he pulled the magazine from the submachine gun, cleared the chamber, and checked to make sure the barrel was clear of dirt, reloaded and recharged the weapon, then returned to where Paco sat. He handed him his Winchester.

~ * ~

Steve had followed Hasteen to the nearest car and found him sitting beside a body, reloading one of his revolvers. Hasteen glanced up at him and gestured at the broken line of cars. "Follow me by a car's length or so, in case someone gets the bright idea to come in on me from behind."

Steve nodded at the holes in Hasteen's shirt and the

spots of blood. "Are you sure you're up for this?"

Hasteen stared down at the marks as though they were of complete disinterest to him. "It only stings a little. Follow me."

Steve let Hasteen move ahead of him, watching as he warily approached a car, crouching and looking under it. When he reached the door he carefully reached up and snatched the door open, examined the rotted and corroded interior, then crept to the back of the car to test the trunk.

As Hasteen approached the third car in line a man sprang out from behind it. The ambusher had almost brought his shotgun to bear when Hasteen thumbed off two quick shots that tossed the bandit onto the hood of the next car, where he slid down to lie in a heap.

Two more men appeared farther down the line. The nearer man fired a burst with an M-16, the bullets chewing a quick line toward Hasteen and Steve then, at the roar of Hasteen's pistol the man spun, still firing, and collapsed. The other bandit managed to snap off one shot with his pistol before Hasteen shot him. The man staggered drunkenly two steps back then fell to his knees, trying to raise his pistol in both hands. Hasteen whipped out his left-hand Colt and fired again. The man's head snapped back as the bullet caught him between the eyes. His pistol barked and a bullet whined off the blacktop and far past them as he toppled.

A dozen feet and a car farther down the line, someone threw a canister at them, something that hit the ground with a thump and, almost a second later, exploded with a bellow. Something hit the grille of the car beside Steve hard enough to dent metal and shatter plastic and he heard other bits of shrapnel clipping weeds and hitting sheet metal.

Hasteen bit back a curse and, after reloading, made his way forward.

Steve followed, stopping at the car Hasteen had crouched beside when the grenade exploded, Hasteen hadn't opened the door of this car. Keeping his Beretta pointed at the windshield, Steve crept forward and snapped off a shot as a head appeared on the passenger side.

A hole appeared in the windshield and the rest of the safety glass shattered into a translucent mosaic. Steve cursed as the head ducked. The bullet must've been deflected by the glass.

Hasteen had halted beside the next vehicle, a pickup, and looked back. Steve motioned him to stay where he was and listened. The covering fire had slackened to an occasional shot or short burst but had done its work. Hasteen and he had only to watch for enemies on the right side of the highway. With the left side secured and Hasteen watching for trouble from the right, Steve slid down the slope of the road and moved ahead. From beside the door and no more than five feet away from it, he fired as rapidly as he could pull the trigger, emptied the magazine into the door. He shoved the hot pistol back into the shoulder holster, drew the single-action revolver, and fired three more rounds into the pattern of holes and tears the bullets had made.

With the cocked pistol in his right hand, he crawled to the door then wrenched at it, having to jerk savagely at it to pull it open, and stared at the corpses. The body in the passenger's seat lay slumped, bleeding from a multitude of wounds. The body behind the steering wheel had fallen in on itself, and was long past bleeding. The jaws, almost bare of skin and the teeth, yawned impossibly wide, the lower jaw muscles having rotted away. From the hair still attached to the head and the color of the rags, he guessed the skeleton had been a woman.

Slamming the door shut, Steve crawled to the back of the car, dragging in deep breaths. When he could talk again, he asked, "Hasteen, how many do you think were in on the ambush?"

"Too many. Don't forget to reload."

"Thanks." Steve ejected the three dead cases, reloaded the revolver and holstered it, then changed magazines in the Beretta and recharged it. "I haven't heard any gunshots in the last few minutes. How many of those goons do you think are left?"

Hasteen glanced at the blood on his pants leg around a hole. "At least one too many. We still haven't gotten the one who threw the grenade."

Steve noticed the fresh wound for the first time. "I didn't know you'd been hit again. How bad is it?"

Hasteen looked at the hole in his pants leg without

expression. "It's—uncomfortable—but it's not serious. Let's finish this." He worked his way back to his feet and limped down the line of vehicles, bent forward at the waist. By walking on the slope of the shoulder he could stay well below the level of the car windows, but otherwise seemed to have cast caution aside.

They covered almost another forty yards when another grenade was tossed. They both hit the ground but Hasteen was back up and charging forward before all the dirt had stopped falling. Steve saw him snap off a shot and a man was thrown, spinning, over the hood of a car and down the slope. As the man fell, something dropped, smoking, from his hand.

Springing forward, Hasteen seized the body and flung it onto the grenade. A split-second later, Steve heard a muffled explosion and the body bounced a couple of inches before settling into a spreading dark pool.

As Steve watched, Hasteen rolled the body over with his foot and dropped a cartridge case into the gaping mouth. "Now we can call it finished."

They heard the sound of boots pacing along the asphalt, coming from the direction of their truck then Wade's voice drawled, "Looks like this little dust-up is over. You boys okay?"

"Fresh as daisies," Steve said, and sat down on the pavement, his back against the fender of the hulk nearest him and rested until his hands stopped trembling. Slightly refreshed, he hauled himself to his feet. "Hasteen, you'd better make it back to the truck. I'll count bodies and pick up booty." He waited only to see Hasteen nod and limp away before he began his grim work detail.

With Wade helping, he counted nine bodies armed with an assortment of weapons, a surprising amount of money, and two of the handmade grenades, one an old aluminum film canister and the other a baby-food jar. Wade only glanced at them. "Probably black powder, likely surrounded by some pieces of metal, all set off with a fuse. Sloppy, but it'll do, if you can drop it within a couple-three feet of whoever you're mad at."

As they approached the truck, Reynaud strode toward them. "One body on the highway, one that Logan shot, and a smear on the blacktop that was probably the guy behind the roadblock when we hit it. How many did you find?"

Wade bit off a chew and got it settled in his cheek. "With

yours, make it an even dozen. Who got hit?"

"Paco's got a nasty cut over his eye, and I saw Hasteen limping." Together, they walked back to the truck. Wade, Steve, and Billy Joe led the horses down the ramp, saddled them or loaded their packs on, while Reynaud attended to the wounded. He spent a few minutes on Paco's cut then turned to Hasteen, who'd waited silently.

"Sweet Jesus!" Reynaud exclaimed when he saw the wounds. "You got enough shrapnel in you to look like a blueberry muffin. Why didn't you say something."

"I was in no hurry to get cut on." Hasteen took off his shirt and displayed what looked like pox across his chest. "The shotgun pellets aren't very deep. They hit the car first and ricocheted."

Robichaux's aid kit contained thin tweezers and Reynaud removed eight deformed pellets from Hasteen's chest, cleaned the wounds as best he could, and bandaged them with compresses over the wounds and some gauze tape, then examined the small, bloody hole in Hasteen's left calf.

"There's something still in there," Hasteen said. "Feels like it's only a half-inch or so in."

Reynaud probed the wound and found a small piece of gravel that required several minutes of tense work to remove then he cleaned the wound out with moonshine and wrapped it.

"How are the horses, Deak?" Reynaud asked as he stood, wiping sweat from his face with a sleeve.

"Two are down," Billy Joe answered. "My horse was shot in the neck and one of the pack animals has a broken leg—" He was interrupted by the sound of a pair of gunshots and Wade walked down the loading ramp, reloading one of his automatics.

"Looks like we're done here." Reynaud paid Robichaux for the trip and Steve handed over another two hundred ROT dollars he'd collected from the bodies. "We'll leave most of the captured long arms for you—to help cover the damages. You want a ride into town?"

"Just to the edge. There's sort of a garage. Smitty's worked on the truck before."

They set out, Billy Joe riding behind Steve and Robichaux riding double with Reynaud. As they rode, Robichaux gave them directions to Baker's place, a small ranch just outside the western edge of Victoria.

As they reached the outskirts, Robichaux pointed out a building with "Messerschmidt's Truck Service" in fading paint and they left him there then let their horses break into a trot down the former main street. Twice they had to stop and ask directions, confused by missing street signs and the fact one of the buildings Robichaux had used as a landmark had been repainted.

Half a block from Baker's house they noticed a pickup parked on the street. Hasteen raised his hand to signal a halt but, before he could dismount, Wade drew his horse beside Hasteen's. "Stay in the saddle. We can take care of it, if you'll hold the horses."

Reynaud drew rein at Hasteen's other side. "I'll help you and the Deacon hold the horses. Paco, Steve, and Logan, you go with Wade."

The men Reynaud had named swung down from their saddles and handed the reins to the handlers, Paco and Steve taking their rifles. Wade waved to Paco and Logan to swing wide around to the stable while he and Steve walked up the gravel footpath to the front porch. Reynaud turned his horse's head and rode to a clump of trees, motioning for Hasteen and the Deacon to follow him. By the time they'd taken cover and drawn their own rifles, Wade had disappeared into the house and Paco had slipped into the stable.

Reynaud took off his hat, feeling the breeze cool his sweat-damp hair then wiped his forehead and the hatband with a spare bandanna.

"Nervous?" Hasteen asked.

"A little. More for Baker and his family than us. That ambush on the highway was set up; it didn't just happen by accident. My guess is Chernikov's come and gone."

Hasteen nodded. "You're probably right."

"What I'd like to know is why they left the pickup." Reynaud wiped his hands on his pants legs.

"We don't know if it still runs," Hasteen pointed out, "and we don't know what vehicles Baker may have had, but it looks as though they left on horseback. The gate of the corral by the stable is open. Taking horses would make sense. This far from the coast, it's easier to cut cross-country."

Wade emerged from the house and swung his arm in an arc. At the signal, the group in the trees rode toward the house at a trot.

"Nobody here." Wade said, "but it doesn't look like they intended to leave. There's a few empty shelves in the pantry but most of the rest of the house is undisturbed. I found this in one of the closets." He handed over a rifle that looked like his own. "This is an M-1A. They used to be a high-dollar piece. If Baker had been planning to go anywhere, he'd probably have taken this with him."

Reynaud gestured at Wade and Steve. "You two find what trail food you can and meet us out back." He reined his horse around and clicked his tongue. Hasteen and the Deacon followed him around the house to where Paco and Logan stood outside the stable door. As the riders approached, they saw the body of a horse lying in a body sling.

"Looks like Chernikov beat us here," Logan said, his face grim. "Paco tells me that wound wouldn't kill the horse right away. Sounds like that bastard, Chernikov, doesn't it?"

Reynaud nodded. "Any sign of how they left, or which way they went?"

Paco indicated the open corral with a jerk of his head. "There's lots of fresh hoofprints, and six sets are headed west."

"Any idea of what's west?"

Paco shrugged. "Mos' of Texas."

Wade and Steve kicked open the back door of the house, their arms laden with dried meat and a number of cans. "I left the rifle and the extra magazines," Wade said, "but I took some ammo. I burned upwards of forty rounds in that firefight we had."

Paco motioned for the Deacon to dismount then he sprang up, kicked a leg over, seated his feet in the stirrups, and untied the thong on the lariat by the saddle horn. "Give that stuff to the others," he told Wade. "Three of the horses are in that hedge at the edge of the pasture, and we need to replace the horses we los'."

He and Wade were gone only a few minutes before they

returned leading a chestnut and a paint. They put the Deacon's gear on the pinto and moved part of the pack load onto the chestnut.

Following the trail Wade and Paco pointed out, they ate lunch in the saddle. Within a few miles, the trail veered northwest. "They're going around towns," Wade observed. "At this point, it looks like your Russian's turned anti-social."

"He's always been that," Reynaud said, "not to mention psychopathic. These men and I know him all too well. He'd kill his own grandmother with no more hesitation or regret than we'd feel stepping on a scorpion."

When neither Wade nor Paco could read the trail in the fading light, they made camp in a hedge grove. Among the trees they collected enough wood for a fire and Reynaud put together a meal from the supplies they'd brought.

They ate in silence, each man with his own thoughts and, from the expressions, the thoughts were all grim. Paco finally stood and stretched some of the knots out of his muscles. "If the trail keeps going this way, we'll be cutting close around San Antonio."

Reynaud suddenly remembered a promise he'd made. He glanced at Logan then remembered the rest of the group had been asleep when he'd promised Mike Teller that he'd see to his family. Finding a place to lay his bedroll, he lay listening to the horses cropping grass. He'd just begun to doze when he heard Hasteen who'd just lay down, roll over with a grunt.

"How're the leg and the chest?" Reynaud asked.

"A little stiff and sore."

Forcing himself to get up, Reynaud rummaged in the packs for the medical supplies. "Let me take a look. You'll need your dressings changed."

Hasteen sat up with a sigh. "If I'd known you were going to make all this fuss, I wouldn't have gotten shot in the first place."

"Think of that next time," Reynaud said, grinning. He examined the wounds in the firelight. "I can't see much tonight. I'll check again in the morning. You need to worry about infection." He swabbed at the pellet pox and the hole in Hasteen's leg with an alcohol-soaked cloth then redressed the wounds. "What's the necklace?" He'd noticed before Hasteen wore a beaded string around his neck.

"Kills."

"What?"

"Kills. When I have to shoot a man, I add another bead to the string. A man should be remembered somehow, even if the only memorial is a bead on his killer's necklace."

"How many beads—"

"Sixty-five. Once I cut notches on my pistols' grips but it became uncomfortable and it seemed like bragging."

Reynaud swirled what was left of the coffee in the pot. There were at least three cupfulls left, easily enough to make it worth re-heating. He set the pot by the embers. "Why are you riding with us? The rest of my crowd and I have a score to settle with Chernikov, but it seems to me there's a lot of other things you could be doing."

Hasteen shrugged. "Like what? And I believe in harmony. People like Chernikov disturb that harmony. Maybe you'd call it justice, or even vengeance but, to me, it's restoring a balance.

"The other reason is the challenge." Hasteen's eyes took a faraway look. "You know what it's like to be in a fight for your life."

"All too well," Reynaud murmured.

Hasteen ignored the comment. "Your whole world narrows down to the enemy facing you, and you can see him so clearly you can count the hairs in his eyelashes. You lose your sense of time. Your reflexes take hold, while some part of you stands aside from yourself and just observes. You don't hear a man shouting in your ear but you clearly hear the tiny click of your enemy cocking his weapon."

Hasteen glanced at Reynaud and showed his teeth in a quick smile. "I've learned to pick my targets before the effect takes hold, so I can shift my focus from one enemy to the next very quickly.

"That feeling, when you put your life on the line, is the greatest thrill I know, and I think maybe I've come to need it." He picked up a cup, held it out, watched Reynaud fill it with coffee.

"An adrenalin junkie, as Logan would say." Reynaud poured himself a cup and set the pot aside. "And what happens if you get shot or, maybe worse, shoot the wrong man?"

"That bothers me a little," Hasteen admitted. He took a

cup of coffee and stared into the cup. "I don't know what I'd do if I killed the wrong man, but I know I've killed sixty-five right ones, and I don't know how many lives that's saved. As for getting killed—well, there's always a risk but can you see me dying in bed, eaten up by some disease, or sitting in a rocking chair listening to my arteries harden?"

Reynaud sipped at his own coffee. "How about Wade and Paco? You think they do it for the same reasons you do?"

Hasteen shook his head. "Paco, a little. We'd both like to be the best man alive with a gun, but mostly he puts himself in harm's way to protect the people who can't defend themselves. Wade's still a peace officer. He wants to make his part of the world safe for women and children and people who don't wear guns. He's someone who's always followed the rules of civilization, and now he has to sort of make up the rules as he goes."

~ * ~

Reynaud was up at first light and found most of the group already up and preparing for another day in the saddle. Hasteen still slumbered, and they let him sleep until breakfast was ready and Reymaud waited until after they'd eaten before he examined the wounds again. Even in the early daylight he could see no signs of infection.

They followed Chernikov's trail until late in the morning, when they found a campfire. Paco paced around the area, examining the ground. Suddenly he held up a two-shot derringer.

"You think there was some action here?" Logan asked.

Paco studied the ground around where he'd found the derringer. "There was a scuffle but no real damage done. Nobody had to drag a body, and no blood. It's a shame Baker wasn' as good a gunfighter as he mus've been a veterinarian."

Hasteen held out his hand and Paco handed him the derringer. After he'd examined it, Hasteen asked, "Do you mind?" After the others had shaken their heads, Hasteen tucked the tiny pistol into the top of his right Navajo ankle-boot. "We're not going to catch them by following them. I'm surprised we've been able to follow them this long. Sooner or later, they're going to follow a highway, and if they follow it for any length of time, we'll play hell trying to find out where they left it."

"Likely," Wade drawled. "We know where they're headed. It makes more sense to try to get ahead of 'em. Looks like they're headed northwest, and they're probably going to rendezvous with Barnes and his gang. Barnes is bound to be a sight easier to find than Chernikov. They ain't but four in this group and Barnes is gonna have a hell of a time hidin' his outfit. You can't just tuck three hundred-odd cutthroats into the shadow of a cactus."

Paco remounted. "Makes sense to me. Let's move."

After they ignored the trail they made better time and drove their mounts until the horses began to balk at putting their hooves down on ground they couldn't see. They camped that night near the ruins of a cabin.

Reynaud cooked dinner again, remembering some of what he'd learned in the family kitchen, and managed to make do with the supplies at hand.

After Logan had stoked his furnace he laid down his plastic plate with a sigh. "Rennie, if you weren't so ugly, I think I'd marry you for your cooking, but you gotta learn to go lighter on the beans, rice, and hot sauce. People are gonna start callin' the trail we're takin' 'Thunder Road,' just from the bean music."

"Would you rather do the cooking?" Reynaud inquired.

"Nah, I'd rather we all got where we're goin' alive." Logan collected the plates, replaced them in the pack then laid out his bedroll.

As Reynaud prepared to bed down for the night, he asked, "How near San Antonio are we going to get?"

"Right by it," Wade replied. "What's so important in San Antone?"

"It's sort of family business." Reynaud lay down on his blanket. "One of the guys we broke out of the prison camp with, fella by the name of Mike Teller, made me promise to look in on his family. Teller didn't make it out. We buried him in Poland." He paused a moment. "You think we might have enough time to try to look them up?"

The silence lasted so long Reynaud was about to repeat the question then he heard Wade clear his throat. "According to Slattery, this manhunt we're on is awful important, but so's this. You make a promise to a dyin' man, and that's a promise you gotta keep. You know where his family was livin'?"

"I think they were on base housing. I thought he said they were at Lackland, though Randolph would be more likely."

"You don' want to go to San Antonio then," Paco said. "The military families who survived the bomb and the plague moved to Camp Bullis Military Reservation. Is jus' a few miles north of San Antonio."

"You know how to get there from here?" Reynaud asked.

"I know the way," Wade drawled. "We can be there the day after tomorrow, bright and early in the mornin'."

"Do you think we might be able to get more supplies there?" Steve asked.

"Not likely," Paco said around a yawn. "They shut down the base hospitals to all but military and their families when the plague hit, then the chicken colonel from Lackland pulled everybody back to Fort Bullis. You ought to get a laugh out of that, Hasteen. This time the paleface soldiers moved themselves to a reservation."

"Are we going to be able to get on the reservation?" Reynaud asked.

"I'd like to see 'em try to stop us," Logan rumbled.

"You can probably get on," Paco said, "and maybe Wade. Hasteen and I will wait for you outside. The soldiers do not like to have much to do with civilians."

~ * ~

They'd long since left the coastal marshlands for heavily grassed prairies, with weeds growing amid crops of corn, sorghum, and soybean gone wild, and they often saw small herds of cattle grazing their way through fields. Most of the few fences they saw were down or cut.

Reynaud nodded toward the cattle. "I thought cattle country was south of here."

Wade peeled off his hat and wiped his forehead and face with a sleeve. "It usta be, until the recent unpleasantness in south Texas. When some of what was left of the Mexican army started headin' north, a lot of survivin' cattlemen shagged their herds north, at least as much as they could drive in a hurry. Ranchin's easier than farmin', and a lot of farmers were already dead."

They swung north, Wade leading the way. "It's probably safer stayin' out of sight of San Antone. The bigger cities became suburbs of hell in a hurry. When the power goes off, and water and sewer services fall apart, and they's food riots and secondary plagues, it don't take long to whittle away upwards of nine-tenths of the population. Most of the rest of them are starin' mad."

They had to cross two major highways on their way around San Antonio and their horses were showing the strain of the day's hard travel. About sundown they saw a spark of fire ahead and to their left.

Reynaud drew up his mount then urged it into a walk toward a lone tree standing in a depression fifty yards to the right. In the wash, he dismounted and tied the horse's reins to a low limb. Leaving the rifle in his saddle boot, he unslung the shotgun and checked the chamber. The rest of the group had drawn up around him and tied their horses to the same tree.

Reynaud glanced at Wade, who was testing the draw of his pistols. "If they're enemies, I'd rather get this settled before we bed down. Sound right to you, Wade?"

"You're doin' good." Wade drawled softly.

The group spread out and paced toward the firelight. Distances were deceptively hard to judge in the dimness, and he guessed they'd covered five hundred yards before they were near enough the camp to hear a sound that made Reynaud suddenly feel cold. It was the wail of a harmonica, and the sound seemed to throw him back into the Russian prison camp. He shook off the instantaneous disorientation but couldn't make himself take cover. There were too many ugly memories, too many debts to be paid.

From somewhere far away, it seemed, he heard Wade murmur, "Lordy, it's the Damnation Army." But Reynaud never slowed, and he strode into the circle of firelight.

~ * ~

Chernikov tested the bindings on the wrists of Baker and his son. It had been a very good thing he'd searched them last night, when he'd found the odd little pistol in Baker's boot.

He glared at Vickers as the Texan laid out his bedroll. "Do not relax yet. You will be guarding the camp until midnight."

"For—" For a moment, Vickers looked as though he wanted to argue, then thought better of it.

Chernikov grinned at Vickers. "I needn't tell you what will happen to you if you go to sleep, need I?"

"Nope." Vickers checked the chamber of his rifle and found a patch of cover from which to observe the plains around them.

"Where you from, mister?" the boy asked him.

Chernikov ignored the bitten-off attempt of Baker to silence his son. "Where do you think I'm from?"

The boy lay silent a moment, then, "Not sure. Somewheres north and east. Sometimes you talk a little like an Englishman."

"You're right," Chernikov said, "I'm from north and east."

Paul Baker had apparently decided not to give him the satisfaction of asking any questions. Since they'd left the ranch, the man had spoken only to his son. This attitude almost amused Chernikov, although he'd have to inspire more fear when they reached the research facilities. For the present, it was better to let the veterinarian maintain some illusions of control; the illusion might keep him from becoming too desperate. They were still looking at a long ride across Texas and desperation could cause him to grasp at any chance to escape. This might result in Baker's death, which would require Chernikov to find another researcher, or the death of Baker's son, which would lessen Chernikov's hold on the man.

"Where are we right now?" Chernikov asked.

He heard Vickers scratching himself then the Texan replied, "About half a day's ride east and north of a military reservation north of San Antone."

"How much longer before we reach your friends?"

"About five more days or so before we'll run into a patrol of them."

Chernikov let himself slip into a doze but was still aware enough that he could hear Vickers approach much later and mumble, "It's midnight."

Chernikov rolled out from under his blanket and stood guard until sunrise painted the eastern horizon pink and gold. He kicked the others out from under their blankets and untied the prisoners' hands. Vickers heated some horrid canned meat, gravy, and coffee.

The sun hadn't cleared the horizon before they were again riding west. Chernikov motioned for Vickers to lead, while he followed the prisoners. By midmorning Vickers held up his hand. "They's a wide spot in the road ahead, place called Camp Verde. We could use more water and oats for the horses, and provisions for ourselves. If you want to take the prisoners around the place, I'll meet you on the other side."

"You take the prisoners. I'll meet you north of there on the highway. It does run north through there, doesn't it?"

"Yeah. Camp Verde's only got a general store. When I was through there the last time the old Nowlin Ranch house was abandoned. The store was still open, though."

"Very good. "I'll meet you on Texas 173 a mile north of the town."

Vickers tugged down the front brim of his hat and motioned for Baker and his son to move ahead of him.

Chernikov stared at the man and his boy and loudly said. "Draw your weapon and keep it at the ready." He rode behind Baker's horse, leaned over, and tied the man's hands behind his back. "If either of them tries to escape, kill the other before you go after the one who's run."

Vickers nodded.

Chernikov urged his horse and the pack animal along the highway toward the windmill in the distance until he could see the ranch house and the general store. As he approached the buildings he noticed four horses tied to a hitching rail in front of the ranch house. He drew rein in front of the store, wrapped the reins and lead lines around the pipe hitching rail, and stepped into the shade of the building.

Just inside the door stood a barrel of water, a dipper hanging on the side of the barrel. Absently, as he studied the man who'd just emerged from the back of the store, Chernikov wiped the dipper off with his handkerchief before bringing up a dipper of water and drinking deeply. As he drank, he continued to examine the store and its owner. The man looked as though the sun and wind had dried him out, leaving only bone and gristle and leather skin behind.

"Mornin'." The man's voice sounded as dry as the rest of him seemed to be.

"I need some supplies." Chernikov glanced back out the door. "I thought I'd heard the ranch had been deserted."

"T'was. Some people from down south moved in last month. They had a few cattle and a flock of sheep. Seem to be good enough neighbors. At least, they ain't any trouble. What do you need?"

"I'll take four of those canteens," Chernikov pointed to where several of the round, flat, blanket-sided civilian canteens hung from the antlers of a mounted deer head. "I'll need enough water to fill them and a few canteens I've got outside. I'd also like oats, beans, flour, and dried meat."

"Beef or mutton?"

"Some of both."

While the shopkeeper gathered the supplies, Chernikov brought in the canteens from his horse and the pack animal and filled them at the barrel, holding them under the water as they bubbled and filled. After he'd carried the freshly filled canteens outside and loaded them on the pack horse, he returned to where the supplies were stacked on the counter. "Let me have three or four blankets."

As the man added the blankets to the pile, Chernikov glanced around the shop again. "What do I owe you?"

The man added up the total on a piece of brown paper. "Looks like about fifty ROTdollars."

Chernikov fished in his pocket and produced a gold coin. "How much do you want for that rifle?" He picked up a lever-action from a rack.

"That's a Marlin thirty-thirty carbine. Just like new. Cost you another hundred."

"Do you have ammunition for it?"

The man wordlessly shoved a box of cartridges across the counter but Chernikov noticed his eyes had narrowed. Chernikov wondered what mistake he'd made. "Is there a place I can try this out?"

"They's a whole prairie out back."

Chernikov opened the box of cartridges, fed four of them into the rifle, then carried the weapon out the back door. He stared out over the plains and noticed a cow's skull on a fence post. He raised the carbine, settled it tightly against his shoulder, levered a round into the chamber, settled the front bead just under the skull, which stood at what he guessed to be seventy-five meters, and squeezed the trigger.

He was hardly conscious of the report or the rocketing sound of the bullet speeding downrange, but the skull wobbled and a horn disappeared. He worked the lever and tried again and this time the skull shattered. He fired the last two rounds into the fencepost then carried the rifle back into the store.

"Shoots good. I'll take it. Do you have a scabbard for it?"

As the man turned around and lifted a worn leather rifle boot off the wall, Chernikov asked, "Did I say something to disturb you before?"

By way of reply, the old man asked, "You ain't from around here, are you?"

"No, I was in the Air Force. Just got discharged and I'm headed back to California."

"Well, you might call it ammunition out there, but around here we call 'em ca'tridges or shells."

Chernikov forced a laugh. "I'm going to need two more boxes of shells for this, if you've got them."

The shopkeeper placed two more boxes of cartridges on the counter. "Expecting trouble?"

Chernikov almost smiled at the opening. "I hear the bandits are getting thicker, and some of Barnes' group is supposed to be drifting this way. I hear they travel in packs, so you might watch out for strangers, especially if there are a group of them."

"Thanks for the advice."

"Not at all." This time Chernikov permitted himself a smile. "We all have to look out for ourselves and each other."

Chapter 6

As Reynaud walked into the camp he still heard the wail of the harmonica and picked out, for the first time, the twang of a Jew's harp and the murmur of conversation. All the sounds died away as Reynaud stopped in front of the man with the harmonica. "I've really learned to hate harmonica music," he said, "and my friends feel the same way. When we hear it, we get mad. Sometimes downright homicidal."

The group of men in the firelight were so stunned by Reynaud's sudden appearance they all seemed rooted to the ground. Slowly, one of them struggled to his feet. "'And the stars of heaven fell unto the earth, even as a fig tree casteth off her untimely figs, when she is shaken by a mighty wind.'

"'And the heavens departed as a scroll when it's rolled up, and ever' mountain and island were shoved out of their places.'

"'For the day of His wrath is come; and who shall be able to stand?'"

The men around the fire stirred themselves to shout a chorus of amens and hallelujahs, and a few of them groped for their weapons.

The man raised his voice to a shout. "In the last days shall He separate the sheep from the goats and those who hear not His call shall be called by the Elect, and that call shall be the voice of the gun."

"First Galatians, verses eight and nine," the Deacon roared as he stalked into the light. "'But though we, or an angel from heaven, preach any other gospel unto you that which we have preached to you, let him be accursed.'" He swung his rifle up and hammered a long burst into the Damnation speaker, who was thrown, geysering blood from a dozen hits, up a slight incline.

Snapping his shotgun to his hip Reynaud popped off a shot at the man who'd dropped his harmonica and snatched up a rifle. The round caught the man in the head, which exploded like a melon dropped forty feet onto a concrete floor. The Cajun flung himself down and to his right, rolling, pumping another round into the chamber.

The Deacon stood like an oak and raked two or three men with another burst, ignoring the bullets that buzzed past him. Reynaud recognized the sound of Logan's AKR as he charged, firing, into the circle of light. Two men who'd already shot at the Deacon spun to face the new threat and were cut down. Steve's AK-74 added its voice to the choir and the last two crazies, unmarked until then, withered under the stream of bullets.

Reynaud dropped his shotgun and clawed at his face, reacting to the sand a near miss had thrown into his eyes. By the time he could see again, Billy Joe had reloaded and was finishing off the wounded with single shots and Hasteen,. Wade, and Paco had strode into the camp from the flanks.

"Anybody hit?" Wade asked.

Logan shook his head then stared at the Deacon. "You sure you didn't take a round or two? You were standing right there in the middle of a firefight."

"The Lord looks after his own," the Deacon intoned.

Logan snorted. "I've heard he looks after children and fools."

"That's not in scripture," Billy Joe snapped.

Logan's eyebrows shot up. "I'm not about to argue the good book with you."

Hasteen disappeared into the night while the rest of the group gathered supplies and weapons. "Don't bother saving the meat," Wade informed them. "You never know where it's been. Or what it came from. Or who it came from."

Logan stared at him. "You mean—?"

"Yep," Wade drawled, "some of these boys develop a taste for long pig."

Logan had reloaded his AKR and counted the rounds left in the magazine he'd removed. "I've got two full magazines and five rounds left."

The Deacon checked his own clips. "Two full magazines and two-thirds left in the one in the weapon."

"I've got three full mags and about twenty rounds more." Steve said. "This Russian ammo is going to be awfully hard to find. You fellows take my ammo, and I'll pick a booty gun."

"The only real rapid-fire piece they had is this Mexican G-3," Paco said, handing over a light automatic weapon. "Is chambered for the 7.62 millimeter NATO round, same as Wade's M-14. They had a couple of bolt-actions that shoot the same cartridge, so there should be enough shells to last a while."

Steve picked up the G-3, found the magazine release, cleared the action, then began to familiarize himself with the weapon.

Hasteen returned from the darkness. "I hope one of you knows how to deal with mules."

"What do you mean?" Reynaud asked.

"They didn't have horses." Hasteen almost grinned. "They traveled by—I suppose you could call it a wagon." He drew a thick branch out of the fire and led the way to the shell of a half-ton pickup. The engine and transmission had been pulled out and discarded, the firewall had been largely cut away and a hole had been cut in the roof of the cab. Hasteen gestured at where four hobbled mules grazed, also pointing out the crude harness used to hitch them to the front of the truck.

Paco laughed. "We did those *locos* a favor. That thing don' look like it could've done another twenty miles."

"We did the mules a favor, too," Wade said. "Hauling this wreck around was no walk in the park." He approached the mules warily and removed the hobbles, putting a hackamore on the one mule that tried neither to kick him or bite him, and led the animal back to the camp where they loaded on the supplies they'd chosen.

By the time they'd returned to the depression where they'd left their horses, Reynaud's weariness had become trembling exhaustion. The group carefully laid out their bedrolls and set up a schedule for sentry duty. After gnawing dried meat, washed down with brackish water from their canteens, all but Paco, who'd drawn the first watch, lay down to sleep.

As Logan tried to find the least uncomfortable position in which to sleep on the uneven ground, he muttered to Wade. "Yeah, it's pretty ticklish talkin' religion with the Deacon. It's a lot safer talkin' about something less dangerous, like politics. You hear about the Democratic congressman who got caught turning the pages?"

"Down here," Wade drawled, "we take our politics right serious." After a pause, he added, "And I'm a Democrat."

After a long pause, Logan cleared his throat and inquired, "So, how's the weather?"

His only answer was s snore and, after making sure at least two of his weapons were within easy reach, he drifted off to sleep.

~ * ~

After studying the guard shack, Reynaud glanced at Wade, who was also squinting at the shed. "Are you sure you want to come with us?"

Wade pulled a badge out of a shirt pocket and pinned it over the left breast pocket. "Let's get it done. I just wish we'd come in with the sun at our backs. That tends to throw off marksmanship—just in case those soldier-boys are a little trigger-happy."

"You know how to keep a fella cheered up." Reynaud said. "Hasteen, Paco, if we're not in Leon Springs by tomorrow morning, it'll be up to you to run down Chernikov."

"We may as well leave our horses with these boys," Wade said. "Leon Springs is easy walking distance if things go well, and if things don't go well, I'd rather not give the bastards the satisfaction of having my horse."

"Makes sense." Reynaud also dismounted. After thinking a moment, he unslung his shotgun and hung it from the saddle horn. "No percentage in my hauling any long arms, for the same reason,"

"We'll be waiting in Leon Springs," Hasteen promised. "If you can walk out, great. If you have to run for it, we'll be close enough to give you cover."

The others decided to carry their rifles. "It only makes sense," Steve explained. "They'd expect us to have rifles. I'd hate to disappoint them. It might make them suspicious."

"We've been riding along this fence for the last half-mile," Reynaud pointed out. "They're more likely to ask us about our horses than guns."

Wade bit off a chunk of chewing tobacco, settled the wad into his cheek, and nodded toward the gate. "Let's go."

At two hundred yards from the gate they heard the flat, mechanical voice of a loudspeaker. "Lay down all your weapons and walk slowly toward the guard station."

The group laid down their rifles and unbuckled gun belts, although Logan grumbled as though they'd demanded he have both arms amputated, then they advanced to the shack inside the gate. They'd covered half the distance when three men and a woman, wearing Army and Air Force battle uniforms, all carrying M-16s, approached them cautiously, their rifles leveled. "What do you want here?" the Air Force sergeant demanded.

"All of us but the Ranger are U.S. Air Force first lieutenants, and we're here to see the personnel officer." Reynaud had taken a step forward.

The sergeant looked closely at each of them in turn. "What for?"

"That's for us to discuss with a superior officer, sergeant," Reynaud snapped.

"You're not in uniform," the sergeant observed.

"You must be the sergeant 'cause you're the sharp-eyed, quick-thinking one. That's because they don't issue US uniforms in Russky prison camps, asshole," Logan growled. "We've come all the way from Europe to make our reports, and along the way we've had to kick tougher asses than yours. Now, get your superiors on the radio and let 'em know you're keeping four Euro-vets waiting at the god-dam gate."

The woman, who wore corporal's stripes, stepped up beside the sergeant and murmured something to him the group couldn't hear. The sergeant raked his teeth across his lower lip then nodded and the woman trotted back to the shack. They all waited until she returned and muttered again to the sergeant.

The sergeant motioned to them with his rifle. "You can all sit down in the shade of the shack, but sit with your hands flat on the ground behind you. Rawlins, you and Konecny go pick up their guns and bring 'em in."

The men walked through the gate and found space in the shade of the shack in which to sit. The sergeant squatted in front of them, his rifle pointed discreetly past them. "Who were the two men with you?"

Reynaud could guess they had binoculars at this post, or other observers had radioed the information that seven men with horses had approached the base. "They're friends of Wade's, who helped us reach this place," he replied.

The two soldiers had staggered back to the guard post, stumbling under the weight of the group's weaponry. "Sarge," one of them announced, "there's several Russian weapons in this lot."

"I told you we'd come from Europe," Logan said.

"Okay, okay," the sergeant said, "just sit tight. Someone's on the way out here to pick you up."

Nearly a quarter of an hour passed before a dusty army truck pulled up and half a dozen men, led by a master sergeant, piled out and surrounded the group. "What've you got here?" the master sergeant demanded, hands on his hips.

The squad sergeant had stood. "Four of these guys claim to be officers from the European war. The other guy says he's a Texas Ranger."

The master sergeant stared at Wade. "What're you doing here?"

"Just tryin' to make sure my friends got here safe and sound." He spat a stream of tobacco juice at a weed. "Is Colonel Frazier still running the show here?"

"Yeah, he is. What's it to you?"

"He has a rep for bein' a straight-shooter, and he doesn't have a quarrel with the Republic of Texas. That's all."

"How about you guys?" The sergeant seemed to have trouble lowering his voice to any level lower than a bellow. "You reporting for active duty?"

"We'll discuss that with the base Personnel Officer," Reynaud said, trying to keep the annoyance out of his voice.

The master sergeant stared at the group with ill favor, as though they were all a herd of very smelly goats. "Awright," he finally roared, "suit yourselves. Into the back of the truck."

Reynaud led the group to the truck bed. The sides of the tarp had been rolled up. They took seats as near the front of the truck as possible, leaving room at the back for the soldiers. After the last man had climbed in and the master sergeant had joined the driver in the cab the engine coughed and wheezed to life, and the truck pulled away.

Reynaud hardly noticed the land around them. He was thinking hard and fast about their situation. Slattery hadn't mentioned a Colonel Frazier nor the military reservation, so it was unlikely that anyone on the base was part of the reconstructionist network. This could mean several things, some of them unpleasant, many of them very unpleasant. At best, this reservation was a benevolent military dictatorship held together by obsolete loyalties, concerned solely with the welfare of the soldiers and airmen and their dependents. At worst, it could be a full-blown military dictatorship, a replay of Nazi Germany without all the fancy trappings. It was best to keep his cards—and a lousy hand it was—close to his vest.

The truck slowed and stopped. The soldiers in the bed hopped out in sequence, like paratroopers leaving a plane. Wade, sitting nearest the soldiers, waited until the last man had bailed out and turned to face the truck before he stood and strode to the rear of the truck bed.

Reynaud was the last of the group to jump down. He paused and looked around, sensing the similarity of this place to almost every military base he'd ever seen; the same ugly buildings laid out in the same unimaginative patterns across the same boring attempts at landscaping.

The gravel parking lot in which he stood served a building uglier than the barracks lined up in ranks about three hundred yards away, if only because it was larger. In the distance he could see teams of people working in the fields, and he could guess, from the pattern of roads, that a motor pool was located somewhere on the other side of the big building. A few smaller clapboard structures, probably private quarters for some of the officers, stood between the barracks and the office building.

The sergeant waved them toward the door of the office building, which seemed unguarded. One of the sergeant's guards opened the door, two more of them entered the building, and the rest of them followed the group inside.

Reynaud was grateful for the shade but wished for more light than the dimness of the unlit barn-like office.

Their guards had halted at a desk at which sat a grim-faced woman with graying hair and second lieutenant's bars. She looked up from a sheaf of papers she'd been sorting.

"They're here to see Major Wilson." The master sergeant somehow managed to keep his voice at a nearly normal level. "These four claim to be Euro-vets, and the other one seems to know

Colonel Frazier."

The woman stood. "I'll see if the major is able to see them." She walked down a corridor, tapped at a door, opened it, and spoke a few words to someone in the office. She was followed back to the desk by a tall, heavyset man in an Air Force uniform, with a major's oak leaves.

Reynaud and the other former prisoners all saluted as soon as they saw the insignia of rank. The major returned their salutes with a faintly ironic air. "And from whom do I have the honor of receiving salutes?"

"Reynaud Dechaine, Logan Reed, Steven Villareal, and William Joseph McCluskey, all first lieutenants, U. S. Air Force. I was in the 94th Fighter Squadron."

Each of the other former prisoners gave their previous unit. As the Deacon recited his, the major raised his eyebrows. "Was Lieutenant Colonel Shelton still in command of the 384th Bomber Wing?"

"Colonel Shelton earned his eagle before we were deployed in England. I regret he died of plague before my last mission."

"Sorry to hear that, Lieutenant McCluskey." The major turned to the master sergeant. "Your group is dismissed, sergeant. I'll see these men in Captain Fulton's office." Reynaud noticed two of the soldiers carrying the group's weapons to another room in the building. He followed the major down a hallway to a large, open office occupied by four desks and at least eight chairs.

The major grinned at them. "At ease, boys. Grab yourselves a chair." He pulled open the drawers of a desk, found what he was looking for in the second drawer. Pulling out a bottle, he held it up and gazed at the label. "Either Fulton's stockpile is running low or his taste is slipping." He found some water glasses and poured a little of the whiskey for each of the men, except for Billy Jo, who held up a hand to signify refusal.

"I was really sorry to hear about Benny Shelton." The major sipped at his drink. "He and I were classmates at the academy. He was a damn good man." He turned to Wade. "I gather you're a Texas Ranger. What brings you so far out of the republic?"

"Just helpin' my buddies, here. Rennie had sort of a special reason for droppin' by and sayin' howdy."

"And what was that, Lieutenant?"

"Just Reynaud, sir. I didn't come back to re-up. You know what it's really like out there."

Major Wilson's face seemed to slump into a frown, and he nodded. "Yeah, except for a handful of unbalanced types, we all know. What does bring you?"

"The rest of these men and I were shot down in the war and spent six months or so in a Russian prison camp. One of the guys with us in the escape was Lieutenant Michael Teller. He didn't make it. He was wounded in the breakout and died just after we'd gotten across the border into Poland. Before he died, he asked me to look up his family here. He had a wife named Rachel, and a daughter, Ginnie, probably Virginia."

Wilson set down his glass, stood, and strode to the filing cabinets along the partition wall. Opening a drawer, he flipped through the files, pulled one out, read it, replaced it, and returned to the chair. "I'm afraid Mrs. Teller died in the hospital. The daughter, Virginia, was one of the few kids lucky enough to survive the plague."

"Yeah," Steve said bitterly, "lucky. Both parents dead. Real lucky."

Wilson's face kept its grim expression. "At least she's being taken care of. Did you want to see her?"

Reynaud considered the question before he finally nodded. "I guess it's up to me to tell her about her father."

The major drained his glass and put the bottle away. "She should be at school now." His frown deepened. "I think it'd be better if I personally went over and picked her up. Maybe, if she's got a teacher she's close with, or somebody else like that, it'll be a little easier for her to take. You fellows just sit tight here."

Reynaud decided he'd risk telling more that he should. "The reason we're not staying—we have reason to believe the Russian prison camp commandant is here in Texas, and we all owe him a lot, for more than Teller."

Major Wilson's cheek twitched as he clenched his teeth. "If he is, I hope you find the bastard. Kill him once for me, too." He stood. "If Captain Fulton comes in, tell him I should be back in about half an hour."

As the major closed the door behind him the men sat in silence for perhaps five minutes, finishing their drinks. Finally, Reynaud turned to Wade. "This is going better than I'd hoped. This guy, Wilson, seems to be a real human being."

Steve got up and began pacing. "Maybe it's my suspicious nature, but I'd feel a damned sight better if we still had our guns. As it is, the line between guest and prisoner is just a bit too fine to suit me."

Logan opened his mouth to answer but, before he could speak, the door swung open again and the master sergeant, followed by an Army captain, strode into the room. "Tenn-hutt!" the sergeant barked then stepped against the wall to let the captain, a short, corpulent, florid-faced man, stride past him.

The sudden command from the sergeant had brought them all to their feet but, after a startled moment, they all sat down again. The captain's face turned two shades redder. "On your feet!"

"Up your ass," Logan shot back.

The captain's face turned redder yet, and seemed to swell with rage. Reynaud caught himself wondering if this tin soldier were preparing to explode. Finally, the captain managed a choked voice, "Sergeant, I want these men placed under arrest for insubordination."

Reynaud stood. "Major Wilson—"

"Major Wilson didn't give you carte blanche to ignore military courtesy. You're out of uniform and AWOL. After you've been tried, we may take you back—with a reduction in grade. As for this man," he pointed at Wade, "he has no authority on a federal post. He'll be escorted to the gate." As the sergeant hesitated, obviously reluctant, the captain's anger raised his voice to a high-pitched shriek. "Sergeant, I gave you a direct order!"

The sergeant looked like the family dog drawn into a domestic dispute but he stepped toward them, drawing his pistol.

Reynaud wondered if he hadn't led the group into a trap. Had Wilson set them up, convinced them to drop their guard and left, leaving the dirty work to this captain? He glanced at the others, most of them looking to him for orders. Logan caught his eye and one eyelid flickered.

"You gonna put cuffs on us, Sarge? The service is a lot kinkier than I remember but, what the hell, I'll go first." He turned his left side to the sergeant and swung his arms back. The left arm went behind his back but his right hand had swung under the duster. The turn continued, became faster. His left hand chopped down on the wrist of the sergeant's gun hand while his right hand swept out and rammed the barrel of the Bulldog under the captain's chin. "If I was to sneeze right now, it'd blow your head right off, so let's both hope I don't have any allergies. Cap'n. you'd better stay quiet and set your fat butt in that chair to your left, or they're gonna be filin' by you sayin', 'My, don't he look natural.'"

The blood drained from the captain's face, and it went from red to white in seconds. He sat down heavily, as though his knees had lost their starch. Reynaud unbuckled the man's belt, pulled it free, tied the officer's hands behind the back then buckled the ends of the belt around the chair's rung.

Color flooded back into the captain's face, which turned red then purple. "This is worse than desertion," he fumed, "this is mutiny and, in time of war, is punishable by death."

"Oh, shut up," Logan snapped. He grinned at the sergeant. "We need a hostage for a little while and it looks like you're it. I'd take the captain but he seems the kinda guy they wouldn't figure to be much loss. I hope, for all our sakes, you're more valuable to them. You gotta be more popular. Now, we're all gonna walk out of here together, and you're going to lead us to our guns. Got it?"

Slowly and carefully, the sergeant nodded then followed Reynaud to the door, Logan right behind him.

Looking up and down the corridor, Reynaud saw only the woman at the reception desk. He rapped the door frame with his knuckles to get her attention then gestured for her to approach.

As she hesitated, Logan shoved the sergeant out the door. "Lady, I really don't like bein' a nuisance and I don't want to hurt anybody here, but if you don't get over here, pronto, I'm gonna have to show you what the inside of the sergeant's head looks like."

The woman slowly stood and walked toward them.

"Good," Logan said. "Now, Sarge, you need to take us to our

artillery."

The sergeant led them down the hallway to an intersecting corridor and stopped in front of a door. Logan gestured with the revolver and the sergeant opened the door. Their weapons were spread across two tables while more weapons hung on racks on the wall. Most of the racked firearms were M-16s and M-4s but with a scattering of other guns.

The Deacon looked at several American grenade launchers slung under M-16s and one mounted on a similar firearm. "What are these?" he asked.

The sergeant barely glanced at it. "It's an M-203 grenade launcher mounted on a Mexican FN FAL,"

Taking the FAL down, the Deacon studied it. "I see how the rifle works. How do you load the launcher?"

The sergeant cautiously reached over and touched the launcher. "Pivot this little tab down and slide the corrugated part of the tube forward then stuff the grenade into the launcher. Pull the corrugated part back, and you're ready to fire."

"What caliber is this rifle?" The Deacon asked.

"It's 7.62 NATO, also called the .308 Winchester," Wade said. "The same as most of the rifles we're already carrying."

"Luke, chapter 10, verse 7," the Deacon recited. "'For the laborer is worthy of his hire.'" He left his AK and the Russian launcher and slipped into the FAL's sling. Finding a case marked "Grenades," he pried it open and took two bandoliers of grenades. The rest of the group, after recovering their own weapons, pried open another crate and took two cases of 7.62 ammunition.

Logan hefted another FAL. "It's not as compact as the little Russian chopper, but I've been needing something with a little more reach, anyway." He and the Deacon rummaged through the equipment until they found ten more magazines for the FALs.

The group loaded their guns, checked chambers and safeties then Reynaud nodded to Wade. "You take the lead. We need wheels to get out of here. There's a door at the end of the hallway that probably leads outside." He paused. "There may be a guard outside. Don't take any chances."

All their senses alert, they crept to the end of the corridor. Wade glanced out the screen door then grinned back at Reynaud. "The only two men within a hundred yards are working on a truck. They's another truck and a jeep within twenty yards of the door."

"We'll need the truck," Reynaud decided. "Okay, everyone out, walking slow and steady. Ma'am, when we get to the truck, you just stand beside it, and keep standing until we're out of sight."

With Wade still in the lead, they walked across the gravel parking lot. Reynaud saw the two men Wade had mentioned. They wore grease-stained coveralls and their heads and upper bodies were under the gaping hood of a truck. To Reynaud, it almost looked as though the men were being eaten alive by the truck. Two other men, perhaps two hundred yards away, walked briskly from one barracks to another but if they noticed the group emerging from the office building, they gave no sign. Even farther away, a handful of figures toiled in a field.

Wade halted by the driver's cab of the truck, which had a whip antenna mounted at the rear of the cab. "I can drive," Wade said.

Reynaud nodded. "Do it. Sergeant, you know what you have to do." He watched the man climb into the back of the truck, followed by the rest of the group. They'd just settled themselves on the benches when the truck throbbed to life and lurched, then pulled away.

~ * ~

Wilson pulled his jeep into the parking area, having to swerve slightly to avoid a truck barreling out. He glanced at the little girl in the passenger seat, but she was securely buckled in. As he rounded the corner of the building, he saw Lieutenant Olson standing in the lot. She saw his jeep at the same time, and dashed toward him. "Major, the people you were talking to just left. They took Sergeant Devlin with them as a hostage."

"What?! What the hell got into them?"

"Captain Fulton came in just after you'd left. He said he'd see to the problem then he ordered Sergeant Devlin to go in with him."

Wilson bit off the words he'd almost used, in deference to the little girl in the seat beside his. "There wasn't a problem until Fulton made one," he snapped. He snatched up his radio mike. "Alpha Ace, this is Charley Deuce. There's a truck headed toward the front gate. Do not—I say again , do not—attempt to stop the truck or fire on it. Take cover, but do not fire on the truck, even if the people in the truck fire on your station. Do you copy, Alpha Ace? Over."

For a moment he listened to static before a metallic voice replied, "Alpha Ace here. Affirmative, Charley Deuce, we are to take cover but not fire on the vehicle. Over."

"Affirmative. Charley Deuce Out." He slammed the mike back onto its hook, unbuckled his seat belt, and sprang out of the jeep. "Lieutenant, I want you to take care of this little girl and to call the ready room. I need a squad. Make the girl comfortable, and I'll get back to her as soon as I can." He turned and dashed into the building. By the time he reached Fulton's office, he was breathing hard and remembering he was no longer young.

Fulton struggled against his bonds as he saw Major Wilson tear into the room. "Those renegades pulled a gun on Sergeant Devlin and I."

"You tell them they were back in the Air Force?" Wilson asked.

"Damn right. And then they jumped us."

Wilson kept his voice deceptively mild. "I think I'm going to recommend you for a promotion."

"Promotion, sir?"

"But you're going to have to change your name." Suddenly he raised his voice to a roar that made Devlin's bellow sound like a murmur. "Because when somebody says 'Major Fuckup,' I want everybody to know who the hell they're talking about, you stupid, insensitive sonofabitch. I'm going to have a little chat with Colonel Frazier and, if I have my way, you'll be busted so low you'll be saluting goddam civilians." He spun and strode out of the room, leaving Fulton still tied to the chair.

A squad of troops had gathered in the parking lot. Wilson pointed at several of them. "You five, get inside and draw weapons. Bring me a rifle, too." He hoped he'd judged the Euro-vets well enough to know the sergeant was in no real danger. He'd have bet his own life on it, but he couldn't bet the sergeant's. They'd follow the truck. If they found the sergeant alive and well, he'd write off the truck. No, not write it off. He'd add it to Fulton's account. If the sergeant wasn't all right—no, better not to think about that possibility.

~ * ~

Reynaud was slightly surprised to find the guard shack at the gate abandoned, but grateful not to have to shoot at men wearing his country's uniform. They continued the short distance to the ruins of Leon Springs, the truck finally jerking to a stop among the tumble-down buildings. Logan waved his revolver at the back of the truck. "Everybody out. That includes you, Sarge."

As they jumped out of the back of the truck, Reynaud asked, "Would you really have popped the sergeant?"

Logan grinned at their prisoner. "Probably not, but I'm damn glad the matter never came up. Wade left the keys in the truck. You." He indicated the sergeant with a bob of the head, "had probably better get back before that asshole captain decides you're AWOL."

Paco and Hasteen rode toward them, leading the other horses. "Looks like you boys wore out your welcome," Hasteen observed, "unless that sergeant was an honor guard." He tossed Logan the reins of his horse. "Was it something you said?"

"Like they say, everybody likes a little ass but nobody likes a smartass." Logan grabbed the saddle horn and heaved himself into the saddle. "Let's get the hell out of here."

~ * ~

Major Wilson had to shout to be heard over the noise of the Hummer. "Hold up at the guard station." He'd seen the missing truck parked by the guard shack, its nose pointed back toward the gate. As his vehicle rolled to a halt he jumped out and strode to the guard post, returning the salutes of the men and women on duty and stopped in front of Sergeant Devlin. "Are you okay?"

"Just fine, sir. A little shook, but fine. I don't think they'd have shot me."

"I didn't think so, either. I'm just glad we were right. Do you feel up to driving the truck back yourself?"

"No problem, sir." The sergeant snapped another salute.

Wilson waved a salute back and strode back to the Hummer.

Now that the excitement was over, he felt a let-down, knowing the only thing left for him to do was to go back to the office and explain to a little girl that her father was gone. Fulton was really going to pay. God, how he was going to pay. Wilson grabbed the window frame of the Hummer. For a moment he looked back at what was left of Leon Springs and a dust cloud rising beyond the shattered buildings. "Good luck, guys," he muttered, then climbed into the Hummer.

~ * ~

"Where to now?" Reynaud asked, as Leon Springs fell away behind them.

Wade gestured at the way ahead. "If we push, we can make it to a place called Camp Verde before nightfall. I know a man there—he has the sweet disposition of a Gila monster with a toothache, but he's a sharp old bird who keeps his ear to the ground. He might even be able to give us a lead on the Barnes gang."

Well before noon the riders had all tied bandannas over their lower faces and peered at the trail ahead through slitted eyes. Logan gestured at the barren land around them dotted with only occasional clumps of drab greenery. "Jeez, it looks like hell opened a branch office."

It was impossible to tell whether Wade was grinning under his bandanna. "You oughta see it in summer. The hot winds feel like they left open the iron door of the blast furnace of Hell. In really tough years, you can spot the buzzards carryin' canteens. But it's God's country."

"Probably because He's the only one who might want it," Steve suggested.

The light was beginning to fade when they saw, in the distance, a windmill. "We'll be in Camp Verde before nightfall," Wade said.

"I hope so," Reynaud replied, "the animals are about played out." He'd long since donned his jacket to ward off the chill in the air, and was eagerly looking forward to rest, warmth, and a meal. As they approached, they saw the two-storied buildings near the windmill, and the horses, smelling water, managed to move a little faster.

They allowed the mounts and the pack animals to bury their noses in the concrete trough fed by the windmill pump, but pulled them away before they could drink too much.

Groaning at the pain in his back and legs as he dismounted and walking to the section of pipe to tie his horse's reins, Reynaud followed Wade. The two steps up to the porch were even more difficult. Inside the doorway, he waited for Wade to finish drinking from a dipper before taking his turn. Wade had just handed him the dipper when a leather-faced old man shoved open a door behind the counter and stared stonily at them.

"Still workin' for the great Republic of Texas, I see. Dammit-all, Wade, when're you gonna grow up and get an honest job?"

"About the first time I ever hear of your bein' polite to anyone, pointin' a gun at you or not. Nate, you old hossthief, you're lookin' just as wicked as ever."

"You always was a silver-tongued flatterer." Nate leaned on the counter. "What brings you out this way? Business?"

Wade nodded.

"Does that include trackin' four people, one of them a big, finicky fella?"

"How'd you know that?" Reynaud asked.

"Saw the big guy earlier. He sent his three friends around." Nate grinned at the expression of surprise on Reynaud's face. "I got a tellyscope upstairs. Saw you boys comin' from a long ways off. You're still ridin' that hammer-headed gray gelding, ain't you, Wade?"

Wade nodded then frowned. "Nate, if you met the big guy, you don't know how close you come to shakin' hands with an undertaker. He's the kinda bad'un that'd kill you just for practice."

"He thought about it some. I guess he decided not to because he didn't know how many people was at the ranch, and probably figgered it'd leave more of a trail if he killed me than he would by leavin' me alive. I think he figgered me for a dumb hick."

Reynaud noticed the rest of the group had entered the store and had drunk their fill.

"I got cornbread, beans, and jackrabbit enough to feed all you boys," Nate said. "You can put your horses in the stable back of the old ranch house. Miguel'll put out oats for them, if you ask him."

They filed out of the store and led their animals to the stable where they were fed and watered by a middle-aged Mexican. The men rubbed down the horses and mule and Wade paid for the night's care for them.

As the group returned to the store, their bedrolls and long arms slung over their shoulders, Reynaud nudged Wade and said, "That old man's one lucky old fart; he met Chernikov and he's still breathing."

"I'm not so sure. Nate's a tough old bird who put thirty years in the Border Patrol: He'd take a lot of killin'. Maybe, if Chernikov had tried him out, it would've made our job easier." Wade led the way into the store, grinned at Nate, and gestured at Paco. "Nate, here's a fella I think you'd be proud to meet. This is Paco Morales."

Nate's eyes widened then crinkled, and he thrust out his hand and shook Paco's hand enthusiastically. "Paco Morales, eh? This is a pleasure. You done run the boys in my old outfit ragged. 'Course, that was after my time. I'd 'a caught you."

Paco flashed his teeth in a grin. "At least you would have made it very interesting."

They followed Nate up a flight of rickety stairs to rooms on the second floor that served as kitchen and bedroom. He let them lay out their bedrolls on the floor while he finished cooking dinner.

Wade looked over Nate's shoulder into the pot Nate was tending. "What are you doin' eatin' jackrabbit when they's gotta be plenty of mutton and beef available?"

"Mutton's for tourists and other payin' customers. 'Sides, I like meat that gives me a fight. Nothin' makes me lose my appetite like food that just sorta lays there dead in your mouth."

Later, as Reynaud chewed on a mouthful of meat and beans he decided the meat had to be jackrabbit or a saddle. "Damn, Nate, if this is your specialty, you must have jaws like an alligator."

Logan had tried a mouthful of beans then taken a bite of cornbread to put out the fire, only to discover the cornbread had also been heavily spiced. He took a long, deep drink of water. "You must also have plumbing of stainless steel." He finished the cup of water and dipped up more from the bucket then gestured at the stove. "Wouldn't it have made more sense to have the stove downstairs? That way, you wouldn't have to haul the wood all the way up here."

"Hell no," Nate growled. "If I heated the store, I'd have people staying around just to warm themselves. I want 'em to buy what they come for then get the hell out."

"Sociable as ever, I see," Wade remarked.

"Look," Nate snapped. "Just 'cause I'm old and alone don't mean I'm lonesome. Most people ain't as good company as a tick. Not much smarter, either." He stood. "Well, about time to turn in."

Reynaud collapsed on his bedroll with a groan. "You said the big guy—his name is Chernikov, by the way, and he's an FSB agent—you said he thought about killing you. What happened?"

"I knew he was a bad 'un when he walked in." Nate had stripped down to his long handles and sat on a bed whose springs creaked and squealed under him. "He had a finicky, uppity way about him. He looked like he'd just opened the door to an outhouse, and he figgered I was just a dumb old coot. I gave him a chance at me by turnin' my back on him."

"That was taking a long chance," Reynaud said.

"Not so much of a one. Like I said, I seen him comin' a long ways off, and I went over and got Miguel. He was in the back room, and when I turned my back to the fella, Miguel had a thirty-aught-six pointed just about an inch above what's-his-name's belt buckle."

"I'm kinda surprised you didn't kill 'im just on general principles," Wade said.

Nate lay on his bed and pulled an ancient patchwork quilt up to his chin. "You been wearin' a badge too long, Wade. I didn't kill 'im 'cause he'd 'a made a mess I'd 'a had to clean up, and 'cause he minded his manners while he was here. What he does someplace else is none 'a my damn business." He blew out the kerosene lamp and plunged the room into darkness.

~ * ~

Breakfast was jackrabbit steak and eggs without the eggs, and some of the most corrosive varnish-remover Reynaud had ever heard called "coffee."

"We got to be on the road thirty minutes ago," Wade said, as Reynaud changed Hasteen's and Paco's dressings.

"You even know where you're goin'?" Nate asked.

"I suppose he followed Texas 173 north."

"Yeah, but to where?"

"We think he's gonna meet Phil Barnes."

"Then if I was you, I'd shag my ass to Sonora." Nate collected the tin plates and cups and pitched them out the back window. "I really hate washin' dishes, so I let the ants get a runnin' start on 'em."

"It's too cold for ants," Reynaud observed.

"Aw, that's all right. They'll be back in the summer."

"You sure Barnes is in Sonora?" Wade asked.

"I'm pretty sure he ain't," Nate replied, "but I'd bet you the King Ranch against a case of the trots an awful lotta his boys are there. Last I heard, Barnes was hanging out around Bakersfield and Fort Stockton, but you'd better be ready from Sonora on west."

Wade bit off his first chaw of the day. "That's about a hundred and thirty miles. Barnes must be a pretty big man to need that much territory to lie down in."

"Ever'thing's pretty scarce in west Texas. With upwards of four hundred or so cutthroats he's got, not counting the wannabees, he needs to keep movin', sorta like a plague of locusts. You can figger he's got a lot of his infantry mounted by now, and he's probably got troops quartered in ever' town around Fort Stockton and Bakersfield, and his cavalry is scouting the country as far as Sonora.

"Sonora's pretty bad by itself. Barnes and his gang gave the place a real thorough goin'-over a couple times. About all the good folks who hadn't died of plague died of lead poisonin'. That, or they headed north or east. About the only ones Barnes left alive were the kinda cutthroats, slatterns, and cheap bullies that kept the jails full in better times."

"Sonora it is, then," Wade said, as he strode toward the door.

"Just be real careful to fill up your canteens," Nate shouted after them, "'cause it's dry country and you gotta long ways to go. And you be careful when you get to Sonora. Them crackers'd kill you quicker than I'd step on a cockroach."

~ * ~

Chernikov was thoroughly disgusted with horseback riding, and their animals were half-dead when they finally stumbled into Sonora. He guessed it was an hour or so before noon. Vickers drew his horse up before a bar called "The Painted Lady." Chernikov waited until the prisoners had dismounted before he swung down out of the saddle. He tied their wrists together again, but in front of them, so they could eat and drink.

As soon as he entered the saloon, Vickers was greeted with friendly shouts.

"Who's the leader here?" Chernikov demanded.

Vickers pointed to a man sitting at a table beyond the end of the bar. The man lounged in his chair, his legs crossed, his boots resting on the table. A thin, balding man with a hooked beak of a nose sat to the leader's left, while the bandit absently fondled the thigh of a really ugly woman wearing half her weight in makeup. Vickers nodded toward the man. "That's Bart Williams. You gotta be a really good friend of his to call him 'Black Bart.'"

"I wouldn't think of it. Order us drinks and something to eat, and have them brought to the table." He motioned for Baker and his son to walk ahead of him. When they reached the table he drew out chairs for them then pulled an empty chair from a neighboring table and sat down, facing Williams.

The bandit glared at him. "Who the hell do you think you are?"

"I think I'm Alex Chambers, and I want to see Phil Barnes pretty damned soon. He and I have some business to conduct."

Williams continued to glower at him. "What do you expect me to do about it?"

"I want you to provide us with something with wheels and a motor. I also want you to get your feet off the table. I've ordered food, and I don't intend to stare at the soles of your boots while I eat."

"He's quite the dude, ain't he, Katie?" Williams remarked to the woman then stared coldly at Chernikov. "Mister, why don't you go fuck yourself?"

Chernikov's left hand shot forward and shoved Williams' feet up and away from the table. For a moment, Williams teetered, his arms windmilling as he tried to keep his balance then he and his chair went over with a crash.

Before the bandit could roll clear of the chair, he found a knife at his throat and the big man grinning ferociously down at him.

"Smile," Chernikov said through his teeth, "and if you don't have a smile of your own, I'll have to give you one." Williams' face twitched before he could finally form a rictus. "That's better. Now, sit nicely in your chair and we'll discuss business."

"Hey!" Something had finally occurred to Williams. "You're the guy we sent Clell, Steve, and Randy to pick up. I see Vickers but where's the other two?"

"I never met this Steve. As for Simmons, he became ambitious. He thought he could rob and kill me, and not have to share with you others."

"You kill him?"

Chernikov nodded.

"All right, what kinda business are we talkin'?" Williams massaged a wrist he seemed to have injured in his fall.

"Guns. U.S. National Guard rifles, machine guns, even grenade launchers and rocket launchers. Ammunition by the case. Even a little gold." Chernikov studied the Texan. The man's eyes were already fixed on a vision of crates of weapons and the kind of havoc they could create. "But first I need to see Barnes, and I'm tired of riding a horse. Also, I think it's in everybody's best interests to get the transaction taken care of as soon as possible."

Williams licked his lips. "Yeah, the sooner the better. I think we can get you a pickup. Will you need anything else?"

For the moment, at least, Williams' greed seemed to have overruled his injured pride. Chernikov nodded. "A driver, and two men to ride in the back with the prisoners." Chernikov indicated, with another nod, Baker and his son. The plates of food arrived at the table, carried by another slattern, and Chernikov began to eat. "Also, while it's unlikely I'm being followed, you'd do well to keep anyone from going west, unless they're part of your group. How soon can we have the use of the truck?"

“Barney!” Williams roared to a tubby man with masses of tattoos on his bare arms, then held up his hand and motioned for the art-lover to approach him. The two muttered, their heads together, then Williams waved a dismissal at the man. “It’s bein’ worked on right now, but the problem’s just a minor one; replacing all the belts and hoses. It oughta be ready to go within an hour.”

“Good. And remember what I said: Nobody is to get through Sonora.”

“If you hadn’t ’a had Clell with you, you wouldn’t ’a gotten through.”

Chapter 7

The sun was beginning to settle itself on the western horizon when the pickup rolled into Fort Stockton and pulled up in front of the Gray Mule. Chernikov climbed out of the cab and stared at the two guards who sat in the pews on either side of the door. They stared back and shifted their shotguns.

Trudging around the front of the pickup, the driver waved at the gunmen. "Got a fella here to talk a little business with the cap'n. Is he inside?"

One of the guards spat out a well-chewed toothpick. "He's in the back room."

The driver led the way into the bar, where a couple of dozen men drank and talked loudly, and approached the bartender who was wiping up a spill. "Okay to talk to the boss?"

Looking up, the bartender's beefy face expressed both boredom and annoyance. "Now might not be the best time to bother him. He's got a hot game goin' back there."

Without waiting for the driver, Chernikov strode to the door set in the rear wall of the barroom, shoved it open, and walked to a table where five men sat playing poker. As player after player raised or folded, a Mexican tossed his cards on the table. "Too rich for me. I'll fold while I still have my saddle."

Two more players dropped out of the hand, so finally only a round-faced man with thinning hair and pale blue eyes and a thin, sandy-haired man with a walrus moustache remained. "What've you got, Dave?"

The walrus turned over the two cards that lay face-down. "Three ladies." He started to reach for the silver coins on the table.

"Don't get too eager," the round-faced man said softly. "I filled that straight." He turned over both his down cards with a snap of the pasteboards, then grinned at the walrus and raked the money on the table toward himself.

The Mexican stood and Chernikov noticed his ornate double holster rig, hand-tooled and with silver trim, which held twin nickel-plated and elaborately engraved revolvers with carved ivory stocks. "I had better get back to Bakersfield," the Mexican said. "My *caballeros* do not take their patrolling seriously unless I ride with them. Sometimes is hard to find good Anglo help."

A sudden outburst of shouting in the bar was punctuated by a knock on the door frame and a man with an immense red beard stood in the door, nervously twisting his hat in his hands.

"What the hell is all that about?" the round-faced man snapped.

"Boss, we got problems. One of our trucks just got hit."

Barnes came out of his chair swearing. "What happened? Give me everything."

"They was at the pumpin' station southeast, turnin' crude into diesel, when somebody opened up on 'em. We found out about it when we run another truck out. The driver saw the smoke and, as soon as he heard the shootin', high-tailed it back here."

Barnes scowled. "Probably riders from the Big Canyon ranch. Get everything together you can scrape up."

Chernikov followed the mob as they all made for the door and, once outside, the Mexican swung up his arm. A mounted man brought him a fine white horse wearing a heavy Mexican saddle with a silver horn almost as big as a saucer. "I have a dozen riders with me," he shouted to Barnes.

"Good. Take old US 285 southeast and circle around the pumping station."

Chernikov observed the disorganized bandits dashing through the streets, shouting for weapons or transportation, with a sneer. Rabble. Undisciplined trash. With a single Spetnaz squad he could wipe this entire mob off the face of Texas. Engines roared and two battered trucks pulled up behind the pickup still parked in front of the bar. Another vehicle rounded the corner and Chernikov was surprised to see a French-built Panhard M-11 three-man armored scout car with an FN MAG machine gun mounted on the gun ring. As the car squalled to a stop in a cloud of dust he noticed the faded Mexican Army markings.

Barnes waved his arms and shouted. "You—" he pointed to the driver of the first truck, "you go directly to the pumping station and try to catch 'em there. Second truck goes southwest of the station. I want the Mex scout car to go wide around. Try to bottle 'em up. Move out!"

While all the Texans scrambled for weapons or into trucks, Chernikov slipped his silenced Makarov out of its shoulder holster and slid it into his waistband, still under his jacket.

Besides the Mexican, who'd led the cavalry out of town, two other former card-players joined the groups piling into the backs of trucks. Short and lean, despite his round face, Barnes stood watching the trucks move out then wheeled to face the men still in the streets. "Tight security. Everyone to their posts." As the crowd broke into its parts, he stared, narrow-eyed, at Chernikov. "Who're you?"

"I'm Alex Chambers. We have some business to discuss."

"Let's do it inside." Barnes trod back into the saloon and back to the gaming room, not having to look back to know he was being followed by half a dozen gunmen. Sitting in the chair he'd left, he asked, "Care for a little poker while we talk? Can you play?" Two of the bandits took empty chairs and sat well back from the table while the others watched from even farther away.

The other card-player, the walrus, had also returned to the table. Chernikov took the remaining empty chair. "I can play."

The walrus tossed a small silver coin on the table. "Ante is a ROT dollar." He shuffled the cards and began to deal.

"Is it the custom here to deal off the bottom of the deck," Chernikov asked, "or are you doing this just for me?"

"Are you accusing me of cheating?" the walrus roared, "you sonofa—" He started to get to his feet, his left hand snatching for the pistol he wore, then he doubled over, stumbling backward, knocking the chair away from the table and clutching his belly with both hands. He raised a trembling left hand and stared in horrified disbelief at the blood on his hand. "I…I…" he stammered, lurching away from the table to collapse on the floor.

The men watching the game began to babble. "What got Dave?"

"I never heard a shot!"

"I thought I heard something but Dave was raisin' too

much of a racket to be sure."

Chernikov raised his silenced Makarov and set it on the table, its muzzle carefully pointed wide of Barnes. He smiled at the bandit, who studied him with wary eyes. "Did you want to deal or did you want me to?"

Barnes stared at the dead man then back at Chernikov. Suddenly he laughed. "I'll deal." Gathering the cards, he began shuffling them.

"Let's make the game worth our time." Chernikov tossed a small gold coin onto the table. He accepted his down card without looking at it, and the seven of clubs, face-up.

Barnes' up card was the jack of spades. "Let's do that again." He added another gold coin to the pile. Chernikov saw the bid and slid his pistol out with the coin. After a second's hesitation, Barnes drew his own weapon, a Smith and Wesson .44 magnum. He snapped the next two cards with his thumb as he dealt them. Chernikov received the nine of clubs while Barnes dealt himself the king of hearts. "Cowboy bets," he said, and tossed yet another small gold coin onto the table. Chernikov matched the bet.

~ * ~

Barnes checked his hole card again—it was still the queen of diamonds—then dealt the next two cards face-up. He drew the ace of spades while the stranger showed the ten of clubs. Again he added a small gold piece to the pot, saw the other man shove his own coin across the table.

"Last one down and dirty." Barnes flicked the other player's second hole card across the table then snapped his own last card up for a look. Keeping his face expressionless, he saw the four of diamonds. He dug through the large silver coins in front of him until he could stack enough to equal a small gold coin.

Almost negligently, the man who called himself Chambers tossed a large gold coin on the pile. "I'll raise you. And add sixty M-16s, ten machine guns, half a dozen grenade launchers, and another half-dozen LAWs."

Barnes stared at the cold eyes. His bluff had been called. Now he could throw good money after bad or fold. Still, there was a chance, a very good chance, that Chambers held a busted flush or a busted straight. There was also a pretty good chance he held at least a pair, which would beat Barnes' ace-high. "What do I bet against that last raise?"

"Bet fifty men for two months' work."

The tone was level and as expressionless as the face, as empty now as when the man had watched Dave stumble his life out. That was the face of a cold-blooded man who was certain of what he was doing, a man who couldn't be bluffed. Barnes turned the faces of his cards down. "I fold."

Chambers picked up his cards, flipped over those that had been face-up, and mixed his cards in with the rest of the deck.

"Hey, hold it, mister," one of the bandits spoke up. "What'd you have?"

Chambers favored him with an icy smile. "The winning hand."

Barnes slapped the table with an open hand. "The man's right. I didn't pay to see his cards, and for damn sure none of you did." He raised his voice. "Billy! Bring us a bottle of the good stuff." Leaning forward, he rested his elbows on the table. "All them guns sound impressive but how do we know you can actually lay hands on 'em?"

"Because I told you I can, and I'll be going with you."

The bartender brought a bottle and two glasses. Barnes made a production of breaking the seal and pouring the drinks. "Where'd you get that Russian popgun?"

"There's a few of them floating around the ports and airfields. Some of the vets from Europe brought them back as souvenirs." He pocketed all his winnings except for the revolver, which he shoved back across the table to Barnes. "Consider it a gift, to cement our business deal." He took a deep drink of the whiskey. "Who're those people your men are chasing?"

"Just a buncha usta-be cowboys. There ain't enough of them to really hurt us. One'a these days we'll get really pissed off and wipe 'em all out."

~ * ~

Chernikov sensed Barnes was lying and wondered whether he was lying to himself as well. Barnes and his men hadn't the firepower, the manpower, or the mobility to win a war against guerillas.

"Back to business." Barnes poured a second glass of whiskey for each of them. "The way I get it, we're supposed to round up some livestock and drive 'em north, and you'll pay us in guns and ammo."

"That's about the size of it. The cattle in Oklahoma have been getting sick and dying; probably some kind of secondary plague. I brought this fellow, Baker, and his boy to inoculate Texas cattle. We're still working on something to counter this new plague, so it'll take us some time before we're ready to move. Most of your cavalry will be needed to move the herd to Oklahoma City. You and I and maybe ten or fifteen men will be going straight to the place. I'll turn the guns over to you and you let your drovers know to bring them in all the way. That's your insurance."

Barnes finished his second drink and poured a third. "That all sounds pretty jake."

Chernikov stood. "If this works out as well for both of us as I think it might, we may be able to do even more business. Some of the people I do business with up north are working on getting ahold of some light armor. With that, and with what you'll get out of this deal, you should be able to clear this part of Texas."

"What about the prisoners you just brought in?"

"I need the veterinarian for a while. He didn't want to give up his practice, so I had to convince him. He's needed to help whip up some of the serum the team's working on, and to help give the shots."

~ * ~

Wade stood in his stirrups and studied the town through his binoculars.

"Well, are we going in?" Reynaud asked. "It's Sonora, isn't it? Chernikov didn't have that much of a head start on us. Maybe he's still there."

"If he's still there, he'll be stayin' till mornin'. Most people around here don't relish a moonlight drive," Wade pointed out. "I figure when Chernikov rode into Sonora, he came from the east. That's why I'd rather come in from another direction. You're the boss, but my advice is to go into a place like that rested, and on a rested horse. If anything goes wrong, we'll want to go through the place like a dose of croton oil, and a horse that can run can make the difference between makin' it out or gettin' buried there." He twisted in the saddle and put the field glasses back into his saddle bag.

Reynaud turned his horse's head toward a stunted copse in a draw and drew up in the shade. "I just wish we had more water." The horses are damn near too dry to sweat."

Wade dismounted and hauled down a large canvas bag canteen from the equipment on the pack mule. He peeled off his white hat, now a dingy gray-brown, and handed the canteen to Reynaud. "Pour. We can give them each about half a hatful. That's another reason for stoppin' in Sonora. We need water."

The animals cropped the sparse grass while the men lay down, sipped at canteens, and gnawed dried meat and hardtack. "We can all get about an hour's shut-eye," Wade said.

Reynaud lay down and closed his eyes. Seconds later, it seemed, someone had kicked the sole of his boots. "Time to arm up and ride." Wade announced. Each man checked his weapons, making sure they were loaded and the actions were clean. Hasteen and Paco paid particular attention to their holsters, making sure their pistols slid out quickly and smoothly.

"I'd go in with my heavy stuff in hand," Wade said, drawing a shotgun from the scabbard on the left side of his gelding's saddle. The weapon's barrel had been cut off at the length of a riot gun. He pumped the action, caught the ejected shell, and reloaded then pointed to the grenade launcher under the barrel of the Deacon's rifle. "Make sure that thing's all primed and ready to go, too."

Mounting, they let the horses have an easy walk to come in from the north and rode into Sonora just as half the sun was below the horizon. Wade and Hasteen rode on either side of Reynaud and they followed the main drag to a handful of raucous bars and taverns clustered together.

As they stopped at a horse trough and let the horses take the edge off their thirst, Wade turned in his saddle. "I want mosta you boys to stay mounted. Chances are, we'll be wantin' to leave in a hurry."

Reynaud kept his head on a swivel, as they used to say in fighter jock jargon, but saw no one in the streets and all the buildings they passed stood dark. Apparently, evening was the time for everyone to gather in the bars. Except for the noise of a badly-played off-key piano, someone strumming a guitar, and the babble of loud talk coming from the taverns ahead, the town seemed dark and silent, deserted.

Wade stopped, took a long cigar out of his saddle bag, broke it in two, handed half to Paco, and lit both stubs. Also from his saddle bags he produced five sticks of dynamite, attached blasting caps with fuses from the other saddle bag, and gave three of them to the Mexican. "If things get excitin', use these wisely."

Paco grinned and puffed on the cigar, making the end glow brightly.

Most of the noises seemed to come from a bar on their left. Turning toward the lights, they rode forward at a walk. Eight or ten horses were tied to a rail in front of the building and, as they approached, a man lurched out the door and weaved down the sidewalk, hardly sparing them a glance.

Reynaud, riding with his shotgun across the saddle in front of him, tasted fear, as sharp and unpleasant as the taste of an old penny. He couldn't even spit to get the taste out of his mouth because his mouth was dry. He rubbed his hands, in turn, on the thighs of his jeans, and tried to remember whether he'd chambered a round in the shotgun.

As they halted in front of the bar, Wade muttered, "Hand your reins to one of the others."

Reynaud swung out of his saddle, handed the reins to Logan then stepped onto the sidewalk and, in two paces, through the saloon's door. The place was crowded with men and a few women, most shouting over the sounds of a guitar and a banjo. Two men wrestled on the floor, watched by a handful of cutthroats, cheering them on, ignored by the rest of the crowd.

A red-eyed man staggered toward the door, saw the strangers, and turned to yell at a small group at the bar. Suddenly, the level of noise dropped, as the level of water drops in a cracked jug.

Without looking to see if any of the others followed him, a tall, broad-shouldered man with a broken nose swaggered toward Reynaud. "Strangers in our fair town?" He turned, playing to the crowd. "Newbies. And I bet they don't know our rules." He pivoted again and showed yellow teeth in a grin. "First rule is; strangers don't pack iron."

Hasteen slowly drew his right hand Colt, twirled and turned it so the butt was extended, then made as if to toss it to the bandit. As his hand swept forward the pistol spun in his hand. Suddenly the tall man and his friends were facing a cocked pistol. "No exceptions?" Hasteen asked softly.

In the sudden silence, Wade murmured, "You see the guy we're lookin' for?"

"Not here," Reynaud muttered. He'd swung the shotgun up to point it at the man facing them, while Hasteen's revolver covered the crowd to the man's left. Reynaud saw sudden movement and squeezed the shotgun's trigger. The blast sounded like the end of the world and left the bandit's chest a ragged, bloody hole. Hasteen's Colt roared and two more men spun and fell. Reynaud jacked the pump action and fired into the mob. Screaming began and more men fell, writhing, to the floor, then Wade shouted, "Out! Get out!"

Reynaud spun and sprang for the door. A bullet tore into the door frame beside him then he was outside and snatching his horse's reins from Logan. As soon as he'd gained his saddle he looked back toward the tavern. Hasteen stood against the wall on the right side of the door, reloading, while Wade, pressed against the other wall, had drawn a stick of dynamite from his shirt. As soon as the end of the fuse sputtered and shed sparks, Wade tossed it into the bar and dashed for his horse.

As Wade moved, Hasteen fanned two rounds into the dust between the hooves of a horse tied to the hitching rail. The horse screamed and reared, taking the rail with him then started to run, panicking the other horses that had been tied to the same bar.

The concussion of the blast in the bar blew out the windows and made Reynaud sway in his saddle and he had to clutch at the saddle horn. As the other horses stampeded, Hasteen caught his horse's mane and flung himself astride. Another explosion echoed down the street, then a third. Reynaud looked around, saw Steve, leading the pack animals, had almost reached the end of the block while Paco had tossed a stick of dynamite into another bar and the Deacon had launched a grenade into a third. The Deacon trained his rifle at the door of the last tavern, where men ran out the door, firing wildly.

Billy Joe hammered off three or four short bursts and the men who didn't fall bleeding into the street ducked back into the building. More staccato gun music broke out as Logan emptied his MAC-10 in a sweep along second-floor windows, then Wade hurled his last stick of dynamite through another opening left by a blown-out window.

The group shot spurs to their horses and raced down the street, firing random shots behind them to discourage the braver souls. As they neared the edge of Sonora they found a large building with an antenna on the roof, flanked on one side by a corral and, on the other, by a parking lot holding half a dozen trucks in various stages of disrepair.

While Hasteen tore a section out of the corral's pole fence and drove the horses into the gathering darkness, Paco used his last two sticks of dynamite to destroy the best-kept trucks. Two men appeared in the door of the building, one still fumbling with his pants while the other fired a pistol, his shots going wide.

Having reloaded his grenade launcher, Billy Joe lobbed a round that sailed past the men into the door before exploding. The bandits were tossed into the street, where they lay moaning and struggling feebly.

"Hit that place again!" Wade shouted.

Billy Joe fumbled with the launcher, worked it open, stuffed in another round, and launched it at the radio tower. The tower wobbled but remained standing.

"Again!" Wade roared. "Once more!"

The next grenade exploded at the base of the tower, causing the framework to twist and buckle.

"Alright!" Wade shouted, "we done wore out our welcome. Let's get some distance."

They raced out of Sonora, driving their animals to a dangerous pace in the fading light of dusk. As the darkness deepened they were forced to slow their mounts and, finally, to dismount and lead the horses and mule. Nearly five miles outside of Sonora they found an abandoned house and tethered the animals under a couple of dead trees near the ruins of the building.

The place had obviously been looted and most of what hadn't been hauled away had been destroyed; even the doors and windows had been taken. The group rubbed down the animals then inspected the house, making sure there were no unwanted occupants. Finding it clear, they spread their bed-rolls in what had probably been the living room. While the others checked their wounds and weapons by flashlights, Wade and Paco explored the rest of the house.

When they rejoined the others their faces were grim. "No water here," Wade announced, "and no way to get any. They had two pumps but they ran off electricity, and they's no way to get the water up manually."

Reynaud held up his canteen and swished the water around I it. Less than half full. "So, how do we get water?"

"We can go prowlin' around some 'a the old ranches, but it's awful risky. "If they's anybody livin' there now, they might be inclined to shoot first and make introductions later. Considerin' the 'good people' of Sonora, you can't blame 'em. And if they's nobody on the ranches, it ain't likely to have water either. They's a town called Ozona about thirty miles down the track. I think we oughta make straight for it at first light. We'll be runnin' on empty by the time we get there, but we should be able to load up then."

~ * ~

"The bacon and gravy are awfully salty," Steve said. "Are you sure eating this stuff is such a good idea?"

"No," Hasteen answered, "but we're going to need something in our bellies, and I'd sooner be rid of this now."

Wade approached from the barn. "I've given the horses as much water as we can spare. That leaves each of us about three swallows of water. Three drinks apiece to last us thirty miles."

"At least the day isn't hot," Logan said, pointing to the jackets they all wore against the morning chill.

"Don't go thinkin' that makes it easy," Wade replied. "We'll be sweatin' in our jackets, and while the wind might be cold, it's also dry, so it'll leach the moisture out of us. Better hurry your eatin'. We want to be movin'."

"Do we stay on the road," Reynaud asked, trying to smother a yawn, "or do we get off it in case we're followed from Sonora?"

Wade considered the question before he answered. "It's up to you. I'd suggest we stay on the road; it's easier travelin'. I think we took out the only radio in Sonora with the range to reach Bakersfield. 'Course I been wrong before, once or twice. I think we stung 'em hard enough in Sonora they're not gonna be real eager to catch us. Nobody wants to grab a handful of pissed-off bees."

"The road it is," Reynaud agreed. He'd finished his breakfast. Taking a small sip of the flat-tasting water in his canteen, he swished it around in his mouth and swallowed. He felt decades older than he had before the plague. Every morning, some new muscle he'd never noticed before had developed an ache, and his back and legs were stiff from riding.

Loading the pack animals, they set out for Ozona. The day began cold and clear, and Reynaud found the cold made all his pangs and aches worse. "Do any of you know this country well?"

Paco shook his head. "I came through here once with some friends, but we were going north, not west."

"I've been through here a few times," Wade said, "but that was before the war; haven't had occasion to travel this way since the recent unpleasantness."

Paco glanced at Wade. "Weren't there some underground caverns around here? Might be some water to be found in 'em."

Wade shook his head. "Caverns of Sonora. Yeah was decent tourist spot before, but after...." He paused for a moment. "Last I heard, the Damnation Army had hit most of the caverns. Entrances to hell, they called 'em. The ones they didn't outright demolish access to they found ways to poison. No, not worth the risk of turning off the trail to search for it and find it was a wasted detour. Best stick to the road and get to Ozona."

To Reynaud, the land seemed utterly inhospitable. Even where greenery softened the harsh lines, it was a stubborn, prickly sort of bush, as though the rugged climate and miserly soil allowed only plants with thorns or knife-edged leaves to fight their way up. He missed the coast with its lush, almost tropical growth and the frequent mists, or even the plains with their thick cover sprouting from soil that held moisture like a sponge.

He was tired, already thirsty, and the breakfast lay in his stomach like a lump of pig-iron. Gazing at the barren country on either side of the road, he wished their mission were finished. Even his hatred for Chernikov seemed to have been tempered. Once, he would've walked barefooted over red-hot razor blades to kill the Russian, with his bare hands, if need be. Now, killing Chernikov was more of a duty; a thing he had to do, not for pleasure but to protect what was left of his country.

"Look sharp, y'all," Wade drawled. "Looks like we got company comin'."

Reynaud's head snapped up and he saw a dot on the horizon.

"Let's get off the road and set up an ambush." Logan began to slide his rifle out of its scabbard.

"Don't bother," Wade said. "Keep the long guns out of sight. They got no reason to think we're not part of the Sonora garrison. Just keep ridin', but space out the line a little better in case they's more than just the two trucks."

Hasteen urged his horse forward, keeping it apace with Reynaud's mount. "Let Paco and I take the lead. He and I will ride on opposite sides of the road and hit the second truck as soon as you go for the first one."

Reynaud took off his hat to wipe his forehead. "Sounds good to me. Wade, you'll be the one to open fire on the trucks." The two vehicles were still a single dot on the horizon to him. "You still think it's just two trucks?"

"Looks like it." Wade rode to the side of the road and unloaded the tobacco he'd been chewing. "I'm gonna hit the first truck from the driver's side."

"I'll take the passenger side, then" Logan offered.

"All right," Reynaud said, "but I'd feel better if we could get those trucks to slow down. As it stands, we get one try, then they're gone. There's no way our horses could keep up with the trucks, even if they were fresh."

"It's a shame horses don't get flat tires," Logan said, with a grin. "Then we'd have an excuse to block the road."

"Good thought," Reynaud said. "They do throw shoes. Steve, you and the Deacon stay back with me. Hasteen, you and the others who're going to hit the trucks, pull back a little.

I don't want you getting too far ahead." He could clearly see the trucks now. Giving his horse a bit of the spur, he trotted to the head of the party, then drew rein and dismounted. As he alighted, he turned the horse so it partially blocked the highway, facing north, keeping his rifle on the side away from the trucks. Bending down, he coaxed the animal to swing up its right foreleg.

"Be careful," Wade warned him, as he rode by at a walk. "That's a good way to get kicked into the middle of next Christmas. Be sure you let go of that leg before the excitement starts."

"Deacon," Reynaud said, "get down and get that grenade launcher of yours ready, and be sure to keep your horse between you and the trucks. You're our insurance policy."

Wordlessly, Billy Joe drew his horse to a halt, dismounted, and unslung his rifle. Steve, leading the pack animals, also stopped.

~ * ~

Wade watched the trucks approach, saw Hasteen and Paco move ahead of Logan and himself. As Hasteen waved a salute to the driver of the nearer truck, Wade grinned. For a change, they seemed to have caught the bad guys with their pants around their ankles. Nudging his horse with his knees, he moved it a little to the left of the truck, which had slowed to a stop, less than six feet away. His left hand, which had touched his hat brim, dropped but, instead of resting on the saddle horn, curled around the grip of his left automatic.

The pistol came up and his thumb snapped the ambidextrous safety down. He squeezed the trigger as the front sight covered the driver's ear, then saw the man's head snap away from the impact, with bone and tissue blown into the cab.

Gunfire erupted around him as he ducked below the level of the door then seized its handle. Somewhere behind the truck he heard the scream of a wounded horse and what sounded like an echo on the other side of the truck.

~ * ~

Logan had decided he'd have to use the Ingram. The silenced Russian pistol was in a flap holster, and drawing it in a hurry was out of the question. The .44 magnum was liable to tear through everything in sight, and might hit Wade or one of the others. That left the MAC, which presented problems of its own; it was, as the

Frenchman had said, a bullet hose and barely controllable. The safest way to use it was from a little in front of the truck, firing though the windshield, so he fell a few feet behind Wade.

As soon as Logan heard Wade's shot his own hand stabbed down and back, swept the duster aside, and snatched up the sub gun. As he swung his weapon up he saw a gun barrel appear in the passenger's side. Tension turned to near-panic and he jerked at the MAC's trigger. The first couple of bullets caromed off the truck's hood before they punched through the windshield, which cobwebbed, then almost vanished in a shower of glittering pieces.

Even as he pulled the MAC's trigger he saw the muzzle of the gun in the truck flicker. His horse screamed in anguish and fear and began to buck. Logan dropped the Ingram to let it hang by its sling while he grabbed the saddle horn with both hands. He was almost thrown at the first buck then was slammed down into the saddle with bone-jarring force. The second bound made him lose the stirrups, then the saddle. He was dimly conscious of sailing through the air, with no sense of up or down. He fell into some brush at the side of the road, coming down on his lower neck and upper back hard enough to make his chest feel as though a ton of lead shot had been dropped on it. The back of his head hit the ground and lights seemed to flash behind his eyes.

He tried to draw a breath but seemed caught in a vacuum, and would've thrashed about but none of his muscles seemed to work. Finally, his vision cleared a bit and he could find a shallow breath of air. A large shape loomed over him and he heard and almost felt the impact as a hoof pounded the ground only a foot or so from his head.

He fumbled for his MAC, pointed it at the shape, pulled the trigger, but nothing happened and he realized he must've fired the entire magazine in a single burst at the truck. The horse seemed to grow larger as it reared again.

~ * ~

As Hasteen passed the first truck, which was slowing, he raised his left hand to his hat brim, did it again as he neared the second truck. As soon as his hand dropped the second time he tossed the reins to his left hand and, at the sounds of the shots behind him, whipped out his right-hand pistol.

He fired across his saddle, his first bullet smashing into the driver's head, splashing blood throughout the cab and all over the inside of the windshield. His second round, snapped off a split-second later, punched through the driver's door, just below the open window. He heard glass shattering and the driver jerked again.

By the time he'd reined his mount and begun to turn, he heard the bellow of a rifle but it cost an instant to twist enough in the saddle to snap off a shot at the bandit in the back of the first truck, then the man dropped and tumbled out onto the highway.

~ * ~

Paco had kept pace with Hasteen until he lost sight of him on the other side of the truck. As soon as he heard the familiar thunder he snatched out his own pistol and fired twice at the gray-haired man in the passenger's seat. The bandit convulsed up and back as the bullet hit and the second slug caught him just in front of the ear, just above the jaw.

Paco twitched his horse's reins to turn him toward the truck then spun in the saddle as a bullet whipped across his thigh and slammed into his mount's neck. The horse screamed and flung up its head then sprang forward, still rearing.

Paco kicked his feet free of the stirrups and, as the horse went down, its forelegs folding under it, he threw himself away from the stricken animal.

Taking the fall on his left arm and shoulder, he managed to roll into it, ending up on his belly. He saw the man in the back of the first truck working the lever of his carbine. With no time to aim his shots, Paco pointed his automatic at the figure and snapped off three fast shots. The bandit jackknifed to his knees then pitched forward, head-first, out the back of the truck.

Paco spun, saw his horse was all but dead, and fired again, putting the beast out of its misery. The animal had gone down on its left side so he was able to snatch his Winchester out of the saddle scabbard then he looked back to where Logan should be.

Reid lay beside the road, trying to point his weapon up at the horse that had thrown him and was thrashing in a frenzy, showering blood over everything around it. Paco swung his carbine to his shoulder, thumbing back the hammer. He saw the horse begin to rear again and knew if Logan didn't move quickly, he'd be chopped to ribbons by the flailing hooves.

Lining the sights, Paco pointed the rifle at the horse's head and squeezed the trigger. Before the sound of the shot had stopped ringing in his ears, he'd cranked the lever open and shut again but the horse was already falling, and a flurry of movement beside the road showed Logan had rolled out of the way.

A dull concussion and the screech of tearing metal drew his attention to the trucks. The second truck had rolled into the rear of the stopped machine then, with a loud knocking noise, the second truck's engine died.

Hasteen rode to the back of the second truck and disappeared into it, a revolver in his hand, then reappeared in less than a minute and lowered himself back into the saddle. "Nothing there but a dozen or so empty barrels."

Paco suddenly remembered his canteen, the strap of which had been looped over his saddle horn. The canteen lay beside the horse, and he was relieved to see it was unmarked. Catching up the strap, he slung it over his shoulder, carefully avoiding the horse's carcass, which still twitched as muscles contracted and relaxed.

Keeping his carbine at his shoulder, Paco strode to where Logan's horse lay. His shot had blown away most of its brain.

Logan slowly worked his way to his feet. "Damned nice shot," he said, "and real well-timed. Thanks."

"What makes you think I was aiming at the horse?" Paco inquired, grinning.

Logan stared at Paco a long moment then threw back his head and laughed. "Then it was a damned lucky accident for me."

Paco nodded down at the dead animal. "I jus' couldn' stand to see the poor animal in pain. You better get your canteen." Paco walked back to the cab of the second truck and turned off the ignition before he dragged the bandits' corpses out onto the pavement and began searching the cab for supplies.

Hasteen joined him. "Nothing in the back of either truck but empty barrels. It looks like they were going to Sonora to pick up fuel."

"They were also primed for trouble," Logan interjected. "You don't have men riding shotgun and tail-gunner if the route's really safe."

Paco looked up from the seat he'd just pulled back. "But not too dangerous, or there would have been more of them. We were lucky."

"Find anything useful?" Hasteen asked.

"So far, only two full canteens and one half empty, and the guns and cartridges." He handed Hasteen the canteens then tossed out a pump shotgun with the stock cut off just behind the pistol grip and the barrel bobbed to the same length as the magazine tube and the driver's weapon, a Tec 9.

The three of them joined the rest of the group around the cab of the first truck. Wade handed Logan an Uzi. "Here's what killed your horse. And we recovered one full canteen, but nothing else."

"So what do we do now?" Reynaud asked.

"We keep on goin'" Wade said. "We take the ammo and trash the weapons, we give the horses and the mule the water from the two full canteens and we share the half-full one, then we help Logan and Paco get their gear on the pack animals and share the pack loads." He again used his hat to help water the animals.

Paco put his saddle on the mule, leaving the horse to Logan.

"Why don't we just take the trucks?" Logan asked.

"We can't haul the horses in 'em," Wade replied, "and, sooner or later, we're going to need these horses."

Transferring the supplies to the saddle horses and wrecking the trucks cost them nearly half an hour before they could get back on the road to Ozona. While the rest of the group made the preparations, Reynaud checked Paco's wound. He used a little alcohol but it seemed hardly to have broken the skin, and was more like a bruise or a burn.

With a clear sky and an unseasonably warm day, running to the seventies, they'd all taken off their jackets, although Logan still wore his duster. By early afternoon, Reynaud found himself squinting through the clear air, almost desperate for the sight of the town and the taste of a deep drink of water. "How much further?" he asked

Wade, in a voice that had become a croak.

"It should be in sight any time now," Wade drawled. "It's about thirty, thirty-five miles west of Sonora, and we've covered about that much distance."

Reynaud found talking painful. Besides costing energy, working his dried lips risked cracking them, and his tongue felt as moist and supple as an old stick. For another half hour the group followed the highway, Reynaud falling into a sort of trance, unable to guess the distance they'd covered or to remember the few features of the land.

Suddenly, Wade stopped, stood in his stirrups, squinting, then dug out his binoculars. Staring through the field glasses, he cursed in a dead monotone then handed the glasses to Reynaud, who looked through the lenses at a dead and blasted landscape. He passed the glasses to Logan. "What do you think happened?"

"I think it's pretty plain," Wade said. "Barnes and his boys must've gotten pissed off about something and burned everything in town that'd catch fire. Looks like they did their damnest to demolish the rest. The scurvy bastards have turned it into a howling wilderness."

"How could they get away with that?" Steve handed Wade back his binoculars. "The town looks like it held between three and four thousand people. I thought Barnes' crowd was a lot smaller than that."

"Probably most of the people there died of plague, and most 'a the survivors cut out for somewhere with more water; probably headed north or east. Besides, Barnes and his boys had an edge; they didn't have to worry about tryin' to save anything. Destroyers and other vandals have that advantage."

"Where'd we be most likely to find water in what's left of the town?" Reynaud asked.

Wade glowered at the smoke-stained ruins. "We probably won't find any, but we can try. We'll check out some of the buildings around the town square."

Their thirst had become desperation, which turned to fury when they saw the devastation the bandits had visited on Ozona. It looked as though everything that could burn had been put to the torch. They found places where mounds of charred skeletons of furniture, and a few human skeletons as well had been thrown in a heap to burn. The fire-blackened hulk of a caterpillar with a blade lay at the end of a trail of apparently random destruction.

"I don't think there's a single unbroken piece of glass in the entire town," Steve observed, shaking his head.

"Jeez," Logan muttered, "I haven't seen this much destruction in one place since the frat party when we invited the football team."

"Remind me not to invite any of your friends to any of my parties." Wade pointed to what looked like a round stone slab barely visible in the heaps of rubble in the store they were exploring. "This looks like a cover for a cistern."

Working together, they cleared away the debris then Wade and Logan gripped the ring handles, their muscles bunched as they threw their bodies into the effort of wrenching the lid up but dropped it with a clatter as an odor hit them with the force of a physical blow.

"Those dirty, rotten, stinkin' sonsabitches," Wade raged. He lapsed into a streak of profanity that held the others awestruck. Finally he ran down and slammed the lid with his fist. "Those motherless bastards dropped a body or two down the cistern. They killed this whole town and wanted to make sure it stayed dead."

Hasteen's face looked grayish as he paled under his tan. "This is a place of the dead. Let's get out of here."

"Might as well," Wade growled. "We won't find anything we can use here. Those bastards were like bulls in a china shop; what they couldn't smash, they shit on."

"We want to get out of here," Reynaud agreed, "but we've also got to have water, for ourselves and our mounts. Wade, you seem to know the area best. Where's the nearest place we can get water?"

"They's a ranch or two around here," Wade replied, "but chances are, Barnes and his crowd took care of them, too. The nearest sure place will be Fort Lancaster, about thirty-odd miles west of here. The water from the Pecos River is undrinkable but Live Oak Creek runs sweet and fresh."

Reynaud squinted at the horizon. "We're not going to make any thirty miles anymore today."

"No we ain't," Wade agreed. "We oughta lay up in the shade till three-thirty or four, then make as many miles as we can while they's still light to see by." He looked back at the stretch of highway they'd traveled. "If I'd known what we were getting' into. I'd 'a suggested we take the trucks, but it's too late now. They're too far back, and even if we could get the trucks runnin' again we might run into some of the hardcases from Sonora."

Steve, using a stick that had once been part of a chair, began to scratch lines in the dirt. "What's our chance of getting some local help? Those truck crews weren't packing all that iron just to look macho for cacti. It suggests there are still people around here who are still fighting Barnes' bandits."

"It's a nice thought but not likely to help us," Paco said. "There is a lot of country around here. We might never find people who mus' be pretty good at staying out of sight. And if we did find them, they might try to shoot with us before they find out we are not more of Barnes' men."

"The only supplies we have left might be of some use," Hasteen held up a jar of preserved tomatoes and a can of peaches.

"We'll save the tomatoes for tonight," Reynaud decided, "and we can have the peaches in the morning. But what about our animals?"

"We give them what water we've got left," Wade said. "We sponge out their mouths with a hanky dipped in water. We'll make it; it's just gonna be a tad uncomfortable. So, we may as well get as much rest as we can right now."

~ * ~

Reynaud stumbled and almost fell as his ankle twisted on another break in the road surface. The sun had gone down, and they were moving in the dim light of a quarter-moon. He tried to guess how many miles they'd covered since they'd left Ozona. From the way his body ached, they could be within a mile or two of where Wade was leading them, or even past it, while, from the harshness of the landscape, they might hardly be out of sight of Ozona. They'd ridden until it was no longer safe, in the dusk, to ride, then dismounted and led their mounts. They often had to soothe the beasts, which shied at each flicker of moon-shadow.

He almost felt he'd become a robot then grinned. He cursed under his breath as the grin cracked his dried-out lips and he tasted blood in his mouth. No, he wasn't a machine, not unless machines became tired and thirsty, and bled.

He stumbled again and this time his ankle was viciously twisted. The pain wrung a cry out of him before he could smother it, and he almost fell. He managed to catch himself but almost tumbled again as his weight shifted to his injured ankle.

"Okay," Wade's drawl came from the darkness ahead. "Time to call it a night. Can you make it to the side of the road?"

"I can make it," Reynaud mumbled.

The Cajun heard a snap and blinked at the flare of a match then a flickering, trembling light as Wade lit a clump of dry brush.

"Wade and I will picket the animals and take care of them," Hasteen said, and took the reins of Reynaud's horse.

Reynaud tried to find the energy to argue. Instead, he collapsed on the ground with a moan. The brush burned fiercely but quickly and, within seconds was reduced to a few points of reddish glow but in the short brightness Reynaud observed most of the group looking almost as bad as he felt. Even Logan looked hollow-eyed and worn. The chill of the ground had begun to seep up into Reynaud's muscles then someone tossed a blanket over him. He managed to sit up, his blanket wrapped around himself.

"Y'know," Logan said, "I miss the finer things. You know you're in stinkin' shape when you'd rather have a drink of water than a woman. And, right now, I'd rather have the water and the chance to get these boots, off."

Steve made sounds as though he were getting to his feet. "Save my place, fellas. I gotta go find Logan a drink of water and a woman. We gotta do something to make him keep his boots on."

Reynaud chuckled. "How far do you think we got today?"

From where he was still working on the horses, Wade's voice replied, "I'd guess we covered all but about fifteen miles. We did pretty well. The old US cavalry covered about forty miles a day. I'd say we at least matched that, maybe a littler better. With a little luck we oughta hit Fort Lancaster and Live Oak Creek sometime between nine and ten in the mornin'."

The Deacon nudged Reynaud then handed him a jar. The Cajun sipped at the tomato juice, feeling the tart, acidic liquid cut the layers of dust in his mouth and throat. He sighed with relief and passed the jar on to the dim shape on his right. The second time the jar went around the juice was gone, and each man took a tomato.

Too tired to eat anything more. Reynaud leaned back again, wrapped in his blanket like a cocoon. "Same rotation of guards as before?" he asked.

"Fair enough."

Reynaud thought it was Paco's voice that replied. He rolled onto his left side and was almost instantly asleep.

Chapter 8

Chernikov followed Baker, directing him to the large, squat white building at the northern edge of Fort Stockton. "This was built before the war by a pharmaceutical company." He'd almost slipped and said "one of your pharmaceutical companies" but had caught himself in time. "They were working on a vaccine to prevent anthrax and several other diseases of cattle and sheep."

As they stepped into a large room, most of it blocked from view by dividers, Baker stared at the computers he could see and at least three men in white lab coats then glared at Chernikov. "So, what do you want me to do? Humanitarianism doesn't seem to be your strong suit. Somehow, I doubt you're working for a vaccine."

"I'm deeply hurt," Chernikov said, in a mock-hurt voice. "You wrong me terribly. Of course I want you to help us prepare a vaccine. I want the anthrax bacteria to have a longer incubation period, to be more virulent, and to be resistant to Cipro and penicillin."

"Go fuck yourself, Chambers," Baker snapped.

The other man smiled and Baker, observing the total cruelty laid bare by the expression, felt his stomach knot. "I'm not sure you understand what is at stake." He turned and led Baker on a sort of tour of the facility. "We have a generator to provide power for computers. Webster, who will be your assistant, can feed data into the system to let us all know if your attempts are successful. But we might need a subject to verify the results.

"I can see by how pale you've become you've understood. If I don't have your complete assistance and participation, I'll have to inject your son with the bacteria. You will be—invited to observe the progression of the disease. We won't use the drug of choice, since that wouldn't give us an index of virulence. I believe you scientists call it 'testing to destruction.'"

"You son of a bitch," Baker said through clamped teeth.

Chernikov looked up from the white phosphorous grenade he'd just picked up and secured to his belt. "You're slow to learn." He gestured toward a bare room that looked as though it had once been a storeroom. "Step inside. You have an hour to make your decision. I want you to take your time, consider all the—" he fumbled, momentarily, for the expression— "outs and ins of the situation. But remember who will pay for your opposition or any attempts at sabotage. Think of your boy experiencing inhalation anthrax.

"You can watch him gasp himself to death while he burns with fever. Or would you prefer that we let him enjoy intestinal anthrax? Then you could see him doubled over, screaming in agony as his belly is eaten out from the inside. Of course, he may not feel it if the fever and shock cause him to go into coma. Septicemia will be what kills him, of course—along with your stubbornness. You might think about that, too." He shoved Baker into the room and locked the door.

Webster, a tall, stooped man with a limp whose washed-out blue eyes stared at the phosphorous grenade at Chernikov's belt and swallowed. "What's that for?"

Chernikov glanced at him. "I don't completely trust Barnes or his rabble. I'll take care of security. You just see that Baker does his work well."

Chernikov studied the assistant more closely. He'd been hired by Artemov when the operation was formed, as were the others who worked in the complex. Artemov had died of plague, leaving an organizational void that had necessarily been filled by less competent men. Webster was one of the less capable ones. He knew enough about medicine to be useful but, aside from his interest in money, he had no loyalties. He was also disposable.

"I'm going to my quarters," Chernikov said. "Call me in an hour."

As he paced to his rooms in the building he admired again the forethought of the people who'd built this complex, who'd constructed most of it underground, making air-conditioning and heating all but unnecessary. Such foresight was similar to his own. The grenade—and several like it hidden in the complex—were kept ready in case of an accident. If the bacteria were released the laboratory it could be destroyed by fire. The destruction of the facilities would set back the operation but losing control of the bacteria could end his activities to crush a weakened enemy, and when the operation was a success he could have the workers inject the cattle and the drovers, then burn the laboratory. In any case, Webster, Baker, and the rest would all go up in flames in an "accident" that would wipe out equipment for which he had no further use.

He opened the door to the room he'd chosen for his personal quarters, closed the door behind himself, and locked it. Lying on the cot, he closed his eyes. He had no orders after Operation Annihilation, and no way to receive orders. He could choose his next project.

He spoke Spanish, but not well, which meant he'd have to go north. What he'd heard about the coasts didn't make them sound inviting. If he went north he might have the opportunity to infiltrate and take over a large enough bandit gang to attack what remained of the NORAD command center in Colorado.

It was unlikely, but possible, that NORAD might have some program to speed rebuilding, although he saw no evidence of its operation.

Still, some organization opposed him. He wondered who the mysterious "Buttercup" might be, and who "Recon 9" might've been. Whoever they were, or had been, they were either dead or wandering around eastern Texas. They'd come by ship, perhaps from Europe. That suggested a large organization with a long reach.

This unknown organization could be a thorn in his side, might even be dangerous. Perhaps after his work was done in spreading a new plague he could devote attention to tracing this organization and its leaders. Assassinating those leaders would deal a crippling blow to whatever government agency had taken over. He was sure it had to be some arm of the defunct government, perhaps the military. The thought surprised him. When he'd come from Europe posing as a returning American veteran, he'd noticed the military bases and posts were disappearing behind the last men out of Europe, that most of the soldiers, sailors, and airmen were drifting away from their posts as the immediate need for their services was gone.

Whoever was leading this organization had to be someone with clout, to be able to bring people back from Europe. With the shortage of fuel, and nothing to trade, Chernikov knew of no commercial carriers who still plied the sea lanes.

An even bigger surprise was to find senior American military officers could be effective. He'd found most senior military officers too bound by tradition and internecine battles over "turf" to actually lead. Some of the junior officers and many of their noncommissioned officers displayed initiative but most of the officers who'd climbed the promotion ladder were too valuable to the FSB to assassinate. They were the ones who made sure the men on operations would have only what maps of the area they could tear out of magazines or find, once they'd been deposited in a strange country. Those self-important buffoons were the ones who made sure the various services' radios were set on different frequencies, so soldiers couldn't coordinate with marines or airmen. There were some of those dinosaurs in the armies of all nations, even in the Russian forces, but the Americans seemed to have built their military around the hidebound fools.

~ * ~

Reynaud woke slowly, his eyes nearly glued shut with a gunk, partly composed of dust, and it felt like sandpaper. More of the same dried paste made his mouth achingly dry and left a taste like forty miles of Texas desert. Hindered by cramped muscles, he dragged himself out of the cocoon he'd made of his blanket. His ankle was stiff and sore but experimentation showed him it'd bear his weight.

"Here." Hasteen nudged his shoulder with the can of peaches then handed it to him. Reynaud took a sip of the juice. Too thick and sweet to banish his thirst, at least it displaced the taste of his morning mouth.

"Sorry, but this is the best we can do for rations." Hasteen handed him a couple of sticks of dried meat. Gnawing the jerky seemed to take most of Reynaud's energy and concentration. As he finished the meat, the can came around again and he ate one of the preserved peaches.

After washing his hands with dust, rubbing away the sticky moisture, he saddled his horse. By the time he'd finished, the others were also prepared to leave. Hasteen's and Paco's wounds seemed to have almost healed, with no sign of infection. He mounted carefully, grateful, for the sake of his ankle, that horses were mounted from the left.

Wade took the lead, Reynaud falling into a position a little behind him and to his left. The rising sun seemed to finally burn away some of the fog in his head. He became conscious of the clatter of shod hooves on pavement and the creak of leather.

The road looked like a black scar running through the angry-colored rock that stretched to the horizon. The whole place looked about as hospitable as a pool table. He rubbed his eyes and tried to stay alert but he seemed to be able to only think about water. He thought he caught the dry scent of pinon in the desert air, but not a hint of moisture. The others must be as uncomfortable as he felt, but the only clues were their squints at the arid land around them and the set of their jaws. Those, and the group's silence. Talking cost energy which was, like moisture, too precious to waste.

As they topped a rise they found themselves at the crest of a slope leading down to a valley rich with plants and trees. Wade stood in his stirrups and spat a stream of brown between his horse's ears and down the steep slope. "Fort's about two miles ahead. We'll hafta lead the horses down or we're liable to lose some of 'em."

Reynaud noticed the animals became harder to handle as they caught the scent of water, and trying to keep them under control while getting them down the steep grade was a bitter struggle.

As the trail leveled off, they remounted and gave the beasts their heads. The same horses and mule that had once had to be forced to plod forward, heads hanging, now threw themselves into a trot down the valley. Reynaud could clearly see real, honest-to-God trees, even oaks, and they looked as though they still lived, although most of the branches were still bare. In spring, this valley might be the only source of life for miles.

Geysers of dust erupted in front of them then they heard three rapid shots. "Pull them horses up!" The voice, coming from the tangle of low walls ahead of them, echoed so the group couldn't tell exactly from where the sound had come.

The group drew reins, having to fight their mounts who were desperate for the water they could smell. Reynaud finally managed to get his blue to stand, although the beast trembled under him, and he glanced at Wade and Paco, both of whom were scanning the rock walls.

"Get down out of them saddles," the voice ordered. As the group hesitated, it continued, "Get down or get shot down. It's all the same to us."

"Dismount," Reynaud ordered the rest of the group, and slid down from his own saddle, still trying to find the position from which the shots had come. Whoever had ambushed them had done a good and thorough job of it. He and the rest of the group were within about fifty yards of a waist-high wall—point-blank range for rifles, and he could still see only one or two heads among the rocks. If they'd tried to fight, they'd all already be dead. Since the ambushers hadn't simply shot them to pieces as they rode to the river, they still seemed to have some hope of getting out alive.

"Awright." Satisfaction had crept into the voice. "Now, take off them gunbelts and hang 'em over your saddle horns."

Reynaud glanced at the others and nodded, then unbuckled the police rig he wore and buckled it around the saddle horn.

A big man stood up behind a lower section of the stone wall. "Jeb, you and Bull go out and collect the horses." It was the man who had shouted to them before. As tall as Wade, he was proportionately as heavily built as Logan, and wore a wild, grizzled beard. Two bandits sauntered out of another partial building, apparently having left their rifles behind, strolled toward the group until they were near enough to snatch away the reins, then led the animals around the ruins of the fort.

"Ain't got enough water for you boys," the big man called out, "but we can let your horses drink." He laughed for a moment at his own humor then set his rifle against the wall. "'Course, if you're thirsty enough, you can try to come through us to get it."

Logan was striding toward the big man when more of the bandits stood, all with rifles or shotguns pointed at the group. Ignoring the rest of the gang, Logan stopped, pointed at the man who'd done all the talking, and bellowed, "I want you, asshole, and it doesn't matter to me how many of your butt-buddies you hide behind, I'm still gonna wipe that shit-eating grin off your ugly face and kick your ass from here to the Rio Grande."

The big man laughed and looked around at his men. "Right feisty for a sawed-off little dab of mouth, ain't he, boys? Bob, Burt, Sim, you keep your rifles pointed at 'em. Julio, you keep an eye on the other prisoner. If any of the rest 'a you boys want a piece of this, step on out." He unbuckled his gunbelt and laid it on the wall by his rifle and picked up what looked like an ax handle.

More bandits crawled out of the rocks, laying aside their long arms and gunbelts, although several of them carried clubs, knives, or other close-in weapons.

"This is gonna be even more fun than shootin' you," the big man announced. "and a damn sight cheaper. Shells are too hard to come by to waste."

"You talk a helluva good fight," Logan roared. "Now, let's see if you can put your muscle where your big mouth is."

Recon 9 and the bandits formed up in two lines, not more than a couple of yards apart, and Reynaud could count the opposition. Fourteen faced them; two-to-one odds, with four bandits still holding rifles, three of them staring at the group, the other somewhere on the other side of the wall. When the other bandit reappeared he shoved ahead of him a tall, lean man clad in rags, who looked as though the gang had tried to beat him to death and had almost succeeded. And two more of the marauders lurked down by the river with their horses.

~ * ~

Logan had also counted the odds but he didn't hesitate as he stalked toward the big man and his ax handle. "I sure hope you got all the splinters off that thing, asshole, so it won't hurt so bad when I ram it up your ass."

Suddenly, Wade's voice cut across and over the babble. "You're all under arrest."

In that instant of the bandits' stunned disbelief, Logan charged the last few feet. His right arm shot up, driving against the elbow of the arm holding the ax handle while his other thumb was thrust into the bandit's left eye and his right knee slammed up into the man's crotch. Even as he hit the leader, Logan spun away, barely avoiding a slash from the bandit to his right and a club wielded by another bandit on his left. Springing toward the man with the club, Logan drove his fist in just below the buckle of the man's chaps. The bandit folded over. He turned to the leader again and his left hand snatched the section of ax handle just above the bandit's hand and rapped the hardwood against the man's skull.

Between the two men with clubs, Logan slipped past the second man he'd hit, catching the man's head solidly with an elbow, then wrenched away the section of tree branch the man had carried.

Reid charged into the leader's left right side, driving him back, and heard the man gasp, then Logan side-stepped. The man with the knife was pulling his blade out of his leader's right side when Logan thrust with the club and hit the man in the face. The bandit screamed as blood shot from a smashed nose and teeth flew. Logan hit the knife-man again, this time in the throat.

Knowing the riflemen would soon open fire. Logan turned again on the man he'd seized the club from and, putting all his strength into the swing, bludgeoned him in the back of the head. The man was hurled to the ground, face-down, and Logan also dropped, snatching for the Bulldog under his shirt.

~ * ~

Wade had seen Logan charge the center of the bandits' line, and he attacked the two men at Logan's right. He'd noticed many of the bandits wore chaps but none of them wore spurs, a little fact that might prove useful. Then he was closing with two of them and had no more time for thinking. Whipping his hat off, he scaled it at the face of the man to his left, who swung a tire iron. The other bandit was even bigger than the leader, with a flattened nose and an ear that was a cauliflowered mass of cartilage.

As Wade pulled the hat trick he side-stepped and rammed his fist into the brawler's upper belly, just below where the ribs joined. It'd been like hitting a truck tire but it had the desired effect, stunning and partially paralyzing the big man. Even as he hit the thug his cheekbone was grazed by a fist that felt as though it were made of iron. The big man's second punch had already been thrown but Wade's blow to the solar plexus had robbed it of most of its force as it landed in Wade's belly. Wade thought, if either of those hand landed clean—

Immediately he whirled on the man with the tire iron, barely avoiding a frantic swing, then stepped inside the arc and swung an uppercut that caught the man on the point of the chin and dropped him onto the ground.

There were no Marquis of Queensbury rules, and the losers of this fight wouldn't get a re-match. Wade kicked, the pointed toe of his boot driving into the soft skin under the bandit's jaw.

Something hit him like a flying pickup as the brawler took him down with a tackle. The two of them sprawled in the dust and arms like steel bands closed around Wade, trapping his right arm against his side. With his left hand, Wade clawed at the bandit's eyes and was rewarded with a scream then he hooked a thumb in the side of the big man's mouth and twisted the bandit's head to the right.

The brawler bellowed like a bull and tightened his death-clamp on Wade but the Ranger continued to lever the man's head back and away, then managed to get a knee bent enough to shove off and roll the two of them over so Wade was on top.

Gray crept in at the edges of Wade's vision. Shaking his head to clear it, he saw the tire iron dropped by the other bandit, just out of his reach. With another surge, he rolled over again and snatched the tool. As he released the bandit's cheek to grab the weapon, the big man butted him in the face. Everything seemed to explode into molten red pain then Wade gripped the iron tighter. With no room to swing, he stabbed with the end and, from far away it seemed, heard a scream as the other man stiffened. He stabbed again and again, and he began to fear the bandit, even dead, might crush the life out of him.

He felt and tasted blood in his mouth and he could hardly breathe. He wasn't sure whether the blood on his face was his own or that of his enemy but he struggled, with fading strength, against the locked arms, then he heard gunshots.

~ * ~

Steve had moved to Wade's right, trying to remember everything he'd learned about hand-to-hand fighting. As a boy, he'd taken some classes in karate, although he'd learned just enough for his friends to call him a dojo ballerina.

The bandit to Steve's left had a knife, which he tossed from hand to hand while the one on the right gripped a pair of flattened iron rings. Steve feinted at the knife-fighter, who seemed to be a show-off, and lashed out with a kick that caught the other bandit on the side of the knee.

Poorly delivered, the kick landed with little force but it caused the man to stumble back. It'd also, unfortunately, cured the knife-fighter of his overconfidence. He slashed out in a silvery blur, cutting a slice in Steve's jean jacket and left a line of blood on his forearm.

Steve circled left to try to keep the knife man between himself and the other bandit then, as the knife swept across again, blocked inside then caught the elbow and levered the arm against its natural bend. The man screamed and dropped his knife. Quickly shifting his weight to the other side, Steve threw the bandit to the ground with a broken arm. As he spun on the other man he barely ducked a flailing right fist as the other man got back into the fight. Ducking again, Steve caught up the knife then tried a side-kick, which his enemy took on the hip.

The man seemed unfazed by the kick, just shrugging it off and continuing to advance, both arms cocked to throw punches. They swung at the same time and the knife was battered from Steve's hand and his fingers numbed but as the broken blade dropped the other man cursed and backed away, clutching at his bleeding fist.

Steve felt some little satisfaction but remembered he'd been cut, too, and he knew this fight wouldn't last long enough to become an endurance contest. The man he'd thrown came up from the ground, roaring, his left fist windmilling.

Trying to ignore the pain in his ribs as a blow landed, Steve caught at the chest of the man's shirt and went over backward, his legs propelling the bandit up and over him. As soon as he'd flung the bandit away he rolled to the left.

The second man had rushed and tried to kick him while he was down. Steve snatched the man's boot and shoved it upward, overbalancing him, dumping him onto his back. Keeping the foot trapped, Steve gained his feet, stamped down into the man's crotch then stamped again on the man's throat. The bandit emitted a bubbling scream and thrashed in the dust.

The other man had staggered to his feet again but only

stared at Steve, his right arm hanging useless, naked fear in his eyes. He charged again and Steve side-stepped and tried another kick, which missed because the bandit had dodged past him and made a dash for the stone wall and the men with rifles.

Gunshots erupted then, and Steve dropped to the ground.

~ * ~

Billy Joe had taken a position to Steve's right. It'd once been a matter of shame to him that when, in young manhood, he'd abandoned his faith. He'd become one of the most notable drinkers and barroom brawlers in Asheville, North Carolina. Now, what had once seemed a fall from grace into the devil's clutches was a past that might save his life and those of his friends, and he marveled at the strange and intricate ways of the Lord.

Both the men facing him stood bare-fisted and cautious. "Are you ready to stand before the Judge of Judges?" Billy Joe demanded,

"Looks like we got us a Bible-thumper here, Archie," one of the bandits crowed, as he moved to Billy Joe's right.

"Looks like, Wes," Archie responded, grinning as he sidled left. "What say, since he's so hot for God, we send 'im to meet Him personally?"

"Blasphemy!" Billy Joe roared. Faking a punch at Archie, he stepped in on Wes, blocking a poorly-thrown punch with his left arm while his counterpunch smashed into the bandit's mouth, mashing and tearing his lips, loosening his teeth, and leaving him stunned.

Something hit Billy Joe behind the ear, almost knocking him down. Whoever Archie was he was faster than Billy Joe had guessed.

"Grab him, Archie!" Wes screamed. "I got some payback for him." The bandit spat blood and a tooth through the ruins of his lips then stepped forward, swinging a haymaker.

Archie had managed to grab Billy Joe but, as Wes swung like a washerwoman, Billy Joe shifted his balance and the fist flew past his head, barely missing Archie. "Dammitall, Wes," Archie shouted, "Hit him in the belly! Hit him in the belly."

Wes pressed the back of his hand against his mouth and stared down at his own blood. "Awright, you psalm-singin' sonofabitch, I'm gonna ruin you. I killed men for less'n this."

"Then you won't find a cool spot in Hell," Billy Joe said, and, as Wes stepped forward, drawing his arm back for a punch, Billy Joe drove his boot into the man's belly, hurling him back and onto the ground. Before Archie had time to take Billy Joe down, he'd stamped savagely on the bandit's instep.

Archie howled as the heavy Russian combat boot smashed the bones of his foot then Billy Joe spun and slammed his elbow into the side of the bandit's head. The man dropped as though every joint had been cut.

With Archie out of the way, Billy Joe strode toward Wes, his fists like living hammers. His first punch smashed the bandit's nose, his second dislocated Wes' jaw, and the third was delivered to the temple. Wes' eyes rolled up in their sockets and he dropped like a bag of flour.

Catching a flash of motion, Billy Joe saw a man running past Steve and saw his friend go down, then he heard the gunfire.

~ * ~

Paco had flanked Logan to the left. One of the bandits facing him held a Bowie knife in his right hand and a quirt dangled from his left wrist, while the other had whipped off his belt, wrapped the leather around his hand, and swung the massive buckle menacingly.

The man with the knife and the quirt, who wore a sombrero, almost danced forward, grinning. "Maybe you've heard of me," he shouted in Spanish, "Rico Sanchez Rojas."

Paco shook his head. "You are not known, but since you gave me your name, I am Paco Morales Esteves."

"Paco Morales?" The bandit's eyes widened momentarily then his grin returned. "I kill you, then I will be a known man. Where do you want to be buried?"

Paco grinned back savagely. "En su madre."

The quirt suddenly flicked out at Paco's face then the knife swept in a vicious arc that almost touched the front of his shirt. As the man slashed backhanded, Paco dodged again then caught the ends of the quirt and yanked the man off-balance.

Before he could follow up the advantage he had to sidestep and duck to avoid the buckle, which hissed over his head near enough for him to feel it graze his hair. Stepping in close, he punched the bandit in the throat then, side-stepping again, grabbed the man's jacket and jerked it down, trapping his arms.

He had to retreat again as he was lashed across the side of his face by the quirt. As the bandit slashed again with his knife, Paco kicked under the arc of sharp steel, catching the bandit in the short ribs, and struck out at the hand holding the knife. The heavy blade fell to the ground but before he could snatch it up, the quirt cut across his face again, this time barely missing his eyes.

He didn't see the kick that knocked him off his feet, then he was face-down on the ground and the bandit was on his back, trying to strangle him with the quirt. Paco struggled then went limp as he saw the knife lying just two feet beyond his reach.

As Paco went limp, Sanchez hesitated just long enough for Paco to catch the base of the quirt and roll, taking the bandit with him. Both men reached for the knife but Paco snatched it up and, twisting in the other man's grip, plunged it to the hilt in the bandit's chest.

Using the knife almost as a pry-bar, he levered the corpse away and rolled to his feet. The other man had finally struggled out of his jacket and brought up an arm—too late. Paco slashed across his enemy's throat. Blood spurted from the severed artery and the man died without a scream.

Paco heard the sound of shots and spun to see the one called Julio, guarding the prisoner, swing up his rifle. Paco flipped the knife, caught it by the blade, and threw it at the guard.

~ * ~

Reynaud tasted bile in his mouth as he limped toward the bandits. Out of the corner of his vision he saw a man move toward Paco, on his right, while a large, stocky man confronted Hasteen on his left.

"I ain't killed an Injun before," the man grunted. "You two dance with the hydromatic coon-ass; I want this 'un myself."

One of the men whirled the stick he carried so the Cajun could clearly hear the noise it made. Reynaud was afraid; he knew he was facing pain and, perhaps, death. With his ankle, he couldn't run, and knew he couldn't run anyway because his friends needed him and whatever he could do to help, even if it was only to stall the two facing him, to keep them from being able to immediately attack the others.

The man with what looked like a sledgehammer handle sprang forward, swinging wildly, and Reynaud was forced to give ground, almost falling with the pain in his ankle, then his fear was transmuted. The unfairness of this battle burned. These bastards, who outnumbered him and his group, were going to beat them to death without even allowing them a drink of the water flowing less than a hundred feet away. The fear had all been burned away by his fury. After dodging another swing, he rushed.

He drove his fist into the bandit's belly then screamed as he was kidney-punched by the bandit who'd circled behind him. A strong arm caught him around the neck. The Cajun kicked back, slamming his spurs into the bandit's shin and raking his leg then swung his elbow back, catching the man in the pit of the belly. The hold on him loosened.

The man with the stick stepped forward and swung again, giving Reynaud just enough time to duck before the club whistled over him and struck the other bandit with a cracking sound. Reflexively, Reynaud tried to move back but tripped on the corpse still clinging to him, and fell. Twisting as he went down, he fell to his hands and knees. He'd just started to roll to his right when a kick landed along his ribs and lateral muscles and threw him back to the ground.

Rolling again, he snatched at the ground, his clawing hand clutching up some loose sand and dust, which he flung into the face of the man with the club. The man howled and, after wiping his face, changed his grip so he was holding the haft near the ends with both hands. With a curse, the man threw himself at Reynaud, his arms extended. With desperation lending strength, Reynaud managed to catch the stick with both hands and tried to keep it away from his throat but slowly, inexorably, the outlaw pressed down.

Whipping his leg around, Reynaud raked the man's leg with his spurs. The man stifled a moan but he flinched from the pain of the gash in his leg. Reynaud felt one end of the stick tremble and he shoved up on that side.

It was enough to overbalance his enemy and Reynaud rolled on top, frantically twisting at the sledge handle. For a long moment they struggled for the stick then it spun away.

The fury had risen in Reynaud until he was almost blind in his rage. His hands groped and fumbled until they found the bandit's throat then they seized it, trying to crush the windpipe. The Cajun heard a growling noise then realized it was coming from his own throat.

His grip tightened and he felt a fist crash into the side of his head as the man under him fought for his life. The pain seemed to madden Reynaud even more and he decided if he died he'd take this bastard to Hell with him, his fingers still locked on the bandit's throat. Another blow hit him just over his left eye and blood ran, obscuring what little vision he had with a veil of red, but he knew there was nothing the man could do, short of killing him, that would make him release his grip. The man under him convulsed until it was like riding a thunderhead but his hands only clamped tighter.

Still clutching his enemy's neck Reynaud pounded the man's head against the ground twice then, at the third time, heard gunshots. He realized the shots were coming from his right then he rolled to his left, taking cover behind the bandit, his hands still locked on the man's throat.

~ * ~

As Hasteen moved to Reynaud's left, he tried to think of some way to reach the derringer in his ankle boot without attracting the attention of the riflemen. He also had another problem. He'd never really learned to fight with his hands. All the trouble he'd survived had ended, and almost began, in gunfire. His only possible advantages were his reflexes and his quick hands.

When he heard the heavyset man single him out, he immediately stepped forward. The outlaw came to meet him, his right fist cocked back, then suddenly his left had shot out at Hasteen's face.

Hasteen was barely able to see the trick in time to catch the man's fist in his hand, slowing the punch and directing it to the side then doubled over in pain as the stocky man drove his knee into Hasteen's crotch and followed through with his right fist to Hasteen's head.

Hasteen gasped as the knee slammed into him and the world seemed to explode into star-shot black as the side of his head was hammered. Losing his grip on the bandit's left hand, he sprawled on the ground. Some part of him knew he had to keep moving, and he tried to roll into the fall.

A boot hit him a glancing blow along the side of the head and he rolled again, trying to get distance and a chance to let his head clear. He saw the boots striding after him. Crooking one of his own feet behind the nearer boot, he kicked out at the knee with his other foot.

The outlaw went down and Hasteen scrambled after him. Remembering how he'd been hurt, he slammed his knee into the bandit's groin. The outlaw screamed like a gutted horse and flailed with his fists. Hasteen tried to blink away a constellation as a punch split the skin over his cheekbone.

The fist opened and the fingers probed at his eyes. Hasteen jerked his head away and, as the hand fumbled after him, snatched the joint of the thumb in his teeth and bit down.

Hasteen suddenly realized he'd forgotten the derringer in his boot. He raised his knee again but this time the bandit blocked it with a leg. Still, bending his leg was enough to raise the bottom of his jeans over the top of his ankle boot. His teeth still clamped on the outlaw's thumb, he reached toward his boot but felt the derringer slip out and fall to the ground.

The man tried to jerk his thumb away and Hasteen bore down harder. Suddenly, the man was pummeling with both hands and Hasteen spat out the end of the thumb. The derringer was somewhere on the ground, and he was in a battle for his life. Hasteen got his arms up and blocked most of the blows, lashing out twice to slap the bandit across the eyes with stinging force but the man struggled on.

Hasteen saw the derringer just as he heard the shots.

~ * ~

As Logan went down, he groped under his Hawaiian-print shirt and whipped out the Charter Arms .44. The nearest bandit on the wall had started to swing up a shotgun and Logan fired rapidly, his third shot leaving a dark stain spreading across the front of the man's shirt. The shotgun bellowed and a minor dust storm erupted a couple of yards away.

Someone less than twenty feet away ran toward the wall

and Logan snapped off another shot. The body ran for two more steps before pitching forward. Seeing another guard ducking for cover, Logan fired his last shot, which kicked up a puff of rock dust a few inches from the bandit's arm.

~ * ~

Hasteen seized the derringer before Logan's third shot and, at point-blank range, shot the bandit still struggling with him. The bullet hole connected the heavy bars of the man's eyebrows. Still on the ground, Hasteen steadied his arm against his bent leg and put his second bullet into a bandit turning his rifle toward Logan. The slug went lower than Hasteen had intended, hitting the outlaw in the belly, just above his belt buckle.

~ * ~

The knife Paco had thrown struck the man called Julio in the chest. The bandit moaned and, with weak, trembling fingers, clutched at the knife's hilt, then stumbled backward, tripped, and fell. The prisoner he'd been guarding swept up Julio's dropped rifle and shot from the hip, finishing Julio, then raised the weapon and snapped a shot at the guard Logan had missed. The bandit, just recovering from dodging behind the wall, brought his own rifle up when the bullet spun him around and slammed him against the wall.

The prisoner worked the lever again, flinging another shell casing tumbling through the air, and fired again. At his next shot the bandit slid slowly down the wall, leaving a deep red smear on the stone.

Paco rushed the wall and caught up one of the carbines leaning there. Flicking the lever, he ejected a live round then swung the gun's sights to where, seventy yards away, the other two outlaws had been watering the horses. The freed prisoner shot one of them just as the man dashed for the cover of an oak. The man went down as though clubbed.

Paco looked for the other bandit, who seemed to have disappeared, then he saw the flash and heard the bark of a pistol. The man had hooked one foot in a stirrup and, clutching the saddle horn with one hand, had fired across the saddle with the other. Using the horse for cover, he presented too little of himself for Paco to shoot at without risking the horse. Instead, Paco sent a bullet into the water under the horse's nose. As the tiny waterspout erupted the horse whinnied and reared, throwing the man off.

The bandit surged to his feet and stumbled awkwardly through knee-deep water until he reached the bank. Paco let the man reach dry land before he squeezed off a carefully-aimed shot that took the man in the back of the head and stretched him out on the bank like a starfish.

~ * ~

Reynaud felt something tap him on the shoulder but only tightened his grip on his enemy's throat, then he heard Hasteen's voice next to his ear. "You can stop now. He isn't going to get any deader."

He finally released the body, although his fingers were almost too cramped to open, and Hasteen helped him to his feet. They looked around to find the others. All the bandits were down, and most seemed dead. Paco, by the wall, laid down a rifle and disappeared from view. Logan had just reached the top of the slope and hauled himself over the wall. Steve and the Deacon were busy peeling a corpse from Wade and were having to struggle to pull the dead man's arms apart. Gasping for air, Reynaud simply stared around him, hardly comprehending, then he broke into a shambling run toward the wall.

The slope seemed steeper than it looked then he clambered over the wall and lurched down to the river. As he neared the water's edge he stumbled and didn't even try to keep himself from falling, sprawling into the blessed clear water.

As he hit the water, all his cuts burned and stung, then the cold water numbed the pain of his torn and bruised skin. Every pore of his body seemed to be sucking up moisture. He had to push himself up out of the water as his heaving lungs demanded air. After several deep breaths he buried his face in the water again then drank from his cupped hands, feeling the relief in his throat and belly.

Hearing another gunshot, he raised himself from the water to look back toward the wall. The prisoner had shot at something on the other side of the wall. Reynaud sucked up one more mouthful of water and reluctantly dragged himself away from the creek. Hasteen and Steve had gathered the horses and the mule and led them away from the water before they could founder. Paco had already reached the wall. Pausing only to wrench the knife from the man he'd killed, he sprang over the wall.

Reynaud wanted to arm himself before facing a possible danger but the horses with their weapons were well out of reach, then he remembered the bandits had left their guns at the wall. Forcing himself into a trot, he found a pump shotgun lying at the base of the wall. Snatching up the gun, he peered over the wall. Paco, the bloodstained knife in his hand, had just turned away from one of the men who'd fought the Deacon. The bandit had been stabbed through the chest.

Paco leaned over another man who'd moaned. Grabbing the man's hair, he pulled the man's head up then plunged the blade into the side of the bandit's neck.

Wade, moving slowly and painfully, had reached the wall. "That's enough of that," he shouted.

Paco turned away from the corpses. "Is done." He bent and wiped the blade on the shirt of one of the bodies then strode toward the wall.

For a moment Wade looked as though he were going to reply then he nodded to the man they'd rescued. "Who're you?"

"Terry Banta." The man looked at his rescuers. "You boys look all done in—like you been rode hard and put away wet. Them bastards had a truck parked back there a ways beyond the crick. Had supplies enough for a couple meals for the lot of 'em."

"Sounds good," Wade said.

"Yeah," Terry said, "we got a little time to get squared away before things get serious."

Chapter 9

Barnes was studying a topographical map of the area when Collins knocked at his door, then stuck his head in. "Sorry to bother you, boss, but Kelly just got something on the radio, and he said I oughta let you know right away."

Barnes frowned at the map then stood and pulled on his heavy jacket. He was beginning to wonder if this Chambers wasn't some kind of Jonah. The day he'd arrived they'd lost a truck and a pumping station was put out of commission, then two trucks, headed for Sonora, had disappeared, and Sonora itself had been off the radio for the last two days. And now they were suffering through a dry Norther. The temperature had plummeted and the wind had risen with a vengeance.

As Barnes strode through the bar he pointed at Carson and gestured for him to follow, then stepped outside and hurried to the old store that served as their radio center. Kelly sat beside his radio, holding a cup of steaming mud that was only called coffee out of habit, and studying a notepad.

"You told Collins it was important. What's up?"

"Got a call from Bakersfield just a little bit ago." He took a sip of the mud. "Somebody from Sonora finally got to Bakersfield. They claimed Sonora got hit by twenty or thirty men on horseback. Had all kinds'a bombs and shit—" Kelly shrugged. "I'm only passing on what they said. That Sonora bunch is like a lazy yaller dog. If they was sittin' on a burr they'd sit and howl, too damn lazy to get off the sticker.

"Anyhow, the Sonora boys said they'd found the trucks. Said the place looked like a regular battlefield. They found the bodies of all five of our boys and two dead horses. And now Sanchez wants to know what you want 'im to do."

Barnes glanced at Carson, who started to roll himself a cigarette. Once it was drawing, Carson scowled at the smoke around his head. "It don't make a lotta sense. The rannies we been chasin' around here couldn't get together a party of more'n twenty or so riders, and they're hurtin' for supplies. We usually keep 'em on the run pretty good, but that's farther afield than they're likely to run."

"Anything else?" Barnes asked the radioman.

"Well, yeah." Kelly drained his cup and set it on the table beside the radio. "Sanchez was sayin' a truck patrol was runnin' late. They was supposed to breeze through Sheffield and check out Fort Lancaster, then sweep back to Bakersfield. They ain't come in yet."

"Get Sanchez on the blower," Barnes snapped.

Kelly picked up the mike and thumbed the transmit switch. "My boss wants to talk to your boss," he said into the mike.

A metallic voice from the speaker told them Sanchez was standing by, that he'd be at the mike in a minute.

Barnes began to pace. By "taxing" the Mex farmers who'd moved in after the plague, he'd been able to keep his men fed and, by leaving the farmers enough to go on with, he'd ensured he'd be able to feed them next year, too. Still, an example had to be made. He knew most of the farmers, although they kept their distance from the cowboys, actually supported them. He hadn't made it dangerous enough. If the farmers knew they'd suffer and their families would suffer for the cowboys' actions, he might be able to drive a wedge between the two groups.

"I'm here."

Barnes recognized Sanchez's voice. Snatching up the mike, he thumbed the switch. "How many riders you got, counting the ones in from Sonora?"

After a pause, "Forty-seven."

"Tomorrow mornin', fair weather or foul, I want you to take your riders to Sheffield and do the town. I don't care what you do there, as long as you don't leave anything alive. I don't even want dogs livin' in that place when you're done. Take everything worth haulin', especially food, and trash everything else."

Again a pause. "We have no trucks in running order."

"Then haul away what you take, even if you have to take it out on horseback and walk back to Bakersfield. I want this done. How many dismounted troops you got there?"

"Sixteen."

"That oughta be enough to hold the town till you get back. Do it." He handed the microphone to Kelly and heard Sanchez's "I understand." Barnes turned on his heel and trotted back to the bar and his office in the back of the building. Carson followed him in, took down a bottle of rye, opened it, and poured a glass for each of them.

Barnes took a deep drink of the whiskey then leaned back in his chair and put his feet up on the table he used for a desk. "How many workin' trucks we got here?"

"Two." Carson sat in a chair across the table from Barnes.

"It's getting' slim. Whether we drive cattle or not, we're gonna hafta ride north before long. Someplace greener."

"East Texas is rich pickin's," Carson observed.

"It's getting' riskier, too." Barnes replied. He finished his drink and refilled the glass, enjoying the warmth in his belly that seemed to be slowly spreading through him. "The Republic's getting' every town under them to form a militia, and they're slowly spreading west. I think it's time to move on."

"What do we do about the men?"

"Leave the barroom sweepin's and take only the best. We got what? Ninety—a hundred men here? Just pull the forty best. We can always get more men. Who wants to bust his back over a plow when he can ride with a gun and take what he wants? We need horses more'n we need men"

"That'd be another reason for headin' north," Carson agreed. After hesitating, he asked, "You want me to tell Chambers any of this?"

"Nah, it might queer the deal. At best, if he knew we were in trouble, he'd cut the price to us. He's the kind that kicks you when you're down, and pisses on you to boot. We don't tell him shit."

~ * ~

Reynaud stared down and ahead through slitted eyes. He was grateful for the dry clothes and the chaps he'd taken from the bandits. The leather leggings cut the wind and saved his legs from the worst of the sandpaper effects of the gale. The wind whistled through the rough country, scouring everything in sight with a fine sand.

They'd sent Terry back to his friends with a load of guns and ammunition they'd found in the bandits' equipment.

According to Terry, there were about thirty men, less one, from the Wilson ranch, the Smoky Mountain ranch, and the Allison ranch staying one step ahead of Barnes' goons and sometimes pulling an ambush. Further south, there were another twenty or so riders from the Longfellow ranch, the Big Canyon ranch, and the Prosser spread, as well as four or five more from the Six Shooter, all waging the same kind of guerrilla warfare.

Terry and his partner, Pete Rodriquez, and three riders had come to Fort Lancaster to water up and had been caught by the bandit patrol. One of the other men had been hit but had gotten away, but Terry's horse had been shot out from under him. Rodriguez had come back to help and been shot out of the saddle and, before Terry could mount, he'd taken a bullet across the side of the head.

When he'd come to, he was being questioned between punches and kicks.

Wade was sure Terry had no broken bones, although he looked as though he'd been pitched off a mountain and dragged.

Terry had grinned at Wade's diagnosis. "Hell, I ain't even spittin' serious blood. I been throwed harder than this and I still went on to ride the horse. The people you oughta worry about are the farmers back in Sheffield. It's the nearest town, and Barnes is a real sore loser. He's gonna hit that place so hard you'd have trouble findin' two sticks together."

Glancing at the others, Reynaud had seen the unspoken agreement. So Banta had been sent, riding Rodriguez' horse and leading the mule carrying some of the booty guns and ammunition, to rejoin his friends, while the group was to ride to Sheffield. Logan was to follow them later, driving the truck carrying supplies and the rest of the captured weapons. According to what Terry had told them, they'd need every gun and every round of ammunition when Barnes' men came calling.

Reynaud tried to adjust the bandana around his face so it chafed his cuts and bruises less, but found his face seemed to be one massive bruise. Some of the others looked even worse than he felt. Both Paco and Hasteen wore faces looking as though they'd been chosen off a butcher's tray, and Wade's nose was swollen from a head-butt. Wade was also moving awkwardly, although he claimed no ribs had been broken.

The storm had cut the visibility to only a few feet, just enough to let them see they were still following the highway. Terry had guessed the town to be about fifteen miles from the fort and Reynaud tried to estimate how much of that they'd covered but gave up. He couldn't be sure how long they'd been riding. The wind might've come straight from the Arctic Circle, and he supposed the temperature was barely above freezing, if that.

The wind finally began to slacken and the visibility improved, although the dust and sand still irritated his eyes. He was simply trying to keep the horse and himself moving when Wade stood in his stirrups and raised his hand then pointed to a dim shape in the curtain of dust. Wade dismounted and the others did the same then walked, leading their horses to a crumbling building of adobe. As they drew nearer they could make out another building beyond it.

Relieved to be out of the wind, Reynaud pulled his bandanna off and tried to wipe his horse's eyes free of dust then untied the cloth over its nose. Turning, he saw the rest of the group also taking care of their horses and most of them had let the bandannas hang loosely at their necks, exposing battered, red-eyed faces.

Reynaud grinned then winced at the pain caused by the expression. "I don't know how much luck we're going to have convincing the locals we're friendly. We might have an easier time scaring them into cooperation." He'd feel better leaving the horses with the Deacon but Billy Joe's distaste for the animals made him a poor choice. "Steve, you stay here and tend the horses. Flag Logan down if he gets here before somebody gets back to you. Wade, what do you think's the best way to find the locals?"

"The easiest way to do it is just walk down the street, line abreast. Whoever's on the ends can listen at the doors and shutters. If they's any trouble, which isn't likely, we'll all be handy. Another question—who talks for us?"

Reynaud nodded at Paco. "According to Terry, the settlers here are Mexicans, and my Spanish is pretty rusty."

Paco, wearing a sombrero taken from one of the dead bandits, drew his pistol, checked the chamber and made sure the action was clear of grit. "If any of Barnes' *porcos* are in town, I'll let this talk for us."

They walked into the street, Paco in the middle of the line, Reynaud on the left flank and Wade on the right. Reynaud had brought his shotgun and the Deacon carried his rifle and its grenade launcher at the ready. The others carried only their pistols, which they left holstered. Reynaud listened at the doors and shuttered windows they passed but heard nothing over the moaning of the wind. Ahead of him, he could just distinguish a taller building than the ones they'd passed by, then saw the building had a steeple.

Abruptly, Wade signaled the rest of the group and stopped beside a door. Hasteen, between Wade and Paco, moved to the other side of the door while the Deacon followed Paco directly to the door. Taking a final look around, Reynaud hurried to follow Billy Joe.

~ * ~

Paco tried the door, swung it open, and stepped inside. Eighteen or twenty men sat around a long table, talking together in low voices. A crude bar stood near the wall to the left and, as he entered, a balding, heavyset man wearing an apron stood. Most of the men looked as though they'd been caught doing something embarrassing while the others stared with hard, bright eyes.

"You'd better be ready to get out of your town, or be prepared to fight for it," Paco said, in Spanish.

For a moment, every man at the table seemed to have something to say then the one with the apron asked, "You're not with the bandits?"

Paco only shook his head.

"Fight with what?" A lean man with a thick, drooping moustache and a scar that left a gap in his left eyebrow slammed his fist on the table. "There are not more than four guns in our entire village."

Paco gestured at the others, who'd followed him into the cantina. "My friends and I can bring guns, if you can bring the courage."

A short man with gray hair and a deeply lined face shouted back, "We have the courage but we also have families. What will become of them?"

"Nothing," Paco replied, "if you get them out of town or have safe places for them here."

The man with the apron walked around behind the bar. "What will you have to drink?"

"What do you have?"

"Homemade beer, a little tequila, and some wine."

"Beer for everyone but him," Paco said, indicating the Deacon. "He drinks only water."

As the bartender set bottles on the bar and removed the caps with an opener he asked, "How soon will the bandits be here?"

Paco sipped the beer which, while thick and with a strong aftertaste, tasted like the best drink he'd ever had. "Not before morning. Probably in the afternoon."

"Why do you think they're coming here at all?" demanded the short man.

Paco turned to face the men at the table, his elbows resting behind him on the bar. "Because they just lost twenty men at Fort Lancaster, and a horseman called Terry Banta said the bandits would have to try to save face by wiping out your town. I believe him."

The babble at the table started again then the short man stood, facing Paco. "You and these others killed some of the bandits and now you want us to share your troubles?"

"No," Paco said in a flat voice. "Barnes will decide about your town, not us, and his bandits will come whether we are here or not. If you wish to leave, then leave. If you want to fight, we are ready to fight beside you."

As the short man stood, undecided, the lean man spoke. "Sit down, Luis. Or go. I will fight, even if I have to fight with a mattock." He looked around at the others at the table. "If I die, I will die quick and all at once. We have been dying here, a little at a time, since the bandits started taking our crops, along with anything else they wanted. I will hide my woman from them one last time, but I will not swallow my pride again."

The other men showed their approval, some with grim nods, one or two of the younger ones with shouts.

"I would not celebrate too loudly or too soon," Paco said. "No one has died yet. It would be wiser to find out how you feel about this battle after it is done. Some of you may die, some of us may die as well. We have not yet won the battle, just made sure it will be a battle and not a massacre." He looked at the men closely then turned to stare at the rest of the group. "Hasteen, go bring Steve in. I'm sure he's thirsty, too."

As Hasteen secured the latigo on his hat more tightly and stepped out into the dying gale, one of the younger villagers asked, "What kinds of guns do you have?"

"You will see when my friend brings our truck and our horses. We do need a place, not far from here, where we can hide the truck and our horses."

"There is such a place, along the river, to the west," the lean man said. "I will show you. I am called Marco Sandoval Garcia."

Paco introduced himself and the rest of the group. They'd just finished when Hasteen returned with Steve and Logan, all laden with rifles and shotguns, which they laid on the bar.

"The wind seems to be dying," Hasteen observed. "If Barnes' cavalry leaves Bakersfield tonight, they might be here at dawn." He went outside again for more guns.

~ * ~

Reynaud, Paco, and Wade passed the weapons around. They had enough long arms to give most of the men in the cantina a rifle or shotgun and passed out pistols to the others. Hasteen chose another pair of single-action revolvers to add to his own. "Reloading takes longer than I like. Any gun battle with this many bandits will likely be brisk work."

Steve helped Reynaud, Paco, and Wade acquaint the farmers with their weapons while one of the older men showed Logan and Hasteen a place to hide the truck and the horses. Most of Steve's help took the form of translating for Wade, whose Spanish was limited and hideously accented, and he became aware of how different his Spanish was from that of the villagers, but he also felt the farmers accepted him.

These villagers were men for whom life had never been easy. They had little education and most of them had been doing men's work since boyhood. Their labor was hot and dry, and the results always in doubt. If the river ran dry their crops would wither in the fields and a wind like the one earlier could flatten most of a season's work, but still they worked on.

He was impressed by their dogged determination. Wade had chosen a life that brought him face-to-face with death daily, but it'd been a choice, and he'd been well-trained for that life. Paco had made much the same choice out of conviction and had learned what he needed to survive. Hasteen, as nearly as Steve could determine, simply worked to be the best man alive with a gun, and he'd absorbed the skills he needed. The rest of the group had been soldiers. Granted, they'd been trained for a different sort of combat, one waged at twice the speed of sound, using electronic eyes and ears, but a soldier is still a fighter. It's what he's paid for.

These people weren't warriors by training or inclination. They fought, or would fight, only because they had to fight for their families and the land and the work they'd return to again—those who weren't killed or maimed. With all these things in mind, Steve felt these farmers were the ones with the truest courage.

By the time the men hiding their horses and the truck had returned, the men in the cantina had been taught to load and charge the guns they'd been given. He noticed Wade and Paco had been careful to give the selective-fire weapons to older men. Paco checked each weapon and had each man dry-fire his gun several times before they finally stopped for dinner.

A middle-aged man, whose gray moustache parenthesized his mouth, introduced himself to Steve as Raul and invited Steve to share dinner with his family and himself, and Steve noticed each of the others had also been offered dinner at the home of a different family.

The wind had indeed fallen, he observed, as he followed Raul into the street and to a small adobe house near the edge of town. The place was dimly lit by a kerosene lamp. Two women, their backs to the door, bent over whatever work they were doing and a boy, who might be eight, jumped up from where he'd sat in the corner to stare wide-eyed at the rifles Raul and Steve had leaned against the wall.

Raul shook his head, a warning to the boy. "Those are not to be touched. They are loaded, and ready for killing."

The house was warm enough to allow them to remove

their coats. "Esteban, this is my wife, Constanza, my cousin Juanita. And the boy is my nephew, Jorge. Constanza, this man and his friends have come to warn us the bandits will come tomorrow to kill us all. He and his friends have brought guns, and they are going to stay to help us fight. After we have eaten, we must return to the cantina to plan for the return of the bandits. You must be ready to go to a safe place before dawn."

Steve warmed to hear his name in Spanish, and he bowed awkwardly to the strangers. "I am called Esteban Villareal Navarro." It felt as though he'd earned the right to the name.

The women turned around and carried hot food from the stove to the table. Constanza was about the same age as Raul, with broad streaks of silver in her heavy black hair, while Juanita was much younger. Steve was struck by her lustrous dark eyes and the grace with which she moved.

"Gracias, senora y senorita," he said.

"De nada," Constanza replied.

Steve noticed how her hands trembled slightly and her face showed strain. He sat in the chair Raul pointed out to him and ate, like the others, in silence. The meal provided only nutrition, companionship being lost in the tension that sat, like an extra guest, at the table.

Juanita finally smiled at Steve, a tentative warming of her face. "You must forgive us, *senor*," she said in Spanish. "We are not used to company, and our cares are usually less immediate."

Steve returned the smile. "You have no need to apologize. The news I bring is not the sort welcome in any home." He wanted to say more but could think of nothing that wouldn't sound like a boast or an empty platitude.

The others at the table only picked at their food but Steve, hungry from the last several days' short rations, and Jorge, who enjoyed the appetite of youth, ate well. Steve was surprised at what could be accomplished with a little cornmeal, rabbit meat, squash, peppers, and *frijoles*. When he'd finished he leaned back with a sigh. "That was excellent. All the meals I've eaten lately were cooked by men, or not cooked at all. Thank you."

"We had best return to the cantina now, *senor*," Raul said.

Reluctantly, Steve got to his feet, put on his coat, and picked up the G-3. "I will hope to see you again later," he said to the women and the boy, then followed Raul back to the cantina.

Inside the cantina, everyone was sitting or standing around the long table, with Reynaud sitting at one end, Wade beside him. Logan gestured at an empty chair beside him. Two of the villagers laid out a map drawn with sand on the table top, with an occasional argument between them or with one of the other farmers, then a line might be brushed away and replaced, until everyone was satisfied it was properly placed.

Finally the men leaned back and pronounced the work finished.

Steve studied the map, recognizing the double row of rectangles as representing the buildings along the street outside. The large rectangle near the middle was obviously the church across the street, the smaller box facing it standing for the cantina itself. At one end lay a broken square that must represent the ruined house in which they'd kept the horses when they'd arrived.

"Which way will the bandits come?" Reynaud asked. "The first thing we must know is the way they will ride into town."

Paco translated for the Cajun, then Marco's reply. "Sometimes they come from the west, but most often they ride in from the east. Once, they came from both sides at once."

Wade took a sip of beer and gestured with the bottle. "They're more likely to come in from the east, if they use the road at all. Remember, they're riding from Bakersfield, which is that way." He indicated what would be the northeast edge of the map. "If they get here early in the mornin', the smart thing would be to come in from the east, to keep the sun at their backs. If they think there's any chance of a fight, they'll want all the odds in their favor. If they come in later in the day, they're prob'ly gonna send some 'a their riders wide around and come in from both sides. That's the easiest way to make sure no one gets away."

"If you were doing it, how would you go about it?" Reynaud asked

Wade stood and walked around the table, pointing out locations as he named them. "If I was Sanchez, the first thing

I'd do is put a few men with rifles in that place we left the horses. I'd also put a couple-three in a coverin' position at the other end of the street, and when I hit town, one'a the first places I'd run people would be the church. A man or two in the bell tower can cover most of the village."

"That makes it tough," the Cajun observed. "If we put men in the places they're likely to post their sharpshooters, we're liable to blow the element of surprise, and if we don't get our people in those places, Sanchez's snipers can shoot us to pieces."

"It's not as bad as that," Wade replied. "We don't need men in those places, just in position to blow the sharpshooters away before they can do too much damage. The only place we really need to have a man is in the bell tower. McCluskey, you've been getting' pretty good with that bloop tube. You think you could lob a long bomb into that place—" he indicated the broken rectangle "—from the bell tower?"

"With His hand guiding me."

Wade suppressed a grin. "I'll take that as a 'yes.' Now, if we leave the three buildin's at the other end of town empty but set up some kinda booby-trap, we got the worst of it taken care of."

"That gives us a fighting chance," Reynaud said. "Nothing more."

"That's right," Wade agreed. "I'm in law enforcement, not the insurance business, and I can't provide us with a sure thing. Now, we'll need at least one good gun in the church, to cover McCluskey. He'll be able to use the tower as a firing platform but he won't be able to cover his own back."

Reynaud placed a beer bottle cap in the square representing the bell tower. "We'll pick the back-up man later. Where else are we going to be needed?"

Wade nodded toward the middle of the table. "The first place most'a them will want to hit'll be the church and the cantina, so they'll be a lotta them clumped in that area. It'd be nice to set up a cross-fire, but it's not gonna be easy. If we all shoot from the same side, we're a lot less likely to wind up shootin' each other and other friends, but we can't afford to turn over half the town to them. An L-shaped crossfire would be almost as good but we can't do that, either."

"As long as they're mounted," Hasteen said, "it'll be easier to shoot the bandits without having to worry about hitting our own people, because we'll be shooting up."

Wade nodded. "Good point."

"I'll take the front of the cantina," Hasteen said, with a glance at Reynaud.

Reynaud said nothing but placed another bottle cap at the front of the square for the cantina.

Logan stroked his beard and grinned. "If it's all the same to you, Rennie, I'd like to cover Hasteen's flank from here." He pointed to the first building west of the cantina.

Paco finished translating and pointed at the church. "We should have a man inside the church, and another man outside. The man outside will try to stop anyone coming in the front door but if we are outflanked, there is a side door. With your permission, I will be in the front of the church. Reynaud, I would want you with your shotgun to cover me and the side door."

Reynaud placed more bottle caps around to show each man at his position.

Steve studied the arrangement and frowned. "We seem to have everyone bunched together. Barnes' men will try to scatter through the buildings at the first sign of trouble, and digging them out again is going to be nasty, dangerous work."

After studying the map, Wade said, "Barnes' men will likely be bunched toward the middle of town, and we've got to protect the Deacon. He's our artillery. But we also don't want the bandits to get a chance to burrow too deeply into the outer sections of town, either. I'll set up shop here." He placed a cap halfway between the church and the eastern edge of town. "Steve, I suggest you take up a position near the two buildin's we're gonna leave empty on that side'a the street. That way, if any of the bandits get inside, you can keep 'em pinned down. I'd feel better, though, if you had a couple men to back you up, one facin' the street, the other coverin' the back door."

"I will stay with him," Raul said.

"Good." Steve had noticed most of the men in the village looked to Marco as a leader. "What do you suggest?"

Marco looked at his hands. "You are the ones who know war best, but the village is ours, and ours is the responsibility for it. I would put the women and children in these buildings," he said, running his finger along the sand lines between the church and Wade's bottle cap. "And here," this time he took in the buildings between the cantina and the house opposite Wade's position. "Each of these houses should have a man at front and back." He named ten of the men to hold those houses. "That leaves Ramon and Jaime to help defend the rest of the village."

Reynaud frowned at the caps and the sand map. "We need another dozen men." He shrugged. "Wade, where do you want those two?"

Wade glanced at each of them. "Jaime, you got an M-16. I want you to take that first house west of where Logan'll be. Use automatic fire to spray down the street between you and the far end of town. Reid, as soon as you've finished your work in the middle of town. You help Jaime. Paco, you do the same on your side'a the street then move east to cover the area between the church and our flank. Deacon, you support them unless Rennie or I call a shot to you. Ramon, you take cover in the house opposite mine and down one. That'll put you with only two buildin's between you and Steve and his back-up. Y'oughta be able to give each other mutual support."

"It's decided, then." Reynaud said. He looked from one villager to another. "I want you all to get familiar with your weapons, know where you're going to be, know what cover you have and what areas you can cover with your fire."

Even the younger men quickly lost their exuberance as they began to fully realize that within hours they'd be in a battle for their lives and the lives of their families and neighbors.

As the men were getting used to the feel of their weapons and trying to absorb the advice he was giving them, Reynaud turned to Wade. "I just wish we could let each of them fire a few rounds, just to let them get used to the noise and the recoil. A gun battle is a sorry place for on-the-job training."

"I'll go along with that," Wade replied, "but we don't have the shells for it. From the ammo we took off the corpses back at Fort Lancaster, I'd guess Barnes and his bully-boys are low on ammo and maybe some other supplies, too. The ones I've seen so far haven't impressed me as prosperous types."

Steve looked back at the farmers practicing snapping the long arms to their shoulders then staring down the sights to see how closely they'd pointed to cracks in the wall and other targets. "Some of them will do pretty well. All the guns they had were ancient, and they still managed to bring in meat for their families."

Stretching, Steve groaned. "It's been a long day and we're going to have to be up before dawn in the morning. And there'll probably be a dozen unexpected jobs to do before the village will be ready for company." He covered a yawn with the back of his hand. "I'm going to turn in before I fall down."

"I know how you feel." Reynaud turned his head, "Paco, please tell everyone here to call it a day. Tell them they must be at their positions half an hour before dawn, and they should have their families in the safe places by the same time."

The group broke up slowly but Steve and Raul were among the first to leave. As Steve followed the farmer out the door, he said, "Your wife seems not to like me."

"It is not you Constanza dislikes," Raul answered slowly. "It is the coming battle. She is afraid."

"She shows good sense." Even in the cold night air, Steve was barely able to keep plodding forward, putting one unsteady foot in front of the other.

After a long pause, Raul said, "Women are very different from men. Women want each day to be very like the day before, even if they must pay a price in hard work each day. We men, we know that if times are good, we will have to fight to keep what we have gained—the good times must end. Even bad times will often be followed by worse. Women fear a battle more than work. For men, as much as they may frighten us, combat is better than a lifetime of hard labor."

Raul chuckled. "For women, the great fear is of the fight, which may take away their loved ones. For men, the greatest terror is that there will be no change at all."

They arrived at Raul's house. Raul opened the door and they saw the women and Raul's nephew waiting for them in the dim light of a candle. Raul explained to them they must rise early and they should take water and food with them to the safe house. "Take water for the entire day, and food that can be eaten cold."

Constanza replied by showing him water jars and packets lined up to be carried out at a moment's notice.

"We can prepare without this man," Juanita said, motioning with her head at Steve. "He needs rest." Taking his arm, she led him to a pallet on the floor.

Steve sank to the mattress. He had no idea what it was stuffed with, but it could've been made of boilerplate and still would have felt as welcome as a downy couch. Taking off his gun belt and shoulder holster, he placed them by his head then bent and worked at pulling off his boots. He struggled feebly with them then Juanita helped, tugging sharply until the boots were finally jerked free. A surge of relief swept through him and he moaned with satisfaction. He heard himself say, *"Gracias."*

From what seemed a great distance, he seemed to hear a soft voice say, *"De nada."*

~ * ~

Paul Baker stared at the lines of the graph, comparing them to bars on graphs from as long ago as three months. Not much difference. He cleared the screen, removed the disc, and powered down the computer. Rubbing his eyes with the heels of his hands, he leaned back in the chair. The man called Chambers strolled into the small computer room and sat down in the chair facing the other console. "How is it coming?"

"We think we can make the bacteria more resistant to penicillin but Cipro is harder, and the virulence and the incubation period are even more difficult to change." Baker stood. "May I see my son?"

Chambers studied him with calculating eyes then shrugged. "For a short time. You may have ten minutes."

Baker considered arguing but knew it was useless, and it might jeopardize even the brief visit. Chambers got to his feet and walked with Baker, staying to his right. Baker had noticed the grenade on the belt, and the pistol, now worn openly in a hip holster.

Apparently, Chambers was cautious about letting Baker too near a weapon. That was interesting and encouraging. Baker had been in the army and he recognized the grenade for what it was. Immediately, he began to play with ideas. If worse came to worst, he could try to find some way to trap Chambers in some situation where he couldn't defend himself.

They'd walked through the lab and reached the living quarters. Chambers took a key from his pocket and unlocked a door, swung it open, and followed Baker into a small bedroom. Wayne looked up from a book he'd been reading then sprang toward his father.

Baker held his son closely for several minutes, time when he couldn't trust his voice. Finally he maneuvered Wayne into a chair and sat down on the edge of the bed, facing him. "How are you doing?" The question seemed foolish to him, even as he asked it, but at least it was something to say, something to break the silence.

"All right, I guess," Wayne mumbled. After a pause, he asked. "Why are we here? What are they doing to you?"

"Not much," Baker replied. "They just needed me to help them develop an anthrax serum. I'm doing some research for them."

"Then why didn't they just ask you, dad? Heck, you'd have helped them if you'd known it was going to do good for people."

Baker gave Chambers, leaning against the wall, an ironic smile. "They just didn't know me that well. I think we're beginning to get things ironed out now, but it may take a while. Are they feeding you all right?"

"Good as can be expected, I s'pose." Wayne said, "but I get bored just sittin' here with nothin' to do. Mosta the books they got are dull."

Chambers stepped away from the wall. "We must be getting back to research right away, Dr. Baker."

Baker ignored the statement and the man. "You just hang tough, Wayne. We'll see if we can't get you out of here pretty soon. You take care." As he stood, he embraced his son again. He wanted to tell Wayne "I love you" but he knew it would embarrass his son, particularly with the other man in the room, so all he said was, "You take care of yourself, y'hear?" He finally released the boy and walked from the room, Chambers at his heels.

"What's the harm in letting the boy go outside once in a

while?" he asked as they walked down the corridor. "Or letting him have something to do?"

"I'm afraid, Dr. Baker, that facilities here are a bit limited. If you do well tomorrow, I will let you have more time with him."

"Look, how long are you going to keep us here? The military was working on the same things you're playing with. They had years to work on it, and I haven't seen any evidence they'd ever gotten much further on it than we have. Hell, they even had equipment for gene-splicing. We haven't got anything like that here, and nobody who could use it if we did. These 'assistants' you've given me seemed to have honed their research skills on a Mr. Wizard science set and never gotten very far past that."

"As for time," "Chambers" answered, "we have approximately two months in which to prepare for the drive."

As much as he was shocked by the short time in which he had to work on a project that could easily take decades, Baker was relieved to learn he had some time to plan a way for his son and he to escape and, if possible, destroy the laboratory and the lethal bacteria in it. In such a span of time, even Chambers must drop his guard for a moment, or make some mistake that'd give Baker a chance to take action.

The biggest problem was finding some way to let Wayne know he must be prepared to run at a moment's notice. Baker accepted the fact his own survival was iffy, and not as crucial as his son's getting away.

Chambers was probably the most dangerous man Baker had ever met. Almost any plan he might devise must involve killing Chambers first. His "assistants" seemed to carry no guns, but Baker knew at least three other men in the compound carried rifles and pistols.

He sat at the computer again, powered up, replaced the disc, and tried to project the results of feeding bacteria killed by penicillin to live bacteria.

Chapter 10

Chernikov stood leaning against the wall, his arms crossed, studying Baker. The man was so transparent, and so easy to manipulate. He'd already become addicted to a lethal drug—hope. Baker would work hard to convince his captor he was docile, while all the time he'd be looking for any opportunity to kill Chernikov and escape.

Had he only needed Baker's presence or some information, it would've been easy enough to break him, but since he wanted the man's cooperation, at least for the next month and a half, hope was the key. At the end of that time he'd provide Baker a chance to attack him then kill the man. It wasn't really necessary to give Baker such a chance but it could provide a bit of diversion.

He had no intention of infecting Baker or his son with anthrax—unless it became necessary. The disease was too dangerous, too difficult to control. No, snapping their necks was efficient and neat.

Chernikov waited over an hour, as motionless and emotionless as a sunning lizard. At last he said, "That is enough for today." He watched closely as Baker took the steps to close down the computer for the night, then escorted him to his room and locked the door behind him.

He had other matters to attend before going to his own bed. He tapped on Robbins' door and walked in. The man who was supposed to be head of security for the compound had just unbuckled his gun belt and laid it beside his cot but, at the knock, he'd moved with commendable speed and pointed his revolver at Chernikov's chest.

"What do you want, Chambers?" The man lowered the pistol but kept it pointed in Chernikov's direction.

"I just wanted to see that you'd been doing your job. I noticed earlier you had no one listening at the radio."

"What's to listen to? The military post by San Antone uses secure radios, and nothing further east is liable to bother us here."

"I don't give reasons for my orders, but what may bother us here is Barnes. That's why I wanted someone to listen in on his frequency." He glanced disdainfully at the pistol, then at Robbins' face.

After hesitating just a moment, Robbins slipped the revolver into his belt. "Barnes ain't likely to kill the goose layin' gold eggs, and if he did, why'd he want anyone to know about it?"

"There are any number of other useful bits of information his men might provide. For instance, I noticed, going through Sonora, they had a radio transmitter there, too. Intercepting radio traffic from Sonora would let us know of anything happening in the east."

Robbins' brow furrowed as he attempted to convey the impression he was thinking. "Yeah, I see what you mean. I'll take care of it, first thing in the mornin'."

Chernikov smiled. "No need to worry about that. I'll talk to your lieutenant—I believe his name is Nagle—about it. I never give the same orders to a man the second time."

Robbins suddenly perceived Chernikov's intentions and his own danger. His hand dropped to the butt of the pistol but, before his fingers could grip it, Chernikov had broken his wrist. A blow to his throat stunned him and made it impossible for him to make any sound louder than a weak croak. He tried to shove the big man away but Chernikov deflected the push and clapped both cupped hands over Robbins' ears.

"Since you couldn't seem to listen to your orders when I gave them to you, we must give you an excuse for not hearing." Chernikov knew he was now speaking only for his own benefit. Blood ran from both of Robbins' ears, and more in a thin stream from the man's nostrils.

Chernikov glanced at the table, on which lay a pen and pencil set and several forms, blank side up. He seized the pen and pencil. "We must do something to clear out those ears." He slammed the pen over half its depth into Robbins' right ear, did the same with the pencil in the left ear.

For almost a full minute Robbins thrashed on the floor before the convulsions stopped and the body was still. Chernikov watched with detached amusement then he left to inform Nagle of his promotion and to order him to have the corpse dragged out and the mess cleaned.

~ * ~

Steve felt someone shake his shoulder and tried to reach his pistols, only to discover he was wrapped in two or three blankets.

"Relax, *senor,*" a soft voice said. "It is only me. It is time to rise."

Steve stopped struggling and crawled out of the blankets, which had been placed over him as he slept. Rubbing the sleep from his eyes, he stared up at Juanita, grinning sheepishly. "I'm sorry. I'm not used to being secure when I sleep."

Juanita handed him a cup of some sort of tea. "We understand, *senor.* For a man who lives with his gun, danger comes at any unguarded moment."

Steve sipped the tea, grateful for the warmth that went to his belly then seemed to spread through his limbs. "It wasn't always that way, and someday it'll be different again. There are many worse ways to live a life than in a village like this, raising a family." His gaze lingered on her face. Even early in the morning she was beautiful, with soft dark eyes and generous lips. Her cheekbones were high, her nose tilted, and her thick black hair flowed like water to the small of her back.

Suddenly, they were both uncomfortable. He tried to hide his embarrassment by checking both pistols before strapping on the holsters while Juanita began, unnecessarily, to rearrange the jars and packets.

After helping the family carry most of the water and food to the house Raul had chosen for his family, he took a single jug of water and packet of food where he was to wait for the bandits.

Finding a low table in the house, he moved it under the window he's chosen. On the table he placed the Beretta from his shoulder holster and the extra magazines for his G-3. Raul carried a chair over for him then crouched by the front door. A young man called Chico placed a pallet by the back door and lay on it on his belly, clutching the lever-action carbine he'd been given.

Steve stared out at the houses he was to watch. He could see most of the alley and the open window of the house to the west. Looking the other way, he could see the dark window of the house to the east, All the curtains had been taken from the windows of all the houses except the safe houses for the families and houses the group and villagers held. Looking out the door he could only see one corner of the house across the street which had been left empty and part of the house Wade had chosen.

After a time he saw wavering lights and once saw Wade's face in the glow and he guessed Wade and another man were moving through the buildings, preparing little surprises for the bandits.

Steve found a comfortable position then looked around the dim room, lit by a pair of candles. Raul and Chico had already stored everything flammable against one of the outer walls. The place was as ready for battle as they could make it.

He found himself thinking again about Juanita and having a real life again. The war was something in the past. Once Chernikov was safely dead, the war would finally be over for him, too. This village would be a good place to which he could return. And Juanita, he thought, might be glad to see him again, and there was no one he'd rather have care for him. There were few who would be glad to see him again, much less care for him.

Watching the sun rise in a sea of crimson, he gave his attention to what he could see of the horizon, watching for dust or any other sign of approaching riders. Several times, each of the men in the house stood and walked in their limited space, trying to warm themselves and exercise muscles grown cramped in what seemed an endless wait. They drank water from the jars and, late in the morning, Steve ate a handful of dried corn, washing it down with more water.

He guessed it was a little after noon when he when he saw dust rising like smoke then, after several minutes, the dust stopped rising. The hands holding his rifle were suddenly damp and he wiped them, one at a time, on his jacket. Minutes later he heard the clatter of hooves on the highway. The bandits were coming in from both sides.

He glanced at the two men with him and saw them cross themselves, and he copied the action.

~ * ~

Reynaud, still half-asleep, stumbled into the church and found Paco and Billy Joe waiting for him. He noticed Paco wore a second

Colt automatic in his waistband.

The Cajun had to fight the temptation, born of years of habit, to genuflect then realized the lamp Paco held and his candle were the only sources of light. No votive light burned by the altar.

"Good morning," Paco said. Glancing around the dark church, he grinned. "If it goes against us, this is as good a place as any to die. And I would have fooled my family. They would never believe I might die in the Church."

"Well," Reynaud said, with an answering grin, "don't be in too big a hurry to confound your relatives. The place may be right, but I'd say the time is wrong by a good twenty or thirty years."

"He will choose the time," the Deacon intoned, with a glance upward.

Reynaud grinned again. "I'm in no hurry if He isn't. Look at it on the bright side, Deak. If you buy it here, up in the bell tower, you'll have a head start to heaven."

The Deacon found the ladder leading to the tower, slung his rifle and a pack of supplies, and climbed into the darkness.

"You've had more experience with this kind of thing than I have," Reynaud said to Paco. "Where should I set up shop?"

Paco held up his lantern and waved it toward the left front corner. "I'll help you move pews for cover. From that position you can cover the front door and the door leading in from the sacristy. It would be better to have another man in the sacristy, but we have more places to defend than men."

They'd just started moving the heavy benches when Wade stepped through the church door. "Paco, I'm gonna need a little help."

"How about me?" Reynaud asked. "I can do anything requiring a middling back and a weak mind."

Wade shook his head. "I want you here. If the party starts sooner than I expect, I want you where you can cover McCluskey. Like I said last night, he's the nearest thing we got to heavy artillery."

While Paco was gone Reynaud finished his mini-fort of

pews and laid his rifle, with four stripper clips of ammunition, just behind the pews while he laid the shotgun and the bandolier across the pew that was the key to his defensive position.

Dawn had colored the sky, making the inside of the church appear even darker when Paco returned. He inspected the position Reynaud had prepared for himself. "Do you feel like Davy Crockett at the Alamo?"

In spite of his nerves, Reynaud laughed. "I didn't think the battle for the Alamo was one of the high points of Mexican history."

"Why not? We won, didn' we?" Paco lifted the water jar and took a deep drink. "When a han'ful of drunk soldiers can make you Anglos rewrite your history books, it is worth remembering."

"I'm not sure what you mean by 'you Anglos,' since I've never been mistaken for one by a real Anglo, but the way I heard the story, Santa Anna and thousands of Mexican soldiers besieged the place for thirteen days before they finally took it."

"It is a common misunderstanding," Paco replied. "That was how long the party last. A han'ful of soldiers were going back to camp from a fiesta in San Antonio when these crazy Texans shoot at them. Naturally, they were angry so they kick the place over."

Reynaud chuckled. "That certainly puts a different complexion on the story." He mused for a moment on history, both ancient and recent, then asked, "What kind of party streamers were you hanging for Barnes' men?"

Paco opened the door and sat down inside it. "Wade had some grenades from your visit to the army post, and set them with trip wires in the three houses on the eastern end of the street and two or three more houses to the west. One of the people who lived there before the war had left an old piano behind. We took some of the wires to use with the grenades, and we used more to stretch across the alleys between some of the houses. We hung them jus' a little higher than a horse's head, so if you go down the alleys. Stay low."

"That ought to discourage the bandits from scattering too much."

"That was our thought."

Until near noon the men sat in companionable silence until Reynaud stood for a drink of water. "What are you in this for?" he asked. "You don't even know Chernikov, so it isn't a personal thing with you as it is for some of us."

"I know the kind of man he is." Paco stood and began to pace, loosening stiff muscles. "And I know men like Barnes even better. They are the bullies, the ones who take from the helpless." He continued to pace, shaking his hands and flexing them. "I suppose I am here because of people like these villagers. Probably they never owned land before. They want only to feed their families and themselves by their own work, and to make life a little better for their children. They are the ones most hurt by men like Barnes and this Chernikov." He took a sip from the jar. "And you? Why are you here? This is not bringing you closer to Chernikov."

"Not directly," Reynaud answered, "but this way I can get rid of some of the men protecting him. If I don't stop them now, I'll almost certainly have to do it later, when they'd have the advantage. But you're right about these people. I don't want to see them victimized by a pack of filthy barbarians."

Paco gestured at a bag of dried corn he'd brought with him. "Eat?"

Reynaud shook his head. "I'm not hungry." After a moment, he grinned at Paco. "All right, I admit it. I'm scared and I don't think I could keep anything down."

"It is nothing to be ashamed of. Everyone has some fear. If your body will take no food, it is foolish to try." He stopped, apparently listening, then returned to the door. "Men are coming." He looked out the door and now Reynaud, too, could hear the bandits riding into Sheffield. They clattered in from both ends of the street and several of them slowed as they approached the church.

Paco set down the rifle he'd just picked up. "Hasteen jus' came out of the cantina. I am going out, too."

~ * ~

Hasteen had slept on the table in the cantina, and he woke to the complaints of sore muscles. Digging out from under the blankets, he accepted a steaming cup from Felipe, the owner of the cantina. He recognized the taste as similar to an herb tea his mother used to make.

He stood and buckled on his gun belts, checked the

chambers and actions of his guns, adding a single action in his belt and another slipped under the belt at the small of his back then practiced his draw until it was smooth and quick and his muscles stopped protesting. He noticed Felipe staring at him but ignored the attention and continued to exercise until his body again felt as if it belonged to a live human being.

Wade appeared at the cantina door. "I'm gonna get Paco and set up a warm welcome for the bad guys. Hold the fort till we get back."

Hasteen nodded then paced restlessly, eating a little dried corn and meat, until dawn, when he saw Paco return to the church. Suddenly, he faced Felipe. Can you warm some water?"

Using the warm water and a cloth, Hasteen cleaned himself, working gingerly around his face and the worst of the bruises on his body, then dressed in the black and orange clothes he'd worn in Freeport, finally putting on the squash-blossom necklace, the concho belt, and, last, the *ketoh*, the bracelet derived from the old warriors' bowguard. After he'd armed himself again he again checked the chambers of all four pistols and made sure the hammers were resting between chambers.

"Beer, *senor*? Felipe offered.

Hasteen shook his head. "Not now. I'm working. A drink of water, *por favor*." He accepted a large jug from Felipe and drank deeply then handed it back. "*Gracias.*" With his fractured Spanish and Felipe's limited English, they could converse a bit, but now it wasn't needed. They both knew what was expected of them.

Hasteen had left the front door of the cantina open and sat three paces inside, knowing he'd be almost invisible in the shade, especially to sun-blinded eyes. Felipe sat with a shotgun a few feet from the closed and barred back door. And they waited.

Hasteen hated waiting. He was ready now. Several times he stood and paced, keeping his body limber. Just after noon he heard the bandits approaching and, minutes later, he watched the first of them ride down the street.

He knew then he'd have to go out onto the street to meet them, both to keep them from dismounting and to draw as many of them as he could into the killing zone around the church and the cantina. Pulling off the jacket he wore, he stepped out onto the porch, his Navajo moccasins making no sound on the stout boards.

Several men drew up in front of the cantina, ready to dismount. At the center of the group sat a man on a white horse, resting on a black, silver-mounted saddle with a flat, round horn. The bandit wore an ornate pair of Colt single-actions and a small chin beard with a carefully-trimmed moustache. Hasteen guessed this man to be Sanchez, and decided he had to be killed first.

The men had all apparently frozen at the sight of Hasteen, and the familiar icy clarity of mind hit him again. His apparently casual glance was enough to let him choose his follow-up targets. The man to Sanchez's right carried a sawed-off double barreled shotgun lying across the saddle in front of him, while the man to the left of Sanchez wore a revolver in an old-style holster covering almost everything but the butt of the gun. The only other immediate threat was the man behind Sanchez carrying a rifle, the barrel pointed up, the butt resting on his thigh.

More riders reined in before the church and Hasteen saw a flicker of movement as Paco stepped out the door.

"Don't bother to dismount," Hasteen said to the bandits. "You're just as dead if you fall down or get down."

He heard a blast from down the street and drew his right-hand gun, firing his first shot almost as soon as the muzzle cleared the holster. The bullet shattered Sanchez's lower jaw, and the round he fanned after it hit the inside corner of the bandit chieftain's right eye, blowing out the eye and taking off most of what was left of the back of his head.

Hasteen's first shot at the man with the shotgun caught the big man just under the breastbone while the next round went higher, centering in the notch of the collarbone. The third man had just gripped the butt of his pistol when Hasteen's bullet slammed in just over his left eye and blew his hat off, along with most of the top of his head.

The man behind Sanchez had thumb-cocked the hammer of his carbine and began to swing down the barrel when Hasteen's last shot caught him in the upper chest,

Dropping the empty revolver, Hasteen whipped out the gun from his waistband, while crowding closer to the horses, which were in a near-panic, providing him cover from the sides. He snapped off another shot as the man with the rifle dropped his gun and reeled in the saddle. The second bullet hit the man in the center of his chest and hurled him off his mount.

The bodies of the bandits were still falling to the street when Hasteen spun to his left and saw Logan spray men and horses with his Ingram. The man nearest Hasteen had a shattered elbow but had just started to draw across with his left hand when Hasteen put a .45 round through his shoulders from side to side, throwing him off his horse.

The tangle of men and horses in front of Logan all seemed dead, wounded, or riderless horses racing away from the gunfire, so he spun to the right just as two riders broke for the edge of town. He shot the man further away first, then drilled the second rider between the shoulder blades as he tried to catch his companion as he fell. The second man toppled, his left foot caught in the stirrup, and the fear-stricken horse ran down the street, dragging the limp body bouncing behind it, leaving patches of red on the asphalt each time it hit.

A bullet buzzed past him then he heard the shot from down the street. Dashing back into the cantina seemed a case of running into a trap, so Hasteen darted to the narrow alley between the cantina and the nearest house to the east. He spun again and fired three quick shots at a man beside the church, saw him go down, dropped his pistol, and drew the weapon from the small of his back.

He chanced a look down the alley then sprang into it as another bullet whined off the wall beside him and he sprinted down the alley. At the end of it he stopped, his back against the cantina wall, and looked around the corner in time to see a bandit yank at the handle of the cantina's back door.

From inside the building he heard the bellow of a shotgun and the bandit recoiled from the door, a few spots of blood on his face and shirt from some few of the pellets that had penetrated the heavy door. The man staggered back, looking stunned, and Hasteen stepped out. "Right here," Hasteen shouted, and shot the man through the head.

Logan and Jaime were likely to have their hands full trying to clear the eastern side of town, and Hasteen decided to help. Trotting behind the cantina, he crossed the mouth of the next alley and worked his way to the east.

~ * ~

For Logan, the wait had seemed endless. He had no one with whom the share the tedium, so he spent the time pacing, drinking water, caring for his weapons, and cursing the bandits, who should've appeared with the dawn.

When he first heard the racket of steel horseshoes on asphalt, he had to stop and decide what the sound meant, having jumped several times at harmless noises or wholly imaginary ones.

As the first of Barnes' cavalry trotted past, he almost whistled in admiration at the white horse the leader rode, then in appreciation of the numbers of their opposition. He glanced across the street to see if Paco was in position then saw the Mexican walk out onto the steps in front of the church.

"Now that's class," Logan murmured. He'd already set his rifle aside as being too long and heavy for close-in work, and he immediately stepped into the street. Three of the riders saw him and turned their horses to face him. Logan heard Hasteen's voice but couldn't make out the words, then the blast of a grenade echoed between the building from down the street and, almost at the same time, he heard the ripping roar of Hasteen's Colt. Logan swept his duster open and swung the MAC up at the horses and men in front of him.

"Hasta la bye-bye, motherfuckers!" Logan screamed as he held the trigger back and sprayed .45 bullets.

A horse screamed and reared then crumpled as a body fell off its back, a second horse collapsed, and the rider twisted in the saddle, his chest a mass of blood. The gun snapped empty just as Logan centered it on the third man, its last round shattering the bandit's right elbow. Logan used his left hand to press the magazine release and tug the magazine free. He dropped the mag and pawed through his duster pocket, reaching for a fresh mag. The bandit reached cross-body for his pistol when he suddenly pitched to the side.

Out of the corner of his eye, Logan saw Hasteen as he spun away to fire to his right. "Nice save, man," Logan shouted, then the new magazine was seated in the Ingram and he jerked the bolt back. Looking to his left, he saw only a dead rider and a wounded horse then Jaime stepped out of the next house, re-cocking his M-16's charging handle.

The wounded horse was screaming, a hideous sound. Left-handed, Logan drew the .44 magnum from its shoulder holster and fired a single shot. The horse's head jerked at the impact then the animal lay still.

Using gestures, Logan directed Jaime to move down the alley to his left while Logan took the alley between them. Keeping the MAC in his right hand and the Redhawk in his left, Logan jogged down the narrow passage. At the end of the alley he swung his guns up as he saw a figure then lowered them as he recognized Hasteen. "Hey, man, nice threads,"

Hasteen must've recognized Logan already and his only reply was a nod.

"Jaime and I can handle this, I think." Logan said. "You're more likely to be needed up front, in case we flush any of these guys. We'll try to run 'em your way. Besides, we'll need somebody to cover our backs if these guys think of going around the front of the buildings while we're creepin' around back here."

Hasteen nodded again and trotted up the alley from which Logan had emerged.

As Hasten rounded the corner to the front of the buildings, Logan heard an exclamation in Spanish and ran to the western corner of the building. As he sprang around the corner he saw Jaime leaning against the wall, looking sick. At his feet lay a body without a head. The missing head lay several feet away. Looking up, Logan saw a wire, all but invisible except for its gore-coated middle.

Logan nudged the head with his foot, observing what seemed a look of perpetual surprise on the dead features. "Sloppy work," he said. "I thought you were supposed to trim those things with a longer stem." He gripped Jaime's arm. "C'mon, *amigo*. Rugby is hell. Let's get into the game."

As they neared the end of the alley, Logan motioned for Jaime to stay back and cover him as he crept along the back of the next house. He could still hear intermittent firing, punctuated by the rare concussion of a grenade, and the screams of wounded horses and men. He'd covered a third the width of the house when three horsemen raced from behind the house at the end of the street.

"Get 'em!" Logan roared and emptied the MAC at the horses and riders. Jaime fired four short bursts and two of the horses went down then, with a terrific blast, dirt geysered and the third horse was lifted , then dropped, kicking.

Logan stuffed a fresh magazine into the Ingram then let it drop to hang by its strap and gripped the Ruger with both hands. He'd just begun to move when a rifle shot made him dive to the ground. An answering burst from Jaime either killed the bandit or forced him into deeper cover.

Judging the distance to the dead horses about a hundred yards, Logan raised the Redhawk and held it high, pointing at where he thought the shot had come from. Concentrating on the source of the gunshots, he didn't notice Jaime until the Mexican was almost halfway to where the carcasses lay. Before he could shout for the farmer to get down, he heard two rapid-fire shots from somewhere to his right, and Jaime was spun around and collapsed.

Rolling and twisting, Logan centered his sights on a man limping out the back of one of the houses. The bandit saw Logan just as he fired. The big .44 slug hit low, just above the belt wrapped around the thigh of the bandit's chaps and the man was spun and hurled against the door frame. Logan shot again, hitting the bandit in the upper belly and the man went down as though he'd been hit with a steel medicine ball.

Hearing something like an angry hornet and feeling a tug at the duster around his shoulder, Logan rolled again and fired in the direction of the dead horses just as another grenade exploded among the bodies, throwing a rifle, with an arm still clutching it, into the air.

Shoving the Ruger back into its holster, Logan rose unsteadily, surprised to find he was panting like a steam engine and sweating profusely. Holding the MAC in both hands, he stalked toward the man he'd shot, who lay face down, in the back doorway. Besides the two leg wounds and an exit wound in his back that looked as big as a grapefruit, the man also had several smaller injuries. Looking through the open back door he could see, silhouetted in the open front door, what was left of another body.

Logan prowled cautiously through the house until he'd

reached the corpse by the front door. The body had been pretty effectively shredded by a grenade and Logan remembered the blast just before the gunfight started. "We have another winner," he announced to no one. "The first on his block to be measured for a box." Returning to the back door, he reloaded the Ruger before returning it to its shoulder holster, all the while watching where the bodies lay.

He was sure Jaime was dead, but Logan still needed to check the body. If there were any more bandits in this row of houses, though, he'd be as big a target as the farmer had been. Bending over, he scooped up the carbine by the body of the man he'd killed, worked the lever, then picked up the live round he'd ejected, wiped it on his duster and shoved the soft-point .30-30 into the loading gate.

Rolling the corpse over, he found another dozen rounds in its coat pocket. He loaded cartridges into the Winchester until it'd accept no more then dumped the rest into his duster pocket.

Still feeling terribly exposed, he dashed toward Jaime, ducking and dodging as he ran, finally throwing himself toward the farmer as though he were sliding to steal second base. The villager laid face-down with blood in his hair and puddles of blood under his head and body.

Logan rolled the body over and wished he hadn't. One of the expanding bullets had hit the Mexican in the head and blown off most of his face, while the other had blown a rib through his side.

Again dodging, running in a crouch, he dashed to the bodies of the horses and bandits. He thought there were three dead men but the grenades had made enough of a mess of the bandits that matching body parts to take a census would take longer than Logan wanted to spend in the open. Using the carcass of one of the horses for cover, he studied the buildings but saw nothing. The sounds of gunfire had almost stopped and the only noises were the sounds of a few shouts.

After catching his breath, he dashed back to the row of houses. He found one of the grenade booby traps and carefully replaced the pin before taking the trap apart, then went looking for the rest of Recon 9. It seemed the battle had ended with neither a whimper nor a bang but had simply run out of steam.

~ * ~

Billy Joe had waited patiently in the tower, alone. The battle was in God's hands and the outcome had already been decided. It was his duty simply to carry out his part of His plan, in faith. Just before noon he saw a cloud of dust in the east, which circled the town, then largely vanished. Training his binoculars on the highway to the west, he could just make out riders. Looking to the east, he saw more riders trotting toward the village, and he realized these men had decided to leave no escape and no survivors.

Carefully, he laid the field glasses on the floor of the tower and raised his weapon. He'd paced off the distance to his first target, the ruined house, and found it to be almost exactly a hundred seventy yards. Riders reached the buildings at the edge of Sheffield and most of them continued toward the middle of town, while a few of them dismounted. Raising his rifle, Billy Joe centered the sights of the launcher on the roofless building.

Three men drew rein beside the ruin and swung out of their saddles, hauling rifles out of scabbards. With a final glance at the street, they loped to the broken wall. Across the street and a house nearer, two more bandits had dismounted and one of them had kicked open a door. The first man was already inside the house when the grenade exploded, and the man just outside was flung into the street.

Billy Joe heard shots then and lobbed his first grenade at the sharpshooters in the ruined house. Watching smoke and dust boil up, he reloaded as quickly as possible. By the time he'd closed the action on the second grenade the street was nearly clear of live bandits and the only movement he saw was the bandit who'd been wounded by the booby trap dragging himself into the door he'd been blown from. The man had disappeared inside by the time Billy Joe brought his rifle to bear.

Again he waited, now listening for orders from below while watching for opportunities.

Three horsemen suddenly made a break from the southwest side of town. Two of the horses went down while Billy Joe was trying to figure the trajectory and the lead he'd have to use, then he simply followed the rider, added lead and

Kentucky windage, and fired. The range was almost at the maximum on the sights, almost three hundred yards, and he waited, not even sure the grenade wouldn't explode prematurely, then he saw the fountain of dirt and the horse was thrown as though swatted by a giant hand.

Ejecting the empty case, he loaded a fresh grenade then looked up to see a villager about halfway between the row of houses and the dead horses. He tried to watch the bodies among the horses while he picked up the binoculars but finally had to look down to see them.

Using the glasses, he peered at the dead horses and the human bodies among them. At first he saw no movement then noticed a man lying just beyond one of the horses move his arm.

He lobbed a second grenade. "And may God have mercy on your heathen soul," he murmured. The blast dismembered the bandit.

By the time Billy Joe reloaded again, Wade was shouting for him to hit the easternmost house on the north side of the street. McCluskey's first grenade blew away most of the flimsy roof and after reloading he sent a second grenade through the hole. Wade shouted for him to cease fire.

Billy Joe had just decided the battle was over when he heard shouts and screams from the second building west of the cantina.

~ * ~

As soon as Paco stepped outside the church door he moved to the right. Hasteen was talking to the bandits across the street, and in those few seconds Paco chose his targets. When the grenade exploded down the street and Hasteen's single-action made its stuttering roar, he reached for his pistol. He squeezed the trigger as the sights came up on the chest of the bandit with a shotgun. A red spot, then another, appeared on the front of the bandit's dirty white shirt and he dropped his shotgun as he was thrown back out of the saddle. The second target wore a battered hat and shoulder-length hair. The hair jumped like something alive and the hat flew away as Paco shot him between the eyes.

The third bandit had almost cleared his revolver of its cross-draw holster before Paco shot him. The first bullet smashed the man's forearm before punching into his belly while the second shot caught him in the bottom of the chest. Paco swiveled to the right to snap off a shot at the fourth bandit when a shotgun bellowed behind him and the man became a mass of bloody rags from shoulders to chest. The body toppled from the horse, which reared in panic.

Paco ejected the nearly-empty magazine and shoved in a fresh one then drew the second automatic from his belt. The first part of the battle had taken no more than three or four seconds. Hasteen and Logan had already moved away from the fronts of the buildings.

"Thanks for the help. Watch the sacristy door," Paco shouted to Reynaud then paced to the building west of the church. The church was set further back from the street, so he only had to face the nearest wall, which had a single window set in it near the middle of the wall. His gaze flicked from the front of the building, to the window, to the rear, then back again.

Creeping around the front of the building he observed the dust he'd strewn in front of the door was undisturbed and the back door of this house was one they'd booby-trapped. He stopped for a moment, peering down the street and wishing he had a man with him he could trust to cover the backs of the buildings.

As he approached the corner of the house he slowed again. Bending over, he picked up a stone about the size of his fist and tossed it around the corner, then followed it almost before the rock had hit the ground. Nothing in the alley moved.

Hearing the sound of running footsteps on the street, he wheeled to face the figure. As he fired, the bandit spun and shot back, then broke into a run toward the next house. Paco hammered off three more rounds as fast as the .45's slide would shuttle and the man tumbled like a gymnast, flipping around and back to fall on his right shoulder.

A bullet grazed Paco's ribs and he heard a shot behind him. Instantly he ducked and whirled, firing even before he saw a figure. Someone at the back of the alley, behind the next house, grunted but the man was already out of sight, hiding behind the building.

The slide had locked back on Paco's automatic and,

favoring his right hand, he changed pistols. His back against the front of the house, Paco suffered a moment's indecision, while he reloaded the pistol in his left hand and recharged it, then heard Hasteen shout to him from across the street.

"Watch the fronts of the buildings," Paco shouted back then started down the alley, stepping as quietly as possible, crouching lower as he passed the place he and Wade had strung a wire. At the back of the building he looked wide around the corner. Nothing offered cover to a man for over a hundred yards, the fields lying fallow. At the sight of a dark spot on the ground he dropped to sit on his haunches. While remaining behind the cover of the corner of the house, he looked a little further and saw more spots. He'd hit the bandit after all, although he could guess, from the blood, the wound was not too serious.

Straightening, he glared at the corner then crossed himself. He swung his right hand around the corner and fired a shot, parallel to the wall and about waist high.

A rifle shot answered his round, and he sprang out enough to see his target and place his next shot. The bandit stood at the next corner, using the wall for cover, showing only the right side of his face and his right shoulder.

Paco shouted to Hasteen. "He's in the nex' alley,"

"Awright," the man bellowed, "keep your pants on. I'm comin' out." He tossed out his carbine, then, with his right hand raised, stepped around the corner.

"Raise both han's," Paco demanded, gesturing with his pistol.

"Think again, *compesino*," the bandit replied, nodding toward his bloody left sleeve. "It's broke."

"Move aroun' here," Paco snapped. He noticed the wound was above the man's elbow, As the bandit walked past him he slid the revolver out of the man's holster and was surprised to find it was a replica of the old percussion .36 Colt Navy. Wade must've been right about the bandits running short of ammunition.

"He's over here, Hasteen." Paco said. "He's given up,"

Hasteen appeared at the end of the alley, his revolvers holstered.

"Turn him over to the Cajun," Paco decided. "The two of you can frisk him and Reynaud can watch him and any other prisoners."

"I'm afraid this fellow is going to be very lonely," Hasteen said, with the ghost of a smile. He looked more serious when he noticed the blood on Paco's shirt. "How bad is that?"

Paco followed Hasteen's gaze and saw, for the first time, the bloodstain. "Jus' a nick. Come back as soon as you have him cleaned."

Paco prowled among the houses, guns in hands, nerves taut, until he reached the wreck of the house where three bandits lay, shattered by a grenade. He started back toward the church, disarming the booby traps as he went. He'd just slipped the pin into the last grenade when he heard the screams from down the street.

~ * ~

Wade watched the bandits trotting down the street in twos and threes, then saw Hasteen walk out of the cantina. To Wade, the blast of the first grenade and Hasteen's shots seemed to come at almost the same time.

Drawing both automatics, he shot the nearest bandit twice. Another man had started to draw rein as Wade cleared the building and their shots went off simultaneously. The Ranger felt the hat whipped off his head while his bullets tore into the other man's chest. Pivoting, Wade fired at the third man who seemed frozen in the saddle, petrified by the unexpected danger. The round from the left-hand gun hit the bandit's saddle horn, peeling the leather away from the steel form and glancing into the man's lower belly, but the right-hand Colt had failed to fire.

The bandit screamed and clutched his belly, swaying in the saddle. Wade took a split-second to use the sights and drilled the man through the mouth. The raider's body jerked upright in the saddle then went over backward.

Out of the corner of his vision, Wade saw three more of Barnes' men shot off their horses, one of them by one of the farmers in the house across the street. He'd just holstered his left-hand Colt and ejected the dud cartridge when a man with a rifle fired at him from between some of the houses across the street. He'd just snapped off a shot to send the man scurrying for better cover then he heard a warning shout from Steve, in the house near the end of the street.

"Here they come!"

Three horsemen, firing wildly, raced down the street toward Wade, riding through equally wild fire from the farmers. The horse in the lead suddenly attempted a somersault and the rider was flung forward. The bandit managed to get his hands out before he kissed the asphalt then the horse came down on him, leaving a broken, bleeding form that screamed for what seemed forever.

The second rider caught most of a pattern of buckshot and dropped his own shotgun to cling desperately to the saddle horn then his horse screamed and went over on its right side, slamming the bandit to the street.

The third man had already been hit once and was bleeding from his nose and mouth when he saw Wade and raised his revolver. Wade fired first, blowing the bandit out of the saddle but, as he died, the man jerked the trigger. The bullet caromed off the street in front of Wade and the Ranger felt a blow to his belly that took all the starch out of his legs and he fell to the pavement.

He tasted bile in the back of his mouth and, unable to think, barely able to move, instinctively rolled away from the horse's pounding hooves. When he could see again, the horse had dashed down one of the alleys and Wade's pistol lay where he'd dropped it, in the street, about six feet away. He threw himself at the gun then emptied it at the alley where he'd seen the man with the rifle.

Still unable to stand erect, Wade stumbled back into the house he'd left and looked down at his wound. He saw no blood, just the nasty imprint of a flattened mass on his gun belt where it was worn over a double thickness of leather on his chaps.

The pain was more bearable now, although he felt nauseated. Sitting on the floor, he reloaded both pistols then grabbed his M-14 from where he'd leaned it against the wall. He was struggling to his feet when a form appeared at the window. Wasting no time in raising the rifle to his shoulder, Wade shot from the hip, firing until the shape was gone. Staggering to the window, he stared down at a dead man, his chest almost shredded, on the ground outside, a carbine lying near his head.

Creeping to the back door, he opened it and, after making sure the way was clear, slipped out the door. He stopped to listen. Most of the gunfire had stopped, although he could still hear an occasional shot or burst of fire.

Staying low, he crept along the row of houses, crouching under each window to listen for any noise that might give away the presence of ambushers. He'd reached the fourth house from the edge of town when he saw a man in chaps and a leather vest dash for the back door of the last house. Swinging up his rifle, he fired four hasty shots. The man stumbled but fell into the building.

As Wade drew nearer, a withering burst of fire drove him back. "McCluskey," he roared, "put a 'nade in the house at the east end, north side."

The flat report of the launcher was followed by an explosion but another shot from the building showed someone was still alive. "Again!" he bellowed.

As the second grenade exploded, the flash was visible through the window.

"Cease fire!" he shouted, and dashed forward as a rifle across the street popped rapidly, three or four times. Kicking open the back door, he found the two men in the building not only dead but spread all over the inside of the house. After shouting his name, he staggered out the front door and saw Steve pointing a rifle at the door and another corpse a few feet away.

Reynaud dashed down the street toward them. "They've got hostages!" he shouted.

~ * ~

As the bandits rode down the street at a trot, peering at the silent, closed buildings, Steve gripped his automatic rifle more tightly and pulled it back hard against his shoulder. Counting the bandits, he stopped after a dozen riders.

A grenade exploded in the house across the alley and he heard more shots, like echoes, from the street, along with what sounded like automatic weapons fire, although he could see no one to shoot at. He swallowed and took a deep breath, wondering if the others felt as nervous as he did, then he heard galloping hoofbeats. He only had time to scream, "Here they come!" before three men flashed by in the street. He held the trigger down and emptied the magazine at the fleeting images then had to duck behind the wall to reload and recharge.

When he looked outside again he saw a man duck into the last house on the other side of the street and fired a short burst after him.

Movement in the window of the house across the alley caught his attention and he ducked, just as a man fired a rifle at him. The bullet buzzed through the open window and tore its way into the opposite wall.

Steve had seen the man dodge back against the wall to the left of the window and fired into the wall until he'd emptied his rifle. After the metallic clinking of his last three cartridge cases hitting the floor, the place was quiet, the silence as sudden and shocking as a dynamite blast, then the silence was broken.

A bandit sprang into the back doorway and fired down at Chico. As he swung up the barrel, he flipped the carbine's lever and shot again.

Raul, just turning to face the man, was spun by a hit.

Steve dropped his empty rifle. The pistol he'd set on the table would take too long to seize and use, and he'd watched Hasteen practice his draw. His hand swept down to the single-action still in its holster then the gun was in his hand and he was almost deafened by it sharp bark.

The bandit was still swinging the lever up when the .357 bullet crashed into his left hip. He stumbled backward, still trying to close the action of his Winchester when Steve raised his pistol, re-cocked, and fired again. This time the man was hit in the chest and he wore the dazed look of a man who's just realized he's forgotten something important.

Steve finally got his left hand up to brace the revolver with both hands and took time to aim. His left thumb stroked the hammer back and he squeezed the trigger as the sights centered on the man's face. The third slug left a small black hole at the bridge of the man's nose and blood shot back and the bandit pitched backward.

Rushing to the back door, Steve saw only the dead bandit.

Chico was still alive but Steve was afraid to roll him over, afraid any movement would kill the farmer.

"I will guard the back. You are needed here," Raul said, moving to the rear doorway.

Snatching up his rifle, Steve dropped the empty magazine,

shoved in a fresh one, drew back the charging handle, and thumbed the selector to semi-automatic. He reached the door just as a grenade hit the last house across the street and he waited. After a second blast he saw a man flung out the door and Steve put three rounds into the body.

Wade shouted from the building then stepped out the front door. Before the Ranger could reach the street, Reynaud raced down the street shouting, "They've got hostages."

Wade and Steve both dashed into the street to meet Reynaud. "Paco sent me down to help Wade clear this end of town," the Cajun panted. "Steve, he wants you to help him keep the villagers back."

"There's wounded here," Steve jabbed a thumb toward the door he'd just left.

"Wonderful," Reynaud snapped. "I'd feel better if I weren't getting so much practice at this. Better hurry. Paco wants to keep everybody away. Hasteen's going in."

Steve trotted past Reynaud and down the street, then broke into a run as he recognized the house the people gathered around as the one to which he'd helped carry food and water for Raul's family.

Chapter 11

Hasteen slid his Colts into and out of their holsters. He was tired, at the near edge of exhaustion. Action always did that to him—left him feeling drained. Now he needed to push just once more.

"Why you and not me?" Paco demanded.

Hasteen pointed to the automatic on Paco's hip. "You risk your life every time you use that. A bad primer, a weak load, and you're holding a useless piece of pig iron. You may gamble your life on that, but do you want to risk theirs?" He nodded toward the house.

Paco stared at him a moment then shouted for the villagers to move away, that there was danger. After he'd convinced the villagers to go to the houses across the street, he turned to Hasteen again. "Is there any other way to kill them? Rifles?"

Hasteen shook his head. "That was a wish, not a question. You can see for yourself, the doors are closed and the windows shuttered, and no lights inside. They hold all the aces." After a pause, "Are you sure it's just two of them?"

"We only heard the two voices. There is another dead bandit by the back door, so at leas' one of the guards paid for himself. You aren't going to try to hide the guns?"

"Too slow. Anyplace I have to put a gun to hide it is going to make it hard to reach in a hurry. Besides, the last time I took off my guns, I had the shit beat out of me. Being shot is no fun, but it's better than being beaten to death."

"You better bring us eight horses," one of the bandits shouted. "You got three minutes to get 'em up here before we kill one'a these people."

"Wait!" Hasteen shouted back. "That gains you nothing. If you kill one of them, that's one less hostage to bargain with. Step back from the front door. I'm coming in."

"If you step through that door, we start shooting."

Hasteen's lips drew back from his teeth in something no one could mistake for a smile. "If you kill me, you'd better hope my friends don't do anything worse to you than shoot you full of a lot of big, ugly, leaky holes. You've got a cougar by the tail, and you're just going to have to learn how to ride it." He began to pace toward the door.

Paco caught his arm. "*Vaya con dios*. And if they kill you, I will try very hard to keep your promise to them."

Hasteen nodded and walked to the door. He opened it slowly, knowing any quick movements could make a nervous finger jerk a trigger, and stepped inside, having to step over the body of one of the guards. Crouching, he touched the farmer's throat but could find no pulse. The man had been shot three or four times.

"Shut the door," one of the bandits rasped.

Hasteen did as he was told, then glanced around the room. Three women and a very young child crouched together on the floor in the southeastern corner, while another woman, with gray in her hair, stood. A man with an automatic pistol stood behind the woman, the muzzle of his pistol pressed against her temple. A second bandit stood beside the other hostages, pointing an M-3 submachine gun at them.

Hasteen ignored them to examine another body, that of a boy perhaps twelve years old. The boy had a massive bruise across the side of his face but his pulse seemed steady. Apparently, one of the bandits had hit the boy across the side of the head with a gun.

A third body lay just inside the back door. A glance was enough to tell Hasteen this villager was dead. He'd been hit at least half a dozen times by a burst from the M-3.

Hasteen slowly rose to his feet and turned to the bandits and their prisoners. In addition to examining the bodies, Hasteen had stalled to let his eyes adjust to the dimness.

The bandit with the pistol was a short, gaunt, blond man, while the one with the grease gun was thickset, with thinning black hair he wore to his shoulders. The distance between them and Hasteen was no more than five yards. Now, he wanted to get their guns pointed away from the hostages, and there was only one other target in the room. "You must be new to this game," he said, gesturing at the hostages. The familiar rush of adrenalin hadn't come, and he was afraid the edge had deserted him. He could face dying, but how many of the hostages would die, too?

"Whattaya mean?" demanded the man with the pistol.

"These people can't hurt you. The only one here who's a danger to you is me." Very slowly he lowered his hands to his belt buckle. The men wavered a moment then he saw the muzzles of the guns start to turn toward him, away from the hostages.

The tachypsychia took hold. He whipped out his right-hand gun. The first shot hit the bandit with the pistol in the right shoulder. As Hasteen's left hand came down to sweep the hammer back, the man was spun, swinging the woman to the right, and Hasteen's second shot took her in the upper center of her chest. Even as he was fighting the recoil, Hasteen twisted the pistol so the third shot went high.

The submachine gun bellowed and put two bullets low and to the left of Hasteen before he hit the gunner in the chest. Another .45 round hit the bandit just below the collarbone, and the hole made by the last bullet looked like a large, garish beauty mark on the man's cheek.

The first bandit had just hit the floor, stunned, his pistol blasting a hole in the ceiling. Hasteen holstered his empty pistol and drew the other weapon. The bandit was just like the first men he'd killed; a scavenger who stole from the weak and the dying. He fanned the shots slowly, almost a second between shots. His first bullet struck the man's crotch and he worked his way up the quivering body until his last two shots took off most of the man's head. He kept stroking the hammer, even after it began to fall on empty cases.

Finally, moving like a robot with the shakes, Hasteen managed to shove the pistol back into its holster and staggered to the door. The odor of burnt gunpowder was suffocating. He began to hear the screaming and wailing of the women, and his stomach was convulsing like something with a life of its own. As he lurched out the door, Paco stared at him as though he'd never seen him before. "What happened?" Paco asked.

"Five out of six ain't bad," Hasteen mumbled, then threw up against the wall.

~ * ~

Paco and Steve rushed into the house. A boy, who Steve recognized as Jorge, lay on the floor. He moaned and struggled feebly, trying to get to his feet. Paco knelt beside him while Steve tried to quiet the wailing and keening women, then he noticed a woman's body being tended by two of the younger women. Looking closer, he recognized the dead woman as Constanza and one of the women holding her was Juanita. He looked back to see Paco helping Jorge to his feet.

Steve crossed himself then shouted at the women in Spanish. "It is done. Go outside." Bending over, he dragged Juanita to her feet. "Go outside. Go to the church or the cantina, but you must leave here." He lifted the other woman to her feet and almost dragged the two of them to the door. When he turned he saw Paco steady the boy and gently push him toward the door.

"Will he be all right?"

"His head will hurt for a time, but he will live." Paco began to examine each of the bodies until he reached the man Hasteen had emptied a pistol into,

Steve swallowed hard as he looked at the remains. "What's the matter with Hasteen?"

Paco kicked the body. "He has much anger. It was Hasteen who shot the woman, and I think he was angry with himself. As for his sickness, he has pushed himself too hard, and his body is revolting against him." Paco looked around. "We let the villagers take the bodies of their own. These bastards," he nodded at the dead bandits, "we drag out into the street."

As they hauled the corpses outside they saw Reynaud and Wade carrying Chico to the church on the long table from the cantina. Steve left his dead bandit by the edge of the street and hurried to catch up to Wade. "Is Chico going to make it?"

"It don't look good," Wade said grimly. "The bullet went through him then ricocheted off the floor and back into his belly. The other fella should pull through, if he don't get an infection. We decided the church was the best place for the wounded and the dead."

Steve looked at the unconscious young man and walked with them into the church, where the Deacon stood guard over a man with a crude bandage and sling made of his own shirt.

As soon as Wade and Reynaud set down the makeshift

stretcher the Ranger said, "Paco and I will try and round up the loose horses. We'll send over anybody who knows anything about medicine."

Reynaud drew his pistol and pointed it at the bandit. "As soon as we get somebody to take care of the wounded, you and I are going to walk over to the cantina and have a little talk."

The bandit eyed the pistol. "Anytime you wanna, I'll feel downright conversational."

"I thought you might see it that way." Reynaud said with a grim smile. "Now, if you really want to do me a favor. Just look like you're thinking about making a break for it as we're crossing the street."

More of the wounded arrived, including Raul, and Steve approached him feeling awkward. He laid a hand on Raul's good shoulder. "I am sorry," he said in Spanish. "There was a house broken into…." Words seemed awkward and cold. Finally, he blurted, "Constanza is dead. She died very quickly, with perhaps no pain—" All words of comfort seemed to escape him or seem mere platitudes as he stared at the farmer's stunned face, and all he could think of was to repeat, "I am sorry."

~ * ~

Reynaud had waved the bandit out the door ahead of him. As the prisoner stepped into the sunlight he glanced across at the bodies Paco and Steve had dragged out. "Looks like what's left of Tom and, probably, Vin. I figgered Tom had been born to hang. Guess he lucked out."

Hasteen stood at the bar sipping at a cup. He stared into the cup and the hand that lifted the drink still trembled.

Reynaud tried to ignore the gunfighter, who clearly didn't want company, and herded the prisoner into a chair at the back of the cantina then sat down, facing him. "How many of you rode into town?"

"All of us," the bandit said with a grin, then, at Reynaud's scowl, admitted, "They was forty-seven of us." He fidgeted with his sling.

Logan walked into the bar, noticed Hasteen and his mood, then joined Steve, the Deacon, and Reynaud. "What have we here?" He turned a chair around and mounted it, his arms crossed over the back. He rested his chin on his arms. "Looks like a guest who didn't stay for the whole party."

"I'd appreciate it if you and the Deacon would get a body-count on the bad guys." Reynaud said. "It's important to find out if any are still hiding or any got away. Steve, would you get us a jug of water and some cups?"

As Logan and McCluskey walked out the door, Felipe carried water and cups to the table. He poured three cups of water, set one of them by Steve and the other two beside Reynaud's chair. "This man is your prisoner," he said. "and if you want him to have a drink, there is water, but I will give him nothing to drink." He turned abruptly and walked, stiff-legged, back to the bar.

Reynaud handed the bandit a cup of water and watched as the man drank it. Reynaud sipped his own water and waited.

Wade and Paco, looking worn, entered the bar half an hour later. Logan and the Deacon followed them in another five minutes.

"Forty-six dead bandits," Logan announced. "Looks like it was a pretty clean sweep."

Wade refilled his cup with more water. "What have you gotten out of him so far?"

"Just that there were forty-seven of them," Reynaud answered. "I assumed everyone would want to be here to hear the answers for themselves." He stared coldly at the bandit. "We're looking for a big man. Cold blue eyes. He's got another man and the man's son with him. Do you know where we can find him?"

"Hell's bells." The bandit stared at him incredulously. "You mean you boys wasted Sanchez and all the rest'a us just to get to Chambers? Shee-it, If I'd knowed somebody wanted the bastard that bad, I'd'a bumped him off myself and saved us all a helluva lotta trouble." He glanced down at his cup and Reynaud refilled it. After a deep drink and a sigh, the man continued, "Yeah, he's in Fort Stockton. Last I heard. He was prob'ly at the old lab just south'a town."

"You seem to know a lot about him," Reynaud observed softly.

"Only rumor." The bandit leaned back in the chair.

"The story went that he was gonna trade us a lotta guns and ammo, even some heavy stuff, for cattle. We was s'posed to drive the herd north, I gather, and he was gonna pay us up there." The bandit chuckled. "If the story was right, that was his plan. I'd bet Barnes was gonna get the guns then take whatever Chambers was gonna get for the cattle."

Reynaud smiled mirthlessly. "You didn't miss out on much. You'd never have made the whole trip. 'Chambers' was going to infect the cattle with anthrax. You'd have died on the way and the only thing you would've done was help spread another plague. Chambers' real name is Chernikov. He's Russian. FSB."

"That double-crossin' sonofabitch," the bandit grumbled. "I hope you boys do catch up with him. Put a bullet through him for me, too."

"This brings up the rather indelicate question of what to do our guest, here." Reynaud said. "We can't just let him go. Too much chance he'd warn his friends. And we can't take him with us. We can't spare a man to watch him. These people in the village have enough to do repairing their place without having to play jailor, and bandit stock would seem to be at an all-time low right now."

"Still," Logan said, "he is our prisoner."

Paco spat. "He is a thief and a murderer. Before the war, he might have been put on trial an' some stinking lawyer might have got him cut loose. Now, the law is made by the survivors. We are the jury, and the only programs we have are a gun or a rope, and either will make sure he don' tell his friends we are here."

"I gotta tell ya, I don't much like the sounds of this," the bandit said. "If I'm gonna buy it, I'd rather have my last drink somethin' stronger'n water."

Wade stood, walked behind the bar, returned with a bottle of tequila. He poured the man's cup full then took the bottle back to the bar.

The bandit emptied half his cup in one swallow, made a face, then downed the rest. "Wish I could die with a better taste in my mouth, but I guess that'll hafta do."

The Deacon leaned closer to the prisoner. "Do you accept the Lord as your savior?"

The bandit's grin was as much an expression of nervousness as of humor. "Might as well. The job's open and nobody else seems to be applyin'."

"I don't like this," Logan growled. "I just don't feel it's right to blow away somebody who's helpless."

"A noble sentiment," Steve said, "but he was ready to come to this town and kill the helpless."

"I kinda agree with Logan." Wade said. "I guess maybe I just don't like ridin' the same trail he took." He gestured at the bandit.

"I hate to, but I have to vote with Paco and Steve," Reynaud said. "There's no law out here, but there's a sort of rough justice, and we don't have the luxury of pretending otherwise."

Paco stood and nodded to the prisoner. "What are you called?"

"Eddie Slocum."

"Well, Eddie Slocum, stand up."

The Deacon also stood. "If this man has truly repented of his evil, then I'll walk with him, offering what comfort I can—words from the good book."

"I'd appreciate that," Slocum said. His legs trembled and Billy Joe had to help him to his feet. Still holding the bandit's hand, the Deacon led him out the back door, reciting the twenty-third psalm, while Paco followed.

After a pause of the time it took for the Deacon to finish the psalm, they heard a gunshot. Moments later, Paco and the Deacon returned. "I think we mus' leave this place very soon," Paco said.

Wade tapped at an old road map one of the villagers had found and given to him. "Accordin' to this, it's almost exactly sixty miles, goin' cross-country, to Fort Stockton, and that's the way we wanta go. If we take the road, it'll take longer—and we'd wind up ridin' through Bakersfield. I don't think we're in good enough shape for that kinda excitement."

"How long do you think we'll have before Barnes starts to get nervous about his missing cavalry?" Reynaud asked,

Wade took a deep drink of water. "I don't think we missed any. Remember, they hit the town after a hard mornin' of travelin', so the horses were tired already, and we caught most of them down by the creek. They ain't likely to try to get too far from water." He groaned as he got to his feet. "We brought our horses and a spare for each of us, along with a pack horse and a relief pack animal. Like Paco said, we'll hafta leave soon, so get your stuff together. Pack as light as you can. The only extra supplies for the pack horse'll be water and whatever we can find to feed the horses. Oh, by the way, Logan, we brought you Sanchez's horse." His eyes crinkled with a hidden chuckle.

"Hot damn!" Logan exclaimed, "I finally get to ride a white horse."

~ * ~

Steve returned to the house he'd defended with Raul and Chico, and gathered up the empty magazines for his G-3, then to Raul's house where he'd left his supplies. He dropped the magazines in his saddlebags. He'd have plenty of time to reload them on the way to Fort Stockton. He'd just slung the saddlebag over his shoulder and turned to the door when Juanita entered. Steve involuntarily stepped back. "I am sorry about Raul and Constanza."

"It was not your fault. We all knew we might be hurt or killed." She walked past him and began to gather dried meat and corn. "You will need something to eat."

"We can take nothing more from you—you have so little. My friends and I are leaving."

"Then take this food for the road." She handed him a bundle.

Steve was suddenly struck by an attack of shyness as his fingers brushed hers. "*Gracias.*" He accepted the bundle. "I would like to return here, after our business is done in Fort Stockton."

She tried to smile through her sorrow. "I would like that."

As Steve carried his equipment and supplies back to the cantina he tried to analyze his unaccustomed shyness. Many men, after a long time away from women, might become desperate. In his case and, he suspected, that of many others, the long dry spell had given him a fresh perspective of and appreciation for women, and it'd reminded him just how much more to life there was than mere survival.

Several villagers stood outside the cantina, as well as the rest of Recon 9, who were saddling their horses. The horses had been paired up so Steve could see that, besides his long-legged buckskin, he'd also be riding a rugged steel dust gray. As he reached the small crowd he heard Paco trying to politely decline offers of more food from the villagers. The only member of the team not plied with offers of food or beer was Hasteen who, if he noticed the different treatment he received, gave no sign of his feelings.

~ * ~

Barnes paced his office like a caged wolf. He should probably have told Sanchez to send a couple men back to Bakersfield as soon as Sheffield had been leveled. It never paid to assume the people under you had sense enough to pour piss out of a boot. You had to make sure the directions were on the heel. Sanchez and his riders had been gone nearly two full days. Even if they were using travois to drag back more plunder than he'd thought the place could possibly hold, they should've gotten back by now and contacted him.

He cursed, caught up his jacket and walked through the bar to the street outside. The weather was clear again, and the approaching night was going to be crisp and cold, with only a trace of breeze. He looked up and managed to pick out the brightest stars in the sunset sky.

Carson emerged from the tavern behind him. "Still waiting for word from Sanchez?"

"No, I'm waiting for a singing telegram," Barnes growled. "What the hell do you think? They shoulda got back by now."

Carson shrugged. "A lot coulda happened. They might've run into some of the cowboys. Maybe they got better news than we thought. Or maybe the place had more booze than anybody thought. Knowin' Sanchez's riders, they'd'a tied one on as soon as they found the stuff."

"That's even dumber than it sounds. They had almost half a day to get drunk, and a full night to sleep it off. That shouldn't cost 'em time on the way back."

"Y'ever try to ride any distance on horseback with a hangover?" Carson inquired.

"Hell, I could cover thirty lousy miles on a horse if I was half dead." Barnes cursed vividly then hurried off to the storefront radio room. "Kelly," he snapped, "get somebody in

Bakersfield on the blower."

Kelly looked at a clock over the radio. "The generator isn't on, and it's gonna be at least forty minutes before they'll be anybody listenin'. We can only do a five-minute radio wait every two hours unless we pre-arrange a contact."

"Helluva way to run a railroad," Barnes groused.

Kelly shrugged. "We can't afford to run the generators constantly, and radio parts wear out, too. An' they wear out a damn sight faster if we use 'em too much."

"Crap," Barnes said, then strode outside. He stared up into the darkening sky until he sensed Carson standing beside him. "You separated the sheep from the goats yet?"

"Yeah, I've picked the forty best men, if that's what you mean."

"That's what I meant, awright. I want you to put some guards out tonight, and make sure they're some of the sharper ones."

"You think it's that serious?"

"Prob'ly not, but I don't wanna find out the hard way I'm wrong. Look, somebody hit Sonora. It mighta just been half a dozen cowpokes with a mad on. Hell, I know those bastards in Sonora are a crowd of gutless wonders that'd wet their pants at the first sign of a real gunfight, but somebody hit 'em. Then we lose a couple trucks west of Sonora. Again, that mighta been a few of the local rannies. Than Sanchez loses about half his infantry. He claimed that happened somewhere between Sheffield and Fort Lancaster. Now Sanchez's been gone longer than he shoulda been.

"Sanchez ain't like them chickenshit loafers in Sonora. He's seen the elephant. That Mex may like to look flashy, but he's one salty sonofabitch. Now, maybe he's just takin' his time getting' back, but with everythin' else that's happened, I don't wanna leave too much to chance. If somethin's out there," Barnes gestured at the gathering darkness, "it seems to be headed this way. That's one'a the reasons I want to hear from Bakersfield. If they start takin' fire, I'll have this place ready to take on an army. As it is, I want a truckload of the boys ready to leave for there in the mornin'. We'll have the Mex scout car escort 'em then return. I want to keep that thing close to hand. Ain't nothin' around here that can go toe-to-toe with that thing."

"I'll alert the boys. Anything else?"

"Yeah, set up the guards around town. Better make that a full twenty on guard."

"You want us to send a couple of them around so they can cover the lab, too?"

"Nah, that's Chambers' problem. Besides, I still don't wanna worry him."

~ * ~

Chernikov lay, fully clothed, on the cot. He'd make the rounds at least once more tonight. He felt a vague dissatisfaction, an uneasiness, and he examined the feeling and its probable causes. He'd learned in Afghanistan that feelings were never to be ignored, that after a few months in combat a good soldier could feel when he was being watched by the enemy. The best soldiers seemed born with the knack, while most of the survivors learned it fairly quickly. The dead, he thought, had not learned it at all.

His own feelings lacked the force, the immediacy of that combat wariness but they were still enough to make him contemplate his situation.

His biggest source of discomfort was the fact that in this operation he was primarily a coordinator; he actually had to depend upon others for the success of the mission. Baker, Webster, and the other assistants were all necessary for the refinement and production of stocks of bacteria. Barnes and his men were equally essential for rounding up enough cattle to make the project worthwhile and to drive the cattle north, where they could infect the livestock there.

Chernikov had studied the old cattle-drive routes taken by the cattlemen of over a century before. The best route would be to follow the Goodnight-Loving trail to around Fort Griffin, then across to the old Chisholm trail to Oklahoma. This would let him run his cattle closer to the great herds of eastern Texas and then spread the plague north. It might even be possible to carry some of the bacteria with him and try to infect some of the animals even further north.

He'd already decided it would be simplicity itself to get away from Barnes and his men, perhaps even kill them all. He had the advantage of being able to choose the time and place.

No matter how little Barnes might trust him, the bandit would have to generally give him the run of the camp.

Chernikov chuckled. America was a wonderful country. It wasn't even necessary to have money or many weapons, since the promise of reward was both an excellent goad and a way to establish a master-serf relationship with the bandits, even with Barnes himself.

The best escape would be one in which he could steal the French-built scout car. Even with rudimentary maintenance, the vehicle was perhaps the best possible machine for this sort of country. The diesel engine was easier to find fuel for than a gasoline engine. The car was also small and light enough to have comparatively good fuel conservation, while its armor was proof against anything up to and including 7.62 rifle rounds—which was about the heaviest weapon he was likely to see in this part of Texas. A grenade exploding against the skin would do little more damage than scar the paint. The machine had four-wheel drive, which gave it adequate off-road performance, and the tires could be run on even after having been flattened by gunfire.

Yes, any escape from Barnes' cutthroats should involve taking that vehicle.

After that, what? He was eager to go north and find out what he could do to further the cause, but he also hated leaving loose ends; it offended his sense of order. Perhaps it'd be better to use the time to hunt down this "Buttercup." The man had to have some useful knowledge about his superiors and their plans, knowledge Chernikov could extract in any number of amusing ways.

All this was in the future, he reminded himself. Best not to dwell so much on the future that he neglected the present.

How to play cat-and-mouse with Baker to get his maximum effort? The best way might be to mix punishment and reward—perhaps let Baker and his son go outside tomorrow, but only give him a short time after dawn. He should still be too groggy with sleep to form any plan to inconvenience Chernikov.

He'd just decided to make his rounds and had gotten up when he heard a rap at his door. He'd long since learned asking, "Who's there" was bad leadership; it was an admission there was something he didn't know. Had he a desk to sit behind while forcing the subordinate to stand and deliver his report, he'd have ordered the man outside to enter, but these quarters were too Spartan to impress underlings. Instead, he opened the door and stepped into the corridor.

"Nagle," he said, recognizing the heavy features, "your report?"

"Yessir." The man had taken on an almost military bearing since his promotion, and was evidently eager to please Chernikov, both qualities meeting Chernikov's approval.

"I just listened in on the radio, like you ordered. Barnes' men seem sorta nervous. Sanchez and his men ain't got back yet from wipin' out a town and Barnes seems pretty edgy about it. He told the garrison in Bakersfield to report every hour."

"Interesting," Chernikov said. "Was any other reason given for the worry?"

"Nothin' I know of, although the guy on the radio asked about Sonora. I got the feelin' somethin' had happened there awhile back, but they didn't talk about it enough to give me a good idea what it was."

Chernikov stroked his jaw. "Very good. Have one of the others continue to listen. I'll want you up early in the morning to guard Baker and his son. I'm going to give them a short time together. If either of them tries to run, shoot them both. Shoot them in the legs if you can, but it's essential they not get away." He studied the squarish face with its heavy-lidded eyes under thick bars of eyebrows. He was sure Nagle would do what was necessary.

"Should we set up guards around the compound?" Nagle asked.

Chernikov considered the question a moment before shaking his head. "We lack the manpower to have an effective guard, and I suspect Barnes has a deep interest in our well-being. Good night." His tone made it an order, as he strode away to inspect the compound.

Chapter 12

Wade and Paco slipped, lizard-like, back into the arroyo. "We're probably about a quarter mile from the town and a little closer to the compound. This arroyo runs to within maybe a hundred twenty yards of the compound before it peters out. It branches up ahead, another seventy yards or so, and the other branch'll take us to about two hundred yards of the edge of town. I spotted eight guard positions up there, so we gotta be careful."

"Nine," Paco said softly. "There was also a man in the clump of scrub jus' south of the road."

"No wonder we could never catch you," Wade said, "you got a cat's eyes."

Reynaud looked around at the others, mere dark shapes in the late dusk. "What do you think? Night raid?"

"That makes some sense," Wade replied, "since it gives us more time to get away after we wear out our welcome, but we need to hurt Barnes and his crowd pretty bad to discourage 'em, and I'd rather have more light for that. I suggest we hit'em just about dawn."

"Looks like we can rest until about midnight," Reynaud said. "And I can see we're going to have to split up. We're going to need a diversion to keep the bandits busy while we snatch up Baker and his son. And we're going to have to burn the lab; pity they weren't considerate enough to put it in a wood-frame house."

"Why don't you ask for a thatched roof, long as you're wishin'? Logan suggested.

Reynaud grinned. "I didn't want too get carried away—"

Wade chuckled. "I suspect that goes for all of us. We'd all rather leave under our own power. So, who do you want to pull the grab, and who entertains Barnes' merry band?"

"Wade, you take Paco, Steve, and Billy Joe; you make the diversion. How many grenades do you have left?"

"Six. You want everyone but the Deacon to take one?"

"No, we want to burn the lab, not blow it up. That would spread the anthrax. Each of you on the diversion except the Deacon take two grenades. That leaves Logan, who has the only silenced pistol, and I, and I want Hasteen for back-up."

"Wouldn't you rather have somebody less likely to kill the hostages?" The bitterness in Hasteen's voice was evident.

"Listen, *amigo*," Paco said. "none of us could have done any better. You were right when you said, 'five out of six ain' bad. I don' think I could have done what you did."

"The man's right, O'Ryan," Wade growled. "You gave it your level best, and right now we got no time for you to mope around feelin' sorry for yourself. The way I figure it, we can spend maybe ten minutes for you to wallow in self-pity, then we need to get some rest so we can get this show on the road, and we're gonna need every man and every gun."

"Wade's right, Hasteen," Reynaud said. "There are going to be a few people we'd rather not shoot, but there's a bunch of assholes we have to wipe out, too. I need to know right now if you're pulling 'conscientious objector status' or a section eight on us."

After a brief silence, Hasteen said, "I'll go with you."

"All right. Everybody get some rest. Each man guards for thirty minutes, then we start moving." Reynaud tried to find a comfortable place on the cold ground and closed his eyes.

~ * ~

When the last man had finished his turn at sentry duty, Reynaud gathered them close enough they could hear a murmur. "It's going to take some time to set up. We've got to stay quiet to get into position, and we don't know if they've set booby-traps in the arroyo."

The seventy yards to the place where the cleft branched took almost fifteen minutes to cover but they arrived without making a noise and without finding a tripwire.

"We'll try to get in close," Wade murmured, "and come in from the east, to keep 'em from noticing you. We'll go after their vehicles first. If the shit gets deep and, for some reason, we can't make a break for where we left the horses, we'll meet you at the southeastern edge of town. They's a ruined buildin' there—looks like it usta be a big 'un. It's still got most of a low stone wall around it. It's prob'ly the best defensive spot we can find."

Reynaud nodded then realized the others couldn't see it in the dark. "Good luck. Don't start the party until you hear sounds coming from the compound, or the bandits start acting like they've gotten an SOS. How long do you think you can hold them?"

"If we're lucky, we can keep them duckin' for cover for maybe twenty good minutes. Think you can finish the compound that soon after the action starts?"

"Sounds like we'll have to," Reynaud answered and started down the part of the arroyo that would lead them near the compound.

~ * ~

As the three who were to attack the compound slithered away, Steve said, "Let me take point for a while. From what you've said, we've got something like two hundred yards to cover before we're in the open, and I can check for booby-traps as well as anyone."

"Go to it," Wade said. "If you decide to let one of the rest of us take over the lead, just hold up and we'll leap-frog past you."

Steve lost track of time as he probed ahead, caution slowing his advance to inches per minute as he negotiated their way past loose rock, cacti, and dry brush. He had to stop, now and then, to warm his fingers which became numb with cold. He consoled himself with the thought this same cold kept him from having to worry about snakes and scorpions.

His careful advance brought them to the end of the arroyo without any sound that carried more than a few feet, and without finding any traps. Wade crawled past Steve to look around. Reaching the lip, he remained motionless for several minutes then crawled back into cover. He continued a little way back into the cleft then spoke so softly they had to put their heads together to hear him. "They's a guard about sixty feet to our right."

~ * ~

"You wan' him quiet?" Paco asked.

"Not for another hour or so," Wade replied. "If you kill him now, they's a chance he'll be found if they's a relief guard."

Paco drew his head as deeply into the turned-up collar of his jacket and put his hands in his armpits, to wait as comfortably as possible. He even managed to doze a little, knowing he'd need all the energy he could muster later. Within a minute he had dozed off.

Wade shook his shoulder. "If you still want that guard, he's yours," the Ranger murmured in his ear.

Paco slipped the spare .45 automatic out of his waistband and handed it to Wade then made his way to the side of the trench. The weak starlight was barely enough to let him distinguish the guard, who lay in a foxhole made by piling up loose stones. The bandit was silent and motionless, and Paco hoped the man was asleep but unwilling to bet his life on it.

He well knew the way noises, even the faintest of sounds, carried in the desert. Stalking with great patience, moving only one arm or leg at a time, taking care not to let his boots or clothing rub against the rock over which he crept, he swung wide, adding a little to the distance he had to cover but staying in deeper shadows.

As he neared his quarry he was able to see the man silhouetted against a lighter patch of rock and he could see the man's chest slowly rise and fall. The breathing was regular enough he was almost certain the bandit was asleep. He grinned as he wondered if the man's last dream was a pleasant one then he slid the heavy Bowie knife out of its sheath. Moving into position near the man's head, he clamped his left hand over the man's mouth and drove the heavy blade in just behind the collarbone, into the heart.

After a moment's struggle the bandit went limp. Paco kept his hand over the man's mouth for almost a minute then he drew the knife out and wiped it on the corpse's shirt. While he waited for the others he examined the dead man's weapons. He'd been armed with a Mexican G-3 like Steve's, while the revolver looked like an older Smith and Wesson .38. Paco was wondering if the dead man had taken it from a cop or been a cop himself when Wade joined him beside the foxhole.

"Okay, Paco, you opened the door. Now we need to get as close as we can to the large buildin' with the light spillin' out the front. I bet that's the garage. I want McCluskey to be able to put a grenade through that door."

"There is another sentry, about two hundred feet from here," Paco objected. "Let me keep him quiet."

"Sorry, *amigo*, we don't have the time. We gotta get in deep. We'll try to neutralize that guy on the way out."

Paco followed Wade but felt leaving an armed enemy alive behind them was poor tactics. They might try to "neutralize" the guard on the way out but he would be trying to "neutralize" them right back.

Wade stopped at the head of an alley running at a right angle to the street leading to the building he'd decided was a garage. "You stay here," he said, tapping Paco on the arm. "Your job is to cover McCluskey from this angle. If anybody comes out shootin', you either discourage them or draw them after you."

Paco settled in, resting the forearm of the captured G-3 on a length of two by four he'd found in the alley.

~ * ~

Wade led the other two around the block then left Steve facing a large brick building beside the garage. "I think that's a barracks," the Ranger murmured. "I want you to be ready to burn down anybody comin' outa there after the action starts, but don't fire until after we've hit the garage."

With McCluskey following him, Wade wormed partway down the block so they were, he judged, just a hundred yards from the garage door. "When I give you the word, I want you to take out that door and follow it as quick as you can with a second grenade, as deep into the building as you can lob it."

They waited.

~ * ~

Reynaud slowly raised his head to look at their target and his stomach knotted as he could see, in the starlight, nothing but rock for the hundred and twenty yards from the arroyo to the compound. Apparently, Chernikov had caused all the brush to be cut. As the Cajun studied the squat building, which looked as though it were made of concrete, he noticed it had few windows and the few it did have were covered with some reflective coating.

"Shit," Logan said. "I've seen more cover on a bowling lane."

"I'll go first," Hasteen murmured, and slipped out of the crevice. Taking advantage of the slight irregularities of the rockscape to stay, as much as possible, out of sight of anyone who might be at the building's windows as well as any of the sentries around town who might glance toward the compound, he made his way forward.

As Hasteen neared the building, Reynaud nudged Logan. "Cover me. I'm the only one packing a long arm, so it'll probably take me more time to get there." Without waiting for Logan's reply, he cradled his shotgun and began to crawl out onto the rocks, following the same route Hasteen had taken.

Hasteen hadn't made so much as a whisper of sound as he covered the rock but Reynaud, to himself, sounded like an avalanche. Acutely aware of the rubbing sound he made as he sometimes dragged his chaps or part of his jacket over the cold stone, he felt like a fly on a kitchen ceiling. By the time he'd reached where Hasteen lay by the door, his face glistened with sweat, both from tension and exertion.

Swinging the barrel of his bullpup around, he covered the door as Logan started to move. By the time Logan had reached the building, Reynaud had recovered his breath and slowed his heartrate.

They all waited until the eastern sky began to lighten. As soon as he could clearly see the other two, Reynaud scrambled to his feet and nodded.

Hasteen placed his hand, flat, on the heavy door then jerked it back as though he'd been burned and waved to the others to stand back, even as he rapidly side-stepped from the door. Reynaud froze, wondering what had startled Hasteen then saw the handle of the door turn. The door was shoved open and a boy walked out, backlit by the glare of electric lights. The boy was followed by a thin man. As the man emerged from the door, a voice behind him growled. "Better enjoy the time you got. Soon's the sun's up, you gotta get back to work."

The thin man turned his head at the sound of the voice and Reynaud noticed his wire-rimmed glasses, the lenses of which looked like blank goggle eyes. Either the man's eyes hadn't adjusted to the dimness and he hadn't seen Reynaud and Hasteen, or he was an excellent actor. He continued to move away from the door and the man who'd spoken, a tall, heavyset thug with coarse features, stepped out of the door, a shotgun under his arm. The guard turned to close the door, facing the rescuers as he halted.

Logan's silenced Makarov made its popping sound and Reynaud saw a dark spot on the man's chest but the guard started to swing his shotgun up as though he hadn't been hit. Logan's second round struck the man in the head and he jerked as though he'd been punched and stumbled back, dropping his shotgun. The man took a single, staggering step then one of his unsteady legs folded and he collapsed.

"What—?" The thin man spun to face them.

"Quiet," Hasteen said in a sharp whisper as he knelt beside the body to check the throat for a pulse.

Reynaud caught the thin man by the arm. "Dr. Baker?" At the man's nod, Reynaud shoved him in the direction of the arroyo. "You and your son follow that south. Ignore the part that breaks around the town. About three miles due south, at the far end of the trail, you'll find a depression and our horses. Take a couple horses and head east. Stay away from the highway. There's a little village called Sheffield about sixty miles from here. They'll take you in and you can probably get directions for the safest way east."

Baker shook his head. "I've got to finish this first. They had me working on anthrax bacteria to start another plague. I've got to help stop it."

"No,' Reynaud snapped. "You need to get your son out of here. Tearing this place up is our job. Now, move!" Baker grabbed his son and, reluctantly, started for the arroyo. "Run!" Reynaud hissed then they all heard the blast of a grenade in the town. Reynaud saw Baker and his son break into a run for the crevice then turned to look at the rest of the group. Hasteen had plunged through the open compound door, Logan only a step or two behind him. Reynaud dashed in after them and swung the door shut.

~ * ~

As soon as Wade heard the very faint popping sound of a silenced pistol he tapped Billy Joe on the back. "Go!"

The first grenade blew the garage door crooked and opened a large hole near the top. Popping the action of his launcher, McCluskey loaded in a fresh grenade and fired it, all within seconds.

The grenade sailed through the hole and erupted, and they heard screams and a ruddy light flickered in the opening.

"Good," Wade said, "we got their attention."

Two short bursts of automatic rifle fire ripped out behind them and Wade hoped it was Steve. A man ran screaming out of a side door in the garage and fell at the sound of a single rifle shot. That must've been Paco.

"All right, McCluskey, we done our jobs here. Let's fall back." Wade sprang to his feet and pointed his shotgun at the building as Billy Joe trotted down the street.

An engine roared inside the building and an armored scout car burst through what was left of the garage door. It halted a few feet clear of the building then, with the clatter of a hatch, a man appeared behind the machine gun on the car's roof.

Wade fired a shot at the gunner and heard his pellets ricochet off the armored body of the car then, at a single rifle shot, the gunner raised his arms and dropped back into the body of the car. Lurching forward, the car made a hard left to turn into the alley from which Paco had fired. A grenade exploded near the back of the car but seemed to have no effect, as the car reached the alley and disappeared from sight.

Wade, who'd pressed himself against a wall, spun and pelted down the street after Billy Joe. By the time the Ranger had reached the corner, McCluskey had reloaded and reached the mouth of the alley. "You can't hurt that thing with a grenade," Wade shouted. McCluskey ignored him and sighted down the alley, firing his rifle on semi-automatic. As Wade reached the alley, he saw the car halted at the intersection of two alleys. He joined Billy Joe in firing at the car, determined to distract the bandits in their hunt for Paco—if they hadn't already killed him.

The car backed up, turned down one alley, reversed, backed across the alley, then turned toward Wade and McCluskey and another man appeared in the gun ring.

As soon as the scout car had made its turn, Billy Joe launched a grenade that hit the wall beside it. The gunner ducked inside the car as the blast flung shrapnel and bricks and raised a cloud of dust. McCluskey again pumped the launcher open, reloaded, and fired, the shell hitting the other wall, toppling it near the driver's side front.

~ * ~

As soon as Paco had shot the gunner he'd leapt from cover, trying to draw the scout car after him. As soon as the machine began its turn he was already racing desperately down the alley. He knew the Panhard carried a crew of three and was sure, at any moment, another man would replace the gunner and saw him in two as he ran. Hearing the engine stall then recover, he glanced back to see the car bounding down the rough alley after him. He strained, desperate to reach the end of the alley before he was shot or run down, but the alley seemed to telescope away.

A series of rifle shots echoed down the alley and, when he spun to look back, the car had stopped. He finally reached the intersection of the alley and sprang to the alley to his right. The car turned into the alley but had to swing wide, then backed across the intersecting alley, turned again, and moved down the same section of alley headed in the opposite direction. As it passed him, he saw a man throw open the roof hatch and reach for the machine gun.

The concussion of a grenade almost knocked Paco off his feet and he heard the cacophony of a wall collapsing and a hatch being slammed shut. He took a couple of deep breaths, preparing himself for a rush, and saw figures darting and ducking down both ends of the alley in which he crouched.

Another blast and another rumble from the alley caused him to duck back around the corner. The Panhard's engine had died and Paco crept toward it. The collapse of both walls seemed to have partially buried the car under rubble. Then the engine roared to life again and a thrill of fear shot down Paco's spine. The scout car seemed like some monster that wouldn't die and couldn't be killed. With a groan, the hatch swung open, causing a shower of dust and pieces of brick then a man sprang up, opening the machine gun's feed cover to load in a fresh belt of ammunition, while the engine noise rose and fell as the driver tried to rock it free of the rubble holding it.

Setting his rifle against the wall, Paco drew his knife and pulled a grenade from his jacket pocket, then sprang like a tiger, up the heap of rubble and onto the back of the car. The gunner, who'd just drawn back the bolt handle, neither saw nor heard him until the Mexican had driven his knife through the side of the bandit's neck.

He let the body drop into the car and pulled the pin on the grenade, dropped it in, and slammed the hatch shut. The blast, partly muffled, rocked the car and blew open the hatch and the engine, at last, died its final death. Trying to ignore the ringing in his ears, Paco clambered around the top of the car. He saw Wade and the Deacon pounding down the alley toward the car as though every bill-collector in Texas was chasing them. Paco had a general knowledge of machine guns and he quickly inspected the MAG, made sure the feed cover was closed and the bolt drawn back. He swung the machine gun to cover the end of the alley he'd just left.

Figures appeared at the intersection and he hammered off a long burst. The gun yammered and vibrated in his hands and one of the bandits jerked as though he'd been snatched by a rope and fell while another grabbed his arm and screamed but managed to duck around the corner. Paco popped off two or three more short bursts to keep the bandits ducking.

He became aware the car was beginning to burn; the air rushing out of the hatch was almost blast-furnace hot and laced with acrid smoke. He fired off the rest of the ammunition in a single long burst, then jumped from the car.

~ * ~

Steve had kept up the suppressive fire on the barracks, touching off short bursts at anything that looked like a man, or even part of a human body, until he spotted a figure, beside the building, rushing at him. He fired at the shape and thought he heard a yell as the bandit dived into a doorway. Glancing down the street, he saw Wade and the Deacon disappear down the alley they'd been firing into.

Realizing if he stayed where he was, he'd be surrounded within minutes as more bandits appeared from other buildings. Clutching his rifle tightly, he ran toward the alley into which his friends had disappeared. The garage, now burning nicely, gave him enough light to avoid the rubble in the street. By the time he reached the alley corner he heard shots from the area he'd left and bullets clipped the buildings around him.

Once behind cover, he swung his rifle up and, as two men started to dash across the street, he fired a long burst that sent them tumbling, then his gun jammed. Cursing, he frantically jerked at the operating handle but the weapon was stuck tight. He threw the useless gun down and ran headlong into the alley. Two figures stepped into sight and he'd almost drawn his revolver before he recognized Wade and the Deacon.

The alley was largely blocked by rubble and the scout car and Paco was firing the machine gun at the alley ahead. They scrambled over the car, which was hot to the touch as the machine gun fell silent. Wade shouted, "Each of you, throw a grenade at the intersection ahead!"

Three grenades arced through the air and two exploded, causing more shouts and screams and they rushed ahead.

"Wade," Steve shouted, "how far is it to that wall you were talking about.?"

"It's on the other side of a vacant lot just across the street from the far end of the alley. Let's move!"

Paco leapt down from the back of the scout car and cursed as he twisted an ankle on the rubble.

Wade caught the Mexican under the arm. "Can you still run?"

Paco barked a laugh. "Don' slow me down."

As they neared the corner, Wade shouted for the Deacon to fire a grenade back at the far end of the alley and for the others to throw them around both corners before they made their break.

Steve stopped, pulled his second grenade, and, pulling the pin, flipped it as far down the cross-alley as he could. As he glanced down, he noticed another G3 lying where it had fallen and snatched it up and remained behind Wade and Paco as a rearguard while the Deacon stalked ahead of them.

They reached and crossed the street, the bandits apparently regrouping. Wade and Paco checked to make sure the next intersecting alley was clear, while Steve fired at anything behind them that moved. A figure near the end of the alley ducked back as Steve fired off a short burst.

They neared the street, which seemed about four lanes wide, and Steve scanned the area in front of them. Ahead lay a large lot with small heaps of rubble and bent girders lying over and around concrete pads, as though several of the old steel warehouses had stood there before they'd been burned and knocked down. Beyond that, mounds of brick and other debris lay heaped in the middle of an area bounded by the remains of a stone wall, some parts of which still stood five feet high.

Wade chanced a look around one corner while Paco peered down the other, then Wade pointed to the fence. "Make for there. McCluskey, you're our heavy artillery so you go first. Steve, follow him close and watch his back. Paco and I will try to keep 'em off your asses."

Whipping out the automatic from his waistband, Paco set his back against the wall and studied the buildings to his right while Wade slipped out of the alley and began to edge toward his left, stuffing fresh shells into his shotgun.

Steve paused to dump the magazine from the G-3 and load in one of his spares before he followed the Deacon, who loped across the street to the vacant lot. By the time Billy Joe strode among the ruined warehouses, bullets spanged about him, glancing off the girder beside him and Paco whirled toward the sound of the gunshots. In a doorway near the street intersections out of sight of Wade, a man stood firing as though he were on a firing range.

Steve snapped the G-3 to his shoulder, put the front sight on the man's chest, and tapped the trigger for a short burst. The bandit seemed unaware he was being shot at as he continued to fire and Steve heard the Deacon grunt. Snapping off a second burst, Steve swore as the man still stood, although he swung the rifle's barrel to point at Steve.

Steve fired a long burst and, sure the sights were off setting, "walked" the bullets into the man. The bandit finally spun, firing a shot into the air as he fell. Steve ejected the empty magazine and fumbled in his pouches. Only one loaded magazine remained. He shoved it into the magazine well, driving it home with a slap, charged the weapon, and looked for the Deacon.

Billy Joe hauled himself back to his feet. Before Steve could call out to him, the Deacon continued limping toward the wall.

The roar of Wade's shotgun caught Steve's attention

and he saw the Ranger firing into a group of bandits, apparently unaware he'd been flanked by one who'd made it to the lot. Steve snapped off a very short burst and saw the figure spin and fall then opened fire on the same group Wade had been shooting at.

A bullet whipped by Steve's ear and he pivoted to face another man in the same doorway used by the one who'd shot the Deacon, although this bandit used the wall for cover. As he swung up his rifle, Steve felt something like a fist punch him in the left shoulder but he slammed the butt tightly against his right shoulder and fired. Dust and small pieces of brick seemed to explode from the wall and the marauder stumbled into the open with bloody hands covering his face. Steve's vision began to blur but he fired the rest of the magazine and thought he saw the bandit pitch forward onto his face.

Steve seemed unable to catch his breath. Looking down, he saw a hole in the right front of his jacket and felt something wet running down his chest and belly. The rifle became too heavy for him to hold in arms trembling with sudden weakness. He tasted something bitter and wondered, vaguely, whether it was blood or regret. He wanted to draw his pistol so he could at least die with a gun in his hand but as his hand closed on the butt his legs folded under him.

Steve realized he'd never be able to find out if Juanita's lips were as soft and sweet as they looked. That was his last thought before he fell.

~ * ~

Wade tried to flatten himself against the wall as he groped in his pocket and drew out his last three shotgun shells, shoved them into the tube magazine, then glanced around at the others. He saw Steve collapse, drawing his pistol as he went down. McCluskey had almost reached the wall although he'd fallen again, and Paco was shoving a fresh magazine into his pistol.

They were effectively pinned down here. That damned combat car had slowed them down too much. "You can almost hear that bastard driver laughing in Hell," he muttered to himself, then caught a bandit trying to dash from one doorway to another. Wade fired. As the man spun and fell his pistol made the characteristic deep-throated bellow and dense cloud of smoke of a black powder load.

Unfortunately, a lot of them were better equipped. A head

appeared in a window across the alley and Wade fired, shattering the glass. The head disappeared. The sonofabitch had probably ducked, although Wade could fervently hope he'd killed another one. He fired his shotgun's last charge down the street to generally discourage anyone getting too close then dropped his shotgun. By the time it'd hit the pavement, both automatics were in his hands.

They had to fall back. Wade had already given up any hope of surviving the battle but he wanted to send as many of this scurvy lot of marauders as he could to hell ahead of him. It'd be nice to have a lot of bandits on hand to announce his arrival. He doubted he or Paco could reach the wall, but the ruins across the street provided some cover. "Paco," he roared, "time for us to move!"

Paco snapped off a round, ducked behind the wall as the slow-automatic throbbing of an M-3 "greasegun" echoed down the alley, then Paco fired two shots so close together they sounded like a single stutter. He turned toward Wade, who saw blood running down the Mexican's face. "You hit?"

"Jus' chips from the wall," Paco replied, and fired at another bandit who'd appeared from around a corner.

"Time to go!" Wade began to retreat from the corner, falling back at an angle to give up as little as possible of his field of fire. Most of the rounds shot at them had been fired by men too hurried to aim, but the longer they remained here, the more likely it became that some bandits would take positions from which they could steady their weapons and take their time.

Some hunch made Wade look up and he threw a shot at a bandit who'd made his way to a building's flat roof. The man's head jerked at the shot and dropped out of sight. Wade wondered how many more of them were on the roof when a grenade exploded above, sending a leg flying and throwing a body over the wall.

McCluskey had finally reached the stone wall and was covering their retreat. His rifle rang out, the shots coming slowly but steadily, as though the gun were tolling.

Wade continued backing across the street, firing as he went. With a crash of glass a window was broken out of the building to his right and he fired both pistols into the broken pane; he thought he heard a scream.

~ * ~

Paco fired his spare automatic until the slide stayed back, threw down the weapon, and ran to where Steve lay. At a glance, he could tell Steve had taken a round through the heart. Reflexively, Paco crossed himself then took the revolver from Steve's hand and the automatic from its shoulder holster. Kneeling on one knee beside the body, he carefully placed the six shots from the revolver, putting at least three bandits down, then laid the pistol beside Steve.

Paco half-emptied the automatic before he found the pouch with its two extra pistol magazines.

Wade had stopped to reload his right-hand gun, and Paco gave him covering fire then, together, they retreated to a heap of metal siding and girders. The crazy man touched by God had stopped firing by the time they ducked behind the cover.

"How're you fixed for shells?" Wade asked, as he wiped his face with a sleeve.

"Not so good." Paco paused to aim three careful shots at a running man before the bandit fell. "I have only two more mags for this, and the .45 in my holster has a full magazine." He held up the Beretta. "This thing mus' be loaded with military hard bullets. I have to shoot these *porcos* many times before they will fall."

Wade fired his left-hand gun twice then reloaded it. "As soon as McCluskey can give us cover again, we go for it." He wiped his face again. "By the way, if one or the other of us doesn't make it to the wall, it's been nice knowin' you."

Paco smiled mirthlessly. "Is how I feel, too."

Automatic fire broke out and they were forced to burrow into the debris as a machine gun opened fire from their right. Bullets battered the metal around them, some ricocheting, some losing their velocity as they hit one piece of metal after another, and all striking too close.

The chatter of the machine gun ended abruptly in a blast and Billy Joe's FN resumed its almost metronome-like firing. Wade glanced up at the sound of screaming and saw that with the machine gun on the left to provide covering fire, a group of bandits had prepared to rush Paco and he from the right. The attack had been thrown back by McCluskey, and the bandits who could still move scurried for cover.

Paco slid a fresh magazine into the Beretta and nodded. "Now we go."

Before either man could get to his feet a grenade exploded only feet away. They were hammered and stunned by the concussion. The rubble in which they'd taken cover stopped most of the shrapnel, while some of the debris itself became shrapnel, and Paco suffered a gash down his left forearm that wrung a vivid curse from him.

Wade sprang to his feet, pistols blazing, even before the dirt and shards of metal had stopped falling. A handful of bandits on either side of them had used the distraction of the machine gun and the rush to creep in close enough to throw a hand grenade.

Paco also jumped up, covering Wade's back. Two men to his right hid behind heaps of debris, while several more lay on the ground or behind clumps of dead brush. He shot one of the bandits through the head and another in the chest as the muzzle of the bandit's gun flashed. He felt a searing pain in his belly and was spun off his feet.

Paco rolled into the fall, losing the Beretta as he hit the ground. He continued to roll and fetched up on one knee, his hands gripping the .45 from his holster. He cut down two more bandits, heard a rifle shot, and killed the man who'd just shot past him. He never heard the shot that slammed into his forehead. Even as he toppled, his reflexes fired the Colt until it was empty.

~ * ~

Wade put two bullets into a man with a carbine, making the body jump as though stung, caught another man in the belly as he jumped up only to jackknife and drive his face into the rock-hard ground, and fired a hurried shot at a man rolling toward the concrete base of a girder. Before he could get off a second shot, a hot iron seemed to run through him from chest to back and, an instant later, he felt another burning pain in his left thigh.

Wade knew the shot through the chest was mortal and,

with no hope for survival, resolved to die well. The bandit rolling for cover never made it as a slug smacked into the top of his head. The roar of Wade's pistols was almost continuous as he lurched forward. Another bandit jumped to his feet than spun back to the ground, the back of his head gone. Wade traded shots with yet another man, wincing as a pistol round tore through his lower chest as the bandit jerked, then crumpled. The last man he noticed had pointed a submachine gun at him and they fired at the same instant. Two .45 bullets tossed the gunner like a rag doll in a high wind, while the short burst from the M-3 twisted Wade to his left and bowled him off his feet. He coughed blood and tried to raise his right-hand Colt when a bullet crashed into the side of his head.

~ * ~

Billy Joe had already turned the attack when his rifle jammed. He swung the weapon up and jerked at the operating handle but the gun remained jammed. He ducked behind the wall and examined the rifle. The jam was a double-feed, with one round partially in the chamber and a second half-stripped from the magazine.

He managed to press the magazine release with trembling fingers then his hands began to shake uncontrollably, as it sank in that he could probably count his remaining time in minutes, if not in seconds.

Steve was dead, Wade and Paco were pinned down, and more of Barnes' men rushed into the fight with each passing moment, and he was trying to clear a jam in a weapon he'd only recently learned to operate. Words came into his mind and he quoted them; "'My God, my God, why hast thou forsaken me?'" He repeated the words then realized what he was saying.

He'd felt this before, when he'd first been captured by the Russians after bailing out of his stricken B-1. He'd been without the armor of his faith; weak, afraid for his life. He forced himself to relax, to accept, putting his life in God's hands. "'Thy will and not mine be done,'" he murmured.

With the magazine out of the rifle he was finally able to clear the jam and inserted a fresh magazine. Only three left. He groped in his bandolier for another grenade and found he'd launched them all. It was almost enough to make a man take the name of the Lord in vain.

Looking over the wall, he saw first Paco, then Wade, fall. He could only see three bandits around them and he shot all three but bullets struck around him and he was forced to duck again, clawing at his eyes, which had been peppered with rock dust from near misses.

Scrambling perhaps ten feet to his left, he opened his eyes. They still stung and his vision was blurred but he could again try to pick out enemies. He crawled another few feet to a gap in the wall so he could look around the wall instead of over it. A gun muzzle winked light in a window in one of the buildings facing the lot and, although the sights were still a blur, he fired back.

A torrent of gunfire erupted and bullets struck all around him, forcing him to crouch, curled as tightly as possible at the base of the wall. A grenade, thrown short, almost deafened him and rocks toppled from the top of the wall, some of them shattered by the intense gunfire., while the ground a few feet away was churned by flying metal.

Part of him stood aside and watched the action, satisfied. He and the others had done what they'd set out to do. Despite the enormous cost, they'd distracted the bandits. If Rennie, Logan, and Hasteen had done their job as well, the doctor and his son would be gone and the compound on fire.

A voice shouted for the bandits to cease fire, cursing and almost endlessly repeating for them to stop shooting. Crawling four or five feet to a new break in the wall, Billy Joe looked out. At first, he saw nothing then remembered the binoculars Wade had given him in Sheffield. Taking the field glasses out of their case, he noted, almost idly, that the case was blood-stained. The right lens was shattered but he raised the glass and peered through the left side. The gunfire had slackened but he was still unable to find any of the bandits behind their cover.

The voice continued to rant. "I said, 'hold fire,' you stupid bastards. Where the hell d'ya think you're gonna get more shells, raise 'em on a bullet ranch? They ain't but two or three men. You dumb sonsabitches threw enough lead to wipe out a Mex army corps."

Billy Joe scanned the streets and buildings, finally found

a man lying prone and looking back over his shoulder. McCluskey followed the line of sight to the building he'd hit with the grenade, and narrowed down the location of the man shouting to one of two broken windows, side-by-side on the second floor.

Moving slowly and painfully, he crawled up on a small mound of dirt behind the wall. With the bullet hole in his left shoulder, he'd never be able to hold his rifle steady enough for a difficult shot. Instead, he carefully slid the FN up and out, resting the launcher on the wall. Again, he studied the two windows and finally caught a glimpse of a long, grizzled beard. The room behind the windows was backlit by the early sunlight pouring through the holes he'd punched in the roof with the grenade. Lowering the broken binoculars, he lined up his rifle's sights, trying to blink away the blurriness that still plagued him. He tried to move to a steadier position but his wounded shoulder shot a pang down to his elbow. Even as he peered through the rear sight, he lost the figure and blinked but the peep sight darkened the rectangle of window rather than gathered light to illuminate it, as the field glass had.

"Hold fire!" the voice bellowed again. "Don't shoot unless you have a target. Surround the place and we can pick 'em off."

Billy Joe blinked again but couldn't push away the blackness at the edges of his vision. Sighting carefully at where he remembered seeing the beard, he squeezed the trigger slowly, so the crack of the shot surprised him. As soon as he'd recovered from the recoil, he fired again. He was trying to get off a third shot when the darkness rushed in and he was too weak to hold himself up. He was aware of rolling down the bank and he heard a bandit scream, "They got Carson!" before another storm of gunfire broke.

~ * ~

Chernikov had turned on the generator and made sure Nagle had taken Baker and his son outside, then sat at a terminal and scanned the record of progress. He wished the incubation period could be increased. With such a short incubation, he'd have to find some way to have the bandits themselves inject the cattle on the trail. This added complications, and Chernikov deeply resented and distrusted complications. Even the computer before him was a piece of technology he used grudgingly. He was comfortable with nothing more complex than a weapon. Still, he mused, this was a weapon, or something helping forge a weapon.

He was so absorbed in the figures and his own reflections that, at first, he hadn't noticed the sounds, like distant thunder, but suddenly realized it was the sound of gunfire and explosions. Catching up his carbine from the desk, he stalked silently through the aisles of partitions and desks that made a maze of the large, open office area.

He'd just reached the aisle leading to the outside when a man appeared at the corner ahead, a short submachine gun in his hands. Chernikov was well-hidden by one of the dividers, giving him the advantage.

Even as he swung the carbine to his shoulder, something about the man's face tugged at his memory, and he realized he knew that face from Europe. Was this man also FSB?

Chapter 13

Hasteen had followed the corridor to a doorway on his right and slipped into a jumble of office cubicles divided by portable partitions, some with yellowed comic strips still thumbtacked to them. The place made his skin crawl, for it was truly a place of the dead, and he glanced around nervously, feeling that, at any moment, he'd meet someone in a white shirt and a tie.

His feet, in their moccasins, made no sound on the tiled floor as he crept around desks, wiping his hands on his shirt.

Logan had followed the corridor to the next doorway, he guessed, and the clatter of his boots on the tiles had warned the figure raising a carbine to his shoulder. Even as he drew, Hasteen realized that even a hit might make the man jerk the trigger, so he concentrated on the big man's left elbow. His shot broke the arm and the man dropped the barrel so the round hit the floor and whined away.

Panther-quick, the big man spun, his hand snatching for the pistol at his waist and, in that split-second. Hasteen guessed the man to be Chernikov, and knew the others wanted him alive, if possible.

Hasteen slapped the hammer, trying to hit the hand or the pistol but his bullet slammed into the canister at the man's belt. Instantly, the man was engulfed in a sheet of flame from his chest to the floor. Chernikov shrieked, a high, shrill sound that seemed hardly human, as he beat futilely at the flames with a hand that was, itself, like a torch, his skin blackening and shriveling. The heat was so intense that, as the man lurched into a desk and fell atop it, the telephone began to melt, then to burn.

Hasteen caught a glimpse of Logan on the other side of the burning man. The Ingram trembled in his hand and Logan was obviously deciding whether or not to shoot Chernikov, to finish him, then he dropped the MAC to hang by its sling and stared at the FSB officer with bleak eyes. "Helluva time to be caught without marshmallows," he muttered.

Glancing around the room, Hasteen noticed, near the back of the office area, a pair of feet just visible below one of the partitions. He started toward the back of the room then the Cajun's shotgun bellowed twice, two large holes were blown out of the flimsy divider, and a man with a rifle collapsed on the floor.

Another man with a carbine had been hiding behind a desk and now he tried a dash for the door at the back of the room. Hasteen shot him twice before he'd taken his third step.

Smoke rapidly filled the room with a foul, acrid stench, and all three of the team spun when they heard a minor explosion, then Hasteen realized the rounds in Chernikov's pistol, including those in the magazine, had cooked off.

"We've got to find the lab, quick," Reynaud snapped.

Hasteen, prowling along the row of desks, heard someone cough. "All right," he said, "come out with your hands up."

A pair of hands appeared above a divider and a quavering voice replied, "Awright, I'm comin' out. Please, don't shoot...don't shoot."

"Get out here where we can see you," Logan ordered.

Moving slowly, a tall, stooped man sidled out, his hands in the air. "Look, I can show you the generator, fuel, whatever you want. The lab's through that door." Keeping his hands raised, he pointed with an index finger.

"Where's fuel for the generator?" Reynaud demanded.

"I'll lead you to it," the man said. He turned and limped toward a screen of dividers to the left and had almost reached it when they all heard a popping noise and the prisoner went down, kicking. Reynaud fired into the partitions. A man screamed and thrashed, knocking over a couple of dividers, and rolled out onto the floor. He was dressed, as the prisoner had been, in a lab smock and he still clutched a ridiculously small pocket automatic. Hasteen shot him again, through the head, then reloaded and tossed a cartridge case into the corpse's gaping mouth.

Logan knelt beside the dead prisoner. "Belly-shot twice and once in the chest. He's bought it."

Kicking his way through the partitions, Hasteen found a room. Inside stood a diesel generator and two large fuel tanks as well as several drums and several jerrycans. He grabbed one of the jerrycans in his left hand and lugged it out to the others. "We need to hurry," he said, then headed for the door to the lab. Five feet from the door, he stopped, bent over, and slid the can, driving it into the bottom of the door.

A shot from the lab tore a hole in the door and sent splinters flying. "There's at least one left," Hasteen said.

Logan, carrying another jerrycan, set it down and grinned. "Y'know, you have a real gift for grasping the obvious." He crawled to the wall beside the door by the knob and waited for Hasteen to get into position then reached up, twisted the knob, and flung the door open.

One bullet ripped a hole in the door at waist level and two more buzzed through the doorway, then Hasteen had dived into the room and his Colt made another stuttering roar. "It's clear in here," he announced, and returned to the door to pick up his jerrycan and set it down beside the body. Logan set his at the end of a long table and began to twist the cap off his can when Hasteen shook his head. "Takes too much time. Just get some more cans in here."

As he started toward the door, Logan noticed a couple of cardboard drums of chemicals. He peeled off the metal lids then shoved the containers over, spilling the powder across the floor. "I don't know what this stuff is, but it's probably flammable."

Hasteen set several jerrycans around the lab while the other two made a quick examination of the rest of the complex. Logan, who'd appropriated a captured M-1 carbine and several spare magazines, trotted back to where Hasteen finished the preparations. The smoke from the fire around what was left of Chernikov had become even denser, and he had to shout and follow the sound of Hasteen's voice to find him.

"Look what I found!" He raised his hands, holding up two more canisters like the one Chernikov had worn.

"Good," Hasteen replied, "it's nearly ready."

"Hey," Logan asked, "what's the matter with you? You look like somebody's kicked your dog. Sure, I'd like to have done Chernikov myself, but you gave him a proper send-off to hell."

"I was trying for his pistol."

"You still worried about bein' over the hill, or something? Hell, nobody can do everything exactly right every time. Your average is high enough, if gunfighters had baseball cards, I'd collect yours."

Hasteen snorted. "Do you know how to use these things?" he

asked, indicating the canister.

"Sure thing. It's just a Willie Pete grenade."

"Good. Follow me." Hasteen led the way to the generator room and emptied a pistol into the bottoms of the fuel drums. As the fuel rushed across the floor, he said, "As soon as you hear me start to fire in the lab, chuck a grenade in here, then do the same to the lab. We want to be sure we burn the anthrax out of here."

Working together, they soon had the complex in flames and, with Reynaud, beat a hasty retreat through heavy smoke and oppressive heat. As they rushed out the compound door, Hasteen stopped and braced it open with a rock.

"Well, I guess we're out of here," Reynaud said, listening to intense small-arms fire coming from town.

Taking cartridges from his bandolier, Hasteen reloaded. "The two of you go on. Paco still owes me money."

"Bet I see him before you do," Logan said, checking his weapons.

Reynaud hesitated long enough to be sure his shotgun was fully loaded. "Well, hell, I had to know I wasn't the only sucker around."

Hasteen pointed to a pair of houses still standing between them and the stone wall that was their rendezvous. "You two take the house on the left, I'll get the one on the right. If the place is surrounded, those houses are a natural place for Barnes' men to set up."

"Hold up," Logan said, "let's try to hit them both at the same time."

Hasteen nodded then bent forward at the waist to trot forward at a crouch, using whatever cover he could find.

It cost him at least three minutes he was sure their friends in town could ill-afford but he slipped next to the house unobserved. He crept like a ghost along the front of the house until he reached the front door and listened again. One of the voices he heard seemed to come from near the left side of the door, while the other sounded as though the second man were deeper inside the house.

When he heard a series of shots from the carbine and a shotgun blast he kicked the door open, sprang inside, shot the man in the front room, who was pointing a rifle out a window facing the stone wall, but couldn't see the other man.

"Hold it, fella," a voice grated. "I got a hostage." A man appeared in the door to the back rooms, holding a woman in front of him.

Hasteen noticed the woman was Mexican and her hair was streaked with gray. The blood seemed to have turned to ice in his veins. The bandit's gun muzzle flashed and, in the closed house, the noise reverberated and rang.

Hasteen felt something hit his left side, just above the belt, and he threw himself into deeper shadows, avoiding the next two shots. His own gun was in his hand but he seemed petrified, unable to fire, certain he'd hit the woman. Keeping the woman between Hasteen and himself, the man rushed through the living room and out the door.

Hasteen stumbled after the man and had just reached the door when he heard a single pistol shot. Leaping to the door, he saw the woman lying on the ground and, fifty yards away, the bandit running toward the wall.

Steadying his Colt against the door frame, Hasteen took careful aim and squeezed the trigger. The bandit screeched and fell as the bullet shattered his lower spine.

Hasteen stalked toward the man who was crying, though whether in pain or fear he couldn't tell. He stopped above the man, who stared up at him with tear-filled eyes and trembling lips. He placed the muzzle of his Colt against the man's forehead then swung the gun up. "You don't deserve a quick bullet, woman-killer," he said, his voice sounding cold and flat even to him. "I'm going to let you die in your own time. Maybe one of your friends will kill you. Maybe you'll bleed to death or die of thirst, but take your time." He kicked the man's pistol away, turned his back on the bandit, and walked back to the house.

~ * ~

As Logan and Reynaud reconnoitered the house they were to clear, Logan looked in a side window. "Three of 'em," he muttered. "One's by the far window. Go around the house and when you hear me open up, shoot him through the window. I'll take care of the other two."

While he waited for Reynaud to get into position, Logan looked for Hasteen but the gunfighter was out of sight. After counting to fifty, Logan looked in the window again. Two of the men were still in their same positions but the third bandit, a wiry balding man with a round face, dug at part of the floor. Logan aimed his carbine through the window at his first target, squeezed off a round then hammered three more shots into the man's chest, in case the glass had deflected his first shot.

The bandit staggered a step forward, trying to raise his rifle but dropped it then collapsed while the one Reynaud had shot had been slammed against a table and had taken it down with him.

Logan pushed the carbine's muzzle through the window and pointed it at the bandit on his knees, whose hand moved toward his pistol. "Don't try it unless you want to be sent to your next of kin in a blotter. Put your hands on your head."

As the bandit did as he was told, Logan raised the window and stepped into the house. "Any interesting last words?" he asked the man.

The bandit slowly stood and Logan noticed he was an inch or two shorter than Logan himself. "Killing me ain't gonna help your friends. Likely, it'll make it worse. Maybe we can make a deal. I'm Barnes. Now, if you'll take it easy with that piece, I'll call my men off and let you and your friends—the ones that're still alive—ride outta here. I'll even make the trip worth your while. I've gotta little gold here—"

"Save it," Logan said. "You just hang onta that gold. It might get you a good table in hell's cafeteria." He set the carbine down and poised his hand over the MAC-10's grip. "You wear a pistol. Lower your hands and go for it."

Barnes slowly lowered his arms until his right hand hovered over the butt of the revolver he wore in a fast-draw rig.

"Anytime you're feeling lucky," Logan said softly then, as Barnes' hand shot down, Logan grabbed the Ingram, swung the muzzle up, and pulled the trigger. Barnes caught six or eight rounds through the body and was slammed hard against the wall while his one shot, fired just as the muzzle cleared the front of the holster, tore a long gouge in the floor.

The rest of the Logan's burst made a shambles of the corner, smashing a mantel clock, blowing the mantel itself apart, and knocking a picture from the wall. Glancing at the picture Logan saw it was a photo of a past president, marred by a bullet hole placed neatly between the eyes. "Good thing I used to be a Democrat," Logan observed.

Reynaud slipped in the door. "We'd better move. I thought I saw some men bunching up to make a rush on the wall." He picked up a fallen rifle, a bolt-action with a scope, and slung his shotgun. "We'd better spoil the attack and do it damned fast."

The Cajun took up a position at the window he'd blown in and fired twice. "I think I got one. Where the hell's Hasteen."

"Walking this way," Logan replied, at the other window facing the town. He loaded a fresh magazine into the Ingram and let it hang by its sling while he snatched up the carbine and snapped off half a dozen fast shots before the return fire made him duck. Crawling to the door, Logan said, in a voice scarcely louder than an urgent whisper, "Hasteen, are you crazy? We're takin' fire, and we're just getting ready to make it for the wall, now."

As soon as Hasteen had turned, crouched and loped toward the wall, Logan jumped and ran, ducking and sidestepping as he followed. Reynaud followed him, bringing up the rear and almost tripped over him as Logan fell. Hasteen stopped and dodging and twisting, emptied first one pistol then the other, at the muzzle flashes in the buildings and shooting down the one figure they saw. His shots were close enough that most of the bandits stopped shooting, probably looking for safer cover.

Logan had finally flung himself behind the wall and sprayed off the rest of the rounds in the carbine's magazine while the other two rushed the last few yards to safety. Hasteen had almost made it when he went down and rolled the last few feet through a gap in the stonework.

Logan glanced at him. "How bad are you hit?"

Hasteen paused in reloading his Colts to look down at his leg. "I think it just hit the front thigh muscle."

"There's blood on your jacket by your belly, too," Reynaud observed.

"I've been hurt worse. You two go find the others. I'll hold this position." He watched Logan tying his bandanna around his calf.

"If you can make it."

Logan ignored the comment. "I'm going for that corner over there," he said, pointing at the northeastern corner. "Rennie, why don't you find the others? They're probably somewhere along the northern wall."

~ * ~

Reynaud clutched the rifle and, staying low, dashed to the heaps of rubble at the middle of the square of fence. Halting beside the ruins of a chimney, he studied the area beyond the wall. Three bandits rushed forward, ducking behind cover, then coming on again, Raising the rifle, he settled the crosshairs on the body of the man in the lead then squeezed the trigger, The man went down howling, clutching his belly.

The other two bandits hesitated for a moment and in that time Reynaud had worked the bolt and managed to hit another one in the arm. The two surviving marauders turned and ran and Reynaud worked the bolt again and fired his last shot. Dust kicked up beside one of the men as they dived headlong into a building.

Cursing for having wasted a bullet, Reynaud set the rifle down and drew his shotgun around. After making sure no more bandits were trying to creep up on the wall, he looked inside the stone barrier for his friends, finally sighted a man lying near the wall. It looked like the Deacon.

Staying low, the Cajun made a dash for the wall, hearing a few shots and taking a gouge in his right forearm, then dropped and rolled to where Billy Joe lay in a patch of blood-soaked ground. Reynaud tore off the front of the Deacon's shirt, made pads to cover the holes in McCluskey's shoulder, and bound the wound. Because of the Deacon's dark clothing, the holes in his thigh and calf were harder to find.

When Reynaud had finally bandaged the wounds he could find, he picked up McCluskey's rifle and checked the bore to be sure it hadn't been plugged with dirt. Rummaging through the Deacon's pouches, he was disappointed to find no grenades and only two loaded magazines, with a partially-loaded magazine lying a few feet away. He stuffed the magazines in his coat pocket then crawled to a hole in the wall for a look outside.

From that position he could see nothing moving in the streets or the lot near the wall. If the bandits had decided to wait them out, Reynaud would use the respite to rest and prepare. Showing as little of himself as possible, he kept watch. The sounds of gunfire, which had slackened within minutes after they'd taken cover, had almost completely stopped, and he had the cold, unnerving feeling his Cajun grandmother would've referred to as "feeling someone stepping on your grave."

Reynaud tried to guess at the bandits' next moves. He supposed they'd discovered Barnes missing—if the man Logan had shot had really been Barnes—or maybe they'd found the body by now. It was too much to hope that, without their leader, the marauders would simply drift away. In any such group, there was never a shortage of would-be leaders. The lull was most likely going to last as long as it took the bandits to establish a new pecking order.

Not knowing any of the likely candidates, he couldn't guess what form the attack would take. A rash, aggressive leader might try for a mass rush—if he could get enough idiots for gun-fodder. Someone cautious might decide on a smaller charge with intense covering fire. He preferred not to contemplate other possibilities. There was even a chance someone might try to talk them out of their positions. That would, at least, buy them a little more time.

The gunfire, which had virtually stopped, began again, mostly a series of single shots that built up into an almost steady racket. He tensed then realized few bullets were hitting the wall or around it. Were the bandits having their own civil war?

"Here they come," Logan shouted, and his carbine began a rapid popping.

Bandits rushed from doorways and around corners, all racing toward the wall, many of them firing from the hip as they pressed forward. Reynaud picked a big man in the lead, sighted on his chest, and pulled the trigger. Either he'd missed or the marauder was ignoring the wound. Reynaud aimed a little higher and fired again, and the body whipped back as though the man had hit a clothesline.

Two or three more bandits fell, while some of those rushing spun to fire at the buildings behind them, but Reynaud was too busy to do more than notice it. Throwing the selector to full-auto, he fired short bursts. Catching two bandits in his fire, he cut them down then the rifle fell silent, its bolt open with an empty magazine.

With no time to reload, he dropped the FN, caught up his shotgun, and moved a few feet along the wall. He managed to hit one man squarely with a charge, blowing him backward before bullets pounding around him forced him to duck again. Moving a few feet further from the Deacon, he came up shooting and his second round caught one of them in the groin. The man went down with a shrill scream that ended abruptly.

Ducking again, Reynaud moved a few feet more, to spring up facing a bandit only a few feet from the wall. His blast caught the man in the face, replacing it with a featureless red mask.

Something pinged against a stone and Reynaud felt himself slammed hard in the left shoulder. Swaying on his feet, he found himself no longer able to hold up the shotgun, as pain shot down his left arm to his fingertips.

Letting the shotgun fall, he ducked again, whipping out his pistol. When he looked up again, all the bandits seemed to be down then, five yards away, one of the marauders rolled over the wall to fall heavily just inside the barrier. The man shoved himself to his feet, his right arm hanging useless. The man seemed confused for a moment then reached across his body with his left hand, going for his pistol.

Reynaud raised his own pistol, pointed rather than aimed, and squeezed off three shots as fast as he could recover from the recoil. At the first shot the bandit jerked as though he'd been hanged, and bright red appeared at his throat. The second shot hit him in the upper chest and twisted him around and off his feet. Reynaud had no idea where the third round had gone.

The Cajun lurched forward and sagged against the wall, trying to fight the pain so intense he almost blacked out then slid slowly down the wall. He tried to reload his pistol but the agony became almost unendurable when he tried to move his left arm.

One more rush like the last one and he was dead and, probably, so were his friends.

Dragging himself along the wall he found a section

where it was low enough he could look over it while sitting. The gunfire had stopped and he listened to the sudden silence and the ringing in his ears then a voice shouted from the buildings, "Hold your fire! We're friends of Terry Banta."

The name was familiar but Reynaud had trouble placing it. As if anticipating the lapse, the voice explained, "Terry Banta, the fella whose bacon you saved at Fort Lancaster."

Reynaud digested the idea. It was possible but, after the last year, his trust level was more than a quart low. "Okay," he shouted back, "you can come out, but no more than one man with you." He watched carefully as a tall man with batwing chaps and a duster stepped out the door of one of the buildings. The man walked with a sort of rolling gait, and Reynaud noted he was so bow-legged his legs looked like parentheses. The man was apparently in no hurry, taking his time as he walked across the rubble-strewn lot.

He also appeared to be sight-seeing, looking over the bodies with an expression of profound satisfaction. Still six feet from where Reynaud sat, he stopped. "Okay to step inside?"

"Come on in," Reynaud replied, "but keep your hands well clear of your body."

"Sensible precaution," the Texan commented, and paced through the opening in the wall. After nodding to Reynaud, he noticed the Deacon lying unconscious, then to where Logan was trying to patch up bullet hole in his left forearm. "Where's the resta y'all? Terry said they was seven of you and, from the looks of the place, you done enough damage for a dozen or better."

"Hasteen's on the other side of what's left of that building," Reynaud said. He'd decided he might as well trust the cowboy, especially since the hand holding his pistol trembled with fatigue and weakness. "I don't know where the others are."

"That hole in your jacket don't look good," the cowboy observed. "I left word to send Sam out here soon's he gets done pluggin' the holes in a few of our boys. Sam usta be an army medic. Claims he ain't had but two patients die on him, and he said neither of them was any great loss."

"We'd appreciate that," Reynaud said dryly, looking at the buildings and the corpses. "You fellas seem to have a knack for timing."

"Actually, we wish we'd 'a got here sooner. After Terry found a coupla the boys it took 'im a while to get a bunch of us together. Some of the others and I'd been watchin' Bakersfield and saw Sanchez and mosta his men ride out. We was about ready to hit the place when we got word they was gonna be a really big party here.

"We'd 'a got here sooner but we had to leave our horses well outta sight, so walkin' took us a while. By the time we hit town, you boys had the whole damn place blazin' away at you. It was no trick findin' the place. All we hadta do was head for the smoke and follow the sound of gunfire. They was so busy findin' cover from you, they left their backs wide open."

When the medic appeared he called for blankets for the Deacon and checked Reynaud's wounds. "Broken collar-bone," he announced. "Gonna hafta put that arm in a sling."

Logan had a bullet hole in his left arm, a bullet gouge in his right arm, a hole in the calf, as well as a scalp wound caused by flying rock.

When he examined Hasteen, the medic whistled. "Hole in the upper right chest. Damn lucky if that didn't nip part of the lung. You been spittin' blood?" When Hasteen shook his head, the medic continued. "Prob'ly hafta leave that slug in." He shook his head in his turn. "That hole in your upper leg didn't do much damage, though it sure didn't do you any good. Same goes for the hole in your side. You ain't left many places for new scars, boy. You keep that up and them bullets are liable to go lookin' for fresh hide, and you ain't got many places left you can afford to get shot in."

Binding their wounds with pads and strips of gauze, he said, "This stuff is third or fourth hand. These assholes prob'ly plundered it from the people who looted the drug stores and clinics." He handed each of them a couple of pills. "Accordin' to the labels these are antibiotics. Oughtta help keep you from getting' infected."

~ * ~

The town seemed to be clear of bandits and the cow-boys, working in teams, explored what had once been a good-sized town. One of the groups found a storefront stocked with food while another team discovered a small shop set up as a sort of factory to reload cartridges, although they found only black powder. Weapons and ammunition had been gathered and, after Logan told them about Barnes' stash, three of them returned with rings, watches, old watch cases, some old coins, and assorted pieces of jewelry. Most of the rest of the time was spent dragging dead bandits into an old warehouse and tossing in broken furniture.

"We'll torch the place when we leave," Sam said. "If we don't burn 'em, they're liable to start a secondary plague."

Terry helped find the bodies of Steve, Paco, and Wade. Reynaud could hardly bear to look at his friends dead. Steve had been with the group since the escape from the prison camp, which seemed a decade in the past and, while he'd known the others for no more than a month, losing them was like losing brothers.

Hasteen had hobbled along on the search and knelt by Paco's body. With surprising gentleness, he closed the dead man's eyes. Reynaud did the same for Steve and swallowed hard to get the lump in his throat to go down.

"We'd like to take them back to Sheffield," Reynaud said. "They ought to be buried where they had friends."

"Seems only fittin'," Terry replied, staring at the number of dead bandits around where Wade and Paco lay.

Along with the Deacon, who was still unconscious, and a couple of the cowboys who'd been seriously wounded, they were taken to what had once been an upper-class house. Now it was little more than a shell, whose chief virtue was that it kept out the weather. Mattresses were hauled in, laid on the floor around the fireplace, and the cowboys brought blankets.

"What about the others?" Reynaud asked.

"They prob'ly ain't a coffin in a five-county area," Terry replied. "Best we can do is wrap 'em in blankets. We'll leave 'em outside in the cold, but we'll have somebody watchin' to keep away the coyotes and the wild dogs."

Late in the evening, Dave, the tall, bow-legged leader of the crew of the Six Shooter, and Sam, the medic, brought broken furniture and some supplies and made stew in a kettle in the fireplace.

While the stew was heating, Dave warmed his hands. "Good news, fellas. One'a the boys found an old school bus. He thinks by cannibalizin' ever'thin' else in sight, he can have it runnin'—well, maybe trottin'—tomorrow. We'll have some'a the boys take your horses and gear to Sheffield and meet you there sometime day after tomorrow." He stirred the stew, from which a fragrant steam had begun to rise. "In your shape, bad as the bus ride might be, it beats tryin' to ride a horse or gettin' hauled in a travois."

They were able to rouse the Deacon enough to feed him some broth and help him drink some sweet herbal tea.

Hasteen made a show of eating but Reynaud detected listlessness. "Are you still worried about the woman who died in Sheffield, or is it about Paco? He and the others died the way they would've wanted to; trying to protect friends. Not many people get to go the way they'd choose."

Hasteen ran a spoon through his stew. "I had another hostage problem when we were clearing the houses. This time, I didn't shoot, and the bastard killed her. It doesn't seem to matter what I do, the innocent always wind up dead. Up to now, I've never shot anyone who didn't need killing. Now…" His voice faded and he stared into his bowl.

Logan, who'd finished his stew, set down his bowl. "Look, sometimes, no matter how you grab it, you get the shitty end of the stick. And the only thing you can do is wash your hands afterward."

Reynaud tried to settle the sling more comfortably over his shoulder. "All right, you lost a couple of hostages. All you can do is the best you can do, but you've got to keep doing your best. What would've happened to either of those women if you hadn't tried? Probably, the same thing. And how many more would've died if you hadn't been there, trying? You can't win all the time, you can only try every time. The real shame would be if you stopped trying and stopped caring."

They turned in after the meal. Reynaud woke sometime later and saw Hasteen tending the fire and staring into the flames. When he woke a second time, disturbed by the pain in his shoulder, Hasteen had finally curled up in his blankets and gone to sleep.

~ * ~

In the morning they all gathered outside the building where the dead bandits and broken furniture had been heaped.

Using alcohol-soaked paper and rags and everything else they could find as tinder, Dave set the place afire and they all left, most of the cowboys to hit Bakersfield. Terry, Sam, and three other cowboys, however, joined the dead and wounded in the bus, which was also loaded with food, medical supplies, weapons, some ammunition, and some of Barnes' hoard.

The ride to Sheffield was long and painful, as the worn springs and shocks did little to spare the wounded from the effects of the damage neglect had done to the highway. Despite the mechanic's best efforts, the straining engine was never able to move the bus more than thirty miles an hour, or even less. Thirty minutes out of Fort Stockton, the engine died and the mechanic spent an oil-stained hour and a half coaxing it back to life. After another five minutes following the highway, the driver slowed and left the road and their progress became even more laborious as the engine, its roar rising and falling, with an occasional clashing of gears, negotiated the rocky terrain. Twice more the vehicle broke down, and they barely beat twilight to Sheffield.

Terry got out of the bus a quarter mile from the town and walked toward the houses. Within thirty minutes he rode back on the horse of a dead bandit. "Y'all can c'mon in. They're friendly, but they got a suspicious streak, an' they're armed to the teeth."

Reynaud had the driver stop the bus in front of the church and the villagers helped them carry the bodies inside, where they saw Steve, Paco, and Wade laid out before the altar. The villagers entered the church in pairs and small groups to pray over the dead men and sprinkle the bodies with holy water. Baker and his son had reached the village earlier in the afternoon, and they also came to the church.

Reynaud was about to suggest they leave and go to the cantina when a young and very pretty woman entered alone. After crossing herself, she knelt beside Steve's body. In the light of the candles, Reynaud could see tears glisten in her eyes and on her cheeks, and she began to sob.

Realizing something had happened between Steve and the woman, and without knowing what had been between them, Reynaud felt embarrassed to be in the church. The woman's grief was a private matter and he felt like an intruder. Standing, he gestured for the others to leave then followed them to the cantina.

Baker changed the dressings on their wounds, complimenting

Sam on his work then wiped his hands on the thighs of his jeans. "About the only thing left to do is watch for infection and hope for the best."

"We got some antibiotics in the bus," Sam said. "That oughta help even the odds some."

"Antibiotics?" Baker grinned. "You have got to be the ugliest, hairiest angels I've ever seen. There's a man named Raul who got shot a few days ago. The wound wasn't serious but I was afraid I was going to lose him to septicemia." He followed Sam outside to retrieve the medicine.

Felipe brought them cups and beer and sat at the table with them. He looked older and more worn than Reynaud remembered, and the hand that held his cup trembled slightly. "We los' Chico yesterday." He took a drink and swallowed hard. "What of the bandits?"

"They will not come again," Reynaud replied, and was moved by the expression of relief that crossed Felipe's face. "All dead. *Muerte.*" His Spanish was so rusty it creaked, and he was relieved when Baker and Sam returned. The vet was a good doctor and was also, apparently, fluent in Spanish.

As soon as Baker had sat down again, Reynaud said, "Ask Felipe if my friends and I may stay in their town until we're able to ride again."

Baker interpreted Reynaud's question and Felipe's reply. "He says you and your friends honor the village." After another flurry of Spanish, he added, "He also said they will bury your dead friends in holy ground."

Remembering Paco's comments about being in a church, Reynaud smiled. "I think they'd have liked that, especially Paco."

"If the Deacon's up to it in the mornin', maybe he could say a few words over 'em," Logan said. "He's sure getting' a lotta milage outta the twenty-third psalm."

After a brief conversation with Felipe, Baker said, "There's a house two doors west of the church Felipe says is yours to use. That's where they were going to put up my boy, Wayne, and myself. I guess we bunk together."

Terry and Sam finished their beers and stood. "The boys and I will sleep on the bus," Sam told them. "We got lots of extra blankets."

~ * ~

The next day was perfect for a funeral; overcast, with a sky the color of old lead and a wind that keened like a mourner. Billy Joe had recovered enough to be carried in a chair to where the graves had been dug. He recited the twenty-third psalm and said a few more words that Reynaud, contemplating the men who'd died, didn't really hear. All he could think of was the loss. They'd stopped Chernikov from unleashing another plague and had effectively destroyed the largest gang of cutthroats in this part of the country, but the price had been so high.

Stopping Chernikov was a thing that had to be done, like killing a rabid dog, but it hadn't brought him satisfaction or peace.

During the time they spent in Sheffield, they saw beginnings. Sam remained in the village to learn as much from Baker as he could to treat men and animals. Reynaud also thought he detected the beginning of a relationship between the villagers and the riders. He remarked on it to Logan, pointing out it'd let the villagers eat better and let the cowboys enjoy a more varied diet.

"Well, hell," Logan replied, "if I'd known they wanted more green in their diet, I'd have made them some of my mother's meatloaf."

The villagers treated them with every courtesy but Reynaud noticed a certain distance in their manner and, one night, remarked on it to Baker.

"The way I heard it," Baker explained, "a couple of your friends who were buried were kind of like family to them. Wayne and the rest of you and I, we're all guests. Honored guests, maybe, but not like family."

"I notice they're still afraid of Hasteen," Reynaud said. "And they're calling him something different among themselves. The first time we were here, I heard them speak of him as *el indio*, the Indian. Now they're calling him *el angel*, the angel. What's all that about?"

Baker rubbed his nose, a sign, Reynaud had learned, that he was embarrassed. "That's short for *el angel de la muerte,* 'The Angel of Death.' 'Afraid' isn't quite the right word. 'Awe' might be closer. They think he's a good man, but one who carries death wherever he goes. Look at it from their point of view; would you invite Death to your garden party?"

~ * ~

Four weeks later they prepared to lead their herd of horses east. Reynaud would've preferred waiting another few days or a week, but Logan insisted upon setting out as soon as possible.

"Look," he said to Reynaud, "their idea of night life in this place is to talk about last year's crops, the weather, and next year's crops. I put up with that sorta stimulatin' conversation when I was a kid growin' up on a farm in Kansas. That's why I joined the Air Force; to get away from it. Now, I want some action. There aren't too many things around here to do but procreate, and there's only two unattached women in this whole burg. One of them is in mournin' for a buddy, and if I spend time with the other one, her daddy is liable to give me a white shotgun enema."

Reynaud tried to keep his lips from twitching. "Hell, Logan, I'd think you'd want to marry and settle down. Marriage is a wonderful institution."

"Damn right," Logan growled, but I don't think I'm ready for an institution yet. Besides, I want to be just like my old man—a bachelor."

~ * ~

They took the ride back to eastern Texas slowly, going wide around San Antonio, grateful for the increasing warmth as they moved toward the coast and into spring. They left Baker and his son at the outskirts of Victoria around the end of April and rode into Freeport a week later. After leaving their horses and gear at the stable, they made their way to Slattery's garage.

Reynaud was hesitant about entering a building. The last time they'd bathed was two days earlier, when they'd been caught in a downpour Logan referred to as a "gully washer." While they'd been able to discard their bandages and even Reynaud's sling, they were ragged and unkempt. Logan summed it up nicely; "I think I liked us better when we were still alive."

The garage looked as it had the first time they'd seen it. It might have been the same vehicles, their hoods agape, saying "ahhh" for the car doctors, but when Hasteen opened the office door a blond man with a moustache and glasses stared up at them. "Can I help you?"

"We're looking for Slattery," Reynaud said.

"We're friends of his," Logan elaborated.

"Slattery was called out of town on business," the blond man said. "I expect him back any time now."

Hasteen touched the brim of his hat. "Tell him Hasteen and some of his other friends are staying at the hotel two blocks north of here."

After a bath, a trip to the barber, fresh clothes from Wes' emporium, and another bath, they ate dinner at the hotel. While the others luxuriated in their first night in a real bed in what seemed years, Logan celebrated his return to civilization with a brawl in a bar in the open end of town.

~ * ~

Logan happily provided them a color commentary on the festivities at breakfast the next morning and eating slower than usual because his bruised and skinned hands made handling a fork difficult. Reynaud had finished a plate of six fried eggs and a thick steak, and drank his second cup of the local excuse for coffee when Slattery stepped through the dining room door. The big man glanced once around the room then walked to their table.

"Johnny told me they was a buncha tramps lookin' for me. Didn't take much to figure out who he was talkin' about. Where are the others?"

"Buried in west Texas," Hasteen said brusquely.

Slattery sat down slowly, his face suddenly grave. "Sorry to hear that. They were good men." After a moment, he said, "I'll notify the Rangers about Wade." He sat silent for several minutes then leaned back in the chair, which creaked ominously, looking at each of them in turn. "You want to talk about your trip?"

Reynaud told Slattery about the ride, with others adding details. When he mentioned the military reservation north of San Antonio, Slattery interrupted. "Think they's people there who might be good material for the network?"

"Some," Reynaud said, "but we're not going recruiting there. We had to borrow a truck and a sergeant, and they might not've been amused."

"I can find somebody to check that out." Slattery accepted a cup of "coffee" from the waitress. He seemed to think the matter over in seconds then waved a hand at Reynaud. "Go on."

When Reynaud finished, Slattery considered the report a bit more and seemed to file it away in some other part of his brain. "Rennie, Logan, I'm afraid I got some bad news for the both of you. If any of your families got out of Port Arthur, Texas, or Lawrence, Kansas, they covered their tracks pretty well. With refugees bein' what they are, they're hard to track, but you don't have any relatives livin' within a sixty-mile radius of the old homesteads. McCluskey, I still haven't gotten any word back from South Carolina. It takes a while."

McCluskey gestured dismissal. "It doesn't matter. My family died before I left for Europe."

The tone in which the Deacon said it caused Reynaud to raise his eyebrows, but personal matters were private in the group.

"So, what did you fellas have in mind for the future?" Slattery asked.

After looking at each other they let Reynaud's Gallic shrug answer for all of them.

Slattery sipped his "coffee." "You tired of the wire, Hasteen?"

Hasteen considered the question, shook his head.

"Deacon?"

"His plan for me will be revealed, no matter where I go or what I do."

"How about you, Logan?" Slattery grinned. "You ready to start a farm, get married?"

"I want action. Marriage is either too much action for me, or not enough."

"Well, boys, I gotta little project for you, if you're interested. They's even a little time for some rest and recreation."

"I'm not sure I should ask," Reynaud said, "but what does this little project involve?"

"Takin' a trip to the Ozarks. Summer is comin', and Texas can be awful hot. The mountains, on the other hand, tend to have mild summers. I got a buddy, name of Norton, who can brief you on the details. It's a scurvy bunch that's latched onto some National Guard goodies. They're supposed to be pretty well-organized, but they ain't Texans, so it oughta be a piece'a cake for you boys."

"I'm for it," Logan said.

Hasteen smiled, a rare occasion. "I suppose I'll have to go along to take care of my faithful Caucasian sidekick."

"What about you, Rennie?" Slattery asked.

Reynaud finished his last swallow of "coffee." "Why us? We can't be the only team in the business."

"But you're so good at what you do," Slattery replied through a grin.

Reynaud didn't even try to hide his reluctance, but these men were now his family. "Somebody's gotta try to keep these guys out of trouble."

Logan grinned. "Aw, c'mon Rennie, what could happen?"

"That's a great choice for famous last words," Reynaud said. "That, and, 'Remember, men, take no prisoners.' I think it was Custer who said that."

About the Author

James K. Burk is a sometimes serious writer who enjoys a challenge. He has written five novels and many shorter works. His previous novels from WolfSinger Publications are the first book in the Recon 9 series: THE LONG WAY HOME as well as THE TWELVE, HIGH RAGE, and TAKING HOPE all three fantasies. He's also written two science fiction novels: HOME IS THE HUNTER and REDEMPTION, and a weird western novella, "The Ghoul of Socorro" which is the fourth book in the Night Marshal series.

His shorter works were published in two chapbooks and several anthologies. One of his highlights was "The Trailer Park Vampire Meets the Bubba Yumbie" in THE INTERNATIONAL HOUSE OF BUBBAS.

He doesn't own any cats. His writing tends to be quirky.

In Case You Missed It

The Long Way Home

Book 1 in the Recon 9 Series

A handful of men escape a Russian POW camp and make their way to Poland to alert whatever governments are left that the Russians are planning a strike simply called Operation A, They discover a world that has changed, devastated by plague and war, but where some groups are struggling to rebuild civilization while others continue to serve dead ideologies.

Other Books by James K Burk from WolfSinger Publications

The Twelve

Valtierra, a city-state, is governed by archetypes. Every two years they choose twelve men and women to wear the masks and to become the Wise Old Man, the Fool, the Mother, the Harlot, the Warrior, and the rest of the council. But now Valtierra faces hunger, decay, and an enemy on their border and, when the need for leadership is greatest, one mask is worn by a foreigner and one mask hides a traitor.

High Rage

Scarface, on his way back to a clan stronghold after assassinating a legate, meets and falls in love with a woman even more ruthless than he. To win her, he must reunite an empire and create a kingdom. His only allies are his wits, his sword, and the power in his scars—black marks like the taloned finger prints of a demon.

To achieve his goals, he must deal with old enemies, gods of dubious worth, and his own family—who may be the most dangerous of all.

Taking Hope

The power he once held depleted, Scarface has found contentment as Morgan. No longer seeking power or building kingdoms, he is happy with his current life.

However, when what he most loves is threatened, Morgan must again become Scarface to correct past mistakes. He must defeat a king and a god. Knowing one god can only be beaten by another, he seeks an alliance, but what price will be demanded?

With only a few allies, one of them mad with rage, and the power in his scars returned, he must confront old enemies, including one who knows his deepest secret and greatest weakness. Will he be able to lay to rest his past, defeat his enemies and return to the life he has made for himself. Or will he lose everything and everyone he has come to truly care about?

www.ingramcontent.com/pod-product-compliance
Lightning Source LLC
Chambersburg PA
CBHW061524250926
52052CB00010B/2791

* 9 7 8 1 9 4 2 4 5 0 7 7 1 *